THE MADRINEGA MISSILES

BOOK II: REVOLUTION

DAMIEN HUNTER

THE MADRINEGA MISSILES
BOOK II: REVOLUTION

iUniverse books may be ordered through booksellers or by contacting:

iUniverse
1663 Liberty Drive
Bloomington, IN 47403
www.iuniverse.com
844-349-9409

ISBN: 978-1-6632-4277-8 (sc)
ISBN: 978-1-6632-4720-9 (e)

Print information available on the last page.

iUniverse rev. date: 12/08/2022

To Gabriela Diaz
whose spirit resides in every woman

and to all who stand up
to speak truth to power

CONTENTS

CHAPTER 1
NO LESS A THREAT

The three men marched up a steep hill with grim determination in the brutal tropical heat. The hill contained little cover, marked only by two immature trees at the summit and grass that had been reduced to stubble by grazing cattle. They were violating a cardinal rule by moving in the open in daylight, but the distance to their objective was so great, and the reason for going so urgent, that Mateo made the decision to march by day as well as by night. Neither Leighton nor Camilo had challenged him, but now it was early afternoon and the heat of the day was at its peak. They were hungry, tired, and running low on water.

It was then that Leighton heard the plane.

They were moving through a hilly area where the undulations of the land provided hiding places in the uneven terrain despite what was otherwise a lack of natural cover. The immediate difficulty was that the echo factor in the hills made it impossible to pinpoint the direction from which the plane was coming. They had only another fifty feet to go to reach the hilltop. There was at least a little cover there, and their misery was such that despite the threat of the aircraft they were reluctant to stop, for they desperately craved whatever respite the shade at the summit could offer.

The noise of the turboprop engines grew louder. Leighton searched the sky but kept moving toward the summit, struggling to quicken his pace against the incline of the hill. Camilo did the same. Only Mateo paused, unslinging his FN FAL rifle before moving on.

And then it emerged, bursting forth from behind a hill off to their right, less than a quarter of a mile away, banking in a wide turn as it flew quite close to the ground, knap of the earth, less than a hundred feet high by Leighton's estimation. It was grey rather than green, and was a day plane so it had no radar pod, but it looked dangerous with things hanging beneath its wings, some of which represented death.

It turned toward them, looking something like an insect with its bulbous double-windscreen canopy up front in the nose. The pilot had spotted them and bore down on the trio of guerillas at very low altitude at nearly three hundred miles an hour. Camilo ran to the left, and Leighton to the right, struggling to move rapidly across the steep face of the hill. Mateo dropped to one knee, taking his time as he raised his rifle. The gun pod beneath one of the wings came to life, ripping up the earth in a line moving toward Mateo as he pulled the trigger, sending a three-round burst into the plane's windscreen.

The fire from the gun pod barely missed Mateo as the plane roared by overhead and began another turn. Camilo ran to higher ground to keep it in sight as Leighton reached Mateo and began to pull him toward a depression in the hillside where it might be possible to hide. "You got a death wish?" he shouted.

"There's no cover here. Either we shoot it down or it kills us," Mateo replied calmly.

Leighton cursed and unslung his M-16.

"It's coming!" Camilo shouted, pointing. He too had his FN FAL ready.

Leighton scanned the sky and picked out the aircraft. It was higher now as it turned back toward them; apparently Mateo had reminded the pilot that he was not impervious to ground fire.

As the pilot completed his turn and levelled off for another run at them, Leighton tracked him and shouted, "Camilo! Move away!"

"What is it?" Mateo asked, as Camilo began to disappear around the side of the hill.

"He's getting ready to drop something. I just hope it isn't napalm. Let's move!" Both men leaped from the depression and ran in the opposite direction from Camilo.

Seeing them, the pilot tried to compensate by jinking to the right as, seconds later, something fell from one of the aircraft's wings. Leighton and Mateo flung themselves to the ground as an orange-red explosion burst across the hillside, sending streams of gelatinous fire in all directions. They scrambled to avoid the flaming, clinging gel that set fire to everything it touched, including the two trees at the summit of the hill, which were now in flames.

Leighton noticed some of the fiery gel on the butt of his M-16 and quickly dropped to the ground to smother it in the dirt, being careful not to touch it.

"Camilo!" Mateo yelled, as he scanned the sky. Leighton joined him in looking for the aircraft, but it was nowhere to be seen.

"Camilo!" Leighton called.

"I'm all right," Camilo cried out. In a moment they could see him approaching across the hillside, being careful to avoid the flaming streams of fluid that now oozed downhill. He noticed a nasty chemical stench.

"What's that stink?" Camilo asked.

"Napalm," Leighton replied. "Little like gasoline. We're all damn lucky not to have been hit."

"Let's get out the hell of here," Mateo said, beginning to move. "Don't step in any of it."

"Son of a bitch tried to burn us," Leighton said, inspecting the damage to his rifle butt.

They quickly moved around the flaming summit of the hill to the reverse slope. The plane had gone. They kept moving down into a long ravine, where they found cover among a dense clump of trees that marked the resumption of the jungle canopy. Checking his map, Mateo led them downhill until they came to a stream where they replenished their canteens. It was here that they stopped, protected by the green canopy overhead.

They rested in silence, recovering from the shock of the air attack and feeling fortunate to have survived.

Mateo said, "I thought all the planes were bombing Redención. And there are only three of us. They don't usually attack such small groups."

"Looks like they pried one loose for us," Leighton replied. "The killings at Javadal may have had something to do with it. We can't be much more than twenty miles from there. And our small number may be the only reason he didn't press his attack to make sure of us."

"Twenty-five miles," Mateo corrected. "We've been moving northeast. It may be time to change direction."

"Won't that delay us?" Camilo asked. Zorrita had ordered them to far off Vescambre to disable one of the cruise missiles, and they still had over seventy miles to go, all of it on foot.

"It might, but traveling in a more or less straight line, a predictable course, will be too dangerous now that we've been spotted." Mateo unfolded his map and laid it on the ground to study it in silence.

Leighton cocked his head, cradling his M-16 as he listened for unusual sounds. At the moment, there were none. No aircraft—nothing. He felt anything but reassured. "Whatever we do, we should keep moving," he said quietly. "We're still too close to where the plane attacked us."

"Agreed," Mateo said thoughtfully, still studying the map. He glanced at Leighton and Camilo. They'd had barely an hour's sleep since crossing the Verdelpino River at Javadal the night before. They were all hungry, for their last meal had been the duck they'd eaten hours before the crossing. They could not maintain the pace of their recent march without food. His eyes strayed toward the Panactatlan region on the map. He nodded to himself and stood. "Let's go."

Gathering up their gear, they forded the stream and kept moving.

⁘⁘⁘

They did not stop to rest for nearly twelve hours, well after nightfall when Mateo halted them at a hillside covered in foliage. Only by climbing a tree had he been able to discern the terrain ahead—a descent into yet another valley that had a small village adjacent a stream about three miles away. The heat had taken its toll on them, and no one felt able to move another step.

"We are not walking all the way to Vescambre," Mateo announced.

"What do you mean?" Camilo asked, as he turned on the VHF radio for the 2:00 a.m. broadcast. Leighton was cranking the generator.

"When we saved this one from being killed outside Panactatlan," Mateo nodded at Leighton, "we acquired an Army jeep that we hid in the brush."

"You were there?" Leighton asked.

"You had very nearly just had your head blown off. You were in shock. I'm not surprised you don't remember me."

"I remember Miguel—"

"And I was with him," Mateo interjected. "There were two others. But that is not important. We hid the jeep, and it had nearly a full tank of petrol. If the Army hasn't discovered it, we can ride it to Vescambre."

"How far is it?" Camilo asked.

"From here," Mateo said, studying his map with the penlight, "it will involve a detour of just twenty miles. But we will be able to reach Vescambre and get back to Limado in just a fraction of the time."

"I say yes," Camilo said with emphasis as he put on the headphones. "Palmer?"

"My feet are as sore as yours," Leighton said. "If we can ride, let's do it."

"The first order of business will be to get some food in that village down below. Then we can turn northwest, back toward Panactatlan."

"Shh." Camilo held up a hand. "It's starting." He listened intently as the Morse signal began. It was brief. Decoded, it read:

> *Fighting continues in Redención. Air attacks continue. Guerillas have surrendered two government buildings. Army sending reinforcements. Call for surrender rejected. Previous instructions to all cells stand.*

"All the more reason for us to speed our travels," Mateo said, once he had read it from Camilo's notepad. At Mateo's direction, Camilo sent the following signal:

> *NGX to PDM. Lone aircraft attacked NGX 1300 hours today 25 miles northeast Javadal. No casualties. Please advise of air attacks outside Redención.*

A reply came within five minutes.

PDM to NGX. No reports of air attacks outside Redención except yours. Proceed extreme caution.

"Your hunch was right, Palmer … we were singled out for special attention after all," Mateo said. "Acknowledge the signal, Camilo. There's no question – we have to change direction now."

They quickly packed up the radio and moved down into the valley. The indirect confirmation that the Army was indeed trying to track their movements gave each man the energy he needed to move on. Reaching the valley floor just before 3:00 a.m., they located the creek and replenished their water bottles, although here the water had a brackish odor that made them hesitate. The village was the smallest Leighton had seen, perhaps only a dozen homes, all of them *campesinos,* peasant farmers. To them the civil war was remote, barely a reality, and they were terrified at the sight of armed guerillas, even with Mateo's assurances that they meant no harm and only wanted food.

The first house— more of a shack really— contained a married couple with three small children. Unable to take food from a family that had so little, they moved on to the next home. There an old man and his daughter, a woman of about forty, gave them each the equivalent of a handful of cooked rice. They consumed it gratefully and left the villagers in peace after learning that no Army patrols had been seen in this area for many months. The old man told them about a plateau covered by jungle canopy about three miles to the north that he sometimes used as a hunting blind, where they could rest for the night before moving on. They expressed their thanks and departed.

The old man's plateau was exactly where he said it would be, three miles uphill and slightly to the northwest; only about twenty feet across, it would have been easy to miss without precise directions. It had a lush field of grass that formed a natural bed.

Leighton took the first watch while the others succumbed to the exhaustion brought on by the past twenty-seven hours, most of it spent on the move. Staying awake was an act of will, spurred on by the rare opportunity to send a signal to Headquarters. There was a signal from Miller waiting for him once he activated the laptop, demanding information about the operation he planned against the government. Leighton ignored it and sent the following signal:

> *En route one missile with orders from guerilla leader Zorrita to disable. Missiles apparently dispersed throughout country. Location remaining missiles still unknown. Will give Lang proof disablement if possible.*

Leaving the satellite communicator channel open on a hunch—something he would not have dared do but for the robust snoring of the two guerillas on the grass behind him—Leighton received a reply with surprising speed and thought, *Miller must not be sleeping tonight.*

> *Advise ASAP when missile disabled. Send location others first opportunity. Information Zorrita most desirable.*

Leighton quickly shut down the laptop, puzzled about the last sentence, particularly the words "most desirable." With the missiles recovered or disabled, his assignment would be over. He supposed it predictable that Headquarters wanted as much information on Zorrita as possible, since she might well form a new government in Madrinega in the foreseeable future. But something about it bothered Leighton; it was still on his mind when he fell asleep two hours later, after waking Camilo to take his shift at the watch.

＊＊＊＊＊＠＠＠＠＠＠＠＠＠＠＠＠＠＊＊＊＊＊

Exhausted, they rested for ten hours, and struck out again late the next afternoon. After marching until 1 a.m. they crossed a highway in darkness, then plunged into yet more jungle for another four miles, frequently using their machetes to advance through the bush.

They found the jeep intact and undamaged, sandwiched between two clusters of trees. They all stowed their gear and weapons in the back, and Mateo had Camilo, who weighed the least, sit in it and put it in neutral. Camilo steered while the others pushed it backward out of its hiding place and away from the trees to a point where it could maneuver. Ten minutes later, after pushing it over bumpy terrain to relatively smooth, open ground to save fuel, they piled in. Only then did Camilo start the engine, but he kept the headlights off. There was barely enough moonlight to drive by.

"Avoid the roads," Mateo instructed. "We've got open, hilly countryside that runs east from here for about forty miles at least. Remember: we want to be near cover by daylight. Let's go." Camilo put the jeep in gear and drove off.

Miller steeled himself as he walked down the corridor to the Director's office. He had avoided this meeting as long as he could.

Bypassing the receptionist in the imposing outer office, Miller announced his presence to Cassandra Whitmore, who ruled the second, inner office behind walls of frosted glass. A formidable, attractive silver-haired woman of sixty who looked fifteen years younger, Whitmore was more than the Director's gatekeeper and executive assistant. She knew where a great many bodies were buried. Nodding pleasantly at Miller, she raised the receiver of her telephone and pressed a button; the Director forbade the use of any kind of intercom system in his office as indiscreet.

"Deputy Director Miller is here, sir."

She nodded, replaced the receiver, and, gazing upon Miller with the kindness reserved for those about to receive a severe reprimand, said gently, "You may go right in, sir."

"Come in, Bill," the Director said, too warmly for Miller's comfort, as he closed the door to the inner sanctum behind him. Miller was relieved at least that the Director was alone; if a reprimand was coming, at least it would be in private. "Have a seat."

"Thank you, sir." Miller settled into a plush leather chair opposite the Director's desk.

The Director put down a magnifying glass – a necessity that went with his reading glasses—and said, "Give me the latest. And I hope you can report progress."

"Leighton has infiltrated a cell under the direct control of the national guerilla leader. That leader is female, based on her code name, Zorrita. She has ordered the disabling of at least one of the missiles."

"Do we know why?"

"The guerillas have likely been forced to disperse the missiles to facilitate hiding them. They're hampered by the government's surveillance flights. Our analysts believe that in the wake of Vilar's decision to use his air force to bomb guerilla positions in Redención to quell this latest uprising, Zorrita's concerned that he'll use any weapon he can get his hands on, including the cruise missiles, if he can find them. The surveillance flights, which have been virtually round the clock for several days, have been such a harassment that the guerillas can't move openly day or night in significant numbers without great risk. As a result, at least one of the missiles may be in a place not easily accessible, which would explain the order to disable it."

"How soon 'til Leighton can disable it?"

"There's no way to know for sure, sir. We don't know precisely where Leighton is at the moment, nor do we know the location of the missile—merely that he's headed to it."

"Where are the other missiles?"

"He doesn't know yet."

"He's been in place nearly a month, Bill. Not a very satisfactory state of affairs."

"In fairness, he didn't succeed in making contact with the guerillas until two weeks ago, sir. If you recall, I warned at the outset that the approach of using an agent posing as a journalist would be effective but slow—that it would take time."

"I recall what you said," the Director retorted.

"We tried a direct approach using my first agent, Morales, attaching him to the embassy. He was killed within two days of his arrival."

"I know all that," the Director said, irritated now.

Miller was undeterred. The Old Man needed reminding of some painful facts. "It's going to take time for him to gain their trust, sir."

"But how long?"

"I don't know, but he's making progress. He's part of the group that's been ordered to disable the missile, and he says he has a plan to gain the guerillas' trust. His news stories got him arrested and tortured by the Secret Police for the better part of a week. One of Lang's men saw him afterward, and it was clear that he'd been pretty badly roughed up. We've got to give him the time he needs."

"That may be. But this situation in Redención, do you believe that the guerillas orchestrated that alone?"

Miller shook his head. "I suspect the CIA are working some mischief down there—if nothing else, spreading money among the unions and the Social Democrats. It's the government crackdown on their meetings that has fueled tensions in that city."

"Yes," the Director agreed, "and things are coming to a head. I want those missiles and your agent out of there before they go critical.

"Understood, sir."

"Is that rapid deployment force still on standby in Guatemala to pull the missiles out once you get the word from your agent?"

"Yes sir. On a twenty-four-hour basis."

"Keep it that way. Let's hope you get a signal soon. We need action, Bill."

"I understand, sir." Miller rose to leave.

"By the way," the Director said, remembering something. "Did you mention the name 'Zorrita'?"

"Yes sir."

"Female guerilla leader?"

"Yes, sir."

"The CIA's been hunting her for the past two years—if it's the same person. Chilean by birth, educated abroad ..."

Miller hesitated. "Hunting as in, they've issued a kill order?"

"That's exactly what it means," the Director replied. "Is there a problem?"

"I have no reason to think so, sir," Miller replied.

"Good. Because if your agent has contact with her, we're obliged to seize the opportunity and take appropriate action. Regardless of the risk to your agent."

"I'll get confirmation and relay those instructions, sir."

"Very well. Be nice to upstage the CIA for once."

Within thirty minutes, Miller was at his desk, reviewing the dossier of Gabriela Marcelina Aaima Diaz, the Chilean national known as Zorrita. It was sparse except for a few family details: father a well-to-do physician, mother dead, older brother killed by the DINA shortly after the 1973 coup that ousted Allende. Educated at the Sorbonne and London School of Economics, then appeared soon afterward in El Salvador with the FMLN, then Nicaragua with the Sandinistas. A file photo was included, the same picture that the Central Nacional de Informaciones had provided Colonel Narváez. The dossier ended with this passage: *"This individual is a dedicated revolutionary who poses no less a threat to U.S. interests in the Western Hemisphere than did Che Guevara. She is a clear and present danger to the U.S. and its allies throughout Latin America. Her elimination is of the utmost importance to the peace and security of the region."*

Miller sat back, stunned at the assessment, and let out a breath. He was worried. To his knowledge, Leighton had never killed anyone, on or off assignment. But the Director's meaning had been clear.

Miller took another look at Zorrita's photograph. The slightly grainy black-and-white image yielded a few basics about her. She was young, no more than twenty-five, but according to the dossier had a maturity that belied her youth. She was not merely attractive, but striking, with very alluring facial features: eyes of burning intensity, hair that looked like it might be auburn or reddish brown. And although faintly visible, those freckles.

Miller had to admit, he could not be sure what Leighton would do once he got the order.

CHAPTER 2
DEATH AT VESCAMBRE

Driving at close to top speed over open country, slowing only when the terrain became too uncertain, in a little over an hour Camilo had sliced a day off their march to Vescambre. He leaned close over the wheel, straining to see in the dark without the headlights, while Leighton and Mateo held on tight and craned their necks, scanning the night sky for signs of Owls.

When the terrain grew too rugged, Mateo relented and directed Camilo to the nearest road heading east. They followed it for a good twenty miles until it turned northwest. Confirming the change of direction with his compass, Mateo told Camilo to leave the road and turn north. Here the terrain was the roughest yet as they approached the foothills of the Casavala Mountains.

Suddenly, after they had been driving continuously for two and a half hours, the last thirty minutes at a crawl over broken ground littered with rocks, Camilo braked to a halt and cut the engine.

"The path through the rocks begins not far from here," he said. "It will lead up to Vescambre." Mateo and Leighton got out and unloaded the satchels containing the VHF set and its generator.

Mateo pointed over the hood of the jeep, off to the right, where the terrain sloped down into dark vegetation. "I'll hide the jeep in that ravine and come back on foot. Wait here." Camilo got out and Mateo took his place, starting the engine and driving off slowly over the rocks.

Leighton turned to look at the forbidding mountain of rock towering above them in the moonlight, broken sporadically by the green of jungle foliage along its face. He noticed Camilo checking his weapon, making sure the safety was off.

"Should we expect trouble here?" he asked.

Camilo shrugged, a movement Leighton almost missed in the darkness. "I was out of ammunition after what we did at the mill. I changed magazines two nights ago," he said. "I just don't like it here."

"Why not?"

"I was in a firefight with the Secret Police here. It happened at night. I got shot … some of my friends were killed."

"Maybe Mateo should take point, then."

Camilo shook his head. "The route up through the rocks is treacherous. It's easy to get injured here with a wrong step, especially at night. I'm the only one who knows the way."

Leighton checked the magazine of his M-16. He had been traveling with an unloaded rifle for the past forty-eight hours. Full of adrenaline and fear, he had burned through all twenty rounds firing on full automatic at the soldiers at the mill and never realized it. Fishing a spare out of his satchel, he changed magazines as Mateo approached. Without a word, Camilo pushed past them and began to lead the way up the rocky slope. He paused and said over his shoulder in a firm voice, "Stay close."

After forty minutes of climbing, the rocks gave way to a small, sloped plateau where green foliage burst forth and the ground was more soil than rock. The canopy was just enough to shield them from observation from above in daylight. Leighton stepped on something small and hard, and knelt to pick it up. It was a shell casing. Even in the dim moonlight he could see that parts of the plateau were littered with dozens of them.

Camilo shook off the satchel containing the VHF set, as well as the satchel containing his personal gear. "We must go the rest of the way in daylight. I haven't taken that route before. It's higher up."

"How's the cover higher up?" Mateo asked.

"Sporadic. We'll be dodging in and out of it if we see planes. But once we get where we're going, they won't be able to see us from the air."

"Let's hope our brothers in Redención keep the planes busy one more day at least," Mateo said, shrugging out of his gear.

Despite a previous encounter with the Secret Police here, in this remote place they had little fear of being tracked or stumbled upon, so they all slept after receiving the nightly radio broadcast, which confirmed that fighting in Redención was still raging. Owls continued to bomb the city. The guerillas were holding their own, for the moment.

Camilo woke first at dawn, eager to get what lay ahead over with. As the sun rose, they could see more evidence of the firefight that had taken place here, shell casings scattered about, abandoned empty magazines, a bloody bandage, a live, unprimed grenade that had been overlooked. They collected what useful items they could and moved out, grateful for the cooler air at this elevation. They climbed for about thirty minutes until they came to an entrance to a rocky mountain pass. Looking about, they saw that there was no other route the guerillas who preceded them could have taken.

The pass was relatively narrow, ten feet across, then tightening to six, with walls Leighton estimated to vary between twenty and thirty feet high. They continued on for two miles, then the pass opened up a bit to a space twenty feet wide and nearly oval-shaped, with a few overhangs of rock where it was possible to hide from aircraft.

It was here that they found the bodies.

Camilo had known what was in store. It had been on his mind since they received the order to come to this place. There were six in all, one woman and five men. The woman and one of the men were nearly bald from hair loss, and all of them had large rashes on their exposed skin, red to purple in color. One man's skin was also blistered.

The worst of it was the stench. It was overpowering and seemed to be a combination of rotting flesh and human excrement. It was so bad they could almost taste it, and quickly clapped their hands over their noses, even their mouths.

Suddenly there was movement near one of the bodies on the right. Initially they thought someone was still alive, but the flapping of wings and the appearance of a scrawny, beaked head atop a large neck revealed a vulture. It squawked and tried to take flight but hit the overhang above and fell to the ground. Camilo had his rifle on it in an instant.

"Don't!" Mateo shouted, his voice echoing off the walls of the pass.

Camilo fired, and the vulture flopped over dead before it could take off. Mateo snatched him by his shirt. "Damn it, don't do that again," he said as another vulture appeared and took off. "Look around. All you see is solid rock. If you'd missed, the ricochet could have hit any one of us."

Camilo lowered his rifle and his head sank. He said nothing. Mateo released his grip.

Fighting his own repulsion, Leighton moved closer to examine one of the bodies.

"Looks like radiation sickness," Leighton said. "It's the only thing I know of that could have produced rashes like this. And the baldness."

"We lost a dozen more like this," Mateo said to Leighton, "in the weeks before you came here."

"It was another camp," Camilo added, his voice almost a whisper. "Fifty miles to the southwest in the foothills near one of the big farms. The government sprayed something there, a gray dust, and then people began to get sick."

Leighton remembered the meeting with Dr. Reynoso, the soil samples he talked about.

"We can't help them now," Mateo said. "The pass continues this way." He pointed to the far side of the open space in the pass and moved toward it—a narrower space where it was nonetheless possible to keep moving. Leighton followed. Camilo came last.

About a half mile farther on, they came to the cruise missile lying on its side, still in its nylon sling, wedged between the rock face and a large boulder. Leighton looked up. The rock face rose a bit higher here on both sides, maybe forty feet, and its curvature meant that it was impossible to see the missile from above except at high noon, when maximum sunlight penetrated to the bottom of the pass, and even then only a portion of it would be visible. One of the tail fins had been damaged, otherwise it was intact.

"Well, we found it," Camilo said with an air of anticlimax. "Now how are we supposed to disarm it?"

"I don't know," Mateo replied. "Remove the warhead?"

"You go messing around with that warhead and you could blow us all up," Leighton retorted.

"Have you got a better idea?" Mateo shot back. He thought of Salcedo. "There's a technician at Limado who could possibly walk us through it, but we'd have to hike back out four miles just to get a radio signal."

Thinking of the dossier Miller had given him to memorize, Leighton said, "My job in the Navy was to handle ordnance on aircraft carriers. I may be able to do it."

"Give it a try," Mateo replied. "The sooner we get out of here, the better."

"Amen," Camilo added.

"Have you still got your penlight?"

"Yes."

"Good." Leighton knelt at the missile's nose cone. Using Mateo's knife, he gently cut away the nylon sling. He examined the fasteners around the nose cone where a seam joined it to the shaft of the missile. He leaned back and sighed. "We're done here unless somebody has a Philips screwdriver."

"I have a tool," Camilo answered, going through his pockets. "It's not exactly a Swiss Army knife, but it has a screwdriver on it." He handed Leighton a dull grey metal all-in-one tool that did indeed include a fold-out screwdriver.

"It's the flat head type," Leighton said, "But I think I can use it if it fits."

It was slow going. Several times the screwdriver slipped, damaging the screw heads, but working with the tool, Leighton was able to remove ten of the screws holding the nose cone in place. He paused, for the heat of the sun had found its way down into the narrow pass.

"I need you to help me roll it," he said.

The missile was two feet in diameter and twenty-one feet long, and it was heavy. It took all three of them to rotate it. Leighton resumed work with the tool, and fifteen minutes later he delicately removed the nose cone. The warhead was nowhere in evidence. At the tip of the nose was a metallic blue box about the size of a pack of cigarettes but twice as thick. It was attached by screws to a metal cone with a flat head. At one side of the blue box was a parallel port like that seen at the back of desktop computers. It was attached to the box by two screws, and two thin cables coated with a plastic covering, one red, one black, ran from the back of the parallel port, down the side of the internal metal cone, and down into the bowels of the missile. Near the spot where the two wires disappeared was a stubby, small grey cylinder with a black base.

"What are we looking at?" Mateo asked.

"The guidance system," Leighton replied. "Most of it, anyway." He examined the blue box closely. It bore a metal plate on it that read, "Raytheon INU-9045." He remembered from the dossier's enlarged photos that he was looking at the unit that controlled the missile's inertial navigation system.

"This blue box," he explained, "controls the missile's navigation system, including the ability to follow specific terrain and locate a target. Without this, the whole thing's an unguided rocket – there's no telling where it will come down. I need some light here," Leighton said.

Mateo turned on the penlight, leaning over Leighton as he worked with the all-in-one-tool to unscrew the blue box from the cone underneath it. Next he unscrewed the parallel port and pulled it by its wires until it was out of the way. He reached out for the blue box, but it would not budge. He pulled harder. Still nothing.

"Shoot it off," Camilo said impatiently.

"No guns," Leighton retorted. "Directly behind this guidance section is a fuel tank. All it would take is a spark. The warhead is behind that."

"How do you know so much about it?" Mateo asked.

"I told you. We had these things aboard ship. But I never had to work with one exactly like this, it's a newer model." Leighton studied the all-in-one-tool for something he could use as a wedge. Finding it, he drove the wedge down into the blue box at its base. A gap appeared. He hit it twice more and reached down to grab it, but it still would not come off. He stood up. Using the butt of his M-16, he tapped the blue box once firmly, and it fell free.

"Good. Let's go," Mateo said.

"I'm not finished," Leighton replied, placing the metallic blue box in his satchel. "Give me your knife again." Mateo handed him the weapon. Leighton reached down and, pulling them taut, sliced through the wires of the parallel port. He handed the knife back, then began to examine the stubby grey cylinder on one side of the flat-headed metal cone.

"What is that?" Mateo asked.

"I think it's the gyroscope." Leighton said, looking at it closely. He again examined the all-in-one-tool. "We should take this too, but we can't. It's attached by hexagon screws, and I don't have the right tool to remove it. Let me borrow your rifle."

"What's wrong with yours?"

"Yours is heavier."

Mateo handed the FN FAL over. Leighton used the butt of the rifle to strike the cylinder hard, at an angle calculated not to disturb the fuel tank. After hitting it three times, he stopped to look at it closely. It was badly dented.

"Damaged it anyway," he said, handing the rifle back. Next he began to search the skin of the missile aft of the exposed nose.

Camilo was standing on the other side of the missile, and Leighton asked, "Camilo, do you see how this thing is painted grey all over?"

"Yes."

"Look for a panel on your side that's a different color. Probably plain metal."

"Here it is," Camilo said.

Leighton bent over the missile and craned his neck to see. "I can't get at it from here. We're going to have to roll it again."

Soon Leighton was looking directly at a metal panel. Varying in color between pale and dark aluminum, it stood out against the grey paint of the missile. Borrowing Mateo's penlight, he leaned in close, looking at the panel's seam. It had been attached not by screws, but by what looked like an advanced welding process.

"This is the GPS antenna," Leighton explained, before Mateo could ask. "It helps satellites guide the missile to the target, working in concert with the missile's guidance system and the gyroscope. We can't take the warhead, it's too dangerous and we'd be here all day trying to get at it. But if we can get this off, we've made sure this missile is nothing but junk."

"But this section," Mateo said, touching two points of the missile with both hands. "Didn't you say there's a fuel tank here?"

"Yes," Leighton sighed. "And the GPS antenna is right over it. If I rupture the tank, there'll be fuel everywhere, and that stuff can be toxic. If I create a spark doing it, there'll be an explosion."

Leighton knew there was a small gap between the skin of the missile and the fuel tank, in part to allow space for the wiring, covered by a layer of insulation, that connected the GPS antenna to the rest of the missile's guidance system behind the warhead. But the gap wasn't large, three-quarters of an inch at most. Searching the all-in-one tool for anything sharp and pointed, he found a puncture tool and said to the others, "This will be tricky. You'd better take my gear and move some distance away."

When they had gone, Leighton held the tool and brought his fist down upon the missile's skin so that he punctured it at an oblique angle. He examined the hole he had made, then used the screwdriver to enlarge it. Using Mateo's penlight, he peered into the hole and saw the dark metal of the fuel tank exactly where he had estimated it would be. The all-in-one tool included a thick, curved blade with a blunt tip that looked like a can opener. Leighton used it to cut into the skin of the missile. It was slow going. The blade was quite small, and he had to be careful not to slice open his hand on the jagged metal edges he created as he worked, forcibly parting the metal skin around the GPS antenna. When he had cut three sides open and began to pry the antenna up, Mateo, who had been watching him through his monocular, returned to his side.

The antenna could be pried upward only about three inches, at which point it was held fast by the wiring connecting it to the guidance system. Mateo produced his knife and sliced through the wiring quickly. Leighton, drenched in sweat, continued to slowly cut through the metal until the antenna was free.

Together, they walked to where Camilo waited, and Leighton put the GPS antenna into his satchel along with the inertial navigation unit. No one spoke as they turned to go back the way they had come. The hush that had descended upon them deepened as they passed through the open oval in the pass, too repulsed by the unholy stench to recover the weapons near the discolored dead bodies, or any ammunition they might have, for fear that any items they carried out would bring the stench with them.

They walked in silence until they could begin their descent over the treacherous, jagged rock, past the former guerilla camp littered with shell casings, and continued their climb down the mountain in the oppressive heat. They stopped to drink from their water bottles when they reached the point where they had begun their ascent, then kept moving until they reached the jeep hidden in the ravine nearby. There was a certain risk to driving on the roads in daylight, but no one cared. They were all eager to be away from this place of death. Camilo started up the jeep, and without a word, Mateo consulted his map and pointed the way.

One missile located and disabled. Location Vescambre southeast quadrant Casavala Mountain range in narrow pass. Zorrita born Santiago Chile. Educated Sorbonne and London School Economics. Medium height reddish hair. Estimate age 25. Request handheld transponders preferably magnetized to facilitate tracking remaining missiles. Send Lang ASAP.

With the touch of a button, Leighton sent the signal and shut down the satellite communicator. Now it was merely an ordinary laptop computer, and the screen displayed his article "Portrait of a Guerilla Leader." He had been uncomfortable sending information about Zorrita, and did his best to keep it brief.

Leighton sat looking out at the river from the same spot where he had taken a swim with Zorrita, where the current slowed to a gentle caress. He heard a sound behind him, but he did not turn. He breathed, but he did not move.

"You've been back for hours," he heard her say. "I did not think I would have to come looking for you." Zorrita's voice was soft and almost musical, a welcome sound to Leighton's ears.

"I came here," he said, "to try to recapture the peace I felt here before, with you. I haven't felt it yet."

"Perhaps that is because you came here … alone." She came closer and placed a hand on his shoulder. As she sat down next to him, he turned to her, and they seemed to melt into one another's arms. They held one another in silence for several moments.

"You're different," Zorrita said, her eyes searching his.

Leighton sighed. "I killed … five men," he said, his voice halting as he forced the words out. "Camilo helped with three of them, but the first two were mine alone."

"I know," she replied. "Camilo told me." She held him as they sat together watching the river.

The silence between them grew. Zorrita leaned into Leighton as they sat together on the river bank, slightly behind him, their bodies melding, her arm over his left shoulder and her chin on his right, her cheek against the heat of his neck as the shadows of the trees on the river lengthened and the sun sank toward the horizon. He had never killed before, and he sensed that she knew it—that she felt his sadness.

Word of their journey had spread throughout the camp. To a man, the guerillas were now impressed with the American. From the start, they had been suspicious of him. But now he had their respect; now they had given him a nickname reflecting his exploits and their esteem for him. The guerillas had already begun referring to Leighton as *Machete Negro*," Black Machete."

Zorrita had heard this phrase but would tell him of it later. They sat holding each other, listening to the gentle sound of the river and the nocturnal birds as they began their song at dusk, until slowly, she began to sense the sadness in him subside.

CHAPTER 3
RADIO NIGHT

After the deprivation of the bush, for Leighton the food upon the return to Limado was like a feast. Despite the temporary cessation of the night reconnaissance flights, the guerillas maintained their routine of retiring to the caves in the hills above their camp at nightfall. Still flush with cash from the armored car robbery at Puerto Oeste, Zorrita and Miguel had jointly arranged for a regular flow of food supplies from Limado, whose merchants were only too happy to take the guerillas' money, no questions asked. It was a pleasant change from feeling obliged to provide, for no compensation, foodstuffs to people who often couched their requests in polite terms but who were nonetheless armed.

The evening meal consisted of fish and roast chicken, cooked over actual charcoal, with rice seasoned with sliced lemon, green peppers, and tomatoes. There were also stewed plantains, and to wash it all down, there was even warm beer.

"I have not seen Miguel," Leighton commented when he had finished eating. Zorrita sat around a small fire in their cave with him, Mateo, and Camilo, and the atmosphere was one of a contented reunion, if not a happy one. But at the mention of Miguel, Zorrita's expression hardened.

"He has gone to join the fighting at Redención," she said quietly. "Thirty others went with him."

"Zorrita," Mateo said gently, "let us speak plainly among ourselves. It is only the four of us here. It is clear that the bulk of our force remains

22

here at Limado and that you did not support the idea of joining the fighting down there."

"No, I didn't," Zorrita admitted. "I am convinced that the Americans, for reasons of their own, are behind this so-called uprising. The messages from the leader of the Redención cell to me personally say he is convinced that the CIA is behind it and that he would not have launched this rebellion on his own. I do not believe the *Frente* should be an ingredient in a CIA stew. Vilar is concentrating all his military force down there at the moment. The fact that he has diverted all his air power to Redención"—here she glanced at Leighton—"even if temporarily, is more than just a sign of his struggle to retain control. Half of the Army is fighting there too. We are getting reports from Valmonte, Melilla and other places that the military patrols are suddenly either light or nonexistent. There is a strong possibility that Vilar seeks a decisive, fatal blow against us, and Redención is his opportunity. Even if we pulled every fighter from every cell across the country and poured them into Redención, we would not be strong enough to defeat the Army in conventional combat, even in an urban setting.

"It is possible, even likely," she went on, "that the Americans now want Vilar removed from power, but that does not mean they embrace the *Frente,* the guerillas. We will not have the advantage that Castro had in Cuba when he initially came to power. Redención could be the Americans' ploy to cripple the *Frente* as a viable military force, and I do not intend to play into their hands."

"I think you are right," Camilo said.

"It makes sense," Mateo added, nodding. "But Miguel did not agree?"

"We have different views on the matter," Zorrita replied tactfully. "We discussed it at length. He was determined to join the fighting, and I could not convince him otherwise."

There was an uncomfortable silence in the cave as everyone digested what this meant. There was a rift in the top leadership—something that had never happened before.

"I told Miguel and the others to go with God, and that I would pray for their success. But I will not expend lives in a fight I do not believe we can win. For now, whatever political influence the *Frente* has stems largely from our military strength, and I have a responsibility to use it wisely."

Mateo and Camilo nodded their agreement. "We are with you, Z. To the death."

"Yes," Camilo added. Mateo, Camilo, and Zorrita all stood and embraced. Leighton stood out of respect, having just witnessed what he understood to be a blood pact.

"It means a great deal to me to hear you say it," Zorrita said, visibly moved and near tears. "It was a difficult conversation with Miguel. My obligation," she continued, recovering her composure quickly, "is to see that no one loses his life in vain. And this one," she said, breaking from the three-way embrace to take a step toward Leighton and place a hand on his shoulder, "this one is going to help. I want to hear your plan for attacking the air base. I will not intervene in Redención, but we may still be able to influence events down there."

"Yes, Machete," Camilo said proudly. "Tell us your plan."

Leighton looked sharply at Camilo, stung by the word, and was about to retort when Zorrita shot him a look of warning.

Once they had cleared away the remnants of the meal, Leighton used a stick to sketch out a diagram of the air base at Taramantes on the dirt floor of the cave. Over the next several moments, he told them what he had learned during his reconnaissance of the base.

"It looks like a formidable target, as I expected," Zorrita interjected. "How do you propose to get us in?"

"The plan depends in part on the hills to the south of the base remaining uncovered by sentries. The base of those hills is outside the immediate glare of the searchlights, and from there it's a short distance to a gully. Anyone down in that gully is completely hidden from the view from the base, or even the guardhouses outside the perimeter wire. We first infiltrate four snipers into that gully, on the west side of the road leading up to the base entrance. At a specified time, they would expose themselves long enough to take out the four searchlights on the southern half of the base covering the entrance road, and then a fifth light on the west end of the airfield, one of two that cover the planes."

"Exactly when?" Zorrita asked.

"Once our convoy of vehicles reaches the first perimeter, before it's on its way to the second perimeter fence."

"Convoy?"

"Yes. The plan requires at least five Army vehicles, three jeeps and two three-quarter ton Dodge trucks."

"Where will we get the vehicles?"

"We've seen them patrolling Valmonte, that day at Colinas, and we have one jeep already," Leighton replied, glancing at Mateo. "They shouldn't be too hard to find."

"Taking them could involve shooting."

"There's a good chance, yes," Leighton admitted.

Zorrita looked at Mateo. "What do you think?"

"We'd have to wait until shortly before the operation because there's a question of hiding the vehicles. There's risk involved, but it's possible. Let's hear the rest."

"The convoy would approach at night, only after confirming that the snipers are in place. Our arrival will be timed to catch the maximum number of planes on the ground, after the Owls of the night squadron have returned and before the day squadron takes off. Everyone in at least the three lead vehicles will have to be in uniform. We forge papers ordering the convoy to the air base to beef up security. The orders wouldn't have to be perfect, just convincing enough to have the guards at the outside perimeter gate call the base for confirmation."

Leighton went through his plan in detail, scratching out a surprisingly elaborate sketch of the air base in the dirt, walking them through each phase of the attack. When he finished, Zorrita leaned forward.

"The searchlight in the middle of the airfield concerns me," Zorrita said. "You really need six searchlights destroyed, not five, since the one in the middle of the airfield could blind the drivers and gunners as they near the Owls if it's not dealt with quickly. They'll be headed directly toward it."

"And the snipers," Mateo added. "Not one of them will have a clear view of that searchlight in the center of the field from outside the perimeter. The aircraft hangars directly behind the entrance gate will block their view. And there could be quite a delay while one of them runs from the gully to a point where they'd get a clear shot at that light."

"What if two men in one of the vehicles were assigned to take out the light?" Camilo offered.

"An accurate shot at a searchlight from a moving vehicle will be hard," Zorrita replied. "It might be different if one of the jeeps had a heavy machine gun mounted, but we can't count on that. I'm assuming everyone will have small arms?"

"That's how I planned it," Leighton admitted.

"Then you will need more snipers, at least two more, who will ride in with the convoy and dismount to take out that central searchlight. But they'd have to make a run for it back to the main entrance afterward."

"They won't be likely to survive if they have to go all that way on foot," Mateo said immediately.

"I know," Zorrita replied. "They could be picked up at the entrance, assuming they make it that far, but you're right, they'd likely be killed. The problem will be that if the vehicles are taking fire, it'll be hard for them to slow down long enough to pick up anyone." She thought a moment. "We may need another vehicle, dedicated to eliminating that last searchlight."

She took the stick from Leighton. "When they first drive inside the perimeter here, and turn in a big arc toward the Owls, one of them can instead peel off and head directly toward that searchlight. If they have to, they can stop near the day squadron planes to discourage return fire, just long enough to put that light out. Then they could shoot up the day planes and get out of there. That's better than giving the snipers a suicide mission."

"Suppose someone raises an alarm, though," Camilo said. "Where are the barracks for the troops guarding the planes?"

"One is here," Leighton said, pointing to a rectangle he had drawn near the northern perimeter. "Near the northern airstrip, where the Owls will be parked. But they're one hundred feet away, and there will be a row of Owls between them and our vehicles, so they won't be able to return fire immediately. They'll have to move out onto the tarmac. That'll take valuable time, and by then we should be about finished shooting up the Owls and turning away toward the day squadron. There's another, smaller barracks at the northeast corner of the airfield, but that's over five hundred feet away."

Zorrita studied the drawing in the dirt, illuminated only by their cooking fires. "A great deal will depend on the element of surprise, and split second timing, especially in the first two or three minutes," she said. "It will succeed or fail in those few minutes." She continued to stare at the drawing.

Then she looked at Leighton. "I have anticipated parts of your plan. There is a machinist in Limado who is already making silencers based on drawings I provided him that will fit our M-16's and the Belgian rifles. And for two of our pistols." She looked at Mateo. "Yours and mine. Also our people in Valmonte are working on stealing uniforms. But the vehicles are another matter."

"I can get to work on that tomorrow," Mateo said.

"The plan might work," she said to Leighton with a nod of approval. "I want you to run through it again in the morning."

"Alright."

"You have all done well," she said to the three of them. "Get some rest. But not you, Machete. I will handle the nightly broadcast, and I need someone strong to pack the radio up the hill. Meet me outside." She turned and left the cave.

***

In the darkness outside the cave, Zorrita took Leighton's hand and began to turn to lead him away, but he pulled her back to him and kissed her, hard. She responded, and for a long moment their tongues danced about one another, until she forcibly pushed him away.

"We have a broadcast," she reminded him in a stern tone, surprised at the sudden intensity of his passion. "Are you planning to rip my clothes off?"

"I won't say I never thought of it," Leighton said with amusement.

"Later," she said firmly, and took him by the hand once again. She led him along the hillside in the dark, climbing to a higher elevation until they reached another, smaller cave. Inside, she lit a candle. Here was the powerful radio that made nationwide broadcasts to every guerilla cell in the country, the machine that made *Radio Frente* possible.

It was from this device that Zorrita had ordered Mateo back to Vescambre. It was four times the size of the mobile VHF set Camilo had carried, and more than double the weight. Yet it, too, was mobile, with appropriate sweat and motivation. The radio rested on a rectangular folding table that sagged but did not buckle under its weight. The guerillas had rigged a special canvas harness that allowed a strong man to carry it, with effort. Next to it on the table was a mobile generator similar to the one Mateo had carried into the field, but larger. It was a fraction of the weight of the radio it powered, but Leighton doubted Zorrita could lift it, she was so petite.

"I'm packing *this* up the hill?" Leighton asked.

"Yes," Zorrita replied. "You're strong enough."

"Now I know why Mateo and Camilo were smirking at each other."

"That was one reason," Zorrita said cryptically.

On Zorrita's instructions, Leighton backed up to the radio, slipped on the harness, and held still as Zorrita tightened the straps. "Get under it, bend your knees, and lean forward until you feel the weight of it. Then lift—but using your legs, not your back," she explained carefully. Leighton did as she instructed as she knelt in front of him to steady him with her hands on his shoulders. He groaned as he took the weight of the radio, mostly on his legs initially, then slowly rose. Zorrita quickly bent down and seized the generator, lifting it with apparent ease.

"Follow me," she said.

She moved at the pace Leighton could match, their progress slow and deliberate along a mercifully smooth trail with a gentle incline free of major obstructions. The trail eventually rose to the crest of the hill. Here Zorrita stood behind him and helped him ease the transmitter to the ground. She then busied herself hooking the generator up along with the Morse code key apparatus. Leighton was breathing heavily, still recovering, but she was focused entirely on the task at hand.

"Start the generator," she demanded. Leighton gave her a look but complied as she switched on the transmitter and waited for it to warm up. She pulled a codebook out of the pocket of her dungarees and consulted it by the yellowish light of the transmitter dials. It told her what variation of the *Frente* code to use for this particular broadcast. She flicked a switch and with a series of clicks, adjusted three dials that would automatically encrypt her Morse signals. Once the transmitter began to emit its familiar hum, she set to work with the Morse key:

PDM to all cells. PDM to all cells. Report any new developments.

With a pencil and separate notebook, she jotted down relevant details as, one by one, the individual guerilla cells reported in. Those with no news reported briefly; the longest report by far was from Redención. The process took a full ninety minutes, as she worked furiously decoding each incoming signal in real time. Leighton knew enough about radio procedures and encrypted communications to realize that few people could do what he was watching Zorrita do, and certainly not with her speed. He was developing an inkling of how brilliant she was; he supposed that she had excelled in mathematics at university, since the most gifted cryptographers often did. When the reports concluded, she sent the following signal:

Valmonte cell is to await orders for new operation. Instructions will come within 48 hours direct from NGX.

She then signaled Leighton to stop cranking the generator and began to shut the transmitter down. After waiting for it to cool down a bit, they moved the transmitter and generator a short distance away to a spot where the brush provided them ample cover. Zorrita sat with her back against a tree and rubbed her forehead. Leighton leaned in to kiss her forehead and gently massage her temples, much to her surprise.

"You know just what to do," she muttered in quiet amazement.

"It comes easily," Leighton said, "when I care about someone."

"So…you care about me, then?"

"Yes."

"You aren't falling in love, are you?"

"That's a strange question."

"Not really…Americans are quick to decide they are in love, in my experience."

"Well, in my case," Leighton replied, still massaging her temples, "it takes more than a swim in the nude."

"Hmm, I'll remember that," she said with a smile. "I only brought it up because it can be a dangerous word. A dangerous emotion."

"I'm not afraid of it."

"But you should be. We have no reason to hide behind pretense. There is an attraction between us. You are feeling a surge of chemical and biological reactions. So am I. It's Mother Nature. It's not love."

"Men have become too attached to you in the past, is that it?"

She met his eyes in the darkness. "Yes. Yes, they have."

"Don't worry. I've been told that I'm a survivor."

"What does that mean?"

"It means I'm too cold-blooded to fall in love."

Zorrita cocked an eyebrow, ruminating on that.

"And yet you volunteered the fact that you care about me," she said quietly.

Leighton decided upon a change of subject. "What was the news from Redención?"

She took a breath and let it out slowly, a long exhale. "It isn't good, I'm afraid." She did not elaborate, but instead handed him her little notebook, open to the page containing tonight's Redención report. Leighton fired up his Zippo and read by its light:

> *Fighting continues with increasing ferocity. Frente forced to surrender another government building in City Center today. Casualties mounting, 147 wounded, 76 dead including 9 from Limado cell. Air attacks intensified but shot down government plane today with Stinger missile. Have destroyed several armored personnel carriers with Molotov cocktails. Elements of two infantry battalions totaling estimated 2,500 troops are squeezing our force of 500 plus into a pocket extending from downtown to southern outskirts of city. First tanks appeared today against which we have no defense. Government has shut*

off all water mains in city. Request ammunition as our supply running low.

There was no word of Miguel specifically. It was only a matter of time before the uprising was crushed. Leighton handed the notebook back.

"This is why I did not want to join the fight," Zorrita said sadly, waving the notebook. "We can't help them, with ammo or anything else. It is a fight on Vilar's terms."

"Food is one thing," Leighton said. "But they can't survive long without water."

"Exactly. Vilar knows that—or rather, his generals do. It was an inspired tactic. But I'd rather we had done it to them. My God," she said, shaking her head with her eyes closed. "They're going to be cut to pieces. Annihilated. And Miguel *insisted*. He was adamant. We never had such a bitter argument as that one. I tried to persuade him that this was not the fight, that this was not the time, but he refused to listen. I remember thinking that he would not be so blind to the merits of my arguments if I were a man."

As she spoke, her voice was steady, but tears of frustration began to stream down her cheeks. Leighton watched her closely, instinctively sensing that timing was everything now. He said nothing, inching ever so slightly closer to her, waiting.

She muttered a curse and stood up, and the torrent of tears began in earnest, a reflexive outpouring of frustration rather than grief, an acknowledgement of the lives in jeopardy and soon to be lost, with nothing to be done about it, nothing that could possibly happen in time to prevent disaster. Leighton felt like a trapeze artist waiting for his partner to swing toward him and release the bar, to sail through the air, for only then could he catch her; only then could he be sure of her safety, even if only for the moment. With Zorrita, it was nothing he could see—he could only sense it. The moment came, and he half-seized, half-caught her as she half-fell and half-flew into his arms. He held her tight, squeezing her firmly as her tears slowly subsided, his only thought to give her the one elusive thing she needed most at this instant: Comfort—comfort blended with a strange alchemy of caring and empathy that gave her absolute confidence in his discretion, his silence about this, her most vulnerable and un-leader-like moment.

They were silent for several moments as he eased his grip on her, loosening his arms so that the bear hug melted away and he was merely holding her now, an act of support rather than control. Then he let his hands fall to his sides, still standing so close to her that they could feel one another's body heat, and suddenly she reached out for him and kissed him hungrily. He responded, one hand reaching up to stroke her cheek, sliding over the silky softness of her skin around to the fine down at the back of her neck, reaching up to firmly pull her hair while his other hand roamed her body. She began to grind against him, pushing him against the tree.

She unzipped her dungarees and he continued kissing her as she guided his hand inside her boxer shorts. Leighton's fingers pressed against the source of the heat between her legs, and she moaned. As he knelt, pulling the fabric down toward her knees and touching the deliciously coarse hair of her sex, she whispered, "Gabriela … my name is Gabriela." He smiled in the darkness, sliding her boxers down past her knees and pushing his nose and then his mouth into the little forest of hair, breathing deeply of her intoxicating female musk. His tongue flickered out, and she gasped as he tasted the tangy wetness of her vulva, tucked discreetly between twin folds of tender flesh. Her legs parted slightly as he explored her with his tongue, locating the delicate hood of her clitoris, turning his head to just the right angle to get hold of it with his lips and begin a relentless licking caress.

He continued like that for several moments, until she released his hands and seized the back of his head, as if to pull him into her. She let out a moan, then another, and then a brief, high-pitched scream as her pelvis bucked. Leighton suddenly felt a torrent of viscous fluid on his face and kept hold her buttocks as she convulsed involuntarily. When her tremors stopped, she tugged at his shirt until he stood, and she then kissed him passionately, her fingers moving deftly to open his jeans.

Tugging at his shorts, her hand encircled his erection and squeezed gently. She placed a hand between her legs, and her fingers came away moist and closed upon his erection again, stroking it with the help of her own wetness. She knelt and gave the tip of his penis a small lick. She then kissed it, squeezing it again before enveloping it with her mouth. Leighton moaned as she slowly worked on him, releasing him occasionally to glide her lips along the shaft, slapping it against her cheek before resuming the oral caress, until the excitement was too much for him and he began to move his hips. She yielded to this, and in a short time the fierce pulsing in her mouth told her he was very close. She did not move as he moaned, gripping his hips firmly as he released into her mouth with a low, guttural groan. She continued to hold him there, swallowing and sucking gently until she sensed he could take no more. Only then did she let him go.

She stood and they embraced, kissing for several moments. Using Leighton for support, Zorrita stripped, then waited as he undressed. She took him by the hand and led him a short way along the hillside to a little "bedroom" she had prepared, which consisted of blankets upon the ground on a little oval patch of grass surrounded on three sides by trees, with a bottle of wine.

She stood before him smiling, nude and unabashed. "We have been coming to this moment since that kiss in the tunnel at Colinas," she said softly.

"Then it wasn't my imagination," Leighton said.

"Oh, no. You must have known … that day we went swimming."

"I suspected you don't invite just anyone to go bathing."

"I tried to pretend otherwise, but it was an act that didn't fool anyone. A leader should be more like a sphinx—what you Americans call poker-faced."

"But you're only human," Leighton said, "a flesh-and-blood woman."

"And so was Fidel Castro, and your George Washington, and Alexander the Great. They were only flesh and blood. But I am a woman. I don't have the luxury of being only that, most of the time. Anyway," she said, waving a hand toward the blankets and wine, "I'm sure you have much better in America, but this is the best we can do here."

"I love it."

"Do you?" She took a step toward him, and Leighton reached out and took her firmly by her upper arms, reveling in the feeling of her flesh against his. He kissed her.

"I do," he whispered.

She looked at him in the darkness, her eyes wet with vulnerability and desire. "I know you do not like it, but you must understand; when I call you 'Machete' in front of the others, it only reinforces your reputation with them now, the respect they have for you. It is important. They all know by now that I have chosen you. So everything about you, whether we like it or not, is a reflection on me."

"I know," Leighton said quietly.

"I know you do," she said. "It is important that you embrace the name they have given you, even though you may hate it. You are not the American Señor Palmer anymore. You are the fierce guerilla fighter who singlehandedly killed two soldiers in cold blood with a machete, when he could easily have used a gun. The machismo ethos that so permeates this culture has now settled firmly upon your shoulders. It can benefit you. But you must be seen to embrace it … or you will not be worthy of me in their eyes."

Leighton nodded.

"Do not let my words anger or antagonize you. You are one of us now. Don't throw it away." She hesitated before she spoke again. "I have debated whether to tell you this … I want you to stay with us. With me. I have needed a partner for a long time who was in sympathy with the movement, who believed in it, but who was not of the movement. I have needed someone from outside, who understands other things … the world. Not just Madrinega. Or Central America."

"I want to stay," Leighton heard himself saying. "In a strange way, I feel at home here."

She smiled and caressed his face. "My love, you are being very American at this moment."

"What do you mean?"

"I have decoded your message. In your country, when a man tells a woman he feels at home with her, it is another way of saying he loves her. Love," she said hesitantly, gently, "Love is a bourgeois concept of the Euro-American middle class."

"But Gabriela, you're middle class. Your father is a doctor."

They lay down on the blankets, and she uncorked the wine, offering him the bottle. Leighton drank from it and handed it to her. She took a tiny sip and set it down.

"It's true I was born to privilege. But it has instilled in me more a sense of obligation to do for others than a desire to sit back and wallow in dreams of self-indulgence. Don't be offended; let me explain. When you say to me 'I love you,' I believe what you really mean is 'I desire you.' Perhaps intensely. That makes me happy, because I desire you intensely also. I will tell you honestly I feel that we have a connection that is very strong ... It is something that might last a long time. But to call it love ... love, Brian, is like a mist on the wind. It is hard to catch, and harder still to hold."

"That's the first time you've called me Brian," Leighton said, suddenly wishing that he could tell her his real name. "But you called me 'my love' also."

"Be careful with your 'love,'" she said. "It could hurt us both. Perhaps kill us."

"That's a strange thing to say."

Gabriela smiled. "When I say 'my love,' what I want you to hear is 'my mate.' Because that is how I think of you now," she said, reaching out to playfully tug at his penis. "My mate. Yes?"

Leighton smiled in spite of himself, as he felt another erection growing in her hand. "Yes."

"There, you can see for yourself," she said, pleased. "Your body knows what I mean, even if you don't. Now," she urged, turning her back and getting onto her hands and knees. She turned her head to look over her shoulder at him. "Take me. We have all night ... it would be a sin to waste it."

The noise she made as he entered her was not a gasp; it was a low, brief, trembling squeal more animal than human—but all female. It was a noise that sent a tingle of joy up his spine as he moved deeper into her physical core and began to feel a rapture he had never before experienced. He made love to her slowly at first, trying to savor it, but as his excitement mounted, it became fierce and fast, the gentle beginning quickly giving way to a roughness that seemed to enhance her pleasure.

Afterward they lay entwined together, floating in a blissful torpor on the edge of consciousness. She reached behind her and took hold of his arm. "Stay with me," she murmured, half asleep. "I will," Leighton whispered. "But will you stay here, once Vilar is gone?"

Gabriela did not answer. The beautiful revolutionary was already fast asleep.

CHAPTER 4
THE KILL ORDER

The following morning, Gabriela and Leighton returned to the camp at dawn, replacing the transmitter and the generator in their designated cave before joining Mateo and Camilo as they prepared one of many cooking fires being built around the guerilla camp. This time there were no comments or furtive sideways glances; Mateo now took it for granted that Zorrita would slip away with Leighton for privacy during the hours of darkness, and he greeted them as though it was a long-established routine. Camilo, whom Zorrita had always treated as a little brother, was in favor of anything that brought her safety and happiness. He had accepted the attraction between her and Leighton faster than anyone else.

After breakfasting on coffee, a fried egg, and a thin beefsteak, Leighton revised his article "Portrait of a Guerilla Leader" to add Gabriela's general impressions of the fighting in Redención. Gabriela found him putting the finishing touches on his edits, bent over his laptop computer under what was becoming his usual tree in the camp. He looked up as she approached, trying to contain the rush of well-being he felt at the sight of her. She looked radiant yet serious as she came to stand very close to him, so close that it was easy to see her faint brownish freckles.

"Hello," she said quietly, and Leighton reflected with awe at how a single, formal word of greeting could, with the proper intonation, be made to sound so intimate.

"Hello," he replied, staring into her eyes, feeling disconcerted that he was suddenly very aware of his heart beating in his chest.

"I've been talking to Mateo about your plan for the air base. He'll issue instructions during tonight's broadcast to the appropriate cells about stealing the vehicles we need," she said quietly. "And we should be getting the silencers from Limado this afternoon. When they come in, I want you and Camilo to test them."

"Alright."

"And I want to gather a few more people together in an hour so you can run through the attack plan with them."

"I'll be ready."

"Good," she said, and she looked at her boots, lingering. She continued speaking, her voice quieter still. "And I'd like to know if you want to take another swim with me, at our spot, just before sundown."

"I'd love to," he said at once, pleased.

"It'll have to be a quick one," she cautioned.

"The answer is still yes," Leighton said.

She looked up at him. "Good," she said, allowing herself a tiny smile. The clear brown of her eyes looked a little brighter for an instant but then returned to their normal dark, piercing intensity.

"I made some edits to the article," Leighton explained, turning the laptop around for her to see the screen. "If you have time, I'd like you to read it," he said, offering her the device.

She took it and sat down next to him. "Will you send it to the American newspapers?"

"If you approve it, yes. I'll have to get it to Avellar first."

She nodded as she began to read. Leighton felt exhilarated yet tired, for their night of lovemaking on the hilltop had not allowed him much time to sleep. He lay back, his body touching hers, closed his eyes, and dozed off. When he awoke a quarter of an hour later, she was staring at him.

"What do you think?"

She glanced at the laptop screen and then back at him. "Is this how you see me?" she asked.

Unable to gauge her reaction, he said tentatively, "Yes. Is anything wrong?"

"No … in fact, it's very complimentary. I had no idea you looked upon me as a political chess master."

"Isn't that exactly what you have to be, to do what you do?"

"Well, yes. I'm just surprised that a man—any man—would see me that way."

"I appreciate your beauty. But I see a lot more."

"So it seems," she conceded. "And I like what you've added about my impressions of the struggle at Redención."

"I tried to be accurate, without putting words in your mouth that weren't your own."

"You did an excellent job."

Leighton turned to her. "Gabriela—" She immediately stopped him with a finger upon his lips.

"Not where others can hear you," she said gently. "Only when we are alone."

"Zorrita," he said, "I want to make a suggestion."

"What is it?"

"That we return the missile components we brought back from Vescambre to the Americans."

"Why?"

"As proof that the *Frente* doesn't intend to use the missiles as Vilar has, to cause wholesale bloodshed. It allows you to argue that your primary purpose in seizing the missiles in the first place was simply to deny Vilar further use of them, after what he did at Panactatlan."

She looked thoughtful. "That would be a propaganda victory of sorts," she admitted, "making us look reasonable. But what if it isn't true? What if I intend to use the missiles?"

"I suppose it would depend on how you use them, against what target. But in the short term it wouldn't matter; it would still be a propaganda victory, and it would resonate with people in the United States, undercutting Vilar's claims that the guerillas are no more than criminals."

"What if the Americans just give the equipment back to Vilar?"

"For one thing, I damaged it. For another, I don't see that happening. By now my guess is that the Americans see what a mistake it was to sell the missiles to Vilar in the first place. They want them back. Anyway, no one has to know what your plans are for the remaining missiles."

"I will think about it. As for your article, I approve," she said. She handed back the laptop, then placed a hand on his thigh and squeezed as she rose. Leighton inhaled her scent and watched her walk away, momentarily captivated by the intimate memory of making love to her the night before. Then, looking about to confirm that he would not be observed, he activated the satellite communicator. Miller had sent him a long message:

> You are to terminate, repeat terminate, subject Gabriela Marcellina Aaima Diaz, alias Zorrita, at earliest opportunity regardless of risk. Identify confirmed. This order takes priority over recovery of missiles.
>
> $200,000 CIA bounty on subject has increased recently to $350,000. State Department and CIA confirm assessment subject is high-level threat to U.S. interests and international security in Western Hemisphere. Subject is responsible for multiple assassinations of officers Salvadoran Army allegedly linked to operations of death squads. Most recently subject is believed to have trained special Sandinista teams to strike Nicaraguan Contra base camps in Honduras. Acknowledge upon receipt.

Leighton read the message three times, searching in vain for a loophole, a way out, as a sickly, coppery taste flooded his mouth. He shut the laptop down and stood, letting the device fall to the ground. He began walking, not knowing where he was going. The heat of the day was blistering as usual, and as he stumbled about the camp, he saw many guerillas keeping religiously to the shade, but Leighton was in a cold sweat.

He walked to the river, stripped off his clothes and jumped in. He swam furiously, his mind racing to the point that it could not settle on a single coherent thought. He swam out into the middle of the river and let the current take him. It swept him along for nearly a quarter of a mile, bringing him dangerously close to a series of rocks protruding above the surface. Here the current was too strong to resist by swimming directly against it, and Leighton skimmed by the rocks with minor bruises only by paddling hard in a breaststroke back toward the eastern bank of the river. Downriver the current was stronger still, and he continued to steer his body toward the bank with difficulty, stopping only when he struck a fallen tree and seized one of its branches. He pulled himself up out of the river and sat atop the tree trunk, coughing up river water. When he recovered, he navigated his way along the log until he could drop down on the dry land of the river bank.

He walked back toward his clothing, moving in and out of the brush depending on the proximity of any guerillas he saw, for he had no desire to be seen strolling about nude like a crazy man. It would not reflect well on Gabriela. At last he located his clothing and dressed. He stood there watching the water and then began to pace back and forth along the river bank.

Miller's wording had been very precise; Leighton could never argue that it was anything other than an unequivocal order. Gabriela was perceived as a threat so serious that killing her was deemed more important than recovering the missiles—more important than Leighton's life – that was the meaning of the phrase "regardless of risk." He was used to that, but Miller was now emphasizing the point in light of the opportunity to kill the most important guerilla leader in Latin America since Che Guevara. Miller, who always went out of his way to look after his agents. But not this time.

Only now did he begin to understand the deeper significance of Gabriela's revolutionary beliefs, which she had begun to share with him that day of their first swim together; how profoundly the people in the shadows, those responsible for "national security," feared her. Gabriela scared them shitless.

Drenched once again in his own sweat, no longer cold, Leighton walked back to the camp, where he had abandoned his laptop and carrying case. He took the laptop and stowed it away neatly in the case, patting an exterior pocket of the case and feeling a hard bulge that confirmed the .25 caliber Vesta automatic was still there. Such was the respect the guerillas now felt for him that some had seen him abandon his belongings and simply walk away, yet no one had approached Machete's things.

Leighton found the place where Zorrita wanted the briefing—a little rectangular plateau bordered by fallen trees that the guerillas had placed on four sides to be used as benches. But for the reconnaissance planes, it would have been an ideal place to have large campfires at night. Here Zorrita had gathered Mateo, Camilo, and a dozen other guerillas—the people she decided would help lead the raid against the air base.

Using another stick, Leighton drew a larger map of the air base than before in the dirt and ran through the plan of attack, modified to reflect Zorrita's refinement of a single vehicle dedicated to the elimination of the searchlight in the center of the air base. There was discussion, including several questions. Some were skeptical, but they all understood the significance of crippling the government's force of reconnaissance planes. The entire meeting took close to two hours. In the end, those who would lead the attack all approved.

Leighton had kept his distance from Zorrita the entire time, telling himself he did not want to inadvertently do anything that might compromise her authority. But he went so far as to avoid eye contact. After the meeting, he wanted to flee, but he had some awareness of the effect his behavior was having on her and did not want to make it worse. And so he lingered, against his will, neither approaching her nor running away, busying himself with the many notes he had made during his reconnaissance of the air base while she spoke with Camilo at length. At last Camilo left and they were alone. Leighton forced himself to look her in the eye as she approached.

"Something is troubling you," she said firmly, watching him with those piercing brown eyes.

"The heat seems worse today," Leighton said. "It's almost unbearable sometimes."

"I heard you dropped your laptop and took off for a swim. That's not like you; you carry it everywhere."

"The heat," Leighton repeated, nodding. "You are having me watched?"

She playfully slapped his stomach with the back of her hand. "You misunderstand," she said with a little frown. "You are important to me. They all know that now. So yes, they watch over you. They keep me informed—but without my asking. Our camps have been attacked before. Camilo was wounded in one such attack, before you joined us. I want you to be safe."

"I guess I'm just adjusting to the situation," Leighton said, and Gabriela cocked her head in concern. "I mean, as your ... mate ... I won't have a lot of privacy, will I?"

Gabriela took his hand and said softly, "The same privacy I have, which is not very much ... except when we're alone together." She smiled tentatively, searching his eyes. "Can you live with that?" she asked earnestly.

Leighton sensed what a terrible moment of vulnerability this was for her. Right on the heels of the one she shared last night. He knew that if he allowed doubt to enter her mind now, it would destroy what they had begun together. He looked into her eyes.

"If I can have you, I can live with that until I draw my last breath."

Gabriela stared at him for a long moment. Then she embraced him, hard. Leighton held her tight. He became extremely aware of his heartbeat for the second time that day. Suddenly he realized that Camilo had returned, carrying a satchel and both his FN FAL and Leighton's M-16.

Leighton gently tapped Gabriela's back, and they slowly separated as she looked over her shoulder at Camilo. The youth was unphased; he acted as though he had seen it all before.

"The silencers came in from Limado," he said to Leighton. "Want to help me test them?"

"It looks like you have work to do," Zorrita said, squeezing his hand. "I'll see you later."

And she was gone.

Upon his return to camp with Camilo, Leighton laid his M-16 against "his tree" and fished the inertial navigation unit and the flat GPS antenna with its jagged edges out of his satchel and sought out Zorrita. He found her beneath a group of trees instructing six girls ranging in age from twelve to eighteen how to field strip an AK-47 assault rifle, only one of a handful he had seen in the entire camp.

"Most of the men are reluctant to teach the girls about weapons, so I must do it," Zorrita explained. "They are here because they prefer to be wives and mothers only after they have taken their country back."

"You all have a great deal of courage," Leighton said. Most of the girls were too shy to respond, but one of them met his eye and smiled. "I wonder if I could talk to you a moment," Leighton said to Zorrita. "I'd like to go back to Valmonte."

Zorrita, in the middle of reassembling the AK-47, looked up at Leighton sharply. Turning to the oldest girl, the one who had smiled, she said, "Henrietta, take over. Be sure the others can see everything you're doing."

"Yes, Zorrita," Henrietta replied.

Gabriela took Leighton's arm and led him a few paces away. "Why?" she demanded. "You know how dangerous it is for you there. It's why we brought you out."

"I know. But I need to get the article to Avellar."

"I can send someone else."

"I didn't like the way I left. He was still in the hospital. I need to go back and face him."

"At the risk of your life? If you fall into Narváez' hands again, he will kill you. What else is there?"

"These," Leighton said, raising his hands. "I want your permission to take these missile components back to the Americans."

"Do you feel you owe them?"

"No, I honestly believe it will help the cause."

"Not at the risk of your life. No," she said, visibly disturbed.

"Gabriela, please—"

She immediately shot him an angry look of warning. She walked a few more paces away so that they were behind a tree, out of earshot of the girls. Leighton laid the missile components on the ground and began to embrace her, but she blocked the move with an actual blow against his chest with the flat of her hand. She stared at the ground.

"You want to go away … after last night. What am I supposed to think?"

"I am guilty of terrible timing, and I know it will be dangerous, but do you think I *want* to go? With Avellar it's a matter of honor. And I thought while I was there …"

But Leighton could see that she was not listening. He took a step toward her, and her arms came up reflexively, ready to fend him off, but he did not try to touch her. He leaned in as close as he dared and whispered, "Gabriela … I felt happy for the first time in years last night. I didn't want it to end. I wish we could leave here, right now—leave all this blood and death behind and never come back. You gave me such pleasure last night … but I know you'll never leave until you finish your work here, so I don't ask you to leave. At least not yet. Please, let me do this one thing."

She looked at him, calmer now, more at ease after hearing his words. "I understand matters of honor," she said slowly. "But suppose I never see you again?"

Leighton reached up to her face. This time she made no attempt to prevent his touch as he stroked her freckled cheek. "You will," he said, staring into her eyes. "You will."

"I would like to be as sure as you are," Zorrita said, stepping from behind the tree and turning to see the girls watching her private moment with Leighton and giggling. "And I have no intention of giving the Americans intact parts that can simply be put back into the missile again," she said, stooping down to recover the components and tossing them a short distance away into the dirt. She strode quickly back to the girls.

"Henrietta, the weapon." Henrietta, who had just barely completed reassembling the AK-47, handed it over without a word. Zorrita rapidly checked the magazine, flicked the selector switch to three-round burst, aimed at the missile parts, and fired twice. Frightened at the noise, three of the girls ran, but Henrietta and two others stood their ground.

Several guerillas, including Camilo and Mateo, appeared from out of nowhere, weapons at the ready.

"Do not worry," she told them. "I was only preparing our gift for the Americans." She handed the weapon back to Henrietta.

Leighton walked to the missile parts and picked them up. The GPS antenna had two bullet holes in it, and the inertial navigation system was mangled and still smoking, having been hit multiple times. He rejoined Zorrita, but Henrietta and the other girls had disappeared.

"Will Machete be joining me for a bath, or are you so eager to be away?" Her tone of voice was suddenly cool; her expression told him she was quite unhappy with him.

"I'll be there," Leighton said in a low voice.

⟨ ⟩ ⟨ ⟩ ⟩ ⬛ ⬛ ⬛ ⬛ ⬛ ⬛ ⬛ ⬛ ⬛ ⬛ ⬛ ⟩ ⟩ ⟨ ⟨ ⟨

Miller sat back in his chair and read the latest cable from the SONAI station in Guatemala, which brought the long-awaited good news: a special team in a CH-53 "Jolly Green Giant" helicopter, accompanied by two Cobra attack helicopters, had successfully recovered the first of the cruise missiles from Madrinega.

Flying low enough to hug the terrain and avoid local radar, the three helicopters had penetrated Madrinegan airspace at dawn, located the cruise missile at Vescambre based on Leighton's instructions, recovered it, and flown it back to Guatemala without incident. The team had also discovered the bodies nearby and taken photographs before departing.

Leighton was at last yielding results. In response to his request, Miller had sent three magnetized transponder units, two plus a spare, to Madrinega in the diplomatic pouch addressed to Lang. With the fighting in Redención intensifying, Miller just hoped Leighton could pick up the devices and use them while there was still time.

Miller lifted the telephone receiver to notify the Director of the good news. But his victory lap would be hollow, because nearly twenty-four hours had elapsed since he had sent Leighton the signal ordering him to kill Zorrita. So far there had been no acknowledgment.

CHAPTER 5
CAPTIVE HEART

L eighton stood nude at the river's edge, his clothing, laptop, water bottle, and M-16 laying on the ground a short distance away. The laptop was nearly out of power; he had spent the past three hours working on a story about the discovery of the bodies at Vescambre, doing his best to link them to the information yielded by Dr. Reynaldo. He was planning to share it with Avellar. Together with the notes he had left behind in Avellar's library, it could make for a devastating story. Ultimately Avellar—and his wife Rosa—would have to judge whether it was worthy of publication. But Leighton knew it was the kind of thing that could help bring Vilar down.

The sun was slowly moving toward the horizon, but Zorrita was nowhere in sight. Leighton's back hurt after hours at the laptop, and he took two steps forward and jumped into the water. He did not repeat his mistake of earlier that day and kept close to the shore, where the current was relatively docile. He worried that she might not be coming. She did not want him to leave, least of all to go back to Valmonte.

Leighton wondered whether he had made a fatal mistake in asking to go. 'Asking' was indeed the right word, for he had no doubt that all it would take for the guerillas to prevent him going was a word from Zorrita. In the starkest terms, since she had arranged to extract him from Valmonte, Zorrita had literally held the power of life and death over him. He thought it ironic that he had just been ordered to kill her.

Leighton swam about, with intervals of floating on the water until the pain in his back subsided. As he floated, he let his mind go blank and closed his eyes. He gradually developed a sense that he was being watched. He opened his eyes and turned in the water to see Gabriela staring at him from the river bank, arms folded as she stood there. Her expression was flat and serious as she sat down and began to undress, removing everything but her tank top. She then stood up, bottomless in the twilight, the olive skin of her legs contrasting with the red-brown hair where they met, still watching him with a flat expression until finally she pulled the tank top over her head and slowly entered the water. She was beautiful even with that stoic look on her face.

Gabriela swam past him, keeping fairly close to shore and away from the stronger currents in the middle of the river. She uttered not a word of greeting. He moved back and forth in a lazy backstroke, waiting for whatever was coming. She swam parallel to him and then around him as the sky turned from blue to indigo to black and he could tell where she was only by the splashing of her body in the water. Leighton finally realized that it was she who was doing the waiting, and he swam directly toward her. Their bodies collided, and she pushed away without a sound. He pursued her. When he caught up to her—he sensed that she was the better swimmer and had allowed it—he made no effort to touch her with his hands but glided toward her until their bodies touched along their length. Slowly they embraced, and Leighton felt her body against him as he kissed her. She suddenly broke away and swam rapidly to shore. Leighton followed, noting as he emerged from the water that the night air was so warm he felt no need to dry himself.

"I'm here," Zorrita said, her voice off to his right. Leighton felt his way in the dark until his hand touched her bare shoulder. He planted a kiss on her neck, and his hands slid down her back to her buttocks and squeezed as her hand closed around his penis. Leighton began to stroke her face and moved to kiss her, stopping abruptly when she said firmly, "No. Don't romance me."

With that she turned and bent over, extending her behind until her soft, firm cheeks bumped against his erection. Leighton positioned himself in the dark until he could feel the warm wetness between her legs. He seized her by the hair and pushed, hard. She let out a cry but made no effort to resist him. Still, only when he heard her utter a weak "Si" under her breath did he continue, ravishing her fast and hard until his climax brought even more violent thrusts, shaking her entire body. Afterward, they lay together on the riverbank, recovering in the darkness.

Slowly, they rose and found their clothing and dressed. They then lay together against a tree trunk, looking out at the river as the moon rose over it. Gabriela had a leg over Leighton's and seemed to be wrapped around him tightly. "You're very quiet tonight," he said.

"I do not want you to go to Valmonte," she replied.

"But you are going to let me go," Leighton pressed.

"Yes. I will be very angry with you if you are hurt or killed," she said, her voice deadly serious as she turned to look at him.

"I'll be careful."

"Mateo will go with you—"

"I should go alone," Leighton interjected.

"Mateo will go with you," Gabriela repeated firmly. "Even though I need him here. You will go tomorrow night, after he has issued instructions during tonight's radio broadcast. There has been a change of plans. In addition to delivering the missile parts and the article to Avellar, you will help Mateo bring someone out, just as you were brought out. It might be easier since the local cell reports the patrols there have melted away to nothing with all the focus on Redención. But the Secret Police want the person we are bringing out, very badly. I had a long meeting with Mateo about it today."

"Who are we bringing out?"

"A sniper. Our best."

· · · · ■ ■ ▬ ▬ ▬ ▬ ▬ ▬ ▬ ■ ■ · · · ·

They returned to their cave in time for the tail end of the evening meal: fish soup and rice with cilantro and peas. Afterward, Leighton slept fitfully and finally dozed off about midnight. Shortly before 2:00 a.m., Mateo rose to prepare for the nightly broadcast, along with

Camilo, who had volunteered to join him. Camilo awakened Zorrita before they left.

When they had gone, she awakened Leighton, and they returned to her makeshift bed of old blankets and a plantain sack with a worn ochre velour covering for a pillowcase. With Mateo and Camilo out on the hilltop for the radio broadcast, they would have nearly two hours of privacy, and they made love again, simply because they could. Leighton began as roughly as he had when they were down by the river, but Gabriela stopped him and shook her head in the faint light of the only remaining fire in the cave, her eyes flickering along with the dancing shadows.

"Now," she whispered, "romance me now. Be gentle, and make it last. You will be gone for some days."

And so he was gentle, slow, and passionate, kissing and caressing her until he drove her to an orgasm that left her shaking, just as he shuddered inside her, nearly overwhelmed at the intensity of it. He was unhappy when she told him he had to return to his own bed, but she pointed out that Camilo had volunteered to help Mateo specifically to give them privacy, and it was best not to abuse such consideration. Gabriela gave Leighton a long, deep kiss, then reached behind her and into a satchel, handing him a bulky canvas pouch.

"For Valmonte," she said. "You may need it."

Leighton reached into the pouch and withdrew a leather shoulder holster holding a 9mm Smith & Wesson automatic pistol.

"Mine," she explained. "I rarely carry it. Plus this. It may come in handy." She placed a five-inch metal cylinder in his hand.

"A silencer," he said.

"I tested it today. It works very well."

Leighton looked at her, not knowing what to say.

"You must come back to me safely," she said, her eyes somber. Leighton kissed her, and they embraced. "You must come back to me safely," she repeated.

Leighton then took the gun and returned to his own makeshift bed. He slept soundly until dawn and awoke refreshed, still feeling her kiss on his lips.

·····⚊ ⚊ ⚊ ⚋ ⚋ ⚋ ⚋ ⚊ ⚊ ⚊·····

Leighton and Mateo left the camp that evening as dusk was falling, packing food in their satchels for two days, along with two grenades apiece, their rifles, machetes, and the tin water bottles. Leighton was also packing his laptop, the missile parts, and Zorrita's Smith & Wesson, after adjusting the shoulder holster to fit comfortably. They did not take a radio. Possession and use of such equipment in the city would be very dangerous. Zorrita's only goodbye had been a fierce bear hug in the privacy of the cave. She had no words. She kept her eyes on the ground even as she broke their embrace, and she seemed wary of further physical contact, but she allowed him to take her hand and kiss her palm.

The trail as far as Limado was familiar and by now well worn. They slowed their pace and moved cautiously through the brush as they neared the village, Mateo uttering the bird calls to alert their sentries of their presence as they passed nearby. They crossed the Olmedilla River at the same point seven miles north of Limado, wading across in bare feet with their rifles held above their heads.

They encountered the same rugged terrain on the far side of the river as before but were able to cover it faster. Leighton remembered much of the route and was able to anticipate. In truth, Leighton did not want to be in the brush again so soon; the journey to reconnoiter the air base and back had been an ordeal, not least because of the hunger that had dogged them for a good part of the way. He thought he must be crazy to leave the relatively plentiful food at Limado, and Gabriela. But he needed an excuse to see Lang, who he hoped would have the transponders he needed, and he felt a strange sort of debt to Avellar. The stories he would deliver to him would help perpetuate his identity as a journalist in the collective mind of the guerillas, and, in the case of the Vescambre story, further undermine Vilar. Leighton set to work on devising a pretext to separate himself from Mateo for the meeting with Lang.

The previous night's radio broadcast indicated that the fighting in Redención was drawing to a close. The trade unionists, lightly armed to begin with, had begun surrendering in large numbers once confronted in combat by professional soldiers, leaving the guerillas as the only fighting force in the city capable of continuing to oppose the government. They had been squeezed into six square blocks, and the house-to-house fighting had become bitter, with mounting casualties on both sides. The government continued to pound away at the guerillas with air attacks, but fewer planes had been seen in the previous twenty-four hours as the number of viable targets began to shrink dramatically. Zorrita was convinced that the countrywide surveillance flights in search of the missiles would begin again at any time, possibly by dawn. She had made a point to caution Leighton and Mateo about it.

Mateo took a slightly different route this time that took them farther northwest; it had them out of the worst of the rugged terrain and back under jungle canopy well before dawn. Although they had been marching for hours, they stayed on the move most of the night, stopping only when they heard an airplane overhead just before 4:00 a.m. At that point, they hid and slept until dawn.

Leighton awoke after a fitful sleep. Mateo was already awake and stirring. They moved out immediately, eating roast plantains from their food supplies and drinking from their water bottles as they walked. Coming to an open pasture about half a mile across, they skirted its edge, although cutting directly across it would have been quicker. The trees lining the edge provided cover, and as the sun rose they were mindful of surveillance planes after hearing one the night before.

"We are in a race against time," Mateo said as they walked. "We want to get into Valmonte and out again as quickly as possible before the fighting in Redención is over and the local patrols in the city are back up to full strength."

"We keep walking all day, then," Leighton replied.

"If you can stand it. Until we reach the jeep. As you know, the heat will be terrible. We will stay in the city at least twenty-four hours, hopefully not much more than that. When we arrive, I will have to see about a safe house and contact the local cell leader about getting the sniper out. It would be unwise to use Cabrera's house again, even if he hadn't been arrested. You can meet with Avellar and return the missile parts on your own, but be prepared to meet up with me afterward."

"You're not going with me?" Leighton asked, although privately he was relieved.

Mateo shook his head. "Zorrita trusts you. But she is still not certain about your ability to survive alone in the bush. Or to navigate your way across the country. You will have your job in Valmonte, and I will have mine. But I will need your help to get the sniper out when the time comes. We cannot enter the sewer system as we did before. The Valmonte cell reports the Secret Police have discovered one of the exits, so the whole network is denied us. Our people have sealed the entry point at Villa Palmera."

After walking for nearly two hours, they came to a narrow, disused rock quarry that was barely visible from the air, its entrance entirely overgrown by the encroaching jungle. It was here that they had hidden the jeep upon the return from Vescambre. It sat intact in the shadows, hidden by foliage overhead.

They climbed in. Mateo started the engine and drove the jeep out of the quarry and turned west. After nearly half an hour of driving cross-country, they came to a road. Mateo turned onto it and increased speed. Mindful of spotter planes, he stayed on the road for a mere twenty minutes before turning off at a point where the shoulder drop-off was gentle, sloping down into a series of hillocks and a valley that stretched away to the north. Leighton scanned the skies for planes as the midafternoon sun began to roast them, beating down relentlessly.

***

It was just after 10:00 p.m. as Mateo slid a key into the lock of the front door of the building housing the printing presses responsible for the publication of *El Celador*. The door opened quietly, and he and Leighton slipped quickly inside and shut the door, locking it behind them. Mateo deactivated the alarm and led the way past two offices and down a short corridor, through another door, and into a large, concrete-lined room that housed the printing machinery. The entire interior was dimly lit, but there was sufficient light to see a metal staircase off to the right. Mateo opened the door at the top of the stairs with the second of two keys on the ring; it opened into a twelve-by-eight foot room directly over the reception area and offices below. The room was filled with cardboard boxes and large bottles of printer's ink. On the left were a series of dingy, metal-framed windows that provided a view of the street in front of the building, along with a single side window offering a view of the street as it sloped downhill.

Mateo moved toward the side window and took his monocular from his satchel, using it to observe a building on the opposite side of the street located downhill and one block away. Leighton noticed that he was careful to keep at least four feet away from the window itself. The printers' building was located at the top of a slight rise, and the street stretched downhill to the building Mateo was watching. He could just make out under the illumination of the streetlights the faded wooden sign that read "Villa Palmera" in lettering that had once been bright green.

"No smoking in here," Mateo said, remembering Leighton's cigarette habit. "Under no circumstances are we to be caught here, or seen entering or leaving this building. Avellar doesn't know we're here, but it would be just the excuse the Secret Police need to shut *El Celador* down for good. Any police or soldiers who see us will have to be killed."

"I understand," Leighton replied, unslinging his M-16 and placing it on the floor against the wall.

"The sniper is holed up at Villa Palmera," Mateo explained as he kept watch with the monocular. "The Secret Police suspect she's there, but they've been reluctant to go in because the owner has regularly paid bribes to the government to avoid being raided. Also they aren't sure whether they'll encounter any resistance, since the *Frente* has many friends who frequent the place. Local police, too. It has a reputation as a den of vice, but politics are checked at the door. It's the only place in the city, other than perhaps the church, where such a truce exists. But in this case, the local cell leader doesn't think it will hold. Narváez wants that sniper, bad enough to shatter the truce."

"Why don't we just go in and get the sniper now?"

"The Secret Police have been watching the place, just as we have. The plan calls for getting out of the city immediately, and we don't yet have the means to do that. Tomorrow night we will, so we must wait. Meanwhile, we keep watch and pray nothing happens. Do you know your way to Alturas de Diamantes from here?"

"Yes ... how did you—"

Mateo glanced at Leighton and smiled indulgently. "The guerillas have acknowledged Roberto Avellar as an unspoken ally for some time. We know a great deal about him. We knew when he hired you, within hours of the event. Or did you think it was only by chance that we were operating just south of Panactatlan the day you drove up there?"

"I didn't realize ... the *Frente* has been watching over me from the start."

"Almost. Motivated by self-interest, of course. We didn't interfere when the Secret Police arrested you, because initially we didn't believe they'd move against an American. We assumed they'd target Avellar first."

"Except they went after us both."

"Eventually. The attempt on your life at Panactatlan was due to the stupidity and hastiness of the Army in assuming you were a Secret Police agent. But when the Secret Police themselves went after you, we realized you were in as much danger as Avellar himself, and we stuck close."

"The waiter in the bar ... at La Monarca."

"Yes. And now you had better go. Make the most of your time tonight."

Leighton nodded, screwing the silencer into the barrel of Zorrita's Smith & Wesson automatic. "What if the Secret Police make a move tonight, while I'm gone?"

"I'll do the best I can to get the sniper out alone. You'll be on your own. Try to get word to us through La Monarca or Villa Palmera, and wait to be contacted."

Leighton nodded, emptying his satchel of food and grenades. He would carry only his laptop case, the missile parts, and Zorrita's pistol. Mateo led him downstairs, through the maze of printing machinery, and to the rear entrance of the print shop, which fronted a darkened alley. He shut off the alarm wired to the rear door, then opened it. "Good luck."

Leighton thanked him and was gone.

••••••••••••••••••••••••

Roberto Avellar was abruptly awakened by the high-pitched buzz of his bedside telephone. He rose reluctantly, for he had been in a deep sleep. The house phone was out in the hallway. The phone in the bedroom had been installed to allow instant communication with the bodyguards on the perimeter of the estate. He seized the receiver as Rosa began to stir before it could fully awaken her.

"Yes," Avellar said, glancing at the night table clock. 1:45 a.m.

"Sir, it's Bernardo," the man on the other end said. Avellar recognized the voice. He made it a point to know the names, faces, and voices of all his bodyguards. "Sorry to disturb you at this hour, but there's a man at the front gate who says he's an employee. Brian Palmer. He insists on seeing you. He says it's urgent."

"Palmer? Describe him."

"He's a Black, twenty-five to thirty years old, almost six feet tall, with a beard. Solid figure but a little thin. Looks like he's been living outdoors."

"A beard, you say?" Escort him up to the house." Rosa awoke at that moment.

"He was carrying a pistol. We disarmed him."

"Very well. Arturo will meet you at the east portico."

"Yes sir."

As Avellar hung up, Rosa sat up in bed. "Palmer has returned? What does he want?"

56

"We shall find out, my dear. Or I will do it alone, if you prefer to sleep," he replied, stripping out of his pajamas to put on slacks and a short-sleeved shirt.

"You know better than that," Rosa said, reaching for a housecoat.

Arturo, Luger pistol in hand, met Leighton and Bernardo as they arrived at the south portico on foot.

"This way, Señor Palmer," Arturo said graciously, using the pistol to wave Leighton inside the house. "The Patrón will see you in his study."

Leighton was allowed to lead the way, but Arturo continued to hold him at gunpoint as Bernardo trailed behind them, carrying a machine pistol.

"Must you point that gun at me, Arturo?" Leighton asked, once they arrived at the study.

"Please sit, señor," Arturo said by way of reply, and waited for Leighton to obey. Then he added, "One does not know if you are friend or foe. Caution is best."

"Did you get the Fiat back?"

"Yes, señor. In pristine condition. The Patrón will join us in a moment."

Leighton sat in awkward silence while Arturo stood across the room with his Luger trained on him. The bodyguard had a more relaxed stance but nonetheless projected alertness combined with a certain eagerness to cut Leighton in half with a spray of bullets if he made any threatening moves. Leighton tried not to move at all.

A door opened, and Avellar entered in his bare feet, padding across the room in a beeline to his liquor cabinet. "The prodigal returns," he said with enthusiasm. "You must join me in a drink, Palmer … if that is your real name."

Leighton rose, very slowly. "I'm sorry my deception was necessary," Leighton began, "but I've brought you an exclusive interview with the guerillas' leader, if you care to read it. Plus an article that may explain what happened at Panactatlan."

"First, a drink," Avellar said amiably. He quickly produced two tumblers and poured mezcal as Rosa entered the room, wearing a red housecoat and slippers.

"I apologize for the late hour," Leighton said to them both as Avellar handed him a tumbler. "But it was too dangerous for me to come in daylight."

"Arturo," Avellar said, "I see no need for your gun, although I do appreciate your vigilance. You can return to your bed."

"Patrón, I request your permission to stay. I will not sleep for fear of your safety."

"All right, but please put the gun away. Bernardo here is more than capable of handling the situation should the need arise." Arturo stuck the Luger in the belt of his trousers.

"A toast," Avellar said, "to your safe return, Palmer. Although I must say you look a bit ragged. Thinner, too." They drank and sat down, Leighton in a chair, Avellar on the couch near Rosa.

"So you say it's too dangerous for you in daylight. Why?" Avellar demanded. Leighton sensed he was toying with him.

"If the Secret Police get their hands on me again, they'll kill me," Leighton explained patiently. "It was only your agitation that got the American Embassy to step in to force my release after they grabbed me the last time. If not for that, I'd be dead already. I owe you my life."

"I'm curious about that," Avellar replied. "If you are an American agent"—he paused to sip mezcal—"why did your embassy not intervene on its own?"

"I'm here undercover as a journalist, and they weren't informed. They didn't like that. They expect to be notified if American agents are operating in the country."

"I suppose so."

"The guerillas got a message to me in the hotel and helped get me out of the city. I've been with them ever since."

"And what are you doing here, if not to write stories for me?" Avellar asked.

"It's exactly as I told Rosa. Writing for you was part of it. To gain the guerillas' trust. But I was sent here to recover those cruise missiles they seized."

"And that is all?"

"I have no other assignment." That was no longer true, but it had been when he first said it to Rosa. Leighton knew that muddying the waters now would only damage his credibility.

"You have gone to great lengths, if that is your only purpose here," Rosa said.

"It was necessary."

"Interesting approach. Indirect, but effective," Avellar said.

"But you were nearly killed yourself in the first few days," Rosa interjected, "then arrested and beaten by the Secret Police for your stories—"

"All of which enhanced my credibility with the guerillas," Leighton said. "It was a much slower process, but it helped me gain their trust. But now with the fighting in Redención, there may not be much time. So far there's been minimal loss of life—when the guerillas fired off the first missile, all it did was blow up Vilar's statue."

"Yes," Avellar grinned, "I thought that was a brilliant bit of theatre."

"But the next time they may target a populated government installation."

Avellar looked at Leighton skeptically. "And when you find the missiles?"

"Once I locate them, I'll be going home."

"Just like that," Rosa said.

"I don't say it will be easy."

"Why wouldn't it?"

"I know I've deceived you both. But I know my reporting can make a difference, and I believe in what the guerillas are doing. I don't care for the constant heat, but it's a beautiful country. It's been hard … not to form attachments here."

Rosa Avellar looked at him knowingly. "A woman."

Leighton got up suddenly, and Bernardo swung the machine pistol in his direction. Leighton froze. Avellar, with a wave of his hand, directed Bernardo to lower the weapon.

"Look, that doesn't matter," Leighton said. "I've brought you two articles that may help the guerillas, and help remove Vilar. Please read them."

Avellar studied Leighton closely. "You do care, then, for all your deceit. Where are they?"

"In my case, here. On the laptop." He did not move as Arturo stepped forward and relieved him of the laptop case. Arturo opened it and removed the device. "The battery's gone dead," Leighton explained. "There's a power cord in the case. If you plug it in, you'll be able to read the articles. I've saved everything on a disk. You can take it to *El Celador's* offices and edit it on the computers there. But read them tonight, please. When I leave, I have to take the laptop with me. Rosa, do you still have the notes I put together after our meeting with Dr. Reynoso?"

Rosa walked to a volume on the bookcase and removed it, producing the two typewritten sheets.

"Combine those with the second story on the laptop, and you may have something that will bring Vilar down."

"You look unkempt, Palmer," Avellar said with distaste. "I'll read them now." He took the laptop and its power cord to his desk to plug them in. "I suggest you shower and shave while you wait. Use the guest room, you know where it is. And you look as though you're hungry."

"I'll prepare something," Rosa said. "Bernardo, if you will follow Señor Palmer and keep watch on him." She then turned to Leighton. "Food will be waiting for you in here."

"Thank you," Leighton said.

Once Leighton had departed, Avellar glanced up from the illuminated screen of the laptop. "Do you really think he has a woman? Among the guerillas?"

Rosa turned to the faithful family chauffeur. "Would you excuse us please, Arturo?"

"Of course, señora." Arturo excused himself, and Rosa Avellar advanced toward her husband.

"Roberto, I know men," she said quietly. "Our Señor Palmer may be a deceiver and an American agent, but he is sincere about supporting the *Frente*. He is also, I am willing to bet, a man very much in love. Did you see how he leapt to his feet at the mention of the word 'woman'?"

Avellar, still reading, sat back in his chair, lifting his tumbler of mezcal. "Mmm, yes," he mused thoughtfully. "As if you had struck a nerve."

⋆⋆⋆⋆⋆ ▭ ▭ ▭ ▭ ▭ ▭ ▭ ▭ ▭ ▭ ▭ ⋆⋆⋆⋆⋆

Avellar read "Portrait of a Guerilla Leader" with great interest. Then he turned to Leighton's treatment of the discovery of the bodies at Vescambre and the guerillas' sketchy explanation of the onset of their illness. Finally he read the typewritten notes from the meeting with Dr. Reynoso. By that time Leighton, refreshed from a long shower and the first shave he'd had in weeks, had returned to the study and sat down to eat a plate of roast beef along with vegetables and rice that Rosa had quickly reheated. He washed it down with a cold beer. The meat was excellent, but the beer in particular he found delicious, since it was impossible to get it cold out in the bush.

Avellar poured himself a fresh tumbler of mezcal while Rosa replaced him at his desk to read Leighton's work. "The disc you mentioned," he said to Leighton. "Where is it?"

Leighton rose, Bernardo watching him closely, and moved around the desk to touch a small button on the side of the laptop. A black disk popped out, and he handed it to Avellar, who palmed it and put it in his trouser pocket.

"This Zorrita," Avellar continued, sipping mezcal, "the way you describe her, she is an extremely charismatic woman. She must be to lead so many men, many of whom I am sure are strong-willed, like her."

Leighton nodded. "Yes, all of that is true."

"Will they succeed, do you think?"

"Yes. They're extremely dedicated, and most of them are patient. Zorrita is a strategic thinker. She has the ability to read people, especially adversaries. In my opinion, she's read Vilar like a book. Given time, she'll dismantle him, get inside his head. She can be very analytical. Destroying his statue is just one example of her ability to make him react in way that's against his own best interests."

"Have you spent much time with her?" Rosa asked, still looking at the laptop screen as Avellar cocked an eyebrow at her.

"Well, uhh … no, not really," Leighton replied, though not smoothly enough for his liking. "The guerillas are very careful about who gets access to her."

Rosa merely nodded and continued reading.

Avellar said, "Your CIA has approached me indirectly, asking for any stories you may file."

"What?"

"Yes, I believe they intend to transmit them all to the American wire services, at a minimum. But why do you look surprised? It's every journalist's dream, and they're your own people."

"I don't work for the CIA," Leighton explained. "It's a different agency, although we have to cooperate with them at times."

"Well, no matter," Avellar replied. "I thought you should know. It's an indicator that your government is tiring of Vilar.

"Yes … or the CIA is," Leighton said wryly.

"Do you see any harm in sharing your work?"

"No. In fact, it will make it harder for Vilar to retaliate against you or *El Celador*."

"I had the same thought," Avellar said with a smile. "Your portrait of Zorrita is quite good. It's too late for this morning's edition," he glanced at his watch, "but I'll have them typeset it for tomorrow. Front page. Now, about the Vescambre story … I'd love to, but we don't have enough hard evidence of what the government has been up to, to print it the way you've written it. We can do a piece on the discovery of the bodies and hint that they were exposed to radiation, but that's all."

"But Reynoso's research…"

"We can't print it without putting him in danger," Rosa said sharply. "I can't have that sweet old man's death on my conscience. He would never survive a night with the Secret Police."

"And remember, Palmer," Avellar said, "they tried to kill you for nosing about in Panactatlan, where there must have been some proof. If I could prove that Vilar used radioactive waste against the guerillas, missed most of them, and killed fifty farmworkers instead, I'd love to print that story. But as much as I detest the man, it would be irresponsible to run it without hard evidence."

Rosa had finished reading and looked up from the laptop. "I love it," she said with a smile. "I particularly like the subtle way she fingers the CIA for what's happening in Redención. She's a born leader." She shut down the laptop and closed the lid. "You've captured her quite well in your writing."

"Your machine should be fully charged now," Avellar said.

"Good," Leighton replied, placing it back in its case. "I should be going."

"You should stay the night," Avellar said immediately. "The curfew's still in force, so the streets are quite dangerous this time of night, for anyone."

Leighton shook his head. "There's no choice. I'm on a timetable. It feels good to be clean and have a shave and a full belly for a change. Thank you both."

"One last thing," Avellar said gravely. "You are fortunate that no one in my household is affiliated with the guerillas, including the bodyguards. We will keep your confidence. But do not be so free with information outside this house as you have been with us."

Leighton nodded. "My gut told me I could trust you. I don't know if there will be more stories, but if there are, I'll send a messenger. It's been an honor to have known you both." They all shook hands.

"Vaya con dios, Brian Palmer."

"Zorrita is a most impressive young woman," Rosa said, once Leighton and Bernardo had gone. My woman's intuition tells me she is the one."

"The one?"

"She is the woman who has captured your American friend's heart."

"Rosa, be serious. How can you believe that? An American agent and a revolutionary guerilla leader, the kind of individual his government would like to destroy?"

Rosa nodded, not in the least dissuaded by her husband's skepticism. "Unlikely, but still predictable. I do believe it. I fear for them, Roberto. I especially fear for her."

CHAPTER 6
GABRIELA'S PRAYER

Gabriela awakened from a bad dream. She drank some water from her canteen and tried to calm herself. In the dream, she had been sleeping in a large four-poster bed, the kind she had slept in as a child in her father's house in Santiago. In the dream, she had awakened to find a dark, rectangular metal object on the pillow beside her. She instinctively understood that the object, whatever it was, represented death. In that instant, she had forced herself awake. She rose, throwing off her blanket. With Palmer and Mateo gone, she was alone in the cave with Camilo, who was snoring gently a few feet away.

As she sat there in the darkness, a feeling of foreboding overcame her and she became convinced that the man she knew as Brian Palmer was in danger. She stood and moved outside, stepping over Camilo on her way out of the cave. Palmer and Mateo had not taken a radio, so there was no way to contact them except through the local cell leader in Valmonte. Gabriela had traded messages with him after the nightly radio broadcast; he confirmed only having seen Mateo and providing him the keys to a safe house. He had not laid eyes on Palmer. It disturbed her that Mateo and Palmer had not been together.

She heard a surveillance plane somewhere overhead and immediately ducked back into the cave. The night flights had started up again, making the attack on the air base near Valmonte all the more critical. The guerillas were slowly accumulating the necessary uniforms and vehicles. A critical piece that was missing was a good forger who could effectively falsify Army travel orders.

Salcedo, the soldier who had mastered the intricacies of programming the cruise missiles, had been a gold mine of information about what the travel orders should look like. The only stumbling block was finding someone to produce them, using Salcedo's detailed sketches as a model.

Gabriela experienced something rare for her: fear. What if they could not mount the attack on the air base? What if it failed? What if Palmer, who seemed determined to participate in it, were killed? What if he never came back from Valmonte? Fear rose in her chest and seemed to catch in her throat. For a moment, she felt as if she could not breathe. It was ridiculous: all this because she was missing her lover tonight—not sex, but the comforting presence and heat of his masculine energy beside her, even if only for a few moments. Having experienced such intimate companionship, the first time she had allowed such a thing in years, she now found she did not like having to do without it. She had trained herself not to need anyone, least of all a man. And yet, she felt pangs of loneliness for the first time since she was a teenager in her initial weeks at the Sorbonne.

Gabriela went to her bedding, found her satchel, and fished out a candle, matches, and something she rarely let others see her wearing: her St. Christopher medal. She placed its gold chain around her neck and lit the candle.

She would call on St. Christopher, the patron saint of travelers, to look after Brian Palmer. Gabriela set the candle on a ledge of rock, lit it, then knelt before it and clasped her hands together, saying a long prayer for Palmer in a voice that was scarcely more than a whisper. Completing it, she crossed herself. Only then did she say a separate prayer for Mateo.

* *

John Patrick Lang tapped the accelerator and his car, a silver-grey 1982 Chrysler LeBaron convertible, smoothly rolled into the garage of the condominium he rented in Colinas, the wealthy section of Valmonte. He cut the engine and checked his watch as he pressed the button on the garage door controller, lowering the louvered metal doors into place: 4:11 a.m.

Lang had spent most of the night with his mistress, the wife of the Portuguese ambassador to Madrinega, after meeting up with her at a diplomatic reception.

He opened the door to his condo, stepped into the hallway without closing it, and immediately noticed something amiss. The alarm system wasn't chiming, prompting him to punch in the code to deactivate it, which meant someone else had already deactivated it. Lang was certain of this because he was religious about arming it whenever he left the house. The condominium was uncharacteristically silent. His office and a guest bathroom were on the ground floor, along with a storage closet. Directly ahead of him was a stairway leading up to the kitchen and living area, and a flight above that were the bedrooms. He generally left a light on over the stove, but it was a faint light. Tonight he noticed entirely too much light emanating from the kitchen area. He eased the door to the garage closed and ducked into his office, pulling out the top drawer of his desk, where he kept a .45 caliber Colt automatic. The Colt was gone.

Lang quickly and silently retreated to the garage and felt under the driver's seat of the car for the lever. He pulled it, and a .380 Walter PPK sprang into his hand. He reentered the condo and crept up the stairs, pistol at the ready.

Lang lived alone and his kitchen was small and utilitarian. He had a good view of it from the top of the stairs. In the center of the kitchen stood an island topped with a dark marble counter and housing cabinets for the pots and pans. The SONAI agent Lang knew as Brian Palmer stood behind the island, facing him, calmly peeling a nectarine with a paring knife.

"How the hell did you get in here?" Land demanded, entering the kitchen with the PPK pointed at Leighton's stomach.

Leighton finished chewing a section of nectarine and swallowed. "I wouldn't be very good at my job if I didn't know how to disable a security system as simple as yours. I recommend an upgrade, by the way."

"Alright, smartass, what do you want?"

"I've disabled one of the missiles, and I've brought you proof," Leighton replied, pointing to his satchel, which lay nearby on the marble countertop.

"Show me," Lang challenged. "Slowly."

Leighton laid down the paring knife and opened the flap of the laptop case very deliberately. He then pulled out the bullet-riddled GPS antenna, followed by the damaged inertial navigation system. Lang stepped closer and studied them both carefully.

"Both rendered useless, I see. What about the other two?"

"I'm working on that. I think the guerillas intend to use them, and they may not be in the same place, so the transponder in my laptop may not be enough. I asked Miller to send you two more … Do you have them?"

"Yes, and it's three. They arrived yesterday in the diplomatic pouch."

"If I can have them, I'll be on my way."

"After you answer a few questions. You've been with the guerillas for some time, yet you show up here clean-shaven. Have much time for grooming out there in the bush?"

"I took two stories to Avellar tonight."

"El Celador's publisher?

"Yes. He allowed me a bath and a shave."

"What stories?"

'You'll read about them soon enough. One's a piece on the guerilla leader Zorrita. The other's about bodies we found in Vescambre. Looks like they died of radiation poisoning."

"Did you get access to Zorrita?"

"Just long enough for the interview."

"Could you get it again?"

"I'm not sure. They guard her pretty well. Why so interested?"

"By now Miller must have told you she's a prime target, to be eliminated if you get the chance."

"You mean killed," Leighton retorted.

"Killed. Yes. And we've asked Avellar to share whatever you file with him."

"Why?"

"It's bound to help us create a climate for ousting Vilar. We'll forward it to friendly news outlets in the States via the wire services, if your work has the right slant, and so far everything you've written has given Vilar a black eye. Langley's decided it's time for him to go."

"Don't you mean Washington?"

"Langley, Washington—same difference. He's got to go. About Zorrita. Can you get to her?"

"It'd be suicide to even try. I only got close to her once, for a two-hour interview. There were at least four men within ten feet of her, all of them armed with assault weapons. If I'd made a hostile move toward her, I'd have been dead a second later. Since then they haven't allowed me near her."

"I see," Lang said quietly, as he finally lowered his pistol. "That's too bad. They don't really trust you, then."

"I'm an American."

"True enough. And yet they cut you loose to come into town to see Avellar and then me."

"They know it's to their advantage to get good press. They know I can give it to them. They know there's a very good chance that whatever I write will be picked up by the American papers, and you've just confirmed it."

"So I have," Lang conceded.

"And I told them it would be good public relations to surrender proof that they'd disabled at least one of the missiles. Shows they're not quite as bloodthirsty as Vilar makes them out to be."

"Shrewd move," Lang nodded. "But I didn't think you were sent down here to be their political consultant."

"I know the American mindset, and that's valuable to them. It's all about getting the missiles back, Lang. I'm hoping to learn their location soon."

"Can you get us a fix on Zorrita?"

"Maybe," Leighton said, injecting a note of doubt into his voice. "She moves around quite a bit, and they don't tell me much. I'll be lucky to find the missiles."

Lang moved to his refrigerator, opened it, and pulled out a Tupperware container. He pushed it across the counter to Leighton. "Open it."

Leighton opened the container to see brown rice. "No, thanks," he said.

Lang reached forward and pulled the fake plastic covering of rice away to reveal three dark metal whiskey flasks.

"Your transponders," he said. "The top quarter of each actually contains whiskey. Unscrew the cap counterclockwise like normal if you need to take a swig. Once it's closed again, turn it clockwise to activate the transponder. They're magnetized, as you requested." He took one and tossed it against the refrigerator, and it stuck. Leighton reached over and pulled it free with a little effort. He took the three of them and placed them in the laptop case. Closing it, he slung the strap of his case over his shoulder.

"Palmer."

Leighton looked at Lang as he prepared to go.

"It could save a lot of lives if you can help get her."

"Ours or theirs?"

Lang adopted a quizzical expression that soon became a frown. "Both. Listen, you wouldn't be going native, would you? All that time in the bush, listening to the 'Power to the People' lectures?"

Leighton nodded. "Thanks for the transponders, Lang."

"You're welcome. Try breaking in here again and you'll go home in a body bag."

"You'll find your .45 behind the toilet paper in the cabinet in the guest bathroom downstairs." Leighton walked to the stairs, descended them slowly, opened the door, and let himself out by way of the garage. Lang soon heard the sound of the garage door opening.

Outside, it was near dawn. Leighton removed the snap on Zorrita's shoulder holster, to have the gun ready if he needed it. He moved off down the street quickly and rounded the first corner he came to, certain that Lang was watching him from a window.

Forty minutes after leaving Lang, Leighton was at the back door of the printer's office, pounding on it hard. Eager to be off the street, he had narrowly avoided two patrols of soldiers as he moved through the city on foot, growing ever more nervous as the streetlights went off with dawn fast approaching. After what seemed far too long, Mateo opened the door and pulled him in. "Stop that noise," he said sharply, punching in the code to reactivate the alarm.

"I had to make sure you heard me," Leighton retorted. "I had a close call with a patrol just now. Thought I'd have to start shooting."

"Come on, the morning shift will be here soon." They moved quickly to the staircase, ascending it quickly as they heard the front door open. Mateo unlocked the door of the storage room and they ducked inside, moving well to the back of the room and keeping away from the windows. Within moments, they could hear the din of the printing presses below. Mateo briefly rearranged a few cardboard boxes to shield them from the view of anyone who might come in for supplies. When he turned back to Leighton, he was sitting with his back to the wall, fast asleep.

◆◆◆◆ ▢ ▢ ▦ ▦ ▦ ▦ ▦ ▦ ▦ ▢ ▢ ◆◆◆◆

Leighton awakened in the middle of the afternoon. Mateo was standing with his back to him, watching Villa Palmera's entrance through the window, this time without the monocular. Leighton immediately noticed that his M-16 and Mateo's FN FAL were missing.

"Where are our rifles?"

"They've been placed in cars parked at key points closer to Villa Palmera," Mateo replied. "We'll pick them up on the way. We can't be seen just strolling around town with them, not in daylight."

Leighton looked at this watch. 3:15 p.m. "Anything happening?"

"No. It's been quiet—too quiet. Word's got out about the sniper being holed up down there. It's normally fairly busy out there. People are avoiding this part of town today."

There was a knock on the door of the storage room, and Leighton immediately pulled the Smith & Wesson, the silencer on the end of the barrel requiring an abnormally long draw from the shoulder holster.

"Relax," Mateo said. He opened the door. A young man stepped in carrying a plate covered in foil. He seemed familiar, although Leighton did not recognize him.

"I thought you'd like some hot food," he said. To Leighton he said, "I hear we'll be running more of your stories soon. Glad to have you back in action."

Mateo noticed Leighton's quizzical expression. "This is Guillermo Zaragosa, *El Celador's* dispatch rider."

Leighton nodded. "We've met … sort of. Thank you for the food."

"I'm hungry," Mateo said. "We ate the last of the food we packed yesterday." He uncovered the foil to reveal a plateful of chicken *baleadas*. He and Leighton dug in, devouring the pastries.

"I had to tell the printer that *El Celador* has a government contract to print travel orders," Guillermo said. "They'll be ready by tomorrow morning."

"Thank you, Guillermo, that is a great help," Mateo replied between mouthfuls. "But we'll be gone by then."

"Don't worry … I will send them to you by messenger."

Mateo resumed his vigil at the window. He looked worried.

"What is it?" Leighton asked.

"We've been assuming the Secret Police will strike at night, when the place is open. But why would they? With more people about, some of whom may be armed guerillas, there's that much more chance of opposition. At a minimum there will be more chance for confusion, with all the bodies in there. We might have to do this in daylight."

"That's a problem," Guillermo said. "Transport out of the city is arranged for tonight. Dusk at the earliest."

"We may be forced to improvise," Mateo replied. "I doubt the Secret Police will move at a time that's convenient for us."

"I have to make a phone call, then," Guillermo said. Leighton watched as he opened the door of the storage room and disappeared down the stairs. In a moment, they heard his motorcycle roaring away.

"I'll keep watch for a while," Leighton told Mateo. "Why don't you see if you can sleep?"

"Not likely, but I could use a chance to rest my eyes," Mateo replied, sitting down against the wall and closing them.

"Guillermo seems young to have so much responsibility. He can't be much older than Camilo," Leighton said.

"You think so?" Mateo replied, without opening his eyes. "He's the cell leader here in Valmonte."

"That *kid?*"

"That 'kid' got us the word that you might need help the day you went to Panactatlan."

Stunned, Leighton fell silent.

He turned to the window, keeping an eye on the entrance to Villa Palmera, sensing Mateo's anxiety. Both men had a creeping awareness of what lay ahead: It was going to come down to a shoot-out with the Secret Police.

CHAPTER 7
THE GUNFIGHT FOR ALMA PEREZ

As the afternoon dragged on, a cloud of mounting tension seemed to descend over both Leighton and Mateo. At 4:00 p.m. their getaway vehicle, a weathered Ford pickup truck painted in a two-tone scheme of white and faded teal green, circled the block and pulled up to the rear entrance of the printer's press and parked. The driver got out, knocked, and was admitted via the back door by Guillermo, who had returned. They immediately went up to the storage room.

"This is Benicio, your getaway driver," Guillermo said. Everyone exchanged nods. "The truck is downstairs, out back. He will watch from here and bring it down to you at the appropriate moment." Benicio was short and powerfully built with an alert, almost nervous look about him. A scar on this left cheek and another above his right eye gave him the look of a brawler. "He can be trusted," Guillermo said with finality. "When the time comes for you to leave here, just walk out. The evening shift will be coming on duty soon. When you go, just ignore them. They will ignore you. There are three of our people waiting nearby, who are available to help create a diversion. They're very convincing. They'll move once you get in close. There are also watchers who will not get involved, but they will signal me to come through at the appropriate moment to take the sniper off your hands."

"What about the truck?" Leighton asked.

73

"That's just for the two of us," Mateo interjected.

"Yes," Guillermo confirmed. "The truth is, the sniper is more important than the two of you. She must be gotten away quickly, no matter what, so we'll use a motorcycle for her."

"She?" Leighton looked puzzled.

"It's Alma," Mateo said. "You remember her, don't you? You should. You didn't know?"

"Alma, the waitress at Villa Palmera? She's the sniper?"

"There is more to Alma than her good looks," Mateo said calmly.

"He would not know, Mateo," Guillermo said. He turned to Leighton. "I understand you have met Alma. The *Frente* has many members with different talents. We … develop skills to confront the situation facing us. Alma happens to be good with weapons. Mateo?"

As the afternoon shadows began to stretch across the street, Mateo had taken to the monocular again. He lowered it and looked at Leighton.

"I wish I could tell you that this will be perfectly orchestrated, like a ballet. But the truth is, we're going to have to go in shooting. Head shots if you can. Don't hesitate. They'll all have to be dead within ten seconds of the time we open fire if this is to go according to plan. But under no circumstances is Alma to be hit. Our main advantage will be our silencers, so it may take a few extra seconds for them to realize what's happening. Our success may depend on our ability to drop three or more men apiece during those few seconds." He then told Leighton the route to take to Villa Palmera, and where to find his M-16.

"How many of them will there be?" Leighton asked.

"We don't know for sure. At least six. Possibly more. Narváez wants her in custody very badly."

"Mateo, this sounds like a suicide mission."

Mateo shook his head and said calmly, "We'll have the element of surprise. Now you see why I said I'll need your help. Just keep the faith, compadre. After all, you are Machete."

"I must go," Guillermo said. "Good luck to you all."

"You wouldn't care to sit at a window with a rifle, would you?" Leighton asked, but Guillermo was already closing the storage room door behind him. They heard his footsteps on the metal staircase.

Mateo stiffened and backed away from the window as an Army jeep drove by the front of the printer's office in the street below. He watched as it slowed to a halt directly across the street from Villa Palmera. It held four soldiers, who hopped out and began to mill around the vehicle. They were clearly waiting for something.

Leighton joined Mateo near the window and checked his watch. "They're due to open the club in less than five minutes," he said. "It's nearly five o'clock."

Mateo nodded. "There is one more thing," he said, peering through the monocular. "If I'm killed and you see that we've failed … kill her. It will be a better fate than allowing her to be taken by the Secret Police. You can imagine what they do to female guerillas."

"Yes," Leighton said quietly.

Within moments an armored car with a sloped front end and extra thick, oversize tires rumbled up the street from several blocks down the hill, advancing toward Villa Palmera. They could see that a machine gun was mounted up top, and the gunner, wearing a helmet, was clearly visible through an opening in its roof.

"*Pendejo*," Mateo hissed.

They watched as the armored car came closer and braked to a halt directly in front of Villa Palmera, across the street from the four soldiers and their jeep. Eight men, two in plainclothes and the rest in Secret Police uniforms, got out. Six of them descended the stairs leading to Villa Palmera's front door, and two of the uniformed men remained on guard on the sidewalk, in addition to the man on the machine gun. The four soldiers across the street, visibly more alert now, fanned out down the block with their rifles at the ready.

"Time," Mateo said. "Let's go."

"I'll keep watch," Benicio said as Leighton and Mateo gathered their gear. "Vaya con dios." They quickly descended the stairs and went out the back door. Both men paused at the pickup truck to open the cab and toss in any unnecessary items: satchels, water bottles—after one last swig, for Leighton had dry mouth, and he suspected Mateo did too—the laptop case, machetes, the monocular.

"With that machine gun, we can't take any chances," Mateo said. "I'll take that gunner out first of all. Use side streets to get close. I'll be on the far side of Villa Palmera on this side of the street, and we'll put them in a crossfire. Add to the confusion. Our go signal will be when the three drunks arrive and break a bottle of tequila."

"Got it," Leighton said. He could see that Mateo was shaken, that he had not anticipated the Secret Police would bring so much firepower— so many men. But he was moving ahead with the plan. Leighton himself was not feeling confident about their chances of success; in fact, he believed they both had an excellent chance of being killed. But he trotted off up the alley and turned the corner. Mateo moved off down the alley in the opposite direction.

Leighton felt his heart pounding, knowing it was pure adrenaline and fear – mostly fear. He advanced along the side of the printer's building and moved away from its cover as he passed the corner, stepping out into the open, into the street. The soldiers noticed but did not hail him. He did not look at them but just kept moving. Villa Palmera was a good block and a half away, down the hill to his right, and he walked normally, taking no notice of events down the street.

Reaching the sidewalk on the opposite side of the street, he was soon out of sight of the soldiers down the hill; even the Secret Policeman nearest him, who was scanning the street, had seen him but taken no special notice, for Leighton's shoulder holster was hidden from his view. Ironically, had the Secret Police waited until nightfall as Mateo had initially expected, the curfew would have been in force, giving them a ready excuse to open fire on anyone they saw on the street. But since Villa Palmera had operated with immunity during the curfew, its flaunting of the rules ignored by the authorities, the people being shot at might well be police or government officials, who were known to frequent the place for the music, the alcohol, and the girls just as frequently as the guerillas or ordinary citizens.

Leighton drew the Smith & Wesson, flicked the safety off, and chambered a round. He holstered the weapon and kept walking, feeling the sun at his back as he came to a side street running parallel to the one on which Villa Palmera was located, and turned right. He moved more quickly now, coming to a white Chevrolet parked in the middle of the block with its windows rolled down. Leighton reached in on the driver's side, pulled the lever to open the trunk, and quickly retrieved the M-16 hidden there. He walked away quickly, keeping the M-16 at his side, being careful not to let its long silencer touch the ground. He reached the end of the block and turned right, moving toward Villa Palmera. His heart felt as though it were in his mouth as he set the M-16's fire selector for single shots, remembering how he saw the soldiers near the jeep fanning out.

Leighton neared the corner knowing that just around it, perhaps twenty feet away, stood two armed Secret Policemen and the armored car. On the opposite side of the street, some distance closer, would be the first of the four soldiers. He crouched and waited, grateful that the armored car, by his calculations, would keep at least two of the soldiers across the street from spotting him right away.

He heard loud voices as two or possibly more people advanced toward the soldiers across the street. They passed into Leighton's view and back out again as they crossed the side street, definitely three of them, two men and a woman. All appeared to be inebriated, and one of them carried a bottle of tequila. They had seen Leighton as they passed the mouth of the side street but took no notice. Leighton could hear a slight altercation beginning as another voice—one of the soldiers—told them to quiet down and move along. An argument erupted over their right to be there and to go into Villa Palmera, since the curfew would not begin for two hours. The soldier raised his voice and one of the men threw the bottle of tequila at his feet, smashing it.

"Dear God, don't let me fuck this up," Leighton whispered.

Leighton stepped around the corner in time to see in his peripheral vision the soldier using his rifle to butt the man who had thrown the tequila bottle in the face. The two Secret Policemen nearest to him, on the sidewalk next to the armored car, were distracted by the altercation. Leighton raised the M-16, fired at the first Secret Policeman, pivoted and fired at the second one, both head shots, one round apiece. They slumped to the ground as one of the soldiers across the street cried out. The gunshots had hardly made a noise, but he had seen one of the Secret

Policemen go down. Mateo then fired from a concealed position across the street, silently killing the machine gunner in the armored car. He fired once more, killing a soldier between himself and the jeep as the soldier nearest Leighton cut loose with a burst of fire from his rifle. Leighton dropped to a prone position, firing twice, killing the soldier as bits of brick from the other man's gunfire hit his face and neck. Leighton scrambled for the cover of the armored car as he felt something hit him in the face. Feeling his face, he found that whatever it was had cut him rather than penetrated. Leighton popped out from behind the armored car as the third soldier advanced, catching him by surprise and firing two rounds into his head. The man went down as the fourth soldier fired at Leighton, hitting him in the shoulder and forcing him to retreat back behind the armored car. The fourth soldier, confused, turned to look behind him, for he thought gunfire was coming from that direction, too. He saw Mateo emerging from cover and opened fire. But as he squeezed the trigger, the woman in the group of drunkards stabbed him in the neck, and he sank to his knees as the spray of bullets went wide, smashing into a building.

Leighton, bleeding from the left shoulder, crouched behind the armored car's nose, watching the entrance to Villa Palmera. There was another gunshot as the fourth soldier shot at the woman at point-blank range, missing as blood spurted from his neck. Leighton then heard two small metallic clicks as Mateo in turn shot the fourth soldier dead in the next instant. Mateo advanced into the street, shooting one of the fallen soldiers in the head for good measure, as Leighton spied a boy on a bicycle coming down the hill from the direction of the printer's shop.

Mateo quickly backed away from the jeep and took up a prone position several feet farther down the street, where he had a better view of the entrance to Villa Palmera. As Leighton peered from behind the armored car, Mateo put a finger to his lips. Leighton resumed his position as the boy on the bicycle drew abreast of the jeep, tossing a satchel as he passed. The satchel slid along the asphalt and came to rest beneath the jeep, just beneath its rear axle and fuel tank.

The two male drunkards lay in the street, one of them semiconscious and bleeding from the face after the blow from the rifle butt, the other lying motionless, apparently hit by a stray bullet. The woman helped the bleeding man to his feet, and they fled.

The Secret Policemen inside the nightclub had heard the soldiers' gunfire. They would likely send someone up to check out the situation before they came up with Alma. They would be eager to get out of there and would not wait for backup, given Villa Palmera's reputation as a guerilla-friendly watering hole.

Leighton retreated into the street behind the armored car's massive left front wheel, which would conceal him from anyone coming up Villa Palmera's steps, and listened. He slung the M-16 across his torso with difficulty and pulled out the Smith & Wesson. The long rifle was now too cumbersome with his wounded shoulder, and he sensed the remainder of the gunfight would be at very close range. He looked toward Mateo, who now stood crouching in the middle of the street, silently and urgently signaling him to get down. Mateo dropped back to his prone position and they waited, listening hard.

Leighton presently heard the club's door open, then heard footsteps on the stairs. A uniformed Secret Policeman appeared at the head of the stairs, pistol drawn. He saw the sidewalk and street littered with bodies, but also saw an unobstructed path across the sidewalk to the armored car. He had seen Mateo from his vantage point, but Mateo had had the presence of mind to play dead—something easily done from his prone position.

Leighton froze as the Secret Policeman quickly stepped across the sidewalk, opened the large side door of the armored car, and got in. Leighton flattened himself in the street as the Secret Policeman started the vehicle's engine, then darted back inside the nightclub. Leighton saw him descend the steps through the gap between the sidewalk and the bottom of the armored car, and signaled Mateo, who rose to a kneeling position, aiming the rifle at the top of Villa Palmera's steps. Leighton quickly moved out of the street to the façade of the building and knelt, blocking the pain in his shoulder by thinking of Gabriela. He pressed himself against the wall, just ten feet from the head of the stairs. He heard the door of Villa Palmera opening below.

The group advanced quickly up the steps, then paused, still out of sight. There had been several footsteps. Leighton was sure Alma was with them. He silently retreated a foot or two along the wall, keeping the pistol trained. His shoulder began to ache.

A man stuck his head out, glanced quickly in both directions, then waved the group forward. Then he suddenly swung his head back to the right, raising his pistol as he saw Leighton, and Leighton saw him and Alma behind him, getting just a flash of a blue scarf she wore. The Secret Policeman, Leighton, and Mateo opened fire simultaneously, the same instant as the satchel under the jeep exploded. The blast slammed Leighton against the wall as a bullet nicked his right arm and the Secret Policeman went down. Alma tried to run toward Leighton, but a powerful arm pulled her back. His ears ringing, Leighton fired again as another man raised a weapon toward him, hitting that man in the neck. Leighton felt something strike his head, and although momentarily disoriented, he had enough motor control to lunge toward the sidewalk as a Secret Policeman cut loose with a submachine gun. Mateo, farther back from the blast, took much less of its concussive force and maintained steady aim, putting down three of the men around Alma before any of them realized that gunfire was also coming from his direction.

Leighton rolled on the sidewalk as bullets flew just above him and hit the pavement to his left, firing twice as the Secret Policeman with the submachine gun doubled over and dropped his weapon. There was a pause in the gunfire as everyone ducked when the jeep, inverted, smoking, and still ablaze, came crashing down in a blackened heap in the street very close to the armored car. Leighton's ears were ringing, and he barely heard it.

Leighton looked up to see one of the plainclothesmen gripping Alma by the hair and using her as a shield. Mateo, standing much closer now, had his rifle trained on him but did not have a clear shot. Leighton ducked behind the nose of the armored car as the Secret Policeman who had dropped the submachine gun, badly wounded but not dead, fired at him with a pistol from down low behind the open door of the armored car. But he moved too late to avoid being hit and felt a searing pain in his side as he stumbled and fell to the ground in the street. Cursing and fighting to keep from blacking out, he remembered the gap beneath the armored car and scrambled on his belly along the pavement to see beyond the large front wheel. He then shot the other man in the knee as he knelt on the other side of the vehicle. An unholy scream followed.

Leighton struggled to his feet and moved back around the nose of the armored car to get a shot at the man holding Alma. But the sound of a gunshot and a spark as a bullet struck the metal side of the car near his head forced him back; the plainclothesman had taken a shot at him and nearly got a hit. Leighton forced three words into his brain: *Block the pain.* Mateo and the man holding Alma were at a standoff, as the latter inched toward a side street, keeping Alma between himself and Mateo. Leaning against the nose of the armored car, Leighton slowly crept around it again, ready to shoot whatever moved.

In the distance, they could all hear sirens.

As Leighton came around the front of the armored car, he could see the man he had twice wounded trying to crawl into the car. The plainclothesman holding Alma could see Leighton clearly but now had his hands full trying to keep out of Mateo's field of fire. There was nothing he could do as Leighton took deliberate aim and shot the wounded man through the open door of the armored car twice in the back.

"Let her go," Mateo said. Leighton now had his pistol trained on the plainclothesman's head as well. The sirens were getting louder.

"Fools!" the Secret Policeman shouted. "Those sirens aren't coming to *your* rescue."

From up the hill near the printer's office, a Ford pickup turned into the street and moved downhill toward them. Leighton could also see, from the opposite direction, a motorcycle approaching, beginning to accelerate.

"You won't get away, none of you," the Secret Policeman gloated. "And this whore will be stripped and beaten before—"

Suddenly Alma wrenched herself free of his grip with all her might and elbowed him hard under the jaw before lunging away. He turned to fire at her as Mateo and Leighton both shot him in the face. He fell backward violently and was still.

Alma, wearing handcuffs, stood staring down at the bloody pulp that remained atop the dead man's shoulders. "Murderer," she said under her breath, and spat on the corpse.

"Are you hurt?" Leighton asked.

"No."

"Then let's get the hell out of here." The pickup truck roared to a halt in front of them as Leighton palmed the slide of the Smith & Wesson, which had locked open with his last shot.

"You're bleeding badly," she said, tearing the blue scarf from her head and pressing it against his side. She took his hand and put it over the scarf. "Hold it there, until--"

"Get in, get in!" Benicio shouted.

Alma waved at Guillermo on the motorcycle, who roared up and stopped at her side with a screech of brakes. Mateo stepped forward as Alma hopped onto the back of the motorcycle and put her arms around Guillermo.

"Go east. Use the footbridge at Colinas. Meet us at the power station, about twenty miles north on the far side of the river."

"Okay," Guillermo said. He lowered the visor on his helmet and roared off.

"Let's go," Mateo urged, looking at Leighton. "You've been hit!"

"Just a couple scratches," Leighton said dismissively, although he was concentrating on pressing Alma's scarf against his side. His vision blurred for a moment. "We should take that for the roadblocks." He felt faint as he gestured toward the armored car, its engine still running.

Mateo looked from the armored car to Leighton and back. He turned to Benicio in the pickup. "Follow us. Stick close." Mateo then moved to the armored car and dumped the man Leighton had killed out onto the sidewalk. "Let's go."

They got in. Leighton closed the door behind them as Mateo climbed into the driver's seat, released the brake, and put it in gear. He stomped the accelerator, and the armored car surged forward with surprising speed. Mateo turned to the right down a side street, then left at the first corner with a screech of tires, racing eastward out of the city with the Ford pickup close behind. Leighton started the ride in one of the seats, but soon the pain and loss of blood overtook him and he blacked out and slid to the floor.

● ●

Leighton awoke to the sound of a motorcycle engine starting up. He recovered full consciousness in time to see a red taillight receding in the darkness. He was in the back of the jeep; Mateo stood nearby looking at him with concern as Alma examined his wounds with a penlight, the handcuffs still on her wrists but the chain between them broken by a shot from Mateo's rifle. It was nearly nightfall.

"Looks worse than it is," Alma was saying. "Do you have much pain?"

"In the side," Leighton said.

"That one is a through-and-through," she replied. "It's already stopped bleeding on its own, so I don't think it hit anything vital. I'll clean it and get you sewn up once we get back to camp. You've also got a bullet in your shoulder, but we can't do anything about that right now either. You have a gash in your cheek and another to the back of your head, they both look like shrapnel hits or maybe bullet fragments from a ricochet."

"You sound as if you've treated bullet wounds before," Mateo said.

"A few." Alma took the strap from Leighton's M-16 together with her blue scarf and tied it firmly around his side, easing up a bit on the constriction as he groaned in pain. "It's just until we can get you back to camp, in case you start bleeding again."

"We should go," Mateo said. "We have the night planes to worry about."

"He's ready," Alma said with confidence. She turned to Leighton. "If you sit up again, you may start bleeding. We have you on a makeshift stretcher, but there's nothing to tie you down with. I'll have to ride back here with you. Prepare yourself. It's likely to be bumpy."

● ●

Mateo drove like the wind with the headlights off, taking advantage of the moonlight and avoiding the roads when he could. Consulting his map with the penlight under cover of the trees, he figured a route that would allow him to drive all the way back to Limado. Alma held Leighton in place by throwing her arms over him. They stopped and hid in a ravine when Alma thought she heard a plane. With the engine off, Mateo agreed there was a faint but definite sound. The plane seemed to be circling. They resumed their journey only when it stopped after twenty minutes. Mateo took a detour to the south for ten minutes to be certain, over Alma's protests due to Leighton's condition. When they finally rolled back into the camp at Limado, it was after 3:00 a.m.

Zorrita was awake and there to greet them. Neither she nor Camilo had been able to sleep after the nightly radio message from Valmonte told them Alma had been rescued from the Secret Police and whisked out of the city after a gun battle and an explosion at Villa Palmera. Zorrita hugged Mateo and then Alma, then turned with watery eyes and a concern that robbed her of words to Leighton, listening intently as Alma described the nature of his wounds, nodding frequently.

"His wounds aren't life-threatening, but he's lost a fair amount of blood," Alma said in conclusion. "When it gets light, I want to remove that bullet from his shoulder, but I don't know what equipment you have here."

"We will provide you the best we have," Zorrita said. She helped Leighton, by now feverish but able to walk with effort, to the area they used for briefings, the rectangular plateau bordered by fallen trees, where she had moved both his bedding and hers, anticipating that he might be wounded and unable to make the climb up to the cave. The guerillas retired for the night as Mateo left with the jeep to park it some distance away. Zorrita made Leighton comfortable and gave him water. She noticed Alma lingering. "I will take care of him until you are ready to operate," Zorrita said, her tone carrying authority but also asserting jurisdiction. "You should rest now."

She watched Alma go. Only then, when they were relatively alone, did she embrace Leighton.

"Thank God," she whispered. "Thank God you have come back to me."

"I didn't think we'd get out of there alive."

"But you did," she said, using a cloth to wipe the dried blood from his face as she applied antiseptic to the gash on his cheek. "You did."

Feeling around his head, Zorrita located the other wound in the back and moved around behind him to apply antiseptic there, followed by a bandage.

"We had help," Leighton told her. "A boy on a bicycle with a satchel charge… and three guerillas posing as drunks … I think one of them was killed, another wounded."

"All right, I've bandaged your head. Lie back." Leighton did as asked, and she began to remove the M-16 strap. Zorrita helped him remove his shirt and remained calm as she gently pulled away the blood-soaked makeshift bandage from his side and studied his wound. With a flashlight, she confirmed that his bleeding had stopped and then began to clean the area with a cloth soaked with antiseptic.

"The pain is worse when I lie down."

"Sit up, then. But you'll have to take the pain if you start to bleed again."

Even in his feverish state, Leighton watched her give him first aid and was impressed. "You've done this before."

She looked at him and touched his face. "Yes, my love. I regret to say I have applied many bandages to wounded comrades."

Leighton was drenched in perspiration. Zorrita wiped his forehead and neck with a cloth. "When it's light, when she can see properly, Alma will get the bullet out of your shoulder."

Leighton nodded and closed his eyes. Alma had rigged a sling for his arm, and his left shoulder ached every time he moved, even when he breathed. Looking at him with the bloody bandage on his shoulder, and fresh bandages to his head, face, and side, Gabriela said solemnly, "I should not have let you go."

Leighton opened his eyes, but only briefly, and shook his head. "Avellar will run the story on you. So will the American wire services."

"How do you know?"

"He told me. They've asked him to share any stories I file."

"You are being read in the major American papers?"

"Yes, for the time being."

She dabbed his forehead with a cloth again and kissed him. At that moment, Camilo approached with food and a canteen.

"I have brought you chicken and rice, Machete. And I found something special to dull the pain," he said proudly. Leighton took the canteen first and sipped tentatively. It contained not water but mezcal.

Leighton managed a smile. "A thousand thanks, Camilo. You are a great man." He took a bigger sip.

The youth extended a bowl to Leighton as Zorrita beamed at him. "Alma says you must eat."

"And so do I," Zorrita said, taking the canteen from Leighton. She sniffed the canteen's contents before screwing the cap back on.

"Hey—"

"Eat," she commanded. "Then drink." She held the bowl and fed him rice and bits of shredded chicken with a spoon. "And try to save some of that mezcal for later this morning … when the bullet comes out of you."

Camilo left them alone in the darkness. Zorrita finished feeding Leighton, then sat next to him against the tree trunk and wrapped him in a blanket. Knowing that if he slept at all it would likely be in an upright position, she snuggled close to him so that when he finally did drop off after consuming most of the mezcal, he was able to rest his head on the soft pillow of her shoulder.

CHAPTER 8
CHECKMATE

In the morning, after removing the bullet from Leighton's shoulder, Alma sought out Zorrita. She found her down by the river, making plans with Mateo for the attack on the air base. Concern for Leighton and the occasional drone of surveillance planes had kept Zorrita awake most of the night, and she looked tired. But upon Alma's arrival, she had Zorrita's full attention.

"I've removed the bullet and cleaned the wound in his shoulder. I cleaned and sewed up his side also, and he's resting now. He should be able to sleep much better, and I expect his fever to be gone by tomorrow, possibly sooner."

"Very good," Zorrita said, nodding. "It's our good luck that you have medical training. Are you sure he's in no danger from the wound in his side?"

"The bullet hit him in the side but didn't go very deep, it just ripped up a layer of muscle around his abdomen and passed on through his body without hitting an artery or any of his internal organs. He's lucky. If it had penetrated his intestines or kidneys, we'd have no choice but to get him to a hospital. Even if I were a surgeon, a wound like that would be more than I could handle out here."

Zorrita managed a smile. "We don't have much in the way of facilities out here in the bush. Least of all antiseptic operating rooms. But it sounds as though Machete is in good hands."

"Machete?"

"A nickname. Mateo can explain it to you."

"I should check on those travel orders," Mateo said suddenly, and excused himself.

Alma looked at Zorrita in bewilderment. "Did I -– have I offended him?"

Zorrita smiled broadly and said to her quietly, "He is just intimidated by your beauty, that's all. He'll recover in time."

Alma blushed. Eager to change the subject, she said, "There is one thing about … Machete. Gangrene is a serious risk because of the climate. His dressings will have to be changed twice a day and cleaned with alcohol."

"Well, luckily we have plenty of mezcal and tequila."

"I want to say … it is an honor to be here. One hears a lot about Zorrita in Valmonte. My father, if he knew I were here with you, he would be very proud. There is a growing certainty among the people that you will lead the guerillas to victory and throw Vilar out. Even some of the Secret Police are discouraged."

"Yes, but the fighting in Redención is not going well," Zorrita replied.

"People do not give that any importance. They have faith in you. You have brought many people hope."

"Well, I will do my best to justify their faith," Zorrita said in a somber tone. "I am certainly not here to allow peoples' hopes to be dashed. But you heard all this … where?"

"One hears a great many things working in a place like Villa Palmera."

"Yes. I understand you were intimate with our American patient there."

Zorrita's words stunned Alma. Her mind raced as she struggled to maintain her composure. At last she said, in as dignified a voice as she could, "I'm not sure why you mention that. Is it the *Frente's* concern?"

Zorrita ignored the remark. She looked Alma in the eye and spoke plainly. "When you had him, he wasn't with me. But he is now. He is free to do as he wishes, of course. But I thought you should know."

"I had no idea. But I suspected, after last night. Zorrita, I—"

"You don't have to say anything," Zorrita replied calmly.

"But I was only going to say that I don't want to interfere," Alma blurted.

"I understand. I also know that Vilar had your father killed because of his union activities, and that but for his death there would have been money for you to have completed your medical studies by now. Villa Palmera would never have come into your life. You would already be a doctor."

"That is true, Zorrita," Alma said quietly, her eyes on the ground.

"Do you want him?" Zorrita asked, looking Alma in the eye.

"It was a thing of the moment. I … I never expected to see him again."

"Well … now you have."

"I will leave if you wish. I can go to another cell."

"No," Zorrita said firmly. "We need you here."

"But why?"

"I will tell you in a moment."

"I have no claim on him," Alma said. "It was just … one night."

Zorrita placed a hand on Alma's shoulder. "Don't worry. Living this kind of life, knowing it can suddenly end violently on any given day, you come to think differently about such things. You're an attractive woman, it was natural for him to want you."

"B-but Zorrita …" Alma sputtered, trying to comprehend what she was being told. "I mean to say, I would never … I … last night, it was clear that he … he is your man."

"That may be," Zorrita replied, "but I am not naive. I know things can happen. And whether you are with Machete or someone else, remember that in the bush, being intimate with one man may lead others to have similar expectations. It's different with me. I am the leader."

"Yes," Alma said, confused.

"Have no fear," Zorrita said, taking Alma into her arms. "You are with us now. Take time to think about what I have said, that is all. I will not speak of this again. Come to me at any time if you need help. The day will come when you will be Dr. Alma Perez."

"I can't imagine …"

"But you must, Alma. You *must* imagine it. If it is to become a reality, that is how it starts. You must picture tending the sick and injured in an office that has your name on the door. In gold letters. And you have another skill, which is why we brought you out of Valmonte. I am told you are exceptionally good with a rifle. That you performed extremely well in the attack at Melilla."

"But Zorrita, I only made five shots."

"The number of shots is not as important as who fell once you made them. You targeted machine-gunners. *You saved lives,* Alma. As bad as our casualties were that day, without you they would have been far worse. Do not minimize your actions."

Alma looked up at Zorrita. In that moment, she looked terribly young, almost like a little girl. They were nearly the same age, yet her life experience had given Zorrita the perspective of a much older woman.

"You must remember, Alma … you are going to be a doctor. Vilar and his madness interrupted your course, but that is all it is—a temporary interruption. Just as he is."

"You speak with such confidence," Alma said, amazed.

"Because I can see it," Zorrita said at once. "I can see it very clearly. Vilar will fall away, just as a fever leaves the body. You will become a doctor. Now, I have been told that you are a crack shot." She took three strides to a long wooden box lying where it had been hidden in the underbrush atop a small hillock overlooking the river. The lid of the box was open. Zorrita reached in and lifted out an FN FAL rifle and a box of 7.62mm ammunition. She returned to Alma and handed them to her.

"You will see that this rifle has been fitted with a telescopic sight. I want you to practice with it until you are proficient. You will then see Camilo to get the rifle fitted for a different scope for night operations, called a Starlight scope. We have very few of them, so treat it with care. You will practice until you are proficient with that also. We need your skills for a very special operation. Your role in it will be critical. You will practice by day, but you will spend twice as much time practicing at night."

"At night?"

"Yes. You will soon have the details. The long tube at the end of the barrel is a silencer, so that you can practice at night without disturbing anyone, and get accustomed to using the silencer. We have a place just a few miles from here that we use as a shooting range. Get Mateo to show you," she said with a smile. "It will give him an opportunity to overcome his fear of you. Pick his brain. He is really quite knowledgeable."

"Should I begin now?"

"Yes. Talk to Mateo about selecting a team of at least three other snipers. He will know who our best marksmen are. And Alma?"

"Yes?"

"Welcome to the bush."

• • • • ▪ ▪ ▭ ▭ ▬ ▭ ▭ ▭ ▭ ▭ ▭ ▪ ▪ • • • •

Miller arrived at the office at 7:00 a.m. as usual, and made a beeline for his white porcelain NASA coffee cup, emblazoned with the original 1960's logo and the words "GET WITH THE PROGRAM" in large black capitals. He poured his second cup of Brazilian coffee from the pot on his credenza, primed by Ms. Gradenko upon her arrival, and added cream and sugar. He laid his briefcase on his desk and scanned the headlines of four major daily newspapers, which Ms. Gradenko laid out for him on the couch in his office each morning.

Today was different in that Miller received a rare shock. As the Deputy Director for Operations, reading the newspapers was often no more than an exercise in discovering that which he expected to find— news that in his world had been simmering for days or weeks and had finally been unearthed by the press. But today's issue of the *New York Clarion* ran not one but three stories from Madrinega, two of them authored by his own agent operating as Brian Palmer. He'd expected none of them. A brief notation directly below the first headline, which appeared below the fold, revealed that Palmer was a freelance journalist and that a major wire service had picked up the story and made it available to the *Clarion*:

Portrait of a Guerilla Leader

91

Miller sat down with his coffee to read, utterly fascinated, about the woman he had ordered Leighton to kill, an order Leighton had yet to acknowledge. Pressing the intercom button on a little modular console on his desk, he said, "Ms. Gradenko, hold my calls, and no meetings."

"Yes, sir," came her instant reply.

Reading about the upbringing among the intelligentsia of Santiago, Chile in pre-Pinochet days of the woman identified only as "Zorrita" but whom Miller knew to be Gabriela Diaz, he began to form a hunch about Leighton's failure to respond of late. Leighton had crafted a picture of a brilliant, charismatic young woman, idealistic, educated abroad, whose political beliefs had been radicalized by the excesses of the Pinochet regime, including the murder of her older brother, followed by her time as an exile and student in Europe.

Returning to Chile only briefly, she left home again to take up the cause of leftist guerillas in El Salvador, fighting with them for nearly two years before moving on to Nicaragua, where the regime of Daniel Ortega was still fighting a not-so-secret war launched by the CIA at the direction of President Reagan. Madrinega was her latest venture, and from recent news reports, supported by Leighton's article, the tide was turning in favor of the guerillas there. Miller was aware of the CIA's shenanigans in Redención and saw it as a ploy to weaken the Vilar regime and the guerilla movement at the same time. It was accurate to call the article glowing, yet balanced, in spite of the sense that its author was clearly enamored of his subject.

The second article with a Brian Palmer byline, also below the fold on the front page, was shorter:

Bodies of Six Guerillas Discovered in Madrinega's
Vescambre Mountain Foothills

It was little more than a paragraph but hinted that what was unusual about these bodies, discovered in an admittedly remote location in a country in the midst of a guerilla war, was that none of them had died of gunshot wounds, torture, or anything resembling combat, but rather showed physical signs of what appeared to be radiation sickness. Miller recalled one of Leighton's earlier signals about it.

Only now did Miller turn his attention to the banner headline above the fold, written not by Leighton but by a longtime *Clarion* reporter whose name was familiar to millions:

Weaponized Radioactive Waste Killed Dozens in Madrinega
President Vilar Ordered Its Use Against Guerillas
Special to the New York Clarion

Indisputable information made available to the *Clarion* from a source high in the Madrinegan government details an operation in which radioactive waste was secretly acquired from an American company, placed in a series of aerosol containers by the Madrinegan Army, and used in an airborne spraying operation against the guerillas, much as the U.S. employed Agent Orange during the Vietnam War. Documents obtained by the *Clarion* provide incontrovertible proof that the operation was ordered by President Eduardo Vilar himself in an attempt to terrorize the guerillas and discourage further armed opposition to his regime.

However, during the operation the wind shifted unexpectedly, and only a portion of the intended area received a lethal dose of what was essentially radioactive dust. The wind carried over half of the radiological material up to twenty-five miles to the southwest of the planned target area, toward a large farm near the village of Panactatlan. As a result, over fifty agricultural workers began exhibiting symptoms consistent with radiation sickness in the coming days, and despite going to the hospital in Panactatlan for treatment, many of them died. The exact number of sick and dead is not known, because the only records were in the Panactatlan hospital, which was utterly destroyed in a cruise missile attack also ordered by Vilar once the scope of the disaster became clear. Publicly, the justification for the attack was to destroy a guerilla stronghold, despite the fact that most of the inhabitants of Panactatlan worked on surrounding farms and were not known to be sympathetic to the guerilla cause, due in part to the village's relatively high employment rate. Secret government memoranda shared with the *Clarion* indicate that the missile attack was a deliberate effort to conceal the evidence of the aerial spraying and its deadly results for innocent farmworkers who had no ties to the guerillas.

Officials at the White House, the Pentagon, the Central Intelligence Agency and the International Atomic Energy Commission did not return calls for comment on this story by press time, but Attorney General William French Smith said the Justice Department would investigate the role of Chandelle Disposal of Baton Rouge, Louisiana, the company with the last known legal possession of the radioactive material in question in the United States.

There was more, but Miller laid the paper down and dialed the Director's private number.

"Yes."

"Miller, sir. Have you seen the morning papers?"

"Yes. Get up here, the president's on TV."

Miller entered the Director's office within four minutes. The Old Man was leaning against his desk, watching the television inlaid into his bookcase.

"He'll try to use this scandal as an excuse to invade," the Director said with a world-weary certainty. "Watch." Lifting a remote control device, he turned up the TV volume.

"It is not yet clear exactly how the Madrinegan government got hold of the radioactive material," the President was saying, "but the FBI and the Atomic Energy Commission, at my direction, are investigating the matter, and we will keep you updated."

President Reagan called on a reporter in the front row. "Doesn't the Atomic Energy Commission have to approve the release of such material, sir?"

"Well, as you know, this is a highly sensitive matter, and for security reasons I'm not going to discuss the exact nature of the protocols around movement of radioactive material, but rest assured there will be full disclosure, to the degree that's prudent, once the investigation is completed," Reagan said firmly.

Another reporter asked, "Given the nature of President Vilar's use of the material, sir, has there been any discussion about classifying Madrinega as a rogue nation?"

"It's entirely too soon for such discussions, but one thing that has come up is the question of whether such irresponsible use of highly dangerous material justifies our military intervention to assure the security of the region, a region already under threat from the Sandinista regime in Nicaragua."

The Director shot Miller a look.

"But Mr. President," the reporter pressed, "legally or not, we paid the Vilar government to take possession of the radioactive material. If his actions weaponizing that material are now to be the justification for a U.S. invasion, it raises the question whether it wasn't the administration's plan to invade all along. Was that, in fact, your plan?"

"The transfer of radioactive material to Madrinega was not an act of the U.S. government," Reagan said curtly. "We're not in the business of providing radioactive material to anyone."

"But according to the account in the *Clarion,* sir, both the State Department and the Pentagon were notified of the transfer and did nothing to prevent it."

Reagan deflected the need to comment on the last remark, which after all had not been a question, by calling on another reporter. But if he expected a softball question, he was disappointed.

"Was the CIA aware of the transfer, sir?"

Reagan stared the reporter down, deeply aware that this press conference was venturing into troubled waters.

"Well, that question would seem to be better directed to the Director of Central Intelligence," the president said, with his trademark charismatic smile. "My understanding is that that question has already been put to the CIA by the press, and they have not yet responded.

I'm not prepared to comment until Bill Casey does," he said smoothly. "As for our possible intervention, as you all know, there's been a guerilla insurgency down there for many months which has recently gained momentum, possibly with help from Nicaragua. Now, I've said repeatedly that the United States will not tolerate any attempt to export revolution to the nations of Latin America. Although President Vilar appears to be putting down a large-scale uprising in one of his cities, the city of Redemption, the question remains whether he can maintain order in the long term, and we are monitoring the situation closely. You will all receive a more detailed briefing as soon as the information becomes available. That's all for today, thank you, ladies and gentlemen."

With that, President Reagan waved and stepped away from the podium amid a barrage of follow-up questions, exiting the Blue Room quickly as a phalanx of aides closed in behind him to preclude any physical pursuit.

"Notice how few questions actually got an answer," the Director said, turning the TV off. "I've read today's *Clarion,* Bill. Your agent seems to be determined to prove that the pen is mightier than the sword – but that's not what we're paying him for."

"He's moving on a plan to get the guerillas to lead him to the other two missiles," Miller replied.

"I don't have to remind you, do I, that the missiles now have a fraction of the importance that eliminating that woman, Zorrita, does? Anyway, he's moving too slowly. The CIA has already stepped in to stir things up down there. Redención had their fingerprints all over it."

"Yes, I know."

"Why is that woman still alive?"

"I imagine she's very well guarded, sir."

"Well, if your agent doesn't come through, the whole damn U.S. military may wind up doing the job for him if he continues to dither with his finger on the trigger."

"I understand, sir. He'll do it."

"Tell him not to wait 'til Christmas," the Old Man said testily.

Within hours of the presidential press conference and follow-up news broadcasts confirming the revelations about Madrinega, an international firestorm of criticism erupted. A special session of the United Nations Security Council was convened for the sole purpose of enacting a resolution condemning Vilar's weaponization of radioactive waste. In a rare demonstration of unanimity, the Soviet Union and the People's Republic of China joined the Western powers in supporting the resolution.

At the U.N. General Assembly, shortly following Reagan's broadcast, the Madrinegan ambassador sat mute and humiliated in the face of speeches castigating his government until, approaching the second hour of such oratory, he could take no more. He stood up and walked out.

By midafternoon, telephone calls began to bombard the White House from foreign heads of state. President Reagan initially accepted only three, from Margaret Thatcher of Britain, Francois Mitterand of France, and Helmut Kohl of West Germany. He was persuaded to take a fourth, from Menachem Begin of Israel. Weary of reassuring America's allies, he punted the remainder to James Baker III, his Chief of Staff. In a subsequent meeting, Baker emphasized to the president that even the Soviet Union, China, and the Eastern Bloc nations had signed on to the U.N. resolution of condemnation, underscoring the international community's outrage over Vilar's actions. But, crazy or not, Vilar was a U.S. ally; he had no nuclear weapons, posed no threat to the United States, although at the moment he was an embarrassment, and he was in the final stages of putting down a leftist insurrection in Redención. Baker advised riding out the storm, at least as far as sending in American forces, and the president, feeling less than eager to commit himself, demurred in the face of Baker's analysis. After all, with international pressure escalating, Vilar might resign voluntarily.

But events were taking their own course. Despite American efforts to tamp down the rising sense of outrage, the U.N. followed up its earlier action by voting for a slew of economic sanctions against Madrinega. A bipartisan bill was introduced in Congress to immediately cut off all American aid unless Vilar resigned. This in turn set off alarm bells in the White House, where it was clearly understood that a sudden power vacuum in the Madrinegan government would only benefit the leftist guerillas. A suitable successor would have to be found, and fast.

Then came an announcement from the Organization of American States that it would convene the following day to condemn Vilar's action, call for economic sanctions, and demand Vilar's removal. Belated though it was, the OAS action was a sign of mounting international pressure, particularly in the Americas. In a pointed conclusion, it stated, "We fervently hope that the United States will join us in supporting this humanitarian resolution. What has occurred in Madrinega is an abomination that transcends any political differences between nations in this hemisphere." That night, the OAS action was broadcast on all the major news networks.

After a series of late-night calls during which James Baker conferred with Speaker of the House Tip O'Neill, who confirmed that the Madrinega resolution would pass the House of Representatives by a comfortable margin, including several Republican votes, and Senate Majority Leader Howard Baker, who assured Baker that the optics of trying to stop the resolution in the Senate would be disastrous for the Republicans, Baker reluctantly called Secretary of State George Shultz. The result was that shortly after midnight, a cable went out from the State Department to the U.S. embassy in Valmonte.

٭٭٭٭٭ ▪ ▬ ▬ ▬ ▬ ▬ ▬ ▬ ▬ ▪ ٭٭٭٭٭

The following morning, promptly at 9:00 a.m., the United States Ambassador to Madrinega, Dennis Harwood, met with President Vilar at the presidential palace. Vilar, recently returned to the official residence after an extended stay at Costa Pacifica, the private resort from which he had monitored the fighting in nearby Redención, appeared surprisingly relaxed and confident. After speaking late the night before with General Humberto Pando, the officer in charge of government forces conducting the operation, he felt certain that the guerilla uprising, what remained of it, would be crushed within the next twenty-four hours.

Coffee and cakes were promptly served once the ambassador was seated with the president in his office. Vilar was in a celebratory mood

98

and lit a cigar. He offered one to Ambassador Harwood, who politely declined. Vilar said he had some awareness of the firestorm of media coverage he had received in the United States in the past thirty-six hours, but he dismissed it as so much hand-wringing of the American left, who controlled far too many media outlets. It would soon blow over.

"I'm afraid not, Mr. President," Ambassador Harwood began. "The situation grew much worse during the night. Our Congress is now pushing hard to cut off all aid to Madrinega immediately … unless there's a change of leadership. That is the level of concern my government has over your use, for military purposes, of radioactive material."

"Material which your country paid us to take off your hands," Vilar retorted.

"Yes, we've looked into that," Ambassador Harwood responded. "The contract called for the material to be placed in lead-lined containers and buried underground in a long-abandoned copper mine near the town of Bocuateca, some ninety-eight miles southeast of here. It appears, Mr. President, that the interment of the waste never occurred."

"What of it?" Vilar spat, unperturbed.

"Mr. President, my government has received copies of original documents issued by your Army Central Command—the equivalent of our Pentagon—providing proof that acting on your orders, your military prepared the radioactive material for aerial spraying. They then used an aerosolized radioactive spray in violation of international humanitarian law and an International Criminal Court statute prohibiting the use of weapons which are inherently indiscriminate in their application. The weapon also violated the Geneva Convention and the military practices of over 50 nations, including the United States, the Soviet Union, Spain, Colombia, Ecuador, Mexico, and Peru. My government sees no justification for such an action. I am here to ask you to resign or face the immediate suspension of all American aid."

Vilar seemed not to have heard. "I did only what was necessary to defeat the guerillas," he replied with a wave of his hand. "Just look at what's happening in Redención. By this time tomorrow, they'll be crushed."

"Mr. President, I don't believe you understand the gravity of the situation. This is far bigger than your fight against the guerillas. The United Nations, and now even my government, have condemned your actions and called for your resignation."

"Resignation? Never!"

"Very well, Mr. President," Ambassador Harwood said, steeling himself, "My government has directed me to inform you that you will no longer have American support if you insist on remaining in office. Our Congress is gearing up to cut off all American aid to Madrinega unless you resign."

"Surely your president cannot allow such a thing," Vilar retorted.

"He cannot stop it. Congress controls expenditures regarding foreign aid, and in the past have threatened to cut off aid to the Nicaraguan Contras. That is why I am here. For the good of your country, my government believes it is best that you resign."

Vilar sat ramrod straight as his face reddened with emotion. "Forgive me, Ambassador Harwood," he said with icy calm. "Did you say your government believes that my resignation is in the best interests of Madrinega?"

"I did, sir. That is my government's official position."

Vilar was on his feet. "How dare you! Get out! Get out, do you hear? Get out before I have you shot! You, you *pinche gringo!* Get out!"

Harwood had expected the tirade and was already halfway to the door. He got it open and managed to duck behind it as Vilar hurled a heavy metal paperweight at him.

"I don't need you!" Vilar screamed at the closed door. He moved to his liquor cabinet, poured a tumbler of bourbon, slugged it down, and poured another. He paced his office, fuming.

In a few moments, there was a knock at the door. Meekly, his aide, Ernesto Zambrano, stuck his head in.

"Generals de Santiago and Pando are here, Mr. President."

"What? Why? I did not call for them."

"They say they have news of Redención, sir."

"Ahh, good. Show them in."

General de Santiago, a tall, slender, grey-haired man, erect and immaculate in a khaki dress uniform, entered the president's office with his peaked cap in hand, followed by General Pando. Pando was a stark contrast, a younger, shorter man with a heavyset build wearing a field cap and camouflage fatigues that were torn and visibly dirty. His face was smeared by soot, smoke, and sweat, his boots scuffed and covered in dust. It was clear he had come direct from a battle.

"What news have you of Redención?" Vilar demanded.

"The guerillas in Redención have surrendered, Mr. President," General Pando reported. "All opposition in the city ceased about two hours ago. I flew here directly from the fighting by helicopter to inform General de Santiago."

"Excellent. But either of you could have informed me with a phone call. Why are you here?"

"Since the guerillas in Redención surrendered, and news of the Panactatlan operation has been leaked," General de Santiago said, "we are now facing uprisings in multiple cities." He paused to check his watch. "Six cities, as of thirty minutes ago. We may be able to put them all down, but the scale of bloodshed could turn what is still a growing insurgency into a true civil war, and we may not have the resources to deal with them all simultaneously. I regret, Mr. President," de Santiago said, rapidly unholstering and drawing his pistol, "that I have come to arrest you."

Vilar laughed in his face. "Are you serious, Vicente?"

"Quite serious. With you removed from office, the Army will have a chance of maintaining order. But if you remain …" He shook his head.

"Absurd," Vilar said dismissively. "Guards!"

"Major!" de Santiago bellowed. The door of the office opened, and six regular Army soldiers armed with automatic weapons streamed in. Trailing behind them were three of Vilar's plainclothes security detail, being held at gunpoint by another six soldiers.

"I am sorry, Eduardo," de Santiago said. "We cannot afford to lose the support of the United States, and we are perilously close to doing so because of your actions."

"You won't get away with this, Vicente," Vilar growled. "You think that by arresting me you can save yourself? Save your reputation? Fool! You have blood on your hands, just as I do! Your fingerprints are all over Panactatlan, just like mine!"

"That is true," de Santiago said calmly. "It is my country I am thinking of now, not my own skin. You and I differ in that regard. I do not propose to take power. General Pando will do that. Unlike ourselves, he does not have the stench of the dead of Panactatlan on him."

Vilar stared at de Santiago. It was a look of hate.

"Major Berron," de Santiago said. A young officer stepped forward. "Sir."

"You will place General Vilar under arrest. He is no longer the president. You will confine him in the detention area at Army Central Command until further notice. He is to have no visitors. His bodyguards are to be held as well, for the time being."

"Understood, sir. General Vilar?"

"I will see you dead for this," Vilar hissed.

"You may," de Santiago said wearily. "But you will not resume power. And you may find that revenge is rather difficult when you have to do it yourself. While you were away in Costa Pacifica, Colonel Narváez disappeared."

Major Berron and the other soldiers escorted Vilar and his bodyguards out.

"What happened?" Pando asked. "How did the Americans learn about Panactatlan?"

"My dear Pando," de Santiago said, holstering his weapon, "take my advice, and do not dirty your hands by asking. But I can tell you this. A certain classified dossier has gone missing from Army Central Command headquarters, along with our head of Secret Police."

"I will have to announce the formation of a provisional government," Pando said, "but I am worried. These new uprisings—"

"Why? Vilar's departure will surely ease tensions. Later today I will resign—"

"Yes, but the guerillas will see it for what it is—the military struggling to remain in control. In Redención, I saw something new;

the worse things got for the guerillas, the more their resistance stiffened. I have never seen such fighting spirit on the part of the rebels. We had superior numbers, but we took far too many casualties. At one point, my own command post was nearly overrun. They *knew* they would lose, yet the guerillas mounted that suicidal attack. Many of them seemed to prefer death to surrender. We beat them in the end, but we had to kill far too many for our victory. I tell you, if these uprisings continue, much more blood will be spilled. Redención was bloodbath enough. And on every other wall in the city, there always seemed to be one word, painted or scratched: 'Zorrita.'"

De Santiago nodded. "That Chilean bitch may yet be our undoing."

CHAPTER 9
THE ROAD TO BOCUATECA

L ie still," Zorrita said with irritation as she dripped tequila over the wound in Leighton's side.

"It doesn't just sting, it burns," Leighton complained. "Besides, it's a waste of fine tequila."

"Be quiet," she scolded. "Alma did her best, but the wound has not fully closed, and until it does, this will prevent you from getting gangrene. You call that a waste?" She dabbed the wound dry and put on a fresh dressing, applying surgical tape around his torso to hold it in place.

It was midafternoon and very hot. Camilo sat near them under the trees, shirtless, reading a newspaper that had been brought in from Limado. He had just read to them the news of the radiation poisoning at Panactatlan and Vilar's arrest by the Army to stave off the threatened suspension of American aid and the severing of diplomatic relations by several countries. General Pando had assumed the presidency and announced the formation of a provisional government. There was talk of elections to be held within the year, but nothing had yet been decided.

"And have you noticed that we haven't seen any planes? The surveillance flights have stopped. We haven't heard or seen planes for two days and nights."

"They're regrouping after Redención, after ousting Vilar," Zorrita said. "Trying to decide what to do next."

"And what about us?" Mateo asked, as he looked up from cleaning his rifle. "Do we proceed with the attack on the air base?"

"Vilar's arrest changes nothing," Zorrita said. "The Army only deposed him to appease the Americans and to keep their money and weapons flowing into the country. We are fighting the same beast with a different face. We must go ahead with the attack."

"Well, everything we need is ready," Mateo reported. "We have five vehicles, all with sufficient petrol, the necessary travel orders, even the uniforms."

"Good," Zorrita said. "We must hit them while we can. It will show the world, but especially the Americans, that even after Redención, the *Frente* is not beaten."

"I know you're going to go," Leighton said to Zorrita. "I will go with you."

"No," Zorrita replied. "You are lucky to have survived that gunfight in Valmonte, and you're still recovering from your wounds."

Leighton stood. "I will not sit here while you place yourself in danger."

"Can you handle a rifle with that shoulder?" Zorrita challenged, gesturing toward Leighton's left arm, which still hung in a sling.

With effort, Leighton removed the sling and picked up Camilo's rifle from where he had rested it against a tree. Smothering a groan of pain, he raised it at a forty-five-degree angle and fired it into the tree trunk at a point high above. As he lowered the weapon, the pain was even worse, but he had done it. He set the rifle down.

Zorrita got up from where she had been sitting and helped him back into his sling. "Well done," she said quietly, her voice little more than a whisper. "But I ask you to reconsider."

She turned to Mateo and Camilo. "Pass the word. We will go tomorrow night. After we attack the air base, we will be able to move the missiles into a firing position and use them."

"Against what targets?" Mateo asked.

"The very same air base. And the largest Army base in the country, at Xapaca." All three of her companions reacted with surprise.

"Why the air base?" Camilo asked.

"In case we miss any of the planes. Otherwise, we can send both missiles against Xapaca."

"That could kill many soldiers, Z," Mateo protested. "It's one thing to kill them in the field, while they're fighting us, but to kill them in their beds—"

"I'm not sure I recognize the distinction, Mateo. They would do the same to us if they could. The advantage we have, for the moment, is that they don't know where we are. Besides, I didn't say we'd target their barracks. It's the armory I'm thinking of—their stockpile of weapons and ammunition."

"Do we have a map of the base?" Leighton asked.

"Salcedo has it. He will be more than willing. And we've seen how accurately he can program the missiles' guidance system. Mateo, pass the word. Camilo, please find Alma and her team and send them to me."

Camilo stood. "We should call it Operation Icarus, after the youth who helped his father make wings to fly, then ignored his father's warnings not to fly too close to the sun. He fell to his death when the wax in the man-made wings melted."

Zorrita looked from Mateo to Leighton, who said, "Well … you are trying to cripple Vilar's air force."

"Very well, Camilo. Icarus."

"Yes!" Camilo exclaimed. "I will tell the others." He departed with Mateo.

"I can't believe the things he cares about at times," Zorrita muttered, shaking her head.

"I saw him reading a book on Greek mythology," Leighton said.

Once they were alone, Zorrita turned to Leighton. "I do not want you to go," she said, her voice suddenly harsh. "I will be more effective if I am not worried about your safety."

"Usually it's the man saying that to the woman," Leighton replied.

She shot him a fierce look. "Is your ego involved in this?"

"No. The truth is, I don't want you to go, either. But I'm not going to get what I want, am I?"

"You know that I must go. For me there is no choice. I am the leader."

"But for once, you're not being logical. Wounded or not…how will it look to the others if Machete stays behind?"

"I *must* go," she exclaimed, frustrated. "Don't you see? We all have a purpose."

Leighton took a step toward her, embracing her in his one good arm. She returned his embrace, and they were silent for several moments.

"Then I must go with you. You see? Neither of us has a choice about this."

She broke their embrace and looked into Leighton's eyes. She pressed a hand to his chest, feeling his heartbeat, and said quietly, "Then I suppose we will have to go together."

At that moment, Alma approached, accompanied by two men and a woman. "You wanted to see me, Zorrita?" she asked hesitantly. She was still in awe of the guerilla leader, and not entirely comfortable in Leighton's company. Leighton's approach was simply to pretend that the night with her at Villa Palmera had never happened.

"Yes, Alma. Is this your team?"

"Yes, Zorrita. Four snipers. These are Graciela, Armando, and Timoteo."

"Good. Sit down, all of you. Machete, tell them the plan."

Leighton ran through the attack plan for the air base at Taramantes, emphasizing their role in the critical opening moments and the split-second timing it would require.

"Can you do it?" Zorrita asked.

The snipers looked at one another and nodded. "Yes," Alma replied.

"In the time required? It will be no more than six or seven seconds," Leighton added.

"Yes, we have been practicing often at night, as Zorrita ordered."

"Excellent," Zorrita said. "Go now, and get some rest. We will need you all to be sharp tomorrow night."

When the snipers departed, Zorrita turned to Leighton and stroked the back of his neck.

"Alma is pretty, don't you think?"

Leighton, instantly sensing that he was being tested, said, "No, I think she's beautiful."

"Beautiful? My goodness."

"But no one is as beautiful to me as you are."

Zorrita smiled and continued to stroke the back of his neck. "If you want to be with her again, I won't try to stop you."

"Look," Leighton said, "I know you have a 'live for today' attitude, but don't you think you're carrying it too far?"

Gabriela studied him a moment. "You don't want her," she said under her breath, with a note of surprise.

"No. You're the one I want," Leighton said, genuinely irritated. "Life might be easier if I *did* want her."

Gabriela let out a little laugh. "My, but you're serious. I just thought—"

"I know what you thought. Forget about it. You really—"

She turned to him and put a finger to his lips, pressing close against him. It was so hot that she was not wearing her usual tank top beneath her tunic. The sight of her cleavage was all it took. Leighton grabbed her and kissed her—hard. They embraced, and she let out a little moan as he sucked on her tongue hungrily for a moment then finally he released her and allowed her to catch her breath.

"My goodness," she said quietly. "That's the first time since you got back from Valmonte. I was beginning to wonder."

Leighton kissed her neck. "I've wanted you since the first night I got back. But I was in too much pain."

"You might have told me."

"Told you what? Exactly what should I have said as I sat there bleeding with a bullet in me?"

"Oh, I don't know … a simple statement like, 'I'm dying to fuck you but I'm in too much pain right now.' That would have done very well," she said indignantly.

"But why? If I couldn't."

"Whether you could or couldn't isn't important. A woman likes to hear such things."

Leighton laughed, but her expression told him to stop, and he fell silent. Then Gabriela smiled in a way that accentuated her freckles. She watched him for a moment, eyeing him curiously.

"You are truly mine now." She stared at him until he realized it was a question cloaked as a statement.

"Yes," he said softly. "Didn't you know?"

"So what about tonight?" she asked, her voice husky.

"Tonight it would be nice to have some privacy," he said at once.

"Good." She turned and began to walk back to the camp, confident that he was following her. "Right now I want you to get your laptop and come with me."

Leighton went to recover his laptop and rejoined her as she came upon Mateo, who was talking to a group of guerillas about the air base attack.

"We're taking one of the jeeps to Bocuateca," she said to Mateo. "Will that leave us enough petrol for tomorrow night?"

"Yes," Mateo said, visibly surprised. "We have about thirty gallons in reserve, in case we need it."

"Good."

"Will it be just the two of you?"

"Yes, why?"

"It's at least an hour away. It might be safer to have some of us with you," Mateo said. Leighton noticed that he looked worried.

"I appreciate that, Mateo, but we'll be fine. What can happen to me with Machete with me?"

"No offense, Machete, you know you have my respect. But you are already wounded. Zorrita, neither of you should be away from camp alone."

"We will not be alone," Gabriela replied, amused. "We will be together."

"That's not what I meant."

"I know. We'll be back in time for supper, assuming we don't encounter any planes."

"Please be careful."

"We will."

······ ▪ ▪ ▪ ▪ ▪ ▪ ▪ ▪ ▪ ▪ ▪ ▪ ······

In twenty minutes, they were in a jeep, headed south. Zorrita drove fast and skillfully. Leighton noticed that she wore her 9mm Smith &

Wesson in the shoulder holster and had placed an AK-47 and three spare magazines in the back of the jeep, along with two canteens. The heat was oppressive as usual.

"What's in Bocuateca?" Leighton asked, wiping his brow.

"You'll see."

She drove them down into a valley and eased their speed as the road turned toward the southwest. They were mostly in the open in this part of the country, the comfort of the jungle canopy well behind them, and had a few moments' trepidation when they spotted an aircraft far off to the north. Leighton took a look using Zorrita's binoculars.

"It's a twin-engine transport, probably headed to Valmonte," he said after struggling to focus on it. "Nothing for us to worry about."

"Good," she replied, pressing her foot down harder on the gas pedal. "I wouldn't want to try bringing an airplane down with an AK-47. It's been done, but it's not easy."

"Will it be better with Vilar gone?"

She shook her head. "Somewhat, but the changes will be mostly cosmetic. There's little difference between being ruled by a dictator, and being ruled by what amounts to a military junta. There will still be widespread poverty, illiteracy, lack of health care, education. Political freedom will exist as it does now, in name only. No, with Vilar gone and the generals in charge, there will be no fundamental change."

"Why did Mateo look so worried?"

She looked directly at him. "We're taking a chance driving so far in daylight. I haven't done anything like this since before we seized the cruise missiles." She paused. "But my gut feeling is that we can risk it. The main danger this far from the capital are the planes. And I have a hunch the generals are busy arguing about what to do now with Vilar gone—how best to reassure the Americans. Everything has been paused, but it won't last. That's why we must hit the air base sooner rather than later."

They drove on through the afternoon heat, and after a time they could see through the haze a village several miles distant, farther down in the valley. There was a small hill directly ahead that obscured the village for a few moments, and provided a little shade as the road took them up the hill and into a copse of trees. In what seemed an idyllic moment under the dappled, greenish light, all Leighton could think of was his desire for Gabriela. It consumed him.

He turned to her and asked, "What will you do after the revolution here?"

She thought a moment. "When I was a little girl, my father made me take music lessons. I didn't want to at first. But I was very good at the violin, and just competent at the piano. He wanted me to continue with my music studies, but there didn't seem to be any point to it, trying to create a life of beauty, once Pinochet took power and my brother was killed. But if I could leave this life and do something else, I'd like to take it up again and become a concert violinist. My instructor used to complain to my father that I had the talent to go far but I wouldn't apply myself. I remember Father got very cross with me when he got such reports," she said, smiling at the memory.

The jeep emerged from the trees, and the heat intensified as they left the shade behind and the road dipped, taking them deeper into the valley. Ahead the open landscape on either side of the road grew barren and somewhat rocky. It then yielded to cultivated lands where crops grew on the right side of the road, and the left side lay fallow. It continued like that for another few miles until they could see in the distance ahead that this part of the valley ended abruptly in a sheer cliff that towered over a dense thicket of trees flanking both sides of the road that marked the end of the cultivated land and stretched for miles in either direction. They were soon among the trees, and before long they came upon the outskirts of the village that they had seen earlier from a higher elevation.

"Welcome to Bocuateca," Gabriela said. They drove among the buildings of the village, but many of them appeared to be unoccupied, derelict. "This was once a thriving mining town," she explained. "But once the copper mine nearby was tapped out, the miners left. Only a few families live here now, all of them farmers."

A few children were playing in the dirt road, and a woman came out of a small house to shoo them inside. Gabriela tapped the brake, slowing down, and as they passed the next building, a man with a grey beard stuck his head out of a window, eyed them briefly, then went about his business.

"The government has all but forgotten this place since the mine closed down," Gabriela said. "We occupied a part of the village a few weeks ago—just a handful of guerillas, about three dozen—and once the farmers realized we intended to leave them in peace, they began to share their food from time to time. We try to return the favor by hunting whatever game can be found in the area."

"But why this place? You said there's nothing here."

With a wave of her hand, Gabriela indicated the high cliffs overlooking the village on three sides. She stopped the jeep in front of what appeared to be a cantina and cut the engine. A man who had heard their arrival emerged from the full-length swinging doors.

"Zorrita," he said with pleasure. "We are honored."

"Señor Yarades," Gabriela responded, alighting from the jeep. "This is Palmer. He is a friend." The two men nodded at one another. "Señor Yarades runs this place."

After a cold drink in Señor Yarades' cantina, they went out. Zorrita took Leighton down a side street to a small apartment building. They went up a flight of stairs on the outside of the building to a door on the second floor. Zorrita knocked two times, paused, knocked three times, paused again, then knocked once.

The door opened, just a crack. A man peered out, then flung the door open. "Zorrita!" He stood shirtless in the hot apartment, wearing only shorts and a pair of sandals. Behind him in the one-room studio stood a girl, very young, barefoot in a skirt and bra, cooking at a stove. Looking up, she scrambled for a blouse to put on, and Salcedo looked embarrassed. "I'm sorry. I did not expect—"

"It is alright, Diego," Zorrita said, raising a hand. "It is I who am sorry, to interrupt your meal, but we need to see the missiles. We will wait down in the street."

Diego Salcedo dressed quickly, met them at the corner, and led them to the edge of town and into the trees, a mere four blocks from his apartment. The village of Bocuateca had been built right up against the cliff face. The trees that flanked the sole road into the village closely abutted it on both sides and continued around the village, providing a buffer between it and the base of the cliff on three sides. It was in among the dense concentration of trees on the east side of the village that the guerillas had secreted the two remaining cruise missiles. Zorrita explained that she had ordered the one hidden at Puerto Oeste moved here when the fighting at nearby Redención began.

They had chosen the hiding place well; the proximity of the cliffs meant that aerial surveillance was impossible except from directly overhead or from the south, and the dense trees obscured the missiles even from those vantage points. Finally, the relative remoteness of the village and the single road leading to it, the last mile of which had vegetation and trees almost up to the roadside, would facilitate the ambush of any approaching ground force. The guerillas had a detachment of thirty-six men and women in the village whose sole job was to guard the missiles.

Salcedo let out a bird call as they penetrated deeper into the trees. An answering bird call told them that they could proceed with safety. Bringing up the rear, unnoticed by the others, Leighton quickly opened his laptop case and pulled out a flask, twisting its cap clockwise before sticking it into his right rear pocket. He repeated the procedure with a second flask and tucked it into his left rear pocket and then deftly closed the laptop case. In a moment, they came upon a screen of armed guerillas who had camouflaged themselves so well that they had been invisible until they rose from the ground; two were directly in front of Salcedo's party, and two on either side of them. Recognizing Salcedo and Zorrita, they lowered their weapons.

"I have come to check the missiles," Zorrita said. The guerillas ahead of them moved aside to make way as they proceeded ever deeper into the trees.

"We have kept them in their nylon slings to protect against ground moisture," Salcedo explained, "and they are resting on their sides on top of the launchers, with a layer of thick burlap used as padding," he said.

Presently, they came upon two long objects covered by fabric, tucked in among the trees in what looked like an impossibly tight arrangement.

"We've made the most of the available space here," Salcedo went on. "It looks like they're wedged in here so that we can't get them out, but I promise you we can, on twenty minutes' notice. The trees provide very good cover, but we've also covered the missiles with sheets dyed green using the juice from boiled cornstalks."

Zorrita stepped forward and pulled away a cotton sheet to reveal an intact missile lying on its side. Leighton joined her and looked it over; it was identical to the one at Vescambre.

"The launchers are here also, you said?" he asked.

"Yes, they are underneath," Salcedo replied.

Leighton knelt as Salcedo and Zorrita walked over to the second missile. He could see that the missile was at least three feet off the ground, and beneath it was the side panel of the launcher that it rested on.

"They're both intact?" Zorrita asked. "No problem with ruptured fuel tanks?"

"No, Zorrita," Salcedo responded. "There have been no leaks. Whenever they have been moved, I have personally supervised it. They've been handled very delicately, partly to protect the warheads."

Pretending to examine the underside of the missile, Leighton slipped one of the flasks from his left rear pocket and gently attached it to the underside of the launcher. The magnetized flask held firm. No one noticed. He moved to join Zorrita and Salcedo where they were standing near the second missile.

"And the guidance systems, they are still functioning?" Zorrita asked.

"Yes," Salcedo replied. "There's a way to run a diagnostic on them using a panel on the launcher. I last checked them three days ago. They are ready to be fired at any time."

"Check them again in the next twenty-four hours," Zorrita said. "And be certain that someone monitors your radio during the broadcast for the next couple of nights, for instructions."

"Sounds like we will be firing them off soon."

"Quite soon," Zorrita confirmed. She turned to see Leighton straightening up near the second missile. "Is anything wrong?"

"Just checking for damage. Everything looks intact, just as Diego said."

"We can go, then." She turned to Salcedo. "Thank you for everything, Diego. Your work will pay a dividend soon."

"Is it true the generals have arrested Vilar?"

"Yes, but now we have the generals to contend with. So not much has changed."

Salcedo quickly moved ahead to lead her and Leighton out of the little forest, for with the cliffs so close, blocking most of the light, it was easy to lose one's way once the sun passed a certain point in the sky. They parted company at the edge of town.

It was late afternoon as they drove away from Bocuateca, with the sun dipping toward the horizon on their left. For twenty miles or so, Zorrita was quiet. Leighton looked over at her, the shadow cast by her head shielding his eyes from the sun's glare but placing her face half in shadow, emphasizing what he sensed as her darkening mood. Something disturbed her, and it was only now bubbling to the surface.

"There was a time when I would have said it doesn't matter what happens with the missiles," she said at last. "That it was enough to deny Vilar the use of them, given his bloodthirstiness."

"And now?"

"Now we can use them to our advantage for a proper military purpose, as well an instrument of psychological warfare. Blowing up the national armory and mounting a second strike against Taramantes Air Base will serve the cause well."

"Then why do you look so troubled?"

Gabriela did not respond immediately. They came to the same copse of trees on the hilltop where she had told him about her music lessons, and she drove a few yards into its dappled sunlight and braked to a halt. She shut off the engine.

"Because I didn't quite tell you everything when you asked me why Mateo looked so worried," she began. "He thinks that you may be an American agent."

Leighton sighed. "Even after helping him get Alma out of Valmonte, and getting shot up doing it? Why? What the hell do I have to do?"

"That is exactly what I said. He said you handled yourself so well freeing Alma in Valmonte that you cannot be an amateur, that you are not just a journalist who knows how to handle a gun. He thinks you've done work like the Valmonte operation before."

"That's ridiculous. I never even killed anyone before I came to Madrinega. I had to come here for that."

"Really? Hand me your laptop case."

Leighton kept a blank expression as he reached down between his legs and took hold of the strap of the case and handed it to her. *Could she or one of the other guerillas have searched it? Do they know about the transponders? If so, she surely knows that two of them are now missing.* He fought to stifle a sudden surge of panic as she opened the case.

"Mateo says that if he's right, all that you have done has been done with the goal of getting close to me, getting me alone … so that you can kill me." She paused and stared at him, giving her words time to sink in and studying his reactions minutely. "If you are an American agent, he says, you would stop at nothing, even putting your own life at risk repeatedly, to earn my trust. To get the chance to kill me. After all, your government wants me dead. The CIA has increased the bounty on me to three hundred fifty thousand dollars. It would be very lucrative for you."

She reached into the satchel and pulled out the little black .25 caliber Vesta automatic. Leighton thought for an instant that she was going to shoot him, but instead she checked the magazine to be certain it was loaded, flicked off the safety catch, and handed it to him.

Leighton stared at her. "Gabriela … what are you doing?"

She stared back at him, her open hand extended toward him, offering him the pistol. "You always carry this case with you everywhere. And this gun is always in it. Mateo thinks he knows why."

"Stop it," he said. He would not take the weapon.

"Too small?" she asked, her voice quaking ever so slightly. She put the Vesta down on the floor of the jeep between them. "Want to be sure of a kill? Then take mine. Surely a nine millimeter will do the job."

She flicked off the snap of her shoulder holster and slowly brought out the Smith & Wesson, confirmed that it too was loaded, and this time even chambered a round. She placed the gun in his lap.

"I'll make it easy for you," she said. "I'll turn my back." And she turned in her seat as if to get out of the jeep. "Some people don't have the courage, or the coldness, to shoot a person while looking into their eyes," she said over her shoulder. She got out of the jeep and stood with her back to Leighton. "If you're an American agent, the only other thing stopping you would be waiting to learn where we've hidden the missiles. Well, now you know. You've seen them."

Leighton felt sick to his stomach.

"I don't like wondering whether such a thing will happen, or when," she explained calmly. "Especially after giving myself to you. If you are going to kill me, do it now. No one will see it here. I only ask that it be quick. You can take the jeep and arrange to be out of the country by sundown. The border isn't so very far from here. I'm sure the CIA will help you."

"No," Leighton said firmly. He did not move.

But Gabriela did not move either. She continued to stand with her back to him and replied, "I want an end to the uncertainty I feel about you. I will not go back to Limado unless I can look Mateo in the eye and tell him he is *wrong*. So I'm making it easy for you. If killing me if why you're here … you'll never … you'll never have a better opportunity."

It occurred to Leighton that if he made a move against her, he could be cut in half by a guerilla with an automatic weapon waiting somewhere among the trees. But in his heart he did not believe that. He understood what she was doing, and it was not merely a test or a melodramatic display. She was leaping from the trapeze bar again, this time in a supreme gamble, or perhaps an act of faith, or both, and it was truly life or death for her now … depending on what he did next.

He knew words would be meaningless. Leighton picked up the Smith & Wesson and placed it on her seat and left it there. Slowly, he got out of the jeep and walked around it to where she stood with her eyes closed. She was aware of his presence but would not open her eyes.

She was making an effort to breathe normally. He felt almost a physical pain as he sensed her anguish, her uncertainty about what he would do.

Leighton stood directly in front of Gabriela and removed his sling. He then knelt at her feet and embraced her, his arms around her legs, and closed his eyes, placing his cheek tight against the heat of her abdomen. He felt her start, then heard her gasp. A second later he heard her burst into tears as he felt her returning his embrace.

Sometime later Leighton rose to his feet, and they resumed their fierce, silent embrace under the trees as the sun went down, as if discovering one another for the first time. He had caught her as she let go of the trapeze bar, and now she was snug in his arms for good.

CHAPTER 10
RADIO MADRINEGA

They were late returning to Limado, but upon Zorrita's arrival, she was greeted with more excitement than usual. Leighton sensed that word of Mateo's suspicions had spread throughout the camp; that a collective fear had taken hold among the guerillas that Zorrita might not return at all—that she had gone off to be alone with her executioner. For this reason, she was greeted not merely with joy or adulation, but with what he sensed was an outpouring of relief.

Leighton tried not to take offense. He was the American, the outsider, after all. And in truth, he was walking a fine line, trying to serve two masters, refusing to acknowledge the kill order on Zorrita while working to recover the cruise missiles as initially ordered. He knew he was rapidly coming to a point where he would have to choose, and in choosing, sever all ties with one or the other: Zorrita and the guerillas, or the land of his birth, the country whose flag he served with increasing ambiguity.

He realized that he had passed a test with the guerillas and had again proved himself. But for Gabriela it had not been a test so much as a gamble to force his hand, to finally expose once and for all either his duplicity, or his love for her. He sensed that her motivation was exactly what she had said: she could no longer tolerate the uncertainty. But what a gamble she had made, and she herself had decided upon the circumstances, choosing a scenario that neither Mateo nor any of the other guerillas would have agreed to, had they known in advance.

It was her life, so it had been her choice. But now that it was all over, the guerillas greeted their Machete nearly as warmly as Zorrita herself.

That night, a celebratory mood took hold in the guerilla camp. A bonfire was started and just as quickly extinguished, on Zorrita's orders, for they still had to watch for the Owl planes. Food was a bit more plentiful, and there was more drinking of mezcal and tequila than usual. There was even a little wine. Late that night, a larger group than usual, including Zorrita and Leighton, trudged up the hill for the 2:00 a.m. radio broadcast. Zorrita explained to Leighton that tonight there would be something new.

Camilo tuned the large radio to the appropriate frequency as Henrietta knelt nearby, cranking the generator. Three wooden crates had been lashed together to form a makeshift podium, and on the top crate a microphone rested on a stand, its cord connected to the radio.

Leighton observed that several guerillas were still coming up the hill to crowd around the radio. It seemed the entire contingent of the camp was on the hilltop. He worried about the Owls, since the heat signature of so many bodies, if spotted, was sure to give the existence of the camp away. He mentioned this to Zorrita.

She turned to him in response, and his image seemed to fill her eyes as she clasped his arm. "You are truly with us now, aren't you?" She paused, but not for a reply, for she did not seem to need an answer. "You are right, of course. There is a risk with so many of us up here. But I must allow it just this once. Tonight is special."

Camilo, headphones on but with one ear exposed, heard the familiar hum that told him the radio had warmed up. He made a hand signal to Mateo, who stepped to the microphone and began speaking in a surprisingly resonant voice, reading from a prepared paper that another guerilla illuminated by flashlight. Two guerillas stood around them to minimize the glare.

"This … is Radio Madrinega," Mateo said clearly into the dark, starlit night in a baritone no one had heard before. It was as though he was speaking with a voice not his own, rising to an occasion. Leighton sensed something momentous was coming; despite the heat of the night, he felt a chill. "The voice of the *Frente Popular*," Mateo continued. "The voice … of liberation. Tonight marks our first ever voice broadcast. For this inaugural event, we will hear of recent events that affect us all and are shaping the fate of our nation, directly from Zorrita, our determined, charismatic, and most fearless leader of this, our national movement. She is not of Madrinega. But she is nonetheless our blood sister. A sister who deserves our respect, our loyalty, our love, our obedience, and, most of all, our sacrifice. She has proven not merely by words but by her actions, her own daily sacrifice, that she is one of us. She is from our neighbor far to the south, a land that even now is home to our brothers and sisters who reel under the despotic tyranny and terror of the jackal Pinochet. She has experienced firsthand in her own land terror, political repression, and the murder of loved ones. She knows the agony of the people of Madrinega. It is her most fervent wish to end it. And now… our devoted, fearless leader, Zorrita."

Gabriela squeezed Leighton's hand in the darkness, took a deep breath, and stepped to the microphone as Mateo and the other guerillas moved away. Gone were the flashlight and the prepared text. Suddenly Alma was at Leighton's side, her face full of excitement as she focused on Zorrita. For the moment, she had overcome her desire to avoid him.

"People are listening tonight all over the country," she whispered. "I heard rumors in Valmonte that this broadcast was coming. I never dreamed I would see it happening."

At that moment, Gabriela began to speak into the microphone, into the night, without notes of any kind.

"People of Madrinega … I speak to you tonight in a spirit of hope—a hope that for far too long, has been all but strangled in this land. It has existed as the mere ember of the raging fire that was once your liberty, the eternal flame of the Motherland.

"Tonight I can report to you that the tyrant Vilar has been deposed. But he is not gone. As I speak these words, he is under house arrest, in the custody of the Army. And tonight we hear rumors that the feared head of the Secret Police has fled the country. The oppressors know that their deeds have been exposed to the world, and they are trying to hide, as the cockroach scrambles to hide when suddenly exposed to light.

"The tyrant has only been forced out of power because of his excesses, his efforts to kill by any means those who would take up arms against his tyranny, and end the darkness into which he has plunged beloved Madrinega. He tried to use a perversion of science to reach out and kill us, and by this means to strike fear into our hearts, even at the cost of poisoning the soil of this Motherland so that it will no longer yield the food that feeds us. He is out of power tonight not because the Army learned of his misdeeds, for the Army was the instrument that implemented them. He is out of power tonight in part because of the courage of a lone American journalist, whose investigation into the government's attempt to use radioactive poison to kill our guerillas corroborated information from the government's own files, secret files containing information the Army has killed to keep secret, secret files that were leaked to the American and now the world press.

"Tonight, because the world has vilified the tyrant after learning of his evil deeds, because the American government has threatened to cut off all aid, the generals have arrested Vilar and seized power in a desperate attempt to maintain the flow of American money and weapons into Madrinega, to perpetuate a destructive regime that restricts your freedom and keeps most Madrinegans in a state of poverty. A regime that rules by terror and repression, by the torture, disappearance, and murder of our fathers and mothers, sons and daughters, unionists, clergymen, intellectuals—anyone who dares oppose the regime or even voice a critical thought. The beast that devours us remains in our midst, so our vow to you tonight is that we will continue the fight.

"We have renewed our determination to fight even though we have just lost many comrades, many brave souls in the heroic, bloody struggle for the city of Redención. Their sacrifice has been noted not merely by us but also by the world. Their deaths will not be the last in our movement. But the example of their determination in the face of overwhelming odds has given the generals pause, because it has underscored the depth and intensity of the desire of the people of Madrinega to be free. It has inspired new uprisings, in city after city, village after village, throughout Madrinega. All over this land, people who are sick of the tyranny, sick of their own fear, are rising up, proving that the sacrifice of our brothers and sisters in Redención was not in vain. Our message to the generals, to the government forces who defeated our comrades is this: The fight we waged, and lost, was not the end. It was the beginning.

"Tonight's message for the guerillas, for the men and women, even the children of Madrinega who support them, who pray for their ultimate success, who yearn to be free, is that our fight is not yet over. We will not stop until this land is truly free of the yoke of tyranny, the domination of a military junta that functions as the local representative of a foreign power. We will continue the fight until the military-industrial complex of our powerful neighbor to the north no longer threatens our existence and controls our economic destiny with a mailed fist clenched at our throat. We will not sit passively to one side and observe the transfer of power from one tyrant to another, even if the new one is slightly less evil. We will continue the fight, for ourselves, for our children, for our grandchildren. We will fight until we are free. I say again: We will fight. Until we are free.

"Tonight there is a ray of light penetrating Madrinega's long night of despair. It is but a single flickering flame, but with faith, and perseverance, and sacrifice, and yes, even blood, with your help, we will stoke that flickering flame once again into a fire of liberty, so that we may breathe free in a land where we, and we alone, are the masters of our destiny. Viva Madrinega!"

The guerillas screamed "Viva Madrinega!" in unison—a great cheer exploding from them spontaneously as Gabriela, overcome with emotion and in tears, stepped away from the microphone and moved directly toward Leighton, reaching out to him as a crowd closed around her in adulation to touch and then lift her bodily above them. Between the physical intervention of Mateo and Leighton, she was put down. Pandemonium ensued as the guerillas cheered loudly and repeatedly.

"Take me away," Gabriela said to Leighton.

Mateo began to bellow for quiet and told the crowd to disperse back to their caves. The guerillas quieted down but were in such a state of euphoria that they continued talking and were slow to disband. Leighton gently but firmly forged a path through the bodies and began to make his way down the hillside with Zorrita. She recovered her composure just long enough to shout, "Remember the Owls!" Suddenly the noise level plummeted dramatically as the guerillas quickly dispersed.

Mateo ran to catch up to Leighton and Zorrita, meeting them halfway down the hillside. "May I speak with you, Machete?" he asked.

Leighton immediately looked to Gabriela, who said, "Go ahead. I will be fine. I'll see you in a few moments." She left them quickly as Mateo guided Leighton off the path.

"I owe you an apology," Mateo began.

Leighton immediately shook his head and put up a hand. "Don't apologize. I'd be skeptical too, in your place." He made a point to look Mateo in the eye. "But if you thought I'd ever do anything to harm her, all I can say is you misjudged your man."

Mateo nodded, bowing his head in embarrassed silence.

"Let's forget it," Leighton said. "I feel I have to protect her too."

Mateo managed a smile. "Good luck tomorrow night."

"And to you."

When Leighton returned to the cave, he was surprised to see Gabriela, illuminated by a single candle, standing nude except for her boxer shorts as she lit a second candle with a match. Standing on the blankets that formed her bed, she turned to Leighton and crossed her arms. Her brow was furrowed with an expression of concern, and Leighton sensed that the emotion of the broadcast was still with her. Her head cocked slightly to one side, her expression deadly serious, she asked him, "How was I? Tell me the truth."

Leighton sat down on a rock and focused on her feet, noticing how attractive they were. He said thoughtfully, "The truth is, you were brilliant. It was a powerful, inspiring speech, from the heart—without notes, I noticed. At the end you almost had me in tears."

Gabriela still looked doubtful. "I have to make millions feel that way."

"If I felt it, they will, too. Many of them. You saw how the people here reacted."

"Do you really think so?"

"You may be too close to it, but it was obvious to me. The guerillas here tonight, the way they reacted, tells you everything you need to know. You touched their hearts. I can see you as the next president. It's not a great leap."

"And if I were to tell you I wanted that, what would you say?"

"You're a natural leader. They'd be lucky to have you."

"And you? What would you do?"

"I never thought about it. I honestly don't know," Leighton said, surprised but still staring at her feet. "How would it look? The male equivalent of a first lady who's an American?"

"It's your ego that's worried about appearances."

"Probably," Leighton admitted.

"It doesn't matter," she said, taking a step closer, and Leighton looked up at her as he sensed her mood beginning to lighten. "I told you. As a foreigner, I'm not eligible to lead the government."

"Besides," Leighton said, "after the revolution you're going to be a college professor."

She drew closer still and sat in his lap. "Mmm … it seems you're glad to see me."

"Always, Gabriela."

"And where would you be? Would you still be my mate, if I lived on a university campus?"

"Oh, without a doubt. I would do very well as the arm candy of the most popular professor in the Political Science Department."

She laughed but corrected him. "Music Department." His hand roamed up over her stomach to cup one of her breasts.

"What's happened to Camilo and Mateo tonight?"

"You want to invite them in?" she teased, very much aware of his eyes on her body.

"Ahh, No," Leighton said, kissing one of her nipples. "I love the privacy."

"Camilo told me. They talked and decided we should have our own bedroom from now on. I think it's also part of Mateo's apology."

"You mean from now on this cave is all ours?"

125

"That's right."

"God love them both," he said, and kissed her.

"My love, I'm sorry about today," she whispered, putting her arms around him. "I had to do it. I had to know."

"I know," Leighton whispered back as they embraced. "But please … never again."

"Never." Holding her firmly, Leighton rolled off of the rock and onto her blankets so that she lay on top of him. Leighton kissed her hard and stroked her cheek.

"I would kill or die, to keep you safe," he whispered. He stood and began to undress.

"I know, my love. Can I tell you a secret? It frightens me."

"Why?" Leighton said, rejoining her on the blankets.

"For one thing, it makes me afraid for you."

"Don't worry about me," Leighton said with confidence.

"No one ever loved me that much. Except my father. And with you, it's obviously different. I've never … no man has ever …"

Leighton rejoined her on the blanket and kissed her into silence, but it did not last, for she felt the need to talk, to share. She sat up, and he realized it was time to listen.

"I'm fairly young, I know, but I'm not … I suppose the word is 'innocent.' I've been with … men, and plenty of men have made it clear they wanted me. But none of them was ever willing to sacrifice for me. You're the first. I really didn't know what you'd do out there on the road today."

"Some part of you must have known … to take such a risk."

"I *hoped*. I will admit … I will even admit to you that I prayed about it. But I didn't *know*. I know now," she said, rising to blow one of the candles out. He rose to blow out the other one, but she stopped him. With just the one candle the atmosphere became more intimate, and they embraced in the semidarkness. Leighton kissed her, and they held one another so close they could each feel the other's heartbeat.

Gabriela looked up at him. "I want you to know you can have anything you want."

Leighton looked into her eyes, absorbing the meaning of her words.

"Do you understand?" she asked.

"Yes," he replied quietly.

He touched her chin, inclined her head just a fraction, and kissed her passionately. They sank to the blankets and made love slowly, tenderly, as if it were the first time. Gabriela let go like never before, and Leighton felt himself transported to a state of bliss akin to another plane of existence, where an orgasm marked the beginning rather than the end of physical pleasure. Earlier she had said she had him now, but he realized he had her too … body and soul, he was in her blood … and she was in his. Gasping, still locked in a dreamlike embrace, they clung to each other as their heartbeats and breathing slowly returned to normal, the act of sex complete but the union it birthed only now awakening to life, their souls fused together on a spiritual plane by a joining that began in the physical world. Melded together now, they slept the deep, untroubled sleep of new lovers.

CHAPTER 11
OPERATION ICARUS

Corporal Flavio Martinez was tired. He had drawn the worst shift for guard duty, the 2:00 a.m. to 6:00 a.m. shift, and the less desirable of the two posts, the guardhouse on the outer perimeter gate of Taramantes Air Base. Worse still, he was the senior noncommissioned officer in charge of the shift, as he was accompanied by Private Fuentes at the outer guardhouse, and a private and private first class whom he did not know manned the inner guardhouse some seventy-five feet away.

All day, there had been a measure of disquiet among the security detail, the sixty soldiers charged with guarding the air base. They all knew Vilar had been deposed, and why. It was all over the radio. It had even been on the TV news. But what had everyone even more concerned was that there were rumors of an impending guerilla attack. Their commanding officer, Major Duarte, had informed them at the previous morning's briefing to be on the alert. Army Central Command expected the guerillas to make a move, but they did not know when or where. They simply expected it to occur relatively soon. There were rumors of a radio broadcast in which the guerillas vowed to continue the fight -– clearly Vilar's departure made no difference to them.

When he came on duty, Martinez ordered all the men to be sure to leave the safety catches off their weapons. They obeyed without question, but it made them nervous. *Good,* Martinez thought. *Nervous men tend to be more alert.* Martinez stood in the doorway of the outer perimeter guardhouse and sipped hot coffee and stared out into the

128

night. Fuentes stood at the wooden barrier, no more than ten feet away, holding his assault rifle at the ready, all too aware that he personally was the air base's very first line of defense. Martinez glanced at his watch for the tenth time in the past hour. 3:15 a.m. Dawn could not come soon enough for him.

⁕⁕⁕⁕⁕▬▬▬▬▬▬▬▬▬▬⁕⁕⁕⁕⁕

Alma Perez and her team of three snipers crept on their bellies down from the hill overlooking the southern side of the air base, moved patiently across the few feet of open ground, just outside the glare of the base searchlights, and crept into the same gully Leighton had used to reconnoiter the base. They took careful note, off to their right, of the road leading to the base entrance, the two searchlights just inside the main entrance, and the two floodlights, one on the roof of each guardhouse. Raising her binoculars, Alma also scanned the base inside the perimeter, gauging the distance to the first big searchlight between the perimeter fence and the southern airstrip, the first light the convoy would encounter that was capable of illuminating the planes lined up there. Beyond that was the searchlight at the western end of the air base, situated exactly halfway between the two airstrips. These were the universe of lights that she and her team would have to destroy in the critical first few seconds of the attack.

Alma could also see another light, just north of the end of the northern airstrip, that illuminated the planes of the night squadron. That light would have to be destroyed as well, although there would be more time to spike that one. Spreading out so that they were ten feet apart, Alma and her team kept watch on the two guardhouses, their primary targets. Through the binoculars, she could see a man drinking coffee at the outer guardhouse, and she felt glad that the guerillas in the convoy were responsible for eliminating the guards outside the perimeter. She remembered with revulsion the five men she had killed at Melilla. Using the Morse code key on a walkie-talkie Zorrita had given her, she tapped out three letters: SIP. Snipers in place.

⁕⁕⁕⁕⁕▬▬▬▬▬▬▬▬▬▬⁕⁕⁕⁕⁕

The convoy turned east, having passed along the outer perimeter road of the capital's civilian airport without incident. Leighton and Mateo were in the lead jeep, both carrying silenced pistols, with two other guerillas. Leighton, his sling gone, held a walkie-talkie that had just squawked with Alma's signal. Three more jeeps were behind them, all carrying guerillas outfitted in Army uniforms, followed by a three-quarter-ton Dodge carrying Zorrita and fitted with a canvas covering, packed with guerillas armed to the teeth. Camilo was in the second jeep. His job was to watch carefully the interaction between the guards at the outer perimeter and the guerillas in the first jeep. Once the guards made the decision to phone in to confirm the travel orders, he was to shine a powerful flashlight directly toward the open field to the left and slightly behind them. This was the signal for the snipers to go into action.

"Remember," Leighton said as Mateo drove along the road toward the air base, "we are there on the orders of Army Central Command to beef up their security. They may even be glad to see us. But they won't be expecting us, so once they decide to make a call to check with the base headquarters, we open up. They can't be allowed to complete a phone call, raise the alarm, or get off a shot. We'll be under observation from the second guardhouse, so once we shoot the guards, we'll have to crash that wooden barrier fast. We can expect gunfire from the second guardhouse, but if the snipers do their job, the guards will be firing into the dark and won't be able to zero in on us."

"I just thought of something," Mateo replied. "We've got to kill the guards in the second guardhouse, but we'll be firing in the dark too. How can we be sure we get them?"

"The jeep headlights, if they aren't shot out by then. We may have to do a lot of shooting."

Mateo nodded. "Brilliant plan."

Leighton turned to the other guerillas in the jeep. "Don't worry about wasting ammunition. The guards in the second guardhouse have got to be put down or they'll raise the alarm."

One of the men nodded and cocked his AK-47. "Do not worry," he said.

Mateo came to the final turn, spinning the wheel to the right, and the other vehicles in the convoy followed him neatly. The outer perimeter guardhouse lay less than one hundred feet ahead. As they approached, the convoy was bathed in light from the guardhouse floodlight. Mateo continued forward at the same deliberate pace, coming to a stop about ten feet from the wooden barrier of the outer perimeter as the soldier outside the guardhouse held a hand up. Private Fuentes kept his weapon trained on the lead jeep as he approached. Behind him, Corporal Martinez unsnapped the holster containing his sidearm as he stepped outside the guardhouse.

Mateo extended toward the soldier a small leather folder. The soldier handed it to the man behind him, keeping his weapon trained. Martinez examined Mateo and then Leighton carefully, and he then scanned the other vehicles and the men in them. Finding nothing irregular, he opened the leather folder to see a miliary ID containing Leighton's photograph, identifying him as Lieutenant Colonel Juan Borrero. Martinez withdrew a paper secured by an inside flap that he unfolded and immediately recognized as travel orders. They directed the Second Platoon of the Twenty-First Military Police Battalion to report for duty to Taramantes Air Base to augment existing security. There was an appropriate illegible signature at the bottom of the document, printed on heavy card stock. It appeared to be in order, right down to the seal of Army Central Command at the top.

After studying the document carefully at his leisure for another minute, Corporal Martinez looked up. "You and your men are a welcome sight, sir," he said, addressing Leighton. "We've been told to be on the alert against a possible guerilla attack. But I wasn't told to expect you, so I'll have to check this out. I'm sure it won't take a moment. Please wait here, sir."

"I understand."

Leighton had been sitting with the silenced Smith & Wesson under his left leg, and he eased it out into the open without moving his arm as Martinez turned back to the guardhouse. In the next instant, there was the sound of breaking glass, and the floodlight above the guardhouse went out. Leighton lifted the Smith & Wesson and fired twice through the windshield at the soldier pointing his weapon directly at Mateo. Fuentes went down without a sound. Mateo fired at Martinez twice, hitting him once before he ducked, the second bullet smashing into the guardhouse wall. The light from the second guardhouse was trained on them, but it too went out suddenly with the sound of breaking glass. Martinez had lunged for the ground and had his gun out, returning fire at Leighton blindly—the first audible gunshots. Mateo pointed his silenced .38 revolver in the direction of Martinez' shots and emptied it. Leighton pulled Fuentes' body out of the way and hopped back into the jeep. Mateo gunned it as the vehicle leaped forward and smashed through the wooden barrier. They continued at speed up the road as gunfire from ahead began hitting the jeep and shattered what was left of the windshield. Leighton lifted his M-16 and fired at the muzzle flashes as the two guerillas sitting behind him did the same. One of the jeep's headlights was now out, and Mateo braked to a halt in front of the motorized gate as Leighton and the other two guerillas hopped out. Leighton dashed for the guardhouse as one of the guerillas found a wounded soldier on the ground nearby and finished him off with a short burst from his AK-47. The only illumination was from the jeep's remaining headlight and the interior of the second guardhouse; Alma and her team had already destroyed the two searchlights just inside the perimeter that flanked the main gate.

Leighton found the switch for the gate and pulled it. With a hum, the gate began to move. As he ran to rejoin Mateo and the guerillas in the jeep, a soldier sprang at him, but Leighton was running so hard that the impact of their bodies knocked the gun from the soldier's grasp. Pain rocketed through Leighton's wounded shoulder as the soldier scrambled for his gun, grasping it and turning it on Leighton just as a burst from one of the guerillas in the jeep caught him full in the back. Leighton holstered the Smith & Wesson as he climbed back into the jeep.

Mateo gunned it again, and they roared through the entrance, turned sharply left to avoid the concrete barrier blocking direct access to the hangars immediately ahead, and soon saw the southern searchlight tower—its light disabled—and the southern airstrip, with planes parked on the far side of it. Leighton glanced behind them to see that the other vehicles were keeping pace. Mateo turned back to the right in a wide arc as they passed the concrete barrier, avoiding the planes on the southern airstrip, and they passed quickly in front of the searchlight tower at the western end of the air base. Its searchlight was also dark by now.

Ahead lay the planes of the night squadron, painted a dull black, not easy to see but still visible, neatly lined up at intervals adjacent the northern airstrip in two rows. The canvas cover on the back of the Dodge came down, and Zorrita and several other guerillas readied their weapons. Gunfire erupted from each jeep and the Dodge as they neared the planes, firing mostly at the row to their left and targeting the engines and radar pods. Another searchlight on the far side of the northern airstrip unexpectedly snapped on, bathing the three-quarter-ton Dodge in light as it raced along, coming abreast of the first aircraft in the row of planes. Two men jumped out of the Dodge and charged toward the light, using the shadow of the planes to get closer, as soldiers from the barracks one hundred feet away, also on the far side of the northern airstrip, began to come out and open fire, but they soon stopped for fear of hitting the row of planes between themselves and the guerillas.

The searchlight on the far side of the northern airstrip continued to illuminate the Dodge, which began taking gunfire, until one of the guerillas on foot hurled a grenade and put it out of action. He had ventured past the cover of the aircraft and was quickly gunned down by soldiers from the barracks. In the Dodge, Zorrita's aim was flawless; suddenly one of the planes in the line exploded as its fuel tank was hit, followed by another, and then a third.

The lone remaining guerilla on foot turned and ran back toward the bypassed planes of the southern airstrip, as one of the jeeps peeled out of the line and dashed between two planes to rush the searchlight tower situated in the middle of the airfield. Three guerillas jumped out as it skidded to a halt, and placed satchel charges on three of the tower's four legs. One of them was killed by fire from the northern barracks as they all raced back to the jeep, which was now lit up by yet another auxiliary searchlight that had come on next to the southern airstrip of the base between two hangars. The driver stomped the gas, moving toward the planes of the Day Squadron on the southern airstrip, as the other two guerillas with him began to open fire on the aircraft.

The main column of vehicles, with the Dodge still bringing up the rear, reached the end of the line of aircraft on the northern strip, and began a U-turn. As this happened, the light from the searchlight tower in the middle of the field caught them in its glare, and they began taking fire from soldiers running toward them from the main control tower. Zorrita and others in the back of the Dodge returned fire with deadly accuracy, preventing this new threat from getting too close. Mateo was hit in the arm but completed the U-turn as Leighton and the other two guerillas began raking the second row of planes on the northern airstrip with gunfire. This time it was much more difficult, with soldiers from the northern barracks of the base now rapidly filtering through the planes to fire on the guerillas directly, aided by the fact that the guerillas were now silhouetted by the searchlight tower behind them. The guerillas were now forced to divide their fire between the planes and the soldiers, and they began taking casualties as the men in the second and third jeeps were hit.

Suddenly there was a massive series of explosions and the light silhouetting the guerillas went out as the searchlight tower in the middle of the air base began to teeter toward the planes, three of its legs having been blasted out from under it. Mateo stomped the accelerator, and the jeep raced toward a group of soldiers, hitting one of them before turning sharply away as Leighton ducked down to reload and the guerillas behind him continued laying down devastating fire with their two AK-47s. Leighton slammed a magazine home and turned back and pulled the trigger in time to cripple the radar pod of one last plane with two bursts of fire as Mateo continued turning away. There was another explosion behind them as the tower fell on two of the planes, rupturing the fuel tanks in their wings.

The lone guerilla attacking the planes on the southern airstrip had raked the engines of three of the planes and was now headed toward a fourth. The jeep that had attacked the middle searchlight tower was now laying down fire on the planes from the opposite end of the row as it raced toward him, the driver intent on picking him up. Suddenly the guerilla on foot was hit by gunfire from across the airfield, and the jeep stopped long enough for its occupants to bundle him aboard. Once again illuminated by the searchlight of the southern airstrip, they turned and sped toward the base entrance.

Mateo and the other vehicles now turned toward the Day Squadron parked next to the southern airstrip, but by now several of the guerillas were wounded, and a few were dead. The auxiliary searchlight on the southern airstrip turned toward them, and they began taking gunfire from ahead on their left and from behind as yet more soldiers from the northern barracks poured onto the field. The night squadron lay ruined and in flames. Gunfire from the direction of the one remaining searchlight began to reach out toward the convoy, and Mateo turned sharply left, aborting the attack on the last few planes and smashing between two of them to crash through the line of aircraft and behind a hangar that provided them cover but also marked the way they had come in. The remaining vehicles followed him, doing what damage to the Day Squadron they could as they passed.

Soldiers were waiting at the concrete barrier to fire at the vehicles as they passed, but one of them suddenly fell down dead, bleeding from the head. No one had seen or heard a shot. A second man fell, then a third, and then a fourth, as Alma and her snipers began to whittle down their numbers. Many soldiers broke and ran once the fifth man went down. As the convoy passed the barrier on the way to the main gate, they were harassed only by sporadic, ineffective fire. As the Dodge raced toward the concrete barrier, several guerillas in the back threw grenades, and a series of explosions cut down the soldiers still trying to gather there to stop them. The Dodge raced through both perimeter gates but slowed where the road crossed the gully outside the perimeter long enough for the waiting snipers to run to it and climb aboard.

The convoy roared away into the night, leaving carnage and flames in its wake.

· · · · · ▦ ▦ ▦ ▦ ▦ ▦ ▦ ▦ ▦ ▦ ▦ ▦ · · · ·

The next day, the afternoon edition of *El Celador* ran with a banner headline:

Daring Night Raid Cripples Counterinsurgency Aircraft
By Roberto Avellar, Publisher and Editor-in-Chief

The article detailed the bold guerilla raid that had destroyed seventeen of twenty-two night vision aircraft and damaged or destroyed eight of fifteen daytime surveillance planes. It included the first admission by interim President Humberto Pando that four cruise missiles had been stolen by guerillas several weeks previously, and that the airbase attack compromised the government's ability to stage surveillance flights to search for them. Of special note was a passage explaining that the flights had apparently proved such a harassment to the guerillas and so restricted their movements that they had provoked the previous night's attack, resulting in damage running to hundreds of millions of American dollars. It closed with the following paragraph:

> This attack comes barely twenty-four hours after the inaugural broadcast by Radio Madrinega, the voice of the *Frente Popular,* the Popular Front. In that broadcast, the leader of the *Frente,* identifying herself only as Zorrita, vowed in the wake of the guerillas' bloody defeat at Redención that the fight had just begun. Closing the broadcast, she stated, "We shall fight until we are free."

"This is my greatest work yet, Rosa," Avellar said proudly, standing on the terrace of his home as he looked out at the view of Valmonte. He stood chuckling contentedly as he rolled an unlit cigar between his fingers. "It justifies the existence of the *Frente* very succinctly."

"Roberto, you must be careful," Rosa scolded. "The new men in charge may be better than Vilar, but they are no angels. They will only tolerate so much of your reporting, your telling of their secrets."

"That may be, but you forget that that killer Narváez has gone into hiding."

"I have not forgotten," Rosa retorted. "He is in hiding, not dead. We don't know where. We don't know when he'll be back."

The telephone rang, and shortly Marisol came outside in a state of excitement. "Señor Avellar, you have a telephone call. It is ... señor, it is President Pando."

"Alright, Marisol, alright, please calm yourself," Avellar said gently. "Rosa, my dear, perhaps you can sit her down and make her some tea. I will take the call in my study."

Avellar strode into his study without the use of the walking stick. He moved with pain, but he could retain his balance without that damned stick. He picked up the receiver.

"Hello?"

"Roberto Avellar?"

"Yes ... President Pando?"

"Yes. I wish to talk with you off the record. Do I have your word that I may do that?"

"Yes, Mr. President," Avellar said respectfully.

"I am trying to change things for the better, but I am meeting great resistance. I don't imagine I have to tell you from what quarter."

"No sir."

"Your article about the attack on Talamantes only complicates things."

"Don't people have a right to know what is happening in their own country?"

"Roberto, please listen. I am trying to negotiate a schedule for free elections—to reconstitute the Parliament. These guerilla attacks and your coverage of them are inflaming those I must negotiate with. Please ... consider your actions in the future."

"Or what?"

"Roberto, you are a respected member of the press. Perhaps the most famous journalist in the country. My purpose in calling is not to threaten you, but to ask for your help."

"I would like to help you, Mr. President. But I fear that, although you are a man of good faith, the elements you must negotiate with will undermine and eventually depose you, as they deposed Vilar. Those in the government today are on the wrong side of history."

"You disappoint me, Roberto. Your father was a mentor to me."

"I am aware. You have my respect. I remember you as a guest in my father's house. But for a journalist to remain silent at a time in his nation's history such as this … it would be … it would be criminal. Did you read my article? Really read it? Even a child can see that the guerillas have a superior sense of humanity."

"I hear what you are saying. But you must hear me. If a man such as yourself will not help a man such as me … then there is no hope for the moderates in our government. No hope for those on the General Staff who want to chart a better course for Madrinega."

"I will tell you this, Mr. President. I cannot promise you anything. But I will carefully weigh our conversation in the context of my future decisions as a publisher. And you should be aware that I have been thoughtful in those same decisions to date, with a view, Mr. President, for what is best for Madrinega."

"I suppose that is all I can ask in the final analysis. I bid you a good evening, Roberto."

"And you, Mr. President."

As Avellar hung up, his wife entered the room.

"What did he want, Roberto?"

Avellar stared at the telephone thoughtfully. "He is a man in a very difficult position. He wanted me to stop inflaming the reactionaries on the General Staff."

"Today's article?"

Avellar nodded. "Today's article."

"Oh, Roberto," Rosa gasped.

"He did not threaten, or even imply a threat. His request for my help was genuine. But I don't see how I can help him, Rosa. The fact is, the people he says he's negotiating with to hold free elections, to restore the Parliament—they won't agree under any circumstances. I know that crowd; they were frequent guests at my father's dinner table. He was one of them. I told Pando the government is on the wrong side of history."

"How could you do that?"

"Because it was the truth! Have you heard last night's broadcast of Radio Madrinega?"

"No—"

"You should. I got a copy of it and listened to it this morning while you were out."

"How did you get it?"

"I got it, that is the important thing. I appreciated getting to hear it less than twelve hours after it aired. You should listen to it, Rosa. And the children, too."

CHAPTER 12
THE CHOICE

The convoy had raced through Valmonte at high speed in the predawn hours, carrying a number of wounded and dying guerillas, but the determination had been made in advance that it was too dangerous to stop to get anyone to a hospital. Even with Pando trying to make conciliatory gestures, there was no guarantee that guerillas wounded in an attack on a government installation would not be denied medical care and instead transferred to the custody of the Army or the Secret Police.

There were two fierce firefights on the way out of the city. One broke out when a lone Army truck full of troops tried to set up a roadblock at a critical intersection in one of Valmonte's eastern districts. It was thwarted when the guerillas laid down withering gunfire at the few troops involved and set fire to the truck. The second erupted when two police cars in Colinas, backed up by a police heavy weapons unit, tried to block access to the bridge across the Verdelpino River, but they, too, were badly shot up by the guerillas and rammed. Zorrita had emphasized to the guerillas in the final briefing to tolerate no opposition on the way out of Valmonte, stating that the best way to put it down was with early application of superior firepower. As a result, the convoy was an unstoppable juggernaut as it fled the city – and the guerillas were now dangerously low on ammunition.

No planes gave pursuit. With Mateo navigating, they drove directly to Limado and unloaded the wounded and dead. A small group was tasked with hiding the vehicles while Alma oversaw the work of several first aid teams as dawn approached.

Exhausted but still coming down off an adrenaline high, for many there was no question of sleep for what remained of the night. Leighton joined Zorrita and others in tending the wounded and comforting the dying. They helped Alma as she performed minor surgeries and cleaned and stitched up wounds, including Mateo's. His arm was not broken, but like Leighton, he now had it in a sling. Before trying to sleep, Mateo ensured that the people standing sentry on the camp perimeter were relieved. It was more important than ever that their early warning system function well.

When the work was done for the moment, Alma reported to Zorrita. "There are twelve dead, two missing, and thirty-three wounded. It might have been much worse. Three of the wounded need a hospital or they'll die. The others can remain here in the bush, but we are going to need a lot of medical supplies: bandages, painkillers, and antiseptics. Otherwise, we could begin to see a lot of infections in a few days."

"Gangrene?" Zorrita asked.

"Yes. But it's preventable if we get the supplies."

"You'll have them. We have contacts in the cities that can help smuggle them to us."

"It will save lives," Alma replied.

"Alma, you and your team did extremely well. But for you, we would have far more dead and wounded. Please pass the word to them that I am grateful."

"I will, Zorrita. Thank you."

"Please arrange to disperse the wounded as best you can, and keep them under cover but out of the caves during daylight."

"Yes." Alma nodded.

"Now tell me about the three hospital cases."

"Two have chest wounds, and one has a bullet lodged in his abdomen. That last will likely be a difficult surgery. They're all critical and in severe pain."

Zorrita turned to Leighton. "Machete, find someone unknown to the Secret Police in Valmonte to drive one of the jeeps in with the wounded and leave it at the hospital."

Leighton left to carry out her instructions.

At that moment, Camilo approached, his clothing bloody from helping with the wounded. He and Zorrita embraced.

"You are not hurt, Camilo?"

"Not at all," he replied cheerfully.

"Good."

"Anyway, I wanted to be sure you are all right. I had not seen you since we left."

"Yes, I'm all right. And I have another important job for you."

"What is it?"

"We will soon fire off the last of the missiles. I want you to take a radio set and go to Bocuateca to make sure they are launched when I give the order. No delays."

"When should I leave?" Camilo said, pleased.

"Tomorrow night. Take one of the jeeps. For now get cleaned up and try to rest."

"Zorrita?"

"Yes, Mijito." This was her pet name for him, used only when they were alone.

"Your radio broadcast … it was very good. I was inspired. I will always remember that I watched you make it. I know many others will join us now."

Zorrita smiled at him with deep fondness. "Thank you, Camilo. That means a lot to me, because this fight, this revolution, is really for you—your generation, and your children."

"I will tell them about you … when I have them," Camilo said, beaming. He left to get cleaned up.

Alma, who was tending a wounded guerilla nearby, had heard the entire exchange, and asked, "How old is Camilo?"

"I'm not sure," Zorrita said, leaning back against a tree and rubbing her eyes. "Sixteen, perhaps seventeen. He's an orphan … His parents got in Vilar's way."

"Like mine," Alma said. "He behaves as though he is older. There is something different about him."

"Something special," Zorrita corrected. "He is the smartest of us all. I have great hopes for him, and great hopes for Madrinega because of him. He's a born leader."

"It would be interesting to know him … once he becomes a man."

"I have often had the same thought," Zorrita admitted.

"I must go. There are a few more wounded."

"Get some rest as soon as you can," Zorrita called after her.

Leighton approached Zorrita with a young man in tow. "This is Ricardo Vega," he said. "He's willing to take the wounded into Valmonte. I've explained to him that there's a high risk of being caught by the Secret Police."

"I am not afraid," Ricardo Vega said.

"You should be," Zorrita retorted. "They may torture you with electrodes for the pleasure of it, or do violence to your privates, even if they don't believe you have any valuable information."

Ricardo looked pale for a moment, and then looked Zorrita in the eye. "I am still willing to do it."

"Why?"

"I am not educated. Before this I was a farmworker. But I was here when you made your broadcast. I believe what you said. If things are to change, we all have to help, to sacrifice. Three of us who stood up to the government tonight may die if they don't get to the hospital. I want to help them."

"I see. Did you attack the air base with us, Ricardo?"

"Yes. I was in the third jeep. The man beside me was killed."

"Alright," Zorrita nodded. "You may have to lie low in the city for a few days until we can get you out. Can you do that?"

"Yes. I have friends who will hide me. And I once had a job as a day laborer, painting the inside of Valmonte's City Hall. I know a few hiding places there."

"Don't take unnecessary chances," Zorrita said. "Remember: you may be saving the lives of the people you get to the hospital."

"I will." Ricardo left to prepare for the drive to Valmonte.

Zorrita let out a heavy sigh as she watched him go. Glancing at Leighton, she said, "I just pray I am not sending him to his death."

"He knows the risks," Leighton replied. "If he didn't, you explained them in technicolor."

Zorrita looked around the camp. The wounded were being taken care of, those who had to go to hospital were being loaded onto stretchers and would soon be lashed down to a jeep. And she heard Camilo organizing a burial detail for those who had not survived. She would read over their graves later in the morning. She stood. Looking at the early morning sun, peeking over the horizon as its brilliance penetrated the trees near the river, she realized with surprise that the night had gone. "I'm tired," she said.

Leighton followed her to their cave. Inside she did not even take her boots off. She laid down on the blankets, curled up in his arms, and fell immediately to sleep. He soon joined her.

Leighton awakened in near darkness to find Zorrita next to him, sleeping peacefully. By being very still, he could hear the gentle rhythm of her breathing. He felt around for the laptop case and seized it. Outside, it was nearly dark. He realized he had slept the entire day. Zorrita, who had greater weight on her shoulders, still needed rest.

Fewer guerillas than normal were about. Many were asleep. Some of the wounded, still waiting for sedatives, were trying to rest and occasionally moaning in pain. Leighton moved down the hill to a spot under a tree where he often did his writing and powered up the laptop. He activated the antenna for the satellite communicator and composed the following message:

> *Missiles located in village of Bocuateca, estimate 100 miles southeast of Valmonte, concealed by trees near cliff face. Transponders placed. Unable to gain access Zorrita due to very high security.*

He sent the signal immediately. He realized he needed to request evacuation to delay the moment when Miller realized he had lost an agent to what Headquarters would consider "the other side." He composed and sent a follow-up signal:

> *Request evacuation plan with backup to be ready within 12 hours. Political situation deteriorating.*

Miller might deduce that he had lost his nerve, but he didn't care. It was logical to request evac if the assassination they wanted done was not feasible, and he had already said as much. A reply came through almost immediately.

> *Evac not possible at this time due to fluid situation. Remain in place and await opportunity for access Zorrita.*

Bastard.

Now there was no way back. Leighton had planned and helped execute a major guerilla operation, a fact he had not even touched upon in his signals to Miller. He had no regrets. But with the political situation in Madrinega unstable in the wake of Vilar being deposed, and now Pando struggling to regain control, Miller had to be facing enormous pressure to deliver Zorrita's head. So he was turning the screws on Leighton.

For that, Leighton thought, *they'll have to get themselves another boy.*

He recalled that the last transponder he had could be used to track his movements, and get to Zorrita. Picking his way in the dark, he went down to the river, pulled the flask from the laptop case and unscrewed it. He poured the small amount of liquor it contained out on the ground, screwed the cap on tight, and threw the transponder as far out into the river as he could. The air bubble inside it represented by the empty compartment that had held the liquor made it just buoyant enough to be carried along by the current. By morning it would be well on its way to the Pacific Ocean.

Leighton then thought of the laptop. He remembered that it, too, contained a transponder, and the initial plan, as Miller had outlined it, would have involved leaving the laptop near the missiles, after activating the transponder.

Leighton realized that he still wore Zorrita's shoulder holster and pistol, although he had tucked the silencer into a side pocket of his dungarees. He took out the laptop and laid it on the ground. Then he withdrew Zorrita's 9mm Smith & Wesson and attached the silencer. Checking the magazine, he saw by the faint moonlight that there were at least six rounds remaining. He slid the magazine home, aimed carefully, and pumped all six rounds into the laptop. He then picked it up and tossed it into the river.

Returning to the cave, he found Zorrita sitting with her knees drawn up to her chest by the light of a single candle. She had removed her boots and wrapped her arms around her knees. An AK-47 lay next to her on the blankets. Although she had slept several hours, Leighton could see in the dim candlelight that she needed several more; dark spots, a telltale sign of sleep deprivation, were beginning to form under her eyes.

"I woke up and you were gone."

"I just needed some air," Leighton replied. "I went down to the river."

"Next time wake me." She seemed frightened. Leighton took off the shoulder holster and the Army tunic and sat down next to her, moving the AK-47. He put his arms around her and soon felt her warming to his touch.

"I hated to wake you," he said. "I knew you were exhausted."

"I'm used to having people around me, especially since coming to Madrinega. And …"

"And what?"

"Nothing."

"Gabriela. Tell me. Please."

"The bounty."

Leighton took in a breath and embraced her all the tighter. "I was stupid," he said. "God, I'm sorry."

146

"It's all right. Just try to understand what it's like for me to wake up alone ... especially at night." She took the AK-47 and moved it to her side of the blankets.

Leighton leaned back, studying her. "Next time I'll wake you, no matter what," he said quietly.

"Good," she said, glancing at him with a touch of self-consciousness. "I would like that."

Leighton leaned forward and kissed the side of her neck. She let him fondle her a moment, then held out her left hand, and watched as it shook. It was not a momentary tremor; the longer she watched, the longer it shook. With her right hand, she clutched the left one to her chest, even more self-conscious now.

Leighton said softly, "Gabriela ... when did that start?"

"Last night, during the drive to the air base. I thought it would stop after the attack."

"What would you say to taking off for a rest? A few days on the coast."

"Costa Pacifica is a government stronghold. There's no way—"

"I don't mean Costa Pacifica," Leighton said. "I mean the Caribbean side. Sharks Grotto. It's not exactly a guerilla stronghold, at least not officially. But I'm told we'd be safe there."

"Who told you that?"

"Mateo."

"How can I leave now?"

"Gabriela, after last night the entire cell needs rest, including us. Nearly half of them are wounded," he said, stroking her hair, "and you need the rest more than any of us."

She sighed. "Maybe you're right."

"Mateo told me about Sharks Grotto. Right on the ocean. He said at least half the resort workers there are members of the *Frente.*"

"That can't be. A resort?"

"According to him, they are paid a low wage. They barely do better than farmworkers, most of them. The point is, it's safe. We'd be among friends."

"But with all these wounded—"

"They're in good hands with Alma. You saw her work this morning, she's recruited a team of nurses in training, men and women alike. Don't tell me you don't think you can leave Mateo in charge -- we both know better."

She gripped Leighton's arm. "I would love to go. Let me think it over, and let's talk in the morning."

"Alright."

"Will you take my pants off?"

"I thought you'd never ask."

"My love, I want to, but I must sleep. I'm so tired …" Leighton pulled her dungarees off, then stripped off his own boots and dungarees.

"Hold me?" From where she lay, she reached toward him with outstretched arms.

Wearing only shorts, Leighton blew out the candle and joined her under a single thin blanket. Within moments, she was asleep in his arms.

As sleep claimed him, too, he felt content.

••••••••••••••••••••••••••••

"This is Lang." The long-distance line was secure but still not entirely free of static.

"Lang, it's Miller."

"I've been expecting your call."

"Have you heard from Palmer?"

"Not since the night I gave him the transponders."

"Well, I've had a signal from him. He's finally located the missiles and planted the transponders. They're in a village called Bocuateca."

"I know the place. Practically a ghost town, better part of one hundred miles from Valmonte. But Miller, I have to tell you those missiles aren't important right now—not with the *Frente* gaining momentum, attacking that air base the other night, and this new guy Pando making waves."

"What do you mean?"

148

"I haven't got time to give you all the details, but he's pissing off his own right-wingers on the General Staff and he hasn't been in office a week. He's been personally reviewing individual cases and releasing prisoners in Secret Police custody since yesterday, political enemies of Vilar mostly, and the latest was a co-worker of Palmer's, a reporter on that newspaper. Anyway, between that and trying to negotiate a timetable for free elections and restoration of Parliament, it's hard to know whether Pando's going to last. Seems he's trying to undercut support for the guerillas by tacking to the left, but it's a big gamble, and I'm not sure it'll work. He may be moving too fast."

"Well, things may be getting hot for Palmer with the guerillas. He's requested evac now that he's found the missiles, but for now I've told him to stay put and wait for an opportunity to get at Zorrita."

"Yeah, I mentioned that when I talked to him, but I got the sense he's not too keen on doing the job," Lang replied. "He may have gone native."

"Meaning what?"

"Meaning he could be banging her, or one of the other women in the same guerilla cell, for all we know. If they've turned him, it wouldn't be the first time that's happened to an agent on either one of our payrolls."

"Right now I have enough to worry about without investigating who Leighton's bedding down. I had a rapid deployment team on standby in Guatemala to go in and retrieve the missiles, and they've recovered the first one, but suddenly they're unavailable. I'm told it could be seventy-two hours or longer before they can respond."

"We can't help," Lang replied bluntly. "My information is that every paramilitary and special forces unit in this region that we control is on standby."

"But for what?"

"I've seen cable traffic on Grenada involving the Cubans that have the boys at Langley *and* the White House with their panties in a bunch," Lang said. "We may have to go in."

"An invasion? You can't be serious. Grenada's *tiny*."

"And if it happens, we could be fighting the Cubans. So the Madrinega missiles are just going to have to sit where they are for a while."

"And what if the guerillas fire them off?"

"Well, they're not nukes, so how much damage can they do? I don't know why, but Grenada's what the folks in the White House have a hard-on for right now. Must be the Cuba connection. Anyway, they're not thinking about our problems here. I don't have any resources to spare. There are uprisings in at least six cities down here that make Redención look like the minor leagues, and they weren't our doing. The whole thing could spiral out of control. All hell's broken loose since that Radio Madrinega broadcast and the attack on the air base. If anything changes, I'll let you know. I've got to go."

And with that, the CIA station chief hung up. Miller set down the receiver, staring at a report from an electronics intelligence aircraft he had tasked to do a flyover of Madrinega. It picked up signals from two transponders over Bocuateca, confirming Leighton's intel about their location. It was frustrating, after all this time, to know precisely where the missiles were, and to be denied access to the air assets to get them out. Curiously, the ELINT aircraft had been unable to pick up transponder signals either from Leighton's laptop, or the extra flask that Miller had sent to Lang to give to him.

CHAPTER 13
LOVERS' GROTTO

That night, Mateo took charge of the nightly Radio Madrinega broadcast while Zorrita and Leighton slept. Cells in multiple locations reported clashes with the Army or police: Bernal, Melilla, Macoris, Anselmo, Nogales, Catellan—the list seemed to grow daily. News of the successful attack on the air base at Taramantes had spread throughout the country, emboldening the guerillas everywhere. Curiously, the city nearest Taramantes, the capital, remained quiet. Unrest and bloodshed were spreading to multiple urban locations, but in each case, the Army's response was more measured than in the past. There were no reprisal killings, no roundups, and in one province the governor had arranged for a cease-fire with the guerillas based on certain concessions—quickly followed by a statement issued by President Pando, cautioning that such arrangements would require the approval of his cabinet.

Upon hearing this news the next morning, Zorrita was greatly encouraged. The camp at Limado had so many walking wounded that it now looked like a field hospital, but even the sight of so many comrades in bandages did not dampen her mood. Leighton was pleased, for he was concerned about her state of mind. He took a walk along the river while Zorrita talked with Mateo.

"I am thinking of going away with Machete for a few days to rest," she said tentatively.

"Good," Mateo replied. "I told him about Sharks Grotto on the Caribbean coast. You would be able to get away from the worst of the heat there. And it is far enough away from the capital that the influence of the government, especially now, need not concern either of you. There are many friends of the *Frente* there."

"You would not mind, then, if I left you in charge?"

"No, Zorrita. But I ask you this out of respect, and as a friend: suppose I remain in charge after your return?"

Zorrita regarded him calmly. "Thank you for asking so openly, Mateo. If you are ready for that, then I am ready to pass the baton."

"Just like that? But you would not leave us?" Mateo asked, suddenly concerned.

"We both knew at some point it would happen. I have been a part of struggles for independence in three countries, El Salvador, Nicaragua, and here. Nicaragua was a success, and there are signs that it may soon be a success here. But I confess to you that I am tired. My dearest wish is to liberate my own country, but Pinochet has too much of a stranglehold on everything there. Many who seek change in Chile will have to wait him out. The regime will eventually falter. But for now, here, I need a rest. There is no reason why you cannot lead the movement from now on. Honestly, I thought it would be Miguel, but it appears we lost him in the fighting at Redención."

"Yes, I know," Mateo said, his voice somber. "I have put out inquiries, but have heard nothing. I didn't want to believe it, but it appears he was killed."

Zorrita looked hurt at the words. "I could never lead a government here, but you can."

"What do you mean? Of course you can lead."

"The movement, perhaps, but not a government. I am a foreigner who has been in this country barely a year. But you, you were born here. I ask you, who will the people accept?"

"If they knew what I know, they would pick you."

"But they don't, Mateo. As for the movement, I will leave it to you how and when to announce the change."

"I will announce nothing," he said amiably. "We can discuss it once you are rested, when you return. You may feel differently then." Mateo looked at Zorrita. She did indeed seem tired. "You seem truly happy with Machete," he added. "I am glad."

"He has been an unexpected gift," Zorrita said.

"The plan to attack the air base worked brilliantly ... It has been both a military and a propaganda victory for us."

"We will leave for Sharks Grotto today, but the missiles must be launched before dawn tomorrow. Will you order it?"

"I have a suggestion."

"Yes?"

"Give it at least another day or two. I am thinking of the air base. It will be all the more demoralizing for them if they have begun to make repairs and clear away the wreckage, before they are hit again."

"You have just proven that you are ready to lead. That is the thought of a strategic mind," Zorrita said with approval. "Very well. But no more than forty-eight hours—we may start to see planes again."

"It is a bargain. If you are going so soon, you will need transportation, and the military vehicles at our disposal will be a little conspicuous. Let me send a runner into Limado to find out what may be scrounged up."

"Alright, Mateo." She reached out and touched his face. "Thank you for your friendship."

Zorrita went to see Alma in the aid station she had organized under a large lean-to tent. Alma gave her a satchel bulging with medical supplies for Leighton—bandages, surgical tape, and antiseptic—for ten days. "Be sure to change his bandages and clean the wounds daily," she advised. "You will have a few days' rest away somewhere, then?"

"Yes, on the coast. Sharks Grotto." Zorrita rested on a makeshift bench.

"I have heard good things about it. People call it 'Lovers' Grotto' – it has a reputation as a romantic getaway."

"Hmm ... we shall see," Zorrita responded, pleased at the news but determined not to show much of a reaction. She lingered a moment. "I have a question."

Alma turned to her and waited, her eyes large with anticipation. "Anything, Zorrita," Alma said with reverence.

"What is this?" She held out her left hand, showing Alma the tremor. Alma immediately looked concerned and took Zorrita gently by the forearm. She turned the hand so that it was palm up and looked at the underside of the forearm, studying what she could see of the veins beneath the skin.

"Does this happen all the time?"

"Almost constantly since last night."

"I don't know the medical term, but it looks like an overload of nervous tension. It's the result of ongoing stress, proof that you need rest. The good news is that once you rest, it should pass."

"Rest for how long?"

"Two weeks? Maybe a month. I can't say for sure. But it will pass eventually."

"What if it doesn't?"

"Then it is something more serious. But at this moment I don't think so, especially given your responsibilities. You carry a great weight, Zorrita. There is much pressure. I, for one, could not do it."

"Thank you." Zorrita rose to leave.

"I will speak of this to no one," Alma said intently. Zorrita nodded at her and smiled.

• •

Leighton and Gabriela packed what few clothes they had and a few food supplies. She changed his bandages, then he watched her dress. Leighton was once again treated to the sight of Gabriela in the lightweight blue cotton dress and the sandals she had worn at their first meeting. She had brushed her hair—Leighton was glad she was not resorting to hair dye again—and wore a black bandana as a headband. There were sunglasses too, resting near her purse. Out of habit, Leighton brought the laptop case, although by now it weighed considerably less. They both knew it contained the little .25 automatic. It occurred to Gabriela to leave her Smith & Wesson behind, but he watched as she tucked it, minus the shoulder holster, away in her purse.

"I feel naked without it," she said self-consciously.

"You don't have to explain," Leighton said. "You've lived a certain life for a long time."

"I want to change it," she replied softly, and he embraced her. "Don't let go of me," she whispered.

Mateo poked his head into the cave entrance at that moment and found them still locked in the embrace. He coughed. "We have found you an automobile," he said, pleased with himself.

The car, a crème-grey 1963 Chevrolet Impala with a chestnut vinyl interior, was not far, parked a quarter mile outside the guerilla camp on a bumpy secondary road covered with jungle canopy that eventually linked up with a highway leading east. Mateo and two guerillas accompanied them on the stroll through the jungle to reach it.

Leighton put their bags in the trunk, straining both his shoulder and side, and tossed his laptop case on the front seat through the open window. He could see a map on the seat next to it.

"Keys are in it," Mateo said. "We got it from a merchant in Limado who's willing to part with it for a week or two for the equivalent of three hundred dollars. He even threw in a tank of gas."

Zorrita smiled. "Thank you, Mateo."

"As a going-away present, there's spending money in the glove compartment. When you get there, just ask for Raoul. Mention his cousin from Alturas de Diamantes and you won't get a bill. He'll take care of you."

As a precaution, Leighton was still wearing the lieutenant colonel's uniform, in case they ran into trouble on the road. He planned to discard it once they arrived. He removed his sling and opened the passenger door for Gabriela. "Are you sure you don't want me to drive?" she asked. "Your shoulder—"

"Is just fine. Please get in, señorita."

"Yes, sir." But she got in and slid behind the wheel. "I will drive. You are wounded, and you need rest."

Mateo gave Leighton a mock salute. "Take care of her."

"I will," Leighton said, moving to the other side of the car to get in. Gabriela started the engine, which purred as though it had been recently tuned. "Buckle up," she told Leighton, and she waited while he did it. She fastened her own seat belt, and only then did she drive off.

⬩⬩⬩⬩⬩ ▬ ▬ ▬ ▬ ▬ ▬ ▬ ▬ ▬ ⬩⬩⬩⬩⬩

The drive took two hours and passed uneventfully. The Impala handled well and had been treated with care by its owner, but its air conditioner was not working, and as the sun beat down on the roof of the car it heated up quickly. They did not mind; they simply rolled the windows down and Gabriela drove faster. Leighton opened the glove compartment and found the buff envelope containing the money. He counted out pesos equivalent to three thousand American dollars, enough to keep them for nearly a month if need be. They passed a civilian truck headed east, and a series of other passenger cars, but no military vehicles. Traffic coming from the opposite direction was limited to a bus, and thirty minutes later, an official-looking car of some kind whose occupants took no notice of them. Leighton leaned back and stroked Gabriela's hair idly. Eventually he stopped, and when she looked, he was asleep. The highway stretched out ahead of them, promising a quiet, peaceful drive.

Upon their arrival at an impressive arch covered with vines and decorated with asymmetric images of two large spotted sharks, Leighton awoke. Gabriela drove through the arch and up a small hill until the road levelled off, and she pulled into a large brick turnabout with a small fountain at its center, ringed by a small circular lawn and decorated with hibiscus plants. It was late afternoon, and the air was noticeably cooler here, with a tang of salt in the air.

"Pick a name," Leighton said under his breath. "We can't use our real ones. I have an idea. How would you like to be Brazilian?"

"I want to be Elena," she said smiling from behind her sunglasses. "Elena Da Costa. That is a Portuguese surname, like a Brazilian would be likely to have. I like that name."

"I'll continue to be Juan Borrero, an Army officer on leave with his mistress." He still had his military identification, but had long since discarded the travel orders.

"Do Army officers named Juan have Brazilian mistresses?"

"This one does."

"I'm not sure about this …"

"Gabriela, I didn't say that I'd—"

She cut him off by leaning forward suddenly to peer at him over the tops of her sunglasses. "It's Elena."

She took hold of her purse, which now held their money as well as her gun, and they got out of the car and walked past large sky-blue marble columns into a spacious, open-air lobby covered in aquamarine tile and illuminated by indirect lighting. Directly across from the entrance was the concierge desk. There were quite a few people about, but the new arrivals attracted no special attention; the profile Leighton had devised for them was a common one for Sharks Grotto guests.

Leighton was glad that he'd worn the Army uniform, for it accorded both he and Gabriela, mistress or not, a certain amount of deference. He asked for Raoul, and the young woman behind the desk simply nodded and left to fetch him. Raoul turned out to be a handsome, well-groomed young man wearing a tailored blue suit, shining brown Italian shoes, and a gray silk tie bearing a blue shark logo. He was extremely gracious upon learning that Lt. Colonel Borrero had been referred by his cousin from Alturas de Diamantes.

Leighton told him they wanted a private bungalow on the south beach.

Raoul said simply, "Excellent choice, colonel." He checked a registry book behind the desk and looked up with a smile. "I can put you in Bungalow Nine. Here are the keys. It is very private, with a view of the ocean. You will be delighted to know that it has its own open-air hot tub, in a private enclosure accessible only from the bungalow itself."

Leighton glanced at Gabriela and said, "We can't wait to see it."

Raoul had a bellhop accompany them out to the car. As they passed a rather large shop selling swimwear adjacent the entrance of the lobby, Gabriela turned to Leighton and said in perfect Portuguese, "A moment, my love," and she ducked into the shop.

Gabriela rejoined him in a moment, commenting in Portuguese, "I saw two swimsuits I want to buy." Leighton nodded as they proceeded out to the car. He collected his laptop and opened the trunk, and the bellhop grabbed their bags.

"This is Luis, and he will escort you to Bungalow Nine," Raoul explained. "I will park your car personally. When you want it, just call to the concierge, and we will arrange to have it waiting here for you."

"Thank you very much," Leighton said.

"Enjoy your stay."

Luis guided them through a small sea of palm trees at the side of the resort entrance, down a zigzagging stairway that had been cut into the rock face and let onto a beach about twenty-five feet below. At the bottom, there was a broad walkway of bone-white tile in the sand that passed a series of bungalows, each parcel sixty feet across with its own individual enclosure of thick, pale peach stucco walls about six feet high. Leighton noticed that a series of what appeared to be tiki lamps were positioned every fifteen feet along the walkway. The bungalows were numbered, and he took out the key to the lock in the wrought iron gate that was the entrance to Bungalow Nine. A member of the resort staff was lighting the tiki lamps and seeing the new arrivals, lit the two lamps in the small yard within Bungalow Nine's enclosure. They passed over more white tiles, about twenty feet of them, leading to the front porch of their bungalow. Using the key again, Leighton opened it.

The bellhop entered first and switched on the lights. There was a gleaming floor of dark cocobolo wood polished to a high sheen, plush furniture in what was a small sitting room to the left, and a cozy breakfast nook with windows on two sides to the right. On the right, beyond the breakfast nook, was a small kitchenette. On the left, beyond the sitting room, was a spacious bathroom tiled in aquamarine with brass fittings for the faucets and towel racks. A large shower stall of blue-gray marble with two individual shower heads completed the amenities. The bungalow's interior walls, such as they were, were all of four feet high, with the exception of the bedroom and bathroom, which were fully enclosed with full-length walls. The main hall lay directly ahead, letting onto the large bedroom, which featured a king-size bed, a large window providing a view of the ocean, nightstands, and a small writing desk with a chair. There was a door with a portal window in it on the extreme right of the wall next to the large window. Beyond the door was a red wooden deck with two chairs and a small table outside, and a short staircase that led to the beach four feet below.

Luis set down their bags in the bedroom. "We have room service until two a.m., or if you prefer, the restaurants serve dinner until eleven. If you need anything at all, just dial the concierge. There is a telephone here in the bedroom and another in the sitting room, señor—I'm sorry … Colonel."

"Thank you," Leighton said, tipping him twenty-five pesos.

"Thank you, señor," Luis said with enthusiasm. "My name is Luis. I am on duty until ten tonight, if I can be of further service."

When he had gone, Gabriela laid down her purse on the bed and gave Leighton a bear hug. "I love it. I meant what I said about those swim suits. Come with me," she said, tugging his arm.

"I'm starving. Why don't we shower and then go to the restaurant from the swim shop?"

"As you wish … as long as we go to the swim shop now. They might close soon."

"Alright." Gabriela took her purse, and Leighton fished the .25 automatic out of the laptop case and put it in his hip pocket before locking up.

In the gift shop, Gabriela bought three bikinis, in white, fuchsia, and pale peach, along with a sheer white dress. Leighton satisfied himself with sunglasses, a pair of navy blue swim trunks, an orange short-sleeved shirt, a sleeveless grey T-shirt bearing the Sharks Grotto logo, and a large beach towel in the Sharks Grotto trademark aquamarine color, with the logo bearing two dueling sharks in one of its bottom corners.

They returned to the bungalow, closed the shutters, and were soon making love in the shower as the warm water beat down on them—a quick, almost furious release for them both that was barely satisfying. Only afterward did they wash, and then, as they toweled each other dry, Gabriela looked into his eyes and said simply, "After dinner."

They dressed for dinner. Leighton still had the clothes he had worn that first day at Colinas and was about to put them on, when he saw the garment Gabriela had selected—something he had never seen before. It was a blue-grey dress of a rather dark shade with a captivating sheen to it that hugged her figure. It disturbed him because it made her look even more strikingly beautiful than usual, accentuating both her skin tone and hair color. She had a particularly effective sense of what looked good on her. His disquiet was motivated by concern for her safety rather than jealousy, for she now had a look that would attract the attention of every man in the restaurant, and there was a chance, perhaps not a great chance, but it was nonetheless a degree of exposure, that she would be recognized. He decided to say nothing. They had come here, after all, because it was supposed to be safe here for her. He did not want to sabotage her getaway. The solution was simple: Continue to wear the uniform of a lieutenant colonel in the Madrinegan Army, a man who could not possibly have Zorrita on his arm, no matter how much his Brazilian escort might favor her. It would be her best camouflage.

"Why do you keep wearing that uniform?" she complained. "I thought you would change into something else."

"Whether we like it or not, it commands respect. I will put it in the closet after tonight."

"I'd rather you burned it. How do I look?"

"Utterly devastating. Every woman in the place will be jealous and refer to you as a bitch."

Gabriela laughed so hard that tears came to her eyes. "Good," she said at last. "That is what I want."

She clutched her purse and took his arm. Leighton thanked God she did not have any makeup, for it would have made her look even more alluring. Her hair alone made her appearance striking enough.

"Where did you get that dress?"

"Paris. The last time I wore it I was at a reception in London."

"You look beyond beautiful."

"Thank you, Juan," she said playfully. "I had matching pumps originally, but I've lost them. The sandals will have to do."

"You look magnificent *with or without* the sandals. Barefoot, even."

"You say such sweet things," she said, and she pecked him on the cheek. Leighton grabbed her and kissed her full on the mouth. She returned the kiss, wrapping her arms around him as their tongues performed a long dance together.

"Mmm ... we're ... we're supposed to be going to dinner," she said at last, pushing against him, but not too firmly.

"Yes," Leighton said, recovering his composure as he released her. "I did say I was hungry."

"Yes, but for what?"

"At the moment, it's a toss-up."

Ten minutes later, they were stepping out of the elevator into the foyer of the Sharks Grotto restaurant one floor below the lobby. There was a twenty-minute wait for a table, so they went into the bar. As Leighton predicted, Gabriela turned the head of every man in sight and succeeded in drawing stony glares from a number of the women. Leighton discovered that Gabriela rarely drank alcohol; when the waiter came around, she ordered a Campari and soda, he a gin and tonic. Gabriela commented on the décor, particularly the giant portals in the floor. The sun was down so they could not enjoy the sunset, but Leighton sensed her beginning to relax.

They were called for dinner. They had sea scallops sautéed in lemon and butter as appetizers, and for the main course, grilled Chilean sea bass on a bed of spinach with mashed plantains. Leighton ordered a single goblet of wine, a sauvignon blanc, and Gabriela had bottled water. She tried his wine, but he discovered why she was not a drinker when she became lightheaded after three sips. He suggested coffee. She suggested a sex act. He quickly paid the bill, and they returned to the bungalow, Gabriela leaning against him for support as they descended the steps to the bone-white tile pathway on the sand, which was intermittently lit by tiki lamps.

Once inside the bungalow, she dropped her purse, kicked off her sandals, and teetered to the bedroom. Leighton locked up, carried her purse to the bedroom, and watched as she lay on the bed and propped herself up on her elbows. Tipsy but not quite intoxicated, Gabriela seductively lifted a leg and one side of her dress to reveal a white satin slip and no other undergarments.

"You have permission to ravish me," she said with a regal flair. Leighton stripped, and she cried out in surprise as he pounced on her. Outside, beyond the fine sand of the private beach, the moonlight danced on the waves as he listened for that tiny, incredible, animal noise she made. When it came, it stroked every nerve in his spinal cord on the way to his brain, where once again it caused a kind of explosion.

At some point during the night, as they lay in one another's arms, she whispered, "I think I caught the mist … your mist on the wind." Half-asleep, Leighton nonetheless heard her and understood. He kissed her and held her tighter, until their bodies seemed to melt into one.

They awakened the next morning at ten. Leighton found a few amenities in the kitchen and made coffee, which they drank out on the deck in the morning shade, Leighton wearing only shorts and his new grey shirt, Gabriela in the translucent white dress that he decided she had purchased only to torment him. Now that she had it on, it was every bit as revealing as he anticipated, showing not merely the outline but also the general color of her areolae, and doing precious little to obscure the hair where her legs met. Once the coffee was gone, he telephoned for room service.

The young woman at the concierge desk informed him that breakfast ended at ten but they could get many breakfast items during brunch, which was served until 1:00 p.m. They ordered more coffee, orange juice, and spinach omelettes with pork sausage and sliced pineapples on the side. Gabriela disappeared into the bathroom when the food arrived, which Leighton had the waiter carry to the small table out on the deck, tipping him generously. He had not forgotten what Mateo had said about the wages for resort employees.

They spent the day walking the beach, swimming, and lazing about in the sun on their large blue beach towel. When it got too hot, they opened a large beach umbrella that had been stowed in a nylon sack beneath the deck, and dozed in its shade. Their cottage had its own private section of beach, about sixty feet wide by eighty feet deep, leading to the shore. It was bounded on both sides by a low stucco wall about three feet high with foliage growing up to five feet. The degree of privacy was enough that when Gabriela felt nature stirring her libido, she was ready to make love right there on the beach. A few minutes of kissing was all it took to arouse Leighton. She lifted the dress—the fabric hugged her figure so well that it took some effort to move it up past her hips—and began to mount him. Leighton protested that they should go inside, but she ended the argument before it could begin by straddling him quickly; as she suspected, once she sat on his erection, causing him to penetrate her, his resistance came to an abrupt end. She slowly rode him to a joint orgasm that sent them both back to sleep.

Afterward, they showered and lazed about nude on the bed with no special purpose as late afternoon approached, enjoying what for both of them was the rare sensation of simply floating through the day. Even without sex, Leighton found the touching of their naked bodies in bed intoxicating, but still he wanted a cocktail as 5:00 p.m. rolled around and the sun appeared low in the sky at the window, bathing the bedroom in an orange-yellow glow. He phoned room service and ordered daiquiris—a virgin for Gabriela and a real one for himself. When they arrived, he put on his shorts and received them at the door, tipped the waiter generously, and brought the tray back to her in the bedroom.

"What shall we drink to?" she asked, sitting up in bed.

"A new life. For both of us." They clinked glasses and sipped.

"Would you really come with me?" Gabriela asked, clearly skeptical.

"You haven't said where you'd go."

"Europe, for a start. Just until things cool down here, and by 'here' I mean Latin America. It's wearing, not feeling safe."

"I know."

"I'd want to come back to the Americas. I like parts of Europe, but it wouldn't be my choice to live there permanently. You have no family?"

"No." Leighton said. He did not elaborate.

"You weren't an orphan?"

163

"No," Leighton replied. He had lied to her about so many things about himself that he decided to give her a truth for once. "My mother and sister were killed in a car accident when I was nine. My father died when I was eighteen. I have a cousin, but I haven't seen her for years."

"I have not seen my father in almost ten years. He is ailing now. He will not live much longer. I hate the thought that I may never see him again. I won't even be able to go back to Chile for his funeral."

"And you had a brother."

Gabriela was silent for a long moment. At last she said quietly, "It is still too painful to talk about him. But if he had not been killed, I would not have become a revolutionary. I would be … somewhere … teaching university mathematics, or music. Everything I have done has been for him." She set her drink down on the nightstand and went to Leighton. He put his arms around her.

"But this path is a hard one. I can't stay on it much longer. We have only been here a day, and already I feel that I don't want to go back."

"It's your choice," Leighton told her.

"What if I change my mind?" she said, looking at him sharply. "Would you go back to Limado with me?"

"Yes," Leighton said at once.

Reading him, she replied, "But you'd rather not."

"I can think of an easier life. But I'll go where you go."

She embraced Leighton fiercely, and he returned the embrace. There were no more words between them until after they had watched the sunset together out on the deck.

They debated whether to go up to the restaurant or order room service. They had stayed close to the bungalow all day and decided to dress and go out. Gabriela wore the only other formal wear she had, a sleeveless deep purple gown with a neckline low enough to call attention to her cleavage. It was slightly less formfitting than the blue-grey affair she had worn the night before, but like the other, it, too, complemented her reddish-brown hair. Leighton again wore his military uniform. They arrived a bit early for dinner and did not have to wait for a table. For predinner cocktails, Gabriela ordered a virgin daiquiri, Leighton, a Manhattan.

"No wine for me tonight," Gabriela said with a smile.

"Oh, I don't know … I liked what you were like with a little wine in you," Leighton joked.

"You just want to get something else in me," she retorted.

"True," Leighton replied with a leer. "Feel free to speak up if you have objections."

Gabriela looked at him over her drink and pursed her lips, stifling a laugh.

Leighton covered her hand with his. She was beginning to decompress, he could see it.

She leaned close to him and whispered, "I never thought I would meet a man like you." Her eyes held his for a moment, until the waiter appeared for their order. Gabriela went through the role of the Brazilian mistress, pointing to things on the menu and asking Leighton in Portuguese what they were. When they finished their repartee, Leighton looked at the waiter apologetically and ordered the local paella for Gabriela made with shrimp, sausage, and rice seasoned with saffron, stewed tomatoes, cilantro, and green peppers. For himself he ordered the grilled swordfish and sautéed vegetables with a plantain.

The meal was as delicious as the night before. Leighton sounded her out as to where in Europe she might want to live and teach. France and Italy were her first choices, in part because they were both Latin countries and she would be somewhat less homesick there. Her dream was to teach at her alma mater, the Sorbonne in Paris. Portugal was second, Britain a distant third. Leighton had yet to formally resign from SONAI and had mused during the day about how to do it now that he had destroyed the satellite communicator. He thought about it again as he listened to Gabriela talking about the French educational system.

Watching her, Leighton again became aware of her freckles and reflected on how they provided a subtle complement to her natural beauty. He imagined meeting up with her at a sidewalk bistro in Paris late one afternoon, their work for the day over. He realized he could be happy with her, even as an expatriate. He sipped his Manhattan and wished they could get on a plane and make it happen now, tonight.

CHAPTER 14
THE PRODIGAL

At that moment Leighton saw a man enter the restaurant, look directly at him, and turn sharply to his right to go into the bar as if hoping not to have been noticed. *Christ,* Leighton thought, *not him.* But he was unmistakable, even in an expensive civilian suit: the trim figure, the thinning salt-and-pepper hair, the immaculate mustache, and most of all, the same cold eyes. Only they had been less cold just now. When he saw Leighton, they had registered surprise, perhaps even fear.

"Shit," Leighton said under his breath.

"What is it? What's wrong?" Gabriela asked.

"I'll tell you later. Right now, I want you to get up, walk out of here, and go back to the bungalow. Quickly. Don't look around; just get up and leave."

"But what—"

"Trust me," Leighton said, squeezing her hand under the table. "Go."

Gabriela was rising to leave as the man emerged from the bar and quickly strode directly to their table. His expression was surprisingly haggard. "Please forgive this intrusion, Señor Palmer, I beg of you," he said, seizing a vacant chair from a nearby table and sitting down. Gabriela resumed her seat, sensing that Leighton was coiled like a serpent preparing to strike.

"Colonel Narváez. I wish I could say it was a pleasure to see you." At the mention of the name, Gabriela's expression froze.

166

"I feel the same, but here we are," Narváez replied quickly, his expression wooden. "Initially I thought to hide, but you clearly recognized me. As we are all three fugitives of one kind or another, I thought perhaps we could come to some arrangement."

"This woman is no fugitive. She's just—"

"Señorita Diaz," Narváez said, looking at Gabriela, "I recognized you from a university photo in your dossier. May I say it does not do you justice. You are a great beauty." There was no hint of a threat in his voice, in fact no malice at all. Turning to Leighton, Narváez continued. "None of us should waste time with denials. We are all fugitives."

"We're listening, Colonel," Leighton said, his tone clipped.

"I propose something of mutual benefit—our mutual silence."

"You'll have to explain."

"I do not know your purpose here. Mine is to make contact with persons who can arrange to fly me out of the country," Narváez said in a low voice. "If we let past animosities or a sense of duty drive our next actions, we are on a path to mutual destruction. You, Señorita Diaz, are wanted by my government for your revolutionary activities, and most recently, the attack on the air base at Taramantes. I could turn you in. But in doing so, I might well call attention to myself, which I cannot afford to do. I, too, am wanted by the government, for revealing state secrets to the American press that have brought down President Vilar and damaged the reputation of the Army. It is possible I will be forgiven for the one, but most definitely not the other. You could turn me in, but you in turn might well call unwanted attention to yourselves. If any of us are taken into custody, we are unlikely to survive the experience."

Leighton glanced at Gabriela. Her expression was so cold that it worried him. She stared at Narváez like a cobra awaiting its moment to strike. "So you suggest …?" he asked.

"I suggest that we simply forget we saw one another and go our separate ways," Narváez replied. "I mean you no harm. I have no incentive to turn you in, because I have no guarantee that it would not thwart my own plans for escape. I am hoping you will both see the logic of my argument and conclude that you have a similar outlook. None of us wants the authorities to descend on this resort. I am aware that what I ask may be difficult for you. I am therefore willing to pay for your silence."

"How much?" Gabriela asked.

"Twenty-five thousand dollars. Payable in cash, tonight. You may not know this, but Sharks Grotto has a reputation as a place at which political adversaries have made deals with one another, or at a minimum shared a drink without animosity."

"I will *not* drink with you," Gabriela said coldly, looking away from Narváez for the first time. "That is an honor … I will forgo."

"Very well. You will no doubt want to discuss my proposal. I will be in the resort casino in one hour. I hope to hear from you then." With that, Narváez rose and left.

When he had gone, Gabriela leaned forward over the table. Leighton thought for a moment she was going to be sick. "He must be *killed,*" she hissed. "Tonight."

"First of all," Leighton said quietly, "people are looking, so please wipe that vicious expression off your face and try to *smile*. Make it seem as though he was just a fellow guest asking our opinion about our meal."

"You're serious."

"I am."

She looked into her lap, then looked up at Leighton with a forced smile that nonetheless appeared to be surprisingly genuine. "My love," she began sweetly, in a low, quiet voice that was disturbingly menacing, "That piece of human excrement must *die*. If I have to do it myself, he will take his last breath tonight."

"There may be something in what he says. Let's just consider it a moment."

"Yes," she said, still smiling, "let's by all means crawl into bed with Satan himself, and expect not to be ripped open and devoured like pigs at the slaughter."

"Look, I was arrested and tortured on the orders of that son of a bitch."

"Then you of all people should understand."

Leighton took a breath. "I do. I'm thinking about *you*."

"At this moment, I am not important."

"Bullshit," Leighton shot back. "You are to me."

"I know," she said, her voice and demeanor softening for the first time since Narváez appeared. "But I also know … I knew … people, friends, who were tortured and murdered at his hand. Or by his order."

"I understand. He tried to kill Roberto Avellar, too."

"And didn't he threaten you, to get out of the country?"

"Yes."

"Then I don't see that there's anything to debate."

Leighton paid the bill. "Let's go."

They returned to the bungalow in bitter silence, the joy of the previous hours blasted to pieces like shattered pottery. Once inside, Gabriela pulled the Smith & Wesson out of her purse and began fitting the silencer to it. She then set it down on the counter in the kitchenette.

"We cannot trust him," she said. "For all we know, he is telephoning Valmonte or the local police right now."

"That's a possibility, but I doubt it. That man is afraid."

"Of course he's afraid. He's turned on the government he's done so much dirty work for all these years. He is on the run, and he knows they're out to kill him."

"Exactly. And that one thing may make him trustworthy."

"I will not debate this with you," Gabriela said, her voice taking on an imperious tone. "I have made my decision. You seem to overlook two other possibilities. One is that, because he is a wanted man, he will try to sell me to the Army to get back into their good graces. But they'll never trust him again, and he knows it. For them there is only one solution: kill him. So the stronger possibility is that he will sell me to the CIA and claim the bounty. If he is on the run as he claims, he'll need all the money he can get."

Her argument, as usual, reflected airtight logic. Leighton sat down on the bench in the breakfast nook. "I was right when I called you a political chess master."

"Yes, you were. It is one of the reasons I am still alive."

He looked at her. "Let me do it."

"No, it should be me."

"If as you say he can't be trusted, there's a chance he will have someone waiting for you in the casino. I should be the one to go. And you should be nowhere in sight."

"How will you do it?"

"I'll figure it out. But I'll need your gun."

"No. You need *your* gun." Again Leighton realized she was right. Gabriela was not in a frame of mind to give up her only weapon. And his pistol was smaller, easier to conceal, and just as lethal at close range if one knew where to aim. He retrieved the .25 caliber Vesta from his laptop case and checked the magazine. He had never fired it, so the magazine was full. He next checked the action on the slide, found it butter-smooth, slammed the magazine home, and chambered a round.

"Okay," he said.

"Wait," Gabriela said. She fished a handkerchief out of her purse and handed to him.

"For the noise."

Leighton looked at her and nodded, tucking the handkerchief into his left hip pocket and the Vesta in his right. She stepped close to him and gripped his arm.

"It has to be done," she said, her brow furrowing with sudden anguish. He could see for the first time that in her heart, she wanted no part of any more killing, even of a man like Narváez.

"I know," Leighton said. He went out. There was still half an hour to go, so he went to the Grotto bar and ordered a Manhattan, his second of the evening, but it would not hurt given what lay ahead. He had been sitting there ten minutes when Gabriela walked in. He instantly understood why. She felt safer here, with people around, than alone in the bungalow. And she would be closer to him if anything went wrong.

She approached Leighton, and as she passed by, whispered into his ear, "I'll be waiting in the corner with my virgin daiquiri and my gun."

"And you wonder why I love you," Leighton quipped. Despite his levity, his stomach was in a knot. He finished his drink and walked out.

Leighton strolled into the resort casino fifteen minutes ahead of schedule, presented himself at the cashier's window, and bought $800 worth of chips. It was nearly 9:00 p.m., and the heavy betting was just beginning, with men and women beginning to fill the roulette, baccarat, and blackjack tables. He walked around gazing about as if merely trying to satisfy an idle curiosity, but in reality he was scanning the room for anyone who looked out of place. Within minutes he picked out two men that his gut told him were casino security who were tasked, among other things, with spotting gamblers who were counting cards. No one else tripped his radar.

He found Narváez at one of the baccarat tables, smoking and looking somewhat agitated. Scanning the immediate surroundings, he saw a bar in Narváez' direct line of sight, only thirty feet away. Since the bar also waited the individual gaming tables as a matter of good business, there were no people at the bar itself. Leighton walked up and nodded at the bartender.

"What will you have, señor?"

"Gin martini, with Gordon's if you have it, and a slice of lime."

The bartender had the martini in a prechilled glass in front of Leighton in short order. Leighton tipped him and on a hunch, asked, "Who's the gentleman across the way at the baccarat table? The one with the moustache."

The bartender scrutinized Leighton briefly, registered his uniform, and decided he could talk to an officer of the armed forces. "Ahh, that is Señor Cariño. He has been in here the last four or five nights. He wins, mostly. Seems to have a knack for knowing when his luck is turning. I understand he is a wealthy landowner from one of the western provinces. The rumor is that he sold all his property for fear that the guerillas will win any day now. He has plans to flee, but he is trying to build up a nest egg here at the tables first. He is always alone. A lot of the frequent gamblers who play for high stakes have women on their arms, but not him."

"You'd think a man like that would have plenty of money," Leighton said.

"You would," the bartender agreed with a shrug, "unless he sold his land for less than it was worth."

Leighton sipped enough of his Martini not to spill it, then walked over and sat at the gaming table directly across from Narváez. A hand was just beginning, Narváez was the player, and five other people were betting either on him or the banker. Leighton placed his meager stack of chips on the table but decided to sit the hand out and observe. Judging by the color and number of Narváez' chips, he was playing with an immediate reserve of about $15,000.

Narváez was dealt two cards, one of them face up, a 4 of clubs. The banker was then dealt two cards in the same fashion, one of them a 5 of hearts. Narváez flipped his second card, a 5 of diamonds, for a total of nine. The banker flipped his second card, the ace of hearts, which had a value of zero. The banker asked for a third card and received a 3 of spades. Narváez won the hand.

For the next hand, Leighton joined in. He had a choice of betting on Narváez, the banker, or a tie between the two. He bet $100 on the banker. Narváez was dealt two cards, the visible one was a 7 of spades. The banker was then dealt two cards, one of them a 3 of clubs. Narváez flipped his second card, a 6 of hearts, for a total of thirteen, but when the combined value of the cards was greater than nine, the card with the highest number of the two was by default the player's score. Narváez had a score of seven. The banker flipped his second card, a 5 of spades. The banker's score was eight, and he won the hand. Leighton raked in his winnings and continued to play, sipping his martini and observing Narváez, which slowly began to have the intended effect of wearing on the other man's nerves. He lost the next two hands, stubbed out his cigarette, and nodded at Leighton after raking in his neatly stacked chips. He turned to a casino employee, made arrangements to cash them in, and passed the shoe. Leighton cashed in his chips also, for a net gain of $400.

Leighton returned with his martini to the bar, where Narváez soon joined him, calling to the bartender for a Scotch whiskey.

"We've discussed your proposition, and I'm afraid twenty-five thousand isn't enough. It's rather a low bid, colonel," Leighton said. "A man like you is certain to have abundant resources. I would imagine you've been squirreling it away for years."

"If my resources were that abundant, I would not be here at the gaming tables," Narváez countered. "My opportunities to line my pockets have not been as frequent as you imagine. But you have not rejected the proposition out of hand. What is your counterproposal?"

"Make it fifty thousand and you have a deal."

Narváez sipped his Scotch and blinked. He frowned. "The cashier will balk if I ask for that much."

Leighton looked unsympathetic. "I'm sure you have that much or more on deposit with the casino or in the safe in your room. Do we have a deal or not?"

"Yes, but—"

"Then produce the cash. Tonight."

Narváez was on edge. Leighton sensed that he had pushed the man's back to the wall, for Narváez was visibly trying to control himself, to maintain his composure.

"But I *can't* … the most I can hand over tonight is forty thousand. I could get you the rest—"

"Then we'll have to turn you in and take our chances," Leighton said, his tone one of indifference. "I have no doubt that once you leave my sight tonight, you'll disappear, deal or not. No, payment will have to be tonight," he said, sipping his martini with his left hand as he slipped his right into the hip pocket of his trousers.

"You are shrewd, Señor Palmer," Narváez said with distaste.

"No, I'm just not stupid."

"In any event, you overlook the possibility that if you threaten to make my admittedly desperate situation worse, I could suffer a lapse of judgment and simply kill you." So there was bit of venom in the old snake yet.

"You wouldn't get far, Colonel. Zorrita would see to that. And if I have to, I'll put a bullet in your crotch right now."

Narváez looked into Leighton's eyes. He had the ability to read people, and he knew when a man was bluffing. Leighton wasn't.

Narváez made an offhand gesture. "You would have nothing to gain by that. And while it might be momentarily satisfying, it could well expose you and the young lady to the scrutiny I am sure you wish to avoid."

Leighton smiled unpleasantly and said, "Don't underestimate my ... susceptibility to immediate gratification, Colonel. It might be worth it. You did have me tortured, after all. And I'm not as loyal to the lady as you apparently assume."

Narváez had an excellent poker face when he concentrated on it, but Leighton sensed he was making the other man sweat. Narváez grunted and said, "You're a rather arrogant young man, aren't you? I note that while you intimate that you are perfectly willing to sell the guerillas' messiah for the equivalent of thirty pieces of silver, you seem to be equally confident that she would avenge your death. You seem to rate your appeal to her rather highly. Too high, I think."

Leighton shrugged. "It's your ass on the line, and Zorrita's, not mine. The Army's not looking for me, but they do want the two of you. And with you missing, I doubt the Secret Police care much about my whereabouts at the moment. They've got to be falling all over themselves trying to restore credibility with Pando and the Army. So they too are hunting you, as they're hunting her. If they get me, no one will care. But we digress. You want us to forget we saw you. So are you going to pay the fifty thousand or not?"

"Damn you, yes," Narváez spat. "But it's more than I bargained for. It will delay my escape."

"That's not really my problem, Colonel. But in the interest of saving you from a lapse in judgment and resorting to violence, there is another alternative open to us. A more lucrative one. I share it with you only in the spirit of considering an opponent's position in a negotiation. As much as it might delight me, I know it isn't prudent to force your back to the wall."

Narváez' eyebrows went up. Whatever this was, it sounded like a reprieve. "Lucrative, you say?"

"Suppose," Leighton began, "instead of paying us fifty thousand, you were able to keep that money and in addition receive a net gain of one hundred seventy-five thousand?"

Narváez' eyes lit up, betraying the extent of his desperation. The hook was baited. "How?"

"That would be your half of the CIA's three-hundred-fifty-thousand-dollar bounty on Zorrita," Leighton explained.

"I knew there was a bounty on her," Narváez said slowly. "I didn't know it was that much. But do you expect me to believe you would betray her?"

"We can deliver her to the CIA tonight," Leighton said calmly. "But there's a catch. We can't just kill her. They want her alive, for interrogation. Otherwise they won't pay. They want names of her contacts in El Salvador, Nicaragua, and here. They won't get that information if she's dead. Now, to get her out of here without a lot of fuss, I'm going to need help."

Narváez' eyes narrowed. "But why would you turn her in? A beautiful woman like that? Aside from what I glean to be your politics, judging by your writing, you seem to be enjoying her company."

Leighton tried to wave the question away with a look of disdain, but Narváez was not so easily put off. "I ask again: why would you betray her?"

"For the *money*, colonel," Leighton replied, as though the question were idiotic. "Beautiful women are a dime a dozen. But you don't come across money like that CIA bounty every day. Sums like that don't just drop into a man's lap, and I need money as much as anybody."

Narváez studied Leighton's eyes. He sat back and said, "You are showing a pragmatic side I didn't know existed, Señor Palmer. But then, you are an American. And a Negro at that." Narváez waited for a reaction. When he got none, he asked, "How could we do it?"

"She trusts me," Leighton said with confidence. "I'll go back and distract her, and you chloroform her. I'll call for my car, and we take her up to where it's parked at the roundabout without even having to enter the resort. If anyone asks any questions, she's had food poisoning and we're getting her to a hospital."

"I don't know. She'd be likely to struggle, possibly scream."

"Not if you do it right. Not if I distract her."

"You happen to have chloroform?" Narváez asked, clearly skeptical.

"Next best thing," Leighton said, nodding to the rows of bottles behind the bar. "The one with the green label on the middle shelf, fourth from the left. Menthol Mint liqueur. One hundred proof. One solid whiff of it will stun her at the very least. Then if I have to physically knock her out, I will." They watched as the bartender left to take a break, leaving the bar temporarily unattended.

Incredibly, Narváez looked troubled. "You would do such a thing?"

"I want that money. You can help and get half. Of course, you could take your chances and tip off your pals in the Army about her and try to get back into their good graces, but I think we both know they want you dead no matter what after leaking that Panactatlan dossier. Same with the Secret Police. No, the CIA offers a much better deal. Are you in?"

Narváez lit a cigarette. "Let's get that liqueur while the bartender's away."

Pretending to go out for a breath of air, Leighton walked with Narváez out to the colonnade that marked the entrance to the resort's open-air lobby. Narváez carried the bottle of Menthol mint liqueur along with a rag he had swiped from the bar. Leighton abruptly turned around with the Vesta in his hand as they moved out of the light and into the palm trees at the side of the resort entrance.

"Hands up," Leighton said. "I'll take the bottle."

Narváez was taken aback. No longer the fearsome head of the Secret Police, he was frightened and genuinely surprised. "But why—"

"Forgive me, Colonel, but you have a certain reputation. I want to be sure you're not going to try a double-cross. Maybe grab all the money for yourself?" Leighton said, briskly pat-searching the other man. Pointing the Vesta at Narváez' heart at point-blank range, he reached into the other man's jacket and withdrew a 7.65mm Beretta automatic.

"What nice hardware," Leighton observed.

"I don't like to carry it," Narváez said.

"Of course not."

"Honestly. In my situation, weapons require explanation. Generally money is a much better guarantee of my safety."

"Let's go." Leighton made him take the bottle and lead the way down the steps to the bone-white tiles on the sand.

"She'll be waiting for me in the bedroom," Leighton said in a low voice as they walked past the first tiki lamp. "This should be easy for us. I'll leave the door open for you. Wait in the garden until you see the light on the porch go out. Then come in and head straight back to the bedroom."

Narváez nodded. He produced the rag he had taken from the bar and readied it for the menthol mint liqueur.

They reached Bungalow Nine and found the gate ajar. Two tiki lamps were burning inside the enclosed front yard on either side of the path leading to the porch. As they stepped into the enclosure, Narváez began to turn toward Leighton.

"What about after we—"

But he never finished his question. Leighton swiftly raised the Vesta automatic in his right hand, using his left to muffle its muzzle with Gabriela's handkerchief as he fired two .25 caliber rounds into Narváez' brain in quick succession. As Narváez slowly sank to the ground, Leighton suddenly heard three quick metallic clicks and saw the resulting effect as three more bullets ripped holes into the back of Narváez' jacket. The bottle of menthol mint liqueur smashed as it hit the white tiles. Leighton whipped his head around to see Gabriela's silhouette behind him at the wrought iron gate. She held the Smith & Wesson at her side, the elongated barrel of its silencer still smoking.

Narváez lay crumpled on the ground next to the bottle's shattered remains. The breaking bottle had made more noise than the multiple gunshots and had released the powerful odor of mint liqueur. Leighton knelt to confirm that Narváez had no pulse, then moved quickly to douse the tiki lamps in the yard. He dragged Narváez' body up against the walled enclosure where it could not be seen from the path outside.

Gabriela entered the enclosure as Leighton produced the key to the bungalow. "Come inside," he whispered, gently taking her by the arm. She looked over her shoulder at the corpse, but allowed Leighton to usher her into the bungalow.

"Is he dead?" she asked, once Leighton had closed the door behind them.

"Why ask me?" Leighton retorted with a flash of resentment. "You made sure of it."

Gabriela stared at the floor. She nodded and said pensively, "I had to. We have closed the books on many debts tonight. Many souls will rest easier now."

"Well, before *we* rest, we have to figure out how we get away with this."

"What do we do with him?"

"He's got to be disposed of somehow. I'm going to call Raoul."

"You can't!" Gabriela exclaimed.

"Listen. You said it had to be done, and it's done. My gut is, Raoul can handle this in a way that won't hurt us. Either that, or we start running right now. Mateo said we can trust him. We have to put it to the test."

"All right," Gabriela said, and her shoulders slumped visibly. "But if it goes wrong, I will kill myself before I let anyone arrest me."

"Don't say that," Leighton said, taking her gently by the arms. "Would you rather run? Tell me. Tell me and we'll go right now."

"Where would we go except back to Limado? No. Call Raoul," she said, her voice calm.

◆◆◆◆◙▩▦▦▬▬▬▬▬▬▦▦◙◆◆◆◆

Leaving the Vesta behind, Leighton went outside to the garden and went through Narváez' pockets. He had $900 in cash in his wallet, and a room key for a suite in the Grotto's high-rise towers, along with identity documents certifying that he was Nestor Cariño, a wealthy landowner from the province of Castellas. Leighton took the money and wiped the Beretta down with Gabriela's handkerchief and put it back into Narváez' shoulder holster. He then returned to the lobby and asked to see Raoul at the concierge desk.

The young man on duty replied, "I'm afraid Raoul is off duty until tomorrow morning."

"Well, he told me to call him directly if I needed anything, and this is urgent."

"I understand, sir. Could you tell me what I can do to help?"

"You can get me Raoul. I need to speak with him urgently."

"I will have to call him, sir. Can I tell him what it's about?"

"Unfortunately, no. I need to speak with him."

"I will arrange it, sir," the desk clerk said, reaching for the telephone.

"Please tell him I will wait for him in the bar."

Forty-five minutes later, immaculate as ever in suit and Sharks Grotto tie, Raoul greeted Leighton in the bar. Leighton was nursing his third Manhattan. Ordinarily he might have been intoxicated; tonight it merely served to steady his nerves. Despite the lateness of the hour —it was just after 11:00 p.m.—Raoul was the soul of courtesy. "How may I be of service this evening, Colonel Borrero?"

"I'd like to speak with you outside." Leighton led him outside past the sky-blue marble columns of the resort's entrance. When they were a discreet distance from the columns, Leighton turned to Raoul and said, "I'm afraid I've had to kill someone. He happens to be the former head of the Secret Police."

Raoul stared at Leighton. He blinked. Then he looked down, blinked again, took a breath and whispered a curse as he exhaled. He looked back up at Leighton.

"Did anyone see you?" His calm was impressive, his voice little more than a whisper.

"No."

"How can you be sure?"

"It happened inside our bungalow's enclosure."

Raoul digested that, then asked precisely, "Were you seen with this man anywhere that it would have been captured on our security cameras?"

"The casino. Our longest interaction was there. He spoke to us in the restaurant, and he and I walked through the lobby when we left the casino."

"And are you certain about his identity? He is the definitely the man Narváez, reported missing in the news?"

"There's no question. He once hauled me into his office. I was arrested and tortured on his orders."

"You wanted revenge."

"No. I wanted to be sure he wouldn't turn us in. I know for a fact the Army is looking for him for leaking secret information."

"You are concerned for your companion's safety?"

"Of course," Leighton said.

Raoul eyed him for a moment. "If my cousin sent you, I have an idea who she is. We will keep her safe, I assure you. This must be kept quiet. Take me to him." Leighton led Raoul to Bungalow Nine.

After examining the body, Raoul said to Leighton, "Even military guests such as yourself do not walk around the resort carrying guns. We do not inquire into the backgrounds or affairs of our guests. We had no idea that he was anyone other than who he claimed to be—a wealthy landowner who was here to gamble. It will have to be concealed that this occurred here. My chief concern is the reputation of the resort. Do not trouble yourself, señor. I will see to it that he is moved, and officially checked out, tonight."

"I had no choice," Leighton said.

"If that is true, it is most unfortunate. For many years Sharks Grotto has been a haven from political strife," Raoul explained. "That has been its appeal. In years past, political opponents in Parliament, even guerillas and Secret Police, rubbed elbows here without incident. Until now. But this is a time of upheaval. Many of our employees are in sympathy with the guerillas. There are rumors that the government may fall. That will make the task ahead easier."

Raoul sighed deeply. "Go back inside your bungalow and go to bed, señor. In the morning there will be no trace of this. Do not speak of it to anyone. Ideally I would ask to you to leave, but I dislike having to explain sudden departures to our other guests. His will be challenge enough," he said, nodding at the body. "So you and your lady are welcome to stay as long as you like. In any event, the roads are far too dangerous at night with all the civil unrest in recent days. But I hope, Colonel, that there will be no more incidents like this one."

"No," Leighton said. "And this may help," he added, pressing $600 into Raoul's hands.

"I have just one request. It's vital that I have a piece of information."

"What would that be?" Raoul asked, showing for the first time signs that his patience was not without limit, even as he pocketed the money.

"Could you check and see if he made or received any phone calls in the last twenty-four hours and if so, with whom he spoke?

"Very well, Colonel. I will follow up with you in the morning. Good night."

"Good night," Leighton replied.

Leighton found Gabriela in the bedroom, kneeling and praying by the bed. He left her to finish in privacy, quietly going out the back door and retrieving the nylon tarp from beneath the deck that protected the large beach umbrella. Outside, he went around the bungalow into the front yard, and covered Narváez' body with the tarp. Back in the sitting room, he called room service from one of the large, plush lounge chairs. He ordered hot chocolate for Gabriela and a triple shot of Lagavulin Scotch whiskey for himself. Hanging up, he saw her at the end of the hallway, barefoot in the deep purple gown.

"We're going to be fine," he told her. "Raoul will take care of everything. Like it never happened."

"But why?"

"His main concern, in his own words, is the resort's reputation. They have every incentive to cover it up. According to Raoul, people of different political views have been coming here to relax for many years. They don't want to lose that. Bad for business."

"I might have known."

"We have reason to be grateful," Leighton said. "Raoul also confirmed something that doesn't hurt us—a lot of the staff here are in sympathy with the guerillas. So we can go on like nothing ever happened."

Gabriela literally ran and flung herself into Leighton's lap. She held him, and they sat comforting one another for several moments. There was a knock on the door and she sprang up and ran to the bedroom, emerging with her Smith &Wesson.

"It's probably room service." Leighton peered out through the peephole and saw a rotund young man in a blue Sharks Grotto tunic, holding a tray. He looked at Gabriela and nodded. She hid the gun behind her back as he opened the door.

The waiter came in and set the tray down on a coffee table in the sitting room. Leighton tipped him, and he left.

"You must think I'm crazy," Gabriela said sheepishly.

"I think you're a survivor. And you're understandably jumpy. Seeing that man here tonight was a bad shock. I wish it hadn't happened." She laid the gun down on the coffee table, and he embraced her in a hug.

"This is the only time I feel completely safe," she whispered. "With you."

"I want to *keep* you safe," Leighton whispered back.

"Let's get out of here. Let's go for a swim."

"I ordered drinks." He waved toward the tray.

"We'll have them later. Please, I need to get out of here."

Leighton followed Gabriela into the bedroom. They stripped, the only illumination the small reading lamp on the writing desk. Leighton put on the navy swim trunks, and Gabriela found the white bikini and donned the bottoms only. They went out on the deck, down the steps, and into the night, across the cool sand of the beach and into the surprisingly warm water.

The water calmed and soothed them both. They swam about for nearly an hour, until the ugliness of the night's events melted away almost completely. They walked out of the surf holding hands. Standing on the wet sand, Leighton turned and looked into her eyes. He kissed her and moved farther up the beach, away from the surf, sitting down on the sand. She sat in his lap, putting her arms around him. Neither spoke as he began to rock her gently back and forth, and they listened to the surf under the stars until he felt her rest her head on his shoulder, and later, felt her entire body relax. He could feel that her breathing had become very regular, peaceful. He stopped rocking and waited a few minutes more and then rose, carrying Gabriela, asleep, to bed. He gently brushed sand from the soles of her feet before covering her with a bedsheet and a single light blanket, and opened the window an inch or so until he could hear the sound of the surf outside. He lowered the window shade, left the light on over the writing desk, and put on a robe and went into the sitting room.

Reaching for the telephone and the Lagavulin on the tray, he called the concierge and asked whether it was possible to send a cable to the United States.

"I will check, señor. Please hold."

As he waited, Leighton wondered idly about the missiles that had brought him to this tropical paradise marred with bloodshed, and to the woman sleeping in the next room. But in the next instant, he realized that the missiles were no longer his concern and the woman was all that mattered to him.

"Yes, señor, we can send a cable," came the young woman's answer. "But the service is rather expensive, because it is not direct. It requires us to send your message by messenger to the nearest city with a wire service, Catellan. If you expect a reply, the delay could be three days at least. We can do it, however it will cost two hundred fifty pesos."

The equivalent of fifty American dollars. "I see," Leighton said. "Thank you."

"Do you wish to send a cable, Señor?"

"Not tonight, but thank you for the information."

"Very well, señor."

"Good night."

He took a sip of the Lagavulin. Remembering what Gabriela had said to him about waking up in the cave at Limado alone, he took his scotch into the bedroom. He was not sleepy, but felt a need to watch over her tonight especially, and to ensure she was not in the room alone, whether awake or asleep. He sat sipping from the tumbler, trying to clear his mind of the events of the evening. At some point, he dozed off in the chair at the writing desk. He awoke just after 4:00 a.m. to see Gabriela still sleeping soundly. He watched her for several moments. It had revolted him to execute Narváez—for that was what it had been, an execution—but he knew that for her, he would do it again in an instant.

Leighton got up and padded barefoot into the sitting room. Turning out the lights, he peeked through the wooden shutters and looked into the garden. The resort staff had relit the tiki lamps flanking the path to the wrought iron gate, and removed Narváez' body and every trace of broken glass. The nylon tarp lay neatly folded on the porch.

Returning to the bedroom, he turned off the reading lamp at the writing desk, shed the bathrobe, and got into bed. Gabriela, still asleep, sensed his presence and nestled up against him. He kissed her lightly on the forehead and settled down to try to sleep.

CHAPTER 15
THE CRISIS

The next morning, after their usual coffee out on the deck, Gabriela cleaned Leighton's wounds and changed his bandages. He persuaded her to put on a swimsuit, and under the pretext of sunbathing, they set up station near the Grotto's outdoor swimming pool. The wounds in his shoulder and side were still in need of daily cleaning and bandaging, so to conceal them and avoid unwanted questions, he never appeared shirtless in the daytime. The orange beach shirt he bought upon their arrival had been his frequent companion, and he wore it that morning with the navy blue trunks. Gabriela looked stunning in the fuchsia bikini.

The pool was strategically located within sight of the lobby due to the latter's full-length windows. After they had been there about half an hour, Raoul came out to wish them good morning and ask how they were enjoying their stay. Once assured that everything was to their satisfaction, he sat down briefly and said to them in a low tone, "Regarding the matter that never happened last night, everything is taken care of. We have documented that he checked out last night after his last game in the casino and took a shuttle to the airport in Catellan. He had only one communication in the time period you asked about, and that was an outgoing call to a bank in Valmonte. In fact, I reviewed all his telephone records from the time he checked in last week, as part of the normal check-out procedures. There have been no incoming calls, only outgoing calls to financial institutions to verify bank transfers.

When the body is discovered, it will be many miles from here and will in no way implicate yourselves or this resort."

"We can't thank you enough," Leighton said.

"We're deeply grateful to you. For everything," Gabriela added.

"Please continue to enjoy your stay with us." Raoul smiled, and left to chat with guests on the other side of the pool.

Gabriela watched him. "Do you think he knows who I am?" she asked.

"He may. Mateo's his cousin, remember. Try to relax. We're among friends."

Gabriela looked worried.

Leighton moved to sit on the chaise lounge next to her. He whispered, "Consider what's happened. We killed Narváez last night and he's covered it up completely."

"For the resort. Not for us," Gabriela countered.

"Be that as it may, he still researched Narváez' phone records as I asked, and told us in essence that we have nothing to worry about in terms of his outside communications. He's confirmed everything Mateo told us about him and this resort. So why worry?"

"I'm just so used to being careful. Being just a little paranoid."

"I know you are. It's kept you alive. But you're at the point where it will begin to wear you down unless you can let all that go, at least while we're here. Listen, if Raoul wanted to nail us, he'd have done it last night when I handed him a perfect excuse all tied up with ribbon. If nothing else, he could have kicked us out and made sure we were apprehended once we were away from here, and *still* covered up the killing to protect the resort."

"You're right," Gabriela sighed. "I should have realized that on my own."

"You're under a lot of stress," Leighton said softly, and he kissed her. "It's why you need the rest. Come on," he said, pulling her gently up out of the chaise lounge. "Let's go to the sauna. After that I'll give you a massage."

They spent the next several days in a state of absolute bliss, as bit by bit the ugly memory of Narváez and what they'd been compelled to do slipped away. In the mornings, after they had their coffee out on the deck, breakfast arrived via room service no sooner than nine thirty, and they ate either in bed or in the breakfast nook, depending on their mood. They spent the days swimming and sunning themselves, making love, walking on the beach, and snorkeling. One morning, with Raoul's help, they rented a powerboat for the day and ventured out to nearby Isla de los Cisnes (Swan Island) for a picnic. They got into the habit of showering in the late afternoons, to remove the day's heat, sand, and sweat, often making love afterward. In the evenings, they soaked in the outdoor hot tub and then watched the sunset on the rear deck over cocktails and occasionally, appetizers before ordering dinner via room service.

··· · · ▦ ▦ ▦ ▦ ▦ ▦ ▦ ▦ ▦ ▦ ▦ ▦ ● ● · · ·

Diego Salcedo looked up from the back of the partially dismantled launch console and laid down his tools as he saw Camilo approaching. He had various precision tools and electronic components neatly spread on a cloth on the table before him, along with the manual for the missiles to help him troubleshoot what had gone wrong. He knew the youth meant well, but he had little patience for interruptions of any kind. Mateo had given the order to fire the cruise missiles five days ago, yet they still sat on the ground at Bocuateca. This was Salcedo's fourth attempt to trace what he assumed was a fault in the electronic circuitry that was preventing the missiles from launching, and the previous three diagnostics checks he had run revealed nothing wrong with the launch console, its wiring or any of its components.

Camilo came up the steps of the abandoned apartment that Salcedo had converted into a makeshift workshop on the edge of town, the location closest to the missiles where he could do precision work in relatively clean conditions. He spied Salcedo through the open window, knocked and entered.

"Any luck?"

"No. Everything's in perfect working order," Salcedo said, sitting back with an exasperated sigh. "Yet the missiles won't fire. If there was a fault in the wiring, I could find a way to bypass it, but there's nothing wrong with this equipment. The other panel checked out fine, too."

"Maybe this launch panel isn't communicating with the electronic firing mechanism in the missiles themselves," Camilo ventured.

Salcedo gave him an irritated look. "I thought of that. I've run diagnostics on the missiles, too. There's nothing wrong with them."

"Could it be the diagnostic equipment, then?"

"No, Camilo, there's a way to check that, too, and I already have. The diagnostic gear is fine. But something somewhere is blocking the launch signal."

Camilo gave a loud, exasperated sigh.

"You think I like it?" Salcedo exploded. "I don't like being stuck in this outback any more than you do! There's barely enough drinking water here, and we can't even bathe. The nearest stream is five miles away. Those damn missiles should have flown away at the touch of a button!"

"I don't like to bug you, but Mateo keeps radioing for updates."

"Tell him we'll launch as soon as we can. Now let me get back to work."

• • • • ▪ ▭ ▬ ▭ ▭ ▬ ▭ ▭ ▬ ▬ ▪ • • •

Since the night they had encountered Narváez, Leighton and Gabriela had not returned to the Grotto restaurant and had all their meals brought in by room service. One night Gabriela said she wanted to go back and sit at a window table. It was a significant step in her letting go of her fear, but Leighton nonetheless had mixed feelings about it. While he had been feeling a bit restless keeping close to the bungalow for days on end, in the back of his mind he was still concerned about her safety. He nonetheless encouraged her desire to go out.

Gabriela was at her most beautiful in the blue-grey dress, having found matching sandals and a black headband at a women's shop during a rare drive into Catellan earlier that day in the Impala. They arrived

188

early and had cocktails in the Grotto Bar beforehand, Gabriela feeling adventurous enough to have her first daiquiri containing alcohol. They drank slowly, watching the sunset before being seated for dinner at one of the large, full-length windows. Gabriela had linguini with clams, and Leighton ordered a beefsteak. The meal was delicious, followed by coffee and salted caramel gelato. They took a long walk on the beach afterward in the dark, Gabriela still in her blue-grey gown and Leighton again in the Army uniform. He carried her sandals in his hand and had slung his boots over his shoulder after tying their laces together. They had even gotten into the habit in recent days of leaving their guns behind when they left the bungalow. They walked hand in hand, neither saying a word. Speech between them had often become unnecessary.

Gabriela gradually slowed and then stopped to look at him in the moonlight. "How is your French?"

Leighton regarded her and cocked an eyebrow. "Assez bon pour séduire une femme, je suppose."

"I should slap your face for that," she said, only slightly amused. "I would think there'd be only one woman you'd be planning to seduce."

"In all of France, there would be only one woman for me."

"Only France?"

"In all the world."

"Stop joking; I'm serious. I want to go. Soon. I have a friend who could get me a position at the Sorbonne. Will you come with me?"

"Oui, Gabriela, j'irais avec toi."

"Your French is quite good," she said, smiling at him. "There are many things you could do. Yet you have not even asked about that."

"I'd be with you. I'd find my way."

She turned to go back the way they had come, and Leighton turned with her. "I want to go back to Limado just long enough to tell Mateo," she said. "I've done enough here."

"You're ready to go back, then?"

She placed her head on his shoulder. "Not yet."

The next day, they went out in the speedboat again, this time merely to be on the water. They discovered a dock on the eastern shore of Swan Island, and a little open-air cantina nearby that served lunch at a spot overlooking the ocean. After a luncheon of fish tacos and ginger beer, they returned to the mainland. They picked up the car near a jetty outside Catellan, and drove back to Sharks Grotto. As Leighton pulled the Impala into the roundabout, it was clear that something was happening based on the sheer number of guests milling about in the open-air lobby.

Several people stood crowded around underneath a ceiling-mounted television on the right side of the lobby, where a news announcer was giving an update. In the background was a large photo of a bearded Black man next to Fidel Castro.

"… just confirmed the assassination of Prime Minister Maurice Bishop of Grenada, a small island off the coast of Venezuela, and five others in his government by a counterrevolutionary group led by Deputy Prime Minister Bernard Coard. Coard's group had been a faction of Bishop's Marxist New Jewel Movement and are considered hard-line, doctrinaire Stalinists who see the Party as supreme and the will of the people as subordinate. Bishop, in contrast, since taking power in 1979, pursued policies that were more strictly socialist in nature, and remained focused on improving conditions for workers and farmers in part through mass education and policies moving Grenada toward economic self-reliance. His goal was to give the Grenadian people a sense that they had a stake in the revolution. His administration initiated free health care, launched a massive literacy program, and had an internationalist bent, forging alliances with Cuba, Nicaragua, Libya, and the Soviet Union.

Bernard Coard, if he remains in power, is expected to reorganize the government more closely along the authoritarian lines typically associated with the Soviet Union. We will be back with updates as this story develops."

Gabriela was trying unsuccessfully to choke back her tears. "This is a disaster for them," she cried. "It is sure to lead to an American invasion. The Americans didn't like Maurice ... but they hate Coard. The irony is that Coard has been their tool."

"Did you know Maurice Bishop?" Leighton asked.

She nodded, wiping away tears. "I met him at a conference, in London. We had dinner together. A truly visionary man. This is terrible," Gabriela sobbed. "It's true what the announcer said. He was setting Grenada on a path to economic independence."

They returned to the bungalow in silence. Gabriela called room service and ordered a whiskey, neat. A darkness had overtaken her. Leighton stayed close but sensed she was too distraught to speak. The whiskey arrived, and she began to sip it immediately.

After several minutes, she said, "After dinner ... we talked politics for hours. He was interested in conditions in Chile under Pinochet, what had happened to my family. He told me about his plans for Grenada, how he wanted to form alliances with nonaligned nations, the challenges he faced, how he planned to navigate the antagonism of the United States. He was a brilliant man. We talked all night." She shook her head. "His *mind* ... He left early the next morning. I had coffee with him before he caught a cab to Heathrow. It was the most intellectually intimate experience I've ever had. Soon after that, I graduated, and I went straight to El Salvador ... You could say that my brother and Maurice made me what I am. I can't believe I've lost them *both*."

Sitting on the edge of the bed, she bent down and put her head in her hands and sobbed. Leighton went to her and placed a hand on her shoulder. She did not look up but covered his hand with hers.

"Did you ..." But Leighton could not bring himself to ask.

Gabriela looked up, wiping away tears. "Sleep with him?" Her voice cracked with emotion, and she sniffled. "No ... but I wanted to. If there'd been more time ... He knew that I wanted him."

Gabriela sat sipping her whiskey. "The truth is," she said, her voice rough as the tears began to flow again, "I was a starry-eyed university student, and he was already well on his way to becoming president. If we'd had just a few more hours, it would have happened. I felt it, and so did he. But he filled my head with examples of how my socialist ideals could actually be put into practice to affect change. I would have gone with him, if he'd asked me. He's the reason I went to El Salvador so soon afterward."

⋅ ⋅ ⋅ ⋅ ▪ ▪ ▭ ▭ ▭ ▭ ▭ ▭ ▭ ▭ ▭ ▪ ▪ ⋅ ⋅ ⋅ ⋅

It had taken three days since the airwaves were full of the news of the assassination of Maurice Bishop in Grenada, but Miller had finally gotten through to an officer in the Pentagon who could tell him the status of the helicopters and the missile recovery team that had been sitting on the ground idly in Guatemala for over three weeks. He held the telephone receiver, waiting for that officer to come on the line.

Miller was worried. Leighton had gone completely dark, had not responded to his last three signals. At the moment, he had no proof that Leighton was still alive. He remembered Lang's theory that Leighton might have been turned.

"Mr. Miller?"

"Yes."

"I'm sorry for the delay, sir. This is Colonel Fletcher of the Joint Special Operations Command. I understand you have air assets on the ground in Guatemala that have been on standby for some time."

"Yes, but I haven't been able to use them. I'm told they've been on lockdown because they might be used for the Grenada operation."

"Well, I can't confirm or deny that, sir, but I can tell you that I'm expecting to cut orders within forty-eight hours releasing that hold and freeing up those Guatemala assets."

"Can I have then now?"

"No sir. They have been directed to sit tight until they have orders in hand."

"But I can have them in two days."

"Yes, sir, that's how it looks at the moment."

"'At the moment,' you said. So something could change?"

"Yes, sir, it could, but in my professional opinion, it is unlikely."

"Alright, colonel. Thank you. Is there anything else you can tell me?"

"No, sir, that's about it."

"Very good. Thank you, again."

"Thank you, Mr. Miller. I appreciate your patience."

Miller hung up. He was sure of one thing: multiple sources had confirmed that an American invasion of Grenada was imminent. This meant that for the time being, there would be no invasion of Madrinega. But there was still no word from Leighton. And Miller knew better than to ask permission to send another agent in after him.

••••═══════════••••

The guerillas at Limado, many of them still bandaged and recovering from their wounds after striking the air base at Taramantes, could not believe their eyes. It was Miguel, limping along the main trail through the brush that led back to the village. His clothes were tattered and he was filthy, but it was him, alive and well. They flocked to him in joy and relief. As he came into the main section of the camp, he collapsed, sinking to the ground unconscious.

He was quickly carried to the aid station, and Alma was summoned. Then Mateo.

Mateo came and watched as a team of nurses, under Alma's direction, cut the rags of clothing from his body and cleaned him as best they could using a series of antiseptic wipes. Alma came forward to examine him.

"Bring me light, please," she said. It was not yet dark enough for kerosene lamps – the guerillas had taken to using them on a limited basis since attacking the air base, for they had not seen a single surveillance plane since, either by day or by night. One of the nurses leaned over the area Alma was studying, and shined a flashlight. What Alma had thought to be a scab on Miguel's left leg was actually a bullet wound, and the swelling and redness around it concerned her. As she probed the wound, Miguel, still unconscious, cried out in pain.

Alma straightened up and looked at Mateo, her expression grave. "The bullet's still in him, and there are signs of infection."

Mateo instantly understood the seriousness of what she was saying. If the infection could not be checked—and it was likely well underway, since he had received no medical care for some days in this tropical climate—Miguel could well lose his leg. Mateo nodded. "Do everything you can for him," he said.

"We'll start with getting the bullet out," Alma said to her nurses. "I'm going to need a set of sterilized instruments, clean gauze, and a lot more light."

Knowing he would only be in the way, Mateo took a walk. He was concerned that the missiles had not yet been launched and that Camilo was stuck down there in Bocuateca until they were, since he was now functioning as their radioman. The order to fire had been given, and Mateo knew they would carry it out as soon as they could, but he wanted to know immediately once it was done, and for that reason Camilo had to stay. Mateo had grown to rely on the boy as a junior officer, and he sorely missed his absence. It might be easier now with Miguel back, but for now he was wounded, and in the wake of his break with Zorrita, Mateo was frankly unsure how to treat him. Before, there would have been no question but that Mateo would have relinquished command to Miguel upon his return. But in going to Redención, heroic though the gesture was, he had broken ranks and defied Zorrita, who had correctly predicted the battle's outcome.

This was a critical moment, with the Army on the defensive in multiple cities, and with aid now coming to the *Frente* in substantial amounts from Nicaragua for the first time. Gabriela did not yet know that, and while Mateo had been aware of it for some days, he had been reluctant to announce it on the radio, for fear of provoking American intervention. But Redención, it seemed, while a military disaster for the guerillas, had proved such a bloody fight that it had actually damaged the Army's morale. Mateo had read news accounts in *El Celador* and elsewhere that the government soldiers in Redención had experienced a bad shock upon realizing that many of the guerillas were intent upon fighting to the death, *after* it was clear to them that their position was hopeless. Such a mindset on the part of his opponent in the field gave the average soldier pause. But Redención also amounted to a political setback for the government. The determination Miguel and others had shown at Redención had led directly to the uprisings in other cities, although the attack on the air base had been a factor, too. In terms of his bravery as a soldier, there was none better than Miguel. But Mateo was no longer confident about his abilities as a political leader. Part of him hoped that upon her return Zorrita would decide *not* to pass the baton. Many would want Miguel to have it and would question passing him over to hand control over to Mateo.

Mateo had heard the troubling news about Maurice Bishop in Grenada. His fledgling government had been focused on jump-starting the island's economic development, but Mateo was confident he would have been a staunch ally in future years. He had delayed preparing remarks for a radio broadcast until more information on the situation could be gleaned. There were rumors that Bernard Coard had been a CIA agent, or at the very least that his actions would be exploited by the United States to justify an invasion. The only good Mateo saw in that was that the Americans were unlikely to launch two invasions in Latin America simultaneously, for both political and logistical reasons. If they pounced on Grenada, they would let Madrinega alone.

• • • • • ▬ ▬ ▬ ▭ ▭ ▭ ▭ ▭ ▬ ▬ ▬ ● • • • •

The killing of Maurice Bishop had sent Gabriela into a tailspin. On the first day of learning the news, she had been inconsolable, crying long into the night, refusing Leighton's attempts to comfort her. For the following three days, she had done little but listen to the radio for news, pick over her food, and walk on the beach, often insisting on being alone. She slept very little, and was distant and withdrawn. Most alarming to Leighton, she was suddenly fatalistic about her own physical safety. When he suggested that if she insisted on walking the beach alone, she should be armed, she dismissed the idea with a wave of her hand.

"Raoul says we're safe here, remember?"

Leighton knew she was grappling with a personal crisis in light of the death of not merely a fellow revolutionary, but also a man she had met and personally admired—a man she might have loved, given time. Leighton's empathy told him she had regarded Bishop as both a friend and a beacon, no remote historical figure, but a charismatic, vibrant man whose passing had struck her hard, dimming the light in her own life. Leighton sensed that Gabriela was having serious doubts about leaving the movement and going off to Europe to wait out the storm of controversy around her own revolutionary activities. He suspected that Bishop's death had placed her in fear of her life in a way she had never before experienced, and that her new fatalistic attitude was her response to that fear.

Leighton wanted desperately to comfort her, to pull her out of her funk, but she was not receptive. All he could do was wait and try to protect her. He satisfied himself with trailing some distance behind her when she went on her walks, carrying the Smith & Wesson concealed at the small of his back. This irritated her. He respected the darkness engulfing her, and the likelihood that she would have to navigate her way out of it alone, but he was unapologetic and did not mince words when he told her he would rather have her irritated than dead.

When he followed her, he was careful not to crowd her but also to keep just inside the maximum distance at which he was confident he could get off a fatal shot if he had to. Their romantic getaway was coming to an end, with the tension between them mounting. She was in pain. Leighton knew it, he felt it, yet could do absolutely nothing about it. Being unable to help, hour by hour, despite his own fierce resistance to it, he began to feel a growing pain of his own.

By the morning of the fourth day, he no longer made an effort to interact with her. If she noticed, she gave no indication of it. The silence in the bungalow became a heavy, palpable thing, suffocating them both. He sat alone drinking coffee on the deck, and she stood alone out on the beach, wearing a bathrobe, looking out at the sea.

On previous days, she had refused breakfast, simply starting off on a walk along the beach without a word, sometimes leaving him scrambling to dress and conceal a weapon and then catch her, or at least get to a point from which he could cover her. Today he was proactive. He had dressed early, although with mounting resentment.

He was ready for her if she suddenly decided to dart off on a morning constitutional, right down to the Smith & Wesson lying on the deck beside his chair. He was no longer her lover; he had been relegated to bodyguard, and she did not want even that. It stung.

And still he watched over her.

CHAPTER 16
THE REBIRTH

With the bullet out and the wound cleaned, Miguel improved somewhat, but the infection in his leg was stubborn. Alma had no antibiotics, so she sent a runner into Limado to fetch raw garlic. When it arrived, she sterilized a sharp knife over an open flame and used it to dice the garlic and then crush it into a crude paste. With fine surgical instruments, she troweled the paste into Miguel's wound and bandaged it tightly with gauze. Freshly diced garlic was thereafter applied to the wound whenever the bandage was changed. Within a day, the spread of the infection had been checked, Miguel's fever had broken, and he was both conscious and lucid for the first time. Within two days, although weak from malnutrition, he was able to sit up and speak. He asked to see Zorrita.

"She is not here," Alma said.

"Where is she?"

"She has gone to the coast with Machete, to Lovers' Grotto."

"Machete?" Miguel repeated, his voice hoarse. "I must speak to Mateo." He laid back and closed his eyes.

A few minutes later, Mateo appeared. He came to Miguel's side and managed a smile. "You had us worried," he said. "But it looks like Alma has you on the path to a full recovery."

"Who is Machete?"

"Palmer."

"Zorrita? Lovers' Grotto?"

Mateo lowered his head. He turned to look into Miguel's eyes. "Yes, Miguel. You will have to accept it."

"You think I'm jealous," Miguel scoffed.

"I know you have wanted her," Mateo replied. "Some yearnings are hard for any man to hide."

"He is an American agent," Miguel said.

"What? That can't be."

"Yes."

"I had my suspicions about him too, but I don't anymore. So what are you talking about?"

"In Redención, before we were forced to surrender, we captured an American, fighting with one of the Army units. Severin was his name. CIA."

Mateo was listening intently. "Go on."

"We tortured him. Made him talk."

"You what?"

"Do not waste my time with your moral objections, he was CIA," Miguel spat. "He said Palmer's mission was to recover the missiles."

"You're saying Palmer is CIA," Mateo replied. "I don't believe it."

"What's happened to the missiles?"

"Zorrita ordered us to disable one of them, the one we left at Vescambre. Palmer was the only one who knew how, so he did it."

Miguel emitted a satisfied grunt. "There."

"Miguel, that proves nothing."

"What about the other missiles?"

"Suddenly they won't fire for some reason. Salcedo has been trying to figure it out for days."

"Has Palmer been near them?"

"No ... wait, yes. Zorrita drove down to Bocuateca to alert Salcedo to be ready to fire. Palmer went with her."

"The other missile we fired worked fine. Before Palmer showed up."

"Again, that proves nothing. Palmer has risked his life repeatedly. He planned the attack on the air base near Valmonte and helped lead it. It was a success."

"But the missiles aren't working suddenly."

"Miguel, in the scheme of things, the missiles are not all that important. Your fight in Redención has triggered other uprisings. Vilar has been deposed after a story came out revealing why he attacked Panactatlan. There is much news you have to catch up on."

"I say he is an American agent. He cannot be trusted."

"Get it through your head," Mateo said, beginning to lose patience for the first time. "He *has* been trusted, repeatedly, and he has never let us down. Never. If he were an American agent, he would have killed Zorrita the first time they were alone together for a prolonged period. He didn't. I've seen how he looks at her. He can't hide it any more than you could. He would kill anyone who tried to harm her. And I'm surprised you would take the word of a CIA man at face value … a man you admit you tortured, who therefore had every incentive to undermine someone who has turned out to be a champion of our cause. *To sow division,*" Mateo said with emphasis.

Miguel had not been listening. "How long have they been gone?" he asked.

"I don't know … a week, eight days."

"How do you know she's still alive?"

"Do you think I'm stupid? I sent them to Sharks Grotto because practically the entire staff there are either guerillas or in sympathy with the guerillas, including my own cousin Raoul, who is the manager. She is being closely watched there, I can assure you of that. If anyone moves against her, they will not succeed. Not there. And if she were in any danger, I would have known about it within the hour. It's the one place I know of that's away from here where she'll actually be safe."

Miguel fell silent. Mateo knew he had effectively countered all of his arguments against Palmer. But incredibly, Mateo could also sense that Miguel was not convinced, that nothing would convince him. He would not accept facts that differed with his belief. Something else was driving him, and Mateo could only conclude that it was jealousy.

"We should find out what's happening with those missiles," Miguel said lamely.

"Salcedo is checking them over carefully for defects in the firing mechanism and related computer software. I am in touch with him daily by radio. I'm confident he'll get it solved, so there is nothing left for us do to at the moment but wait."

"You are in touch. You are confident," Miguel mimicked.

"That's right. Zorrita left me in charge," Mateo replied. "You should get some rest and regain your strength. We will talk more later."

"Yes, jefe," Miguel said sarcastically.

"Miguel, I know you are tired and you've been through hell. You have my respect for all that you have done. I ask you not to poison it." Mateo rose and walked off.

As he walked toward the courtyard in the camp, Mateo was taken aback by Miguel's negative energy, and was more convinced than ever that he was unfit to lead, except in purely military matters.

• • • ◦ ◼ ▦ ▧ ◫ ▦ ▦ ▧ ▦ ▦ ◫ ◼ ◦ • • •

It was the morning of the fifth day since the announcement of Maurice Bishop's death. Gabriela had finally slept most of the night. The silence between she and Leighton was becoming more bearable now; it was not as hard or heavy. The impenetrable cocoon of grief in which she had cloaked herself was itself finally beginning to weaken.

But so far their physical routine was the same. Leighton got up, made coffee, and sat alone drinking it out on the deck, while Gabriela stood alone out on the beach, wearing a bathrobe, looking out at the sea.

Still he watched over her.

Leighton also scanned the section of beach he could see for any potential threats. His vision was restricted by the low stucco wall and the vegetation growing above it on either side of their private section of beach, but within that sixty-foot-wide parcel all was clear. Leighton had checked; the adjoining bungalows were occupied by an elderly couple on the left, and a pair of newlyweds on the right. They posed no danger. The only thing to come within thirty feet of Gabriela had been a seagull, diving at the water close inshore in an attempt to seize a fish.

He was dressed in the navy shorts and grey T-shirt and a cheap pair of huaraches he had bought at the resort's gift shop. The Smith & Wesson lay on the deck next to his chair as usual. As he sat sipping his

201

coffee, Gabriela turned and began walking back toward the bungalow. The wind whipped at the white terry cloth robe, but she had belted it tightly and was hugging herself as she walked. The sun was in her eyes, and she squinted against it until she walked completely into the shadow of the bungalow. She came up the stairs and stood in front of Leighton with her arms folded and became still. She gazed down at him, and in that instant she looked exhausted. He noticed that the dark spots he had seen under her eyes at Limado had begun to reappear. He ached to rise and comfort her, but he remained where he was.

Her breathing was heavier than usual, and Leighton sensed she was still in a delicate emotional state. Not knowing what to do, he gazed back at her, his expression one of openness.

She sniffed and rubbed her nose and asked quietly, "May I have a cup of coffee, please?"

Leighton got up, touched her arm, and went into the bungalow to the kitchenette, returning in a moment with a steaming cup of coffee, flavored as she liked it, with cream and just a dash of sugar. He passed the mug to her handle first so that she would not burn her fingers.

She thanked him as he sat down, watching the steam rise from her cup. She kept watching it as she said, "I've been in a kind of hell. I've dragged you through it with me, and I'm sorry."

Leighton waited to be sure she was finished, then replied, "I went through it with you, but you didn't drag me. I love you, Gabriela. When you're hurting, I feel it too."

With the utterance of those words, she put a hand to her mouth, and her eyes teared up. "I know. I'm so sorry."

Leighton stood and kissed her on the temple, stroking her cheek once lightly with the backs of his fingers. He remained very close, leaning against the railing of the deck as she sipped her coffee.

"I don't know how you do it, but the coffee's perfect every time."

"I watched how you prepared it in the restaurant," Leighton said.

He could sense her gearing up to say something else. "It bothered you when I talked about Maurice, didn't it?"

"Only part of it. A little," Leighton admitted with a sigh.

"You asked. And I suppose I needed to talk about him, a little."

"I know," Leighton said.

They stood together until she finished her coffee. She set the mug down on the small circular wooden table between the two chairs, then reached back and took one of his hands.

"Come to bed, I want to talk to you."

They stepped inside and she quickly slipped into bed. Leighton kicked off the huaraches and removed his shirt and joined her. She kissed him softly, and he responded. She had not allowed him to touch her in days.

She looked into his eyes.

"I love you," she began. "But I don't believe I have the luxury of feeling that way. The tension, the pressure of leading, they're wearing me down. I can't explain to you how devastated I am by what's happened to Maurice, but I think you have a sense. I … this is new for me … I'm afraid I'll die like he did. Even still, I feel I must go back to Limado. But I'm concerned that if I tell you I want to go back, you won't come with me."

"But I—"

"Shh, my love, let me finish," she said, putting a finger to his lips. "I have also been concerned that you'll come with me, but do it reluctantly and be unhappy. I'm concerned that if we go to France, I'll be unhappy because I'm not pursuing the destiny that perhaps God has planned for me. And I'm conflicted because I don't truly feel I know what my destiny is. In short, my love, I'm paralyzed, and it is driving me crazy. And to admit to myself that I love you … that complicates everything even more."

Leighton said, "Can I ask a question?"

"Please."

"When you first heard about Maurice, what was your first reaction? In your gut."

"That I had an obligation to go back to Limado, no matter what I wanted personally. That we'd just had a major setback and I couldn't possibly leave. I had a feeling of being trapped."

"Why trapped?"

"Well, just the night before, I'd reached the conclusion that I was exhausted, that it was time to leave. I said it to you, on the beach. The truth is, I'm tired. But so are many others."

"And what was your second reaction?"

"That there are too few people in the world taking on the responsibility to fight injustice, and I was tired of being one of the few. You know, why me? Why do I have to be the one? I would not feel such a responsibility if there were more people willing to do it. But all you have to do is look at what happened to Maurice, and there's your answer. The world is organized in such a way that sometimes you have to pay the ultimate price if you are going to stand up and say 'No' to those who have the power. To challenge injustice and oppression. Everyone is not able, I understand that. But of the many who are able, only a tiny handful, it seems to me, have the courage to step forward, to *do something*. And that is unfortunate."

"Yes, it is," Leighton said with a sigh. He put his arm around her.

"It isn't fair."

"As you know, Gabriela, there's little about this world that's fair."

She snuggled closer to Leighton and sighed, "I still don't know what I'm going to do."

"I know what it is to feel conflicted. You'll eventually decide what's best."

"But I feel that I should *know*. Right now. I should just … be able to choose one path, without any reservations."

"Life is rarely that doubt-free."

"One path may leave me feeling miserable and insignificant, opting for comfort when I could have made a mark on the world, and the other could make that mark and cost me my life."

"That's a hell of a choice to have to make."

"It's been a kind of purgatory, like I said. But what are you going to do? That's been worrying me, too."

"Me? I've told you, but I don't think you believe it. I want to be with you wherever you are, and whatever you decide to do."

"But how can you? You're a man."

"Meaning what?"

"Men have to be the center of attention, they have to feel that they are conquering the world, captain of the ship. They want their women to look up to them, and the woman *cannot, under any circumstances, outshine them.*"

"I'm that way, too," Leighton admitted. "But when I met you, I knew you were an extraordinary woman, of a kind I'd never encountered before. I saw that with you, it would have to be different. So for *you* … and *only* for you," he said, looking into her eyes, "I'm willing to put my ego aside if I can be with you."

Gabriela lay next to Leighton, looking at him with a strange intensity he had never seen before. It was a solemn look, a mixture of love, recognition, and power.

"I want you," she whispered.

CHAPTER 17
THE GO SIGNAL

Miller nearly fell out of bed reaching for the telephone. He had left instructions with the after-hours switchboard to route calls to him at home.

"Hello?" The glow of the digital clock on his nightstand read 2:57 a.m. Not wanting to disturb his wife, he took the telephone into the hallway outside their bedroom and quietly shut the door.

"Mr. Miller?" came a young man's voice.

"Yes."

"Please hold for Major Hardesty, sir." Miller was instantly wide awake. Hardesty was the officer in command of the missile recovery team and, by default, the rapid deployment force in Guatemala.

"Is that you, Miller?"

"Yes."

"Hardesty. We've been cleared to go back into Madrinega."

"What about Grenada?"

"If the powers that be are going to move against Grenada, I got the official word tonight they won't need us. All I need from you now is a 'Go' signal."

"You have it, Major. Go. But there may be opposition this time."

"We'll be ready," Hardesty said confidently. "You'll hear from me once the operation's complete."

"Thank you. Good luck."

At Limado, the morning after his unpleasant confrontation with Miguel, Mateo hiked into the village to use the pay phone at the post office. After talking to Miguel, he wanted to make absolutely certain that Zorrita was safe. He had been adamant with Miguel that that was the case, but there was always room for a last lingering doubt. Depositing the coins into the slot, he suddenly felt anxious as he dialed the number, and his anxiety grew as he listened to the phone ring. *Damn that Miguel.*

"Good Morning, Sharks Grotto."

"Good Morning, I would like to speak to Raoul Estefan."

"Yes, may I tell him who is calling?"

"His cousin Mateo."

"Very well, please hold, señor."

After a few moments, Raoul came on the line. "This is Raoul."

"How are you, cousin? It's Mateo."

"Ahh, wonderful to hear from you," Raoul said, and Mateo could hear the curiosity in his voice. "I am well …"

"I'm just calling to check on the friends I sent your way. Is everything alright?"

"Yes, they are both well and enjoying the Grotto's hospitality to the fullest, I am pleased to say," Raoul replied brightly. But it felt to Mateo like what it was, a prepared answer that Raoul had uttered automatically. He felt the need to prod a bit deeper.

"There have been no incidents?"

"No. Nothing to speak about," he said, cagily referring to communication by telephone.

"But … our sister. She is safe?"

"Yes, perfectly. She is being well looked after. I have seen to it personally."

"That is comforting to hear. And the man, he is well?"

"Oh, yes."

"You have no reason for concern about him?"

"I can tell you that in everything I have seen, he is a doting paramour. They seem quite happy together."

"Excellent, Raoul. Thank you. It has been wonderful talking to you."

"And you, cousin."

Mateo hung up, greatly relieved. As far as Zorrita and Palmer were concerned, reality and appearances matched. They had been alone together for well over a week, and he felt confident that there was no more cause for worry, even in light of Miguel's unsubstantiated suspicions, which were, after all, based on the word of a CIA man he had tortured, a suspect source at best. He walked back to the guerilla camp by the river, eager to find Miguel and tell him so.

When Mateo arrived, he went first to the hospital tent where Alma had been keeping Miguel. He was not there. He next went to the aid station nearby and found Alma.

"Where is Miguel?"

"He has gone."

"What do you mean, 'gone'?" Mateo demanded. "Where?"

"I told him he needed to rest, but he would not listen. He said something about going to Bocuateca."

"Can he even walk?"

"He was limping, but he can move about fairly well. But I don't think he is strong enough to go far. I told him so. You saw how much weight he has lost."

Mateo next found Rafael, the guerilla he had placed in charge of the "motor pool," the collection of vehicles that had been stolen for the air base operation.

"Yes," Rafael said. "He came to see me a little over an hour ago. He wanted a jeep. I gave it to him."

"I know you had no reason to deny him," Mateo said. "But he is not well enough to travel."

"I could see that, Mateo," Rafael replied. "And I'm no doctor. But you know Miguel when his mind is set on something. He is as bad as Zorrita."

Mateo seized the opportunity to plant a seed, for he sensed trouble ahead. "There is one difference between them. Zorrita has better judgment."

Rafael looked at him in surprise, for Mateo had never before leveled even oblique criticism at Miguel. Like a child whose parents are fighting, he simply shrugged, unsure of how to respond.

"Get me a jeep," Mateo said irritably. "With plenty of gas. Siphon it from the other vehicles if you have to."

"Right away, Mateo."

***

Diego Salcedo had come to a decision. Electronic communication between the firing panels and the cruise missiles was being jammed somehow, but there was theoretically still a way to fire off at least one of the missiles, although it would be highly dangerous. He knew which of the two targets Zorrita had designated was the more important. He had been up all night, first programming one of the missiles' guidance systems to target the coordinates of the armory at the Army base at Xapaca, and second, studying the manual to devise a way to fire the missile manually. He had then gone to the guerillas guarding the missiles at 3:30 a.m. and told them to get the first of the missiles into firing position. After some effort, they had one of the missiles out of its sling and erect on its launcher by four thirty. By 5:00, Salcedo had tested the missile's guidance system and confirmed that the Xapaca coordinates had been locked in. All that remained was to get the thing airborne. At 5:15 Salcedo went to work implementing the manual firing procedure.

Salcedo knew he could be badly burned if not killed by the blast of the launch, because he would literally have to be close enough to physically activate the rocket engine. But he was driven by the memory of his mother and sister, killed in the missile strike at Panactatlan. He wanted to ensure the guerillas' final victory, no matter the cost. He stood atop the launcher and used his tools to open a panel along the missile shaft, just below the point of the pivoting gears for the folding wings, which would spring out upon launch. Holding a penlight in his mouth, he began to study the internal workings for the components that the manual indicated could fire the missile's engine without an electronic signal.

***

Major Curtis Hardesty leaned over the pilot's shoulder and took in the landscape rushing past below them through the helicopter's large Plexiglas windscreen. Dawn was breaking as they flew at treetop level with six other helicopters. The little armada consisted of three UH-60 Blackhawks—including Hardesty's—carrying thirty-three troops, two HH-53 "Jolly Green Giant" transports, and two Cobra attack helicopters. Looking at the countryside below, Hardesty could see cows that had been idling on lush green grazing land slowly begin to scatter at the approach of the noise from the sky.

This mission was riskier, involving a far deeper penetration into Madrinega. The first missile they'd withdrawn had been at one end of the Casavala Mountain Range, in one of the northern provinces just twenty minutes' flying time from the border. There had been no opposition. This time the border was over one hundred miles away, and Hardesty had told his men to expect resistance on the ground. Guided by satellite to Bocuateca with the help of signals from the transponders Leighton had planted, they had flown a course directly from the border to the village, keeping below two hundred feet.

Hardesty seized a handhold as the pilot began to climb above an approaching treeline. Beyond the trees, he could see the prairie over which they were flying drop off suddenly, revealing a small village far below.

"Bocuateca," the copilot announced. As the procession of helicopters flew above the cliff overlooking the village and began to fan out, Hardesty looked to his left and identified the thick clump of trees marking the jungle that abutted the village. In the grey light of early morning, he could see that one of the missiles had been removed from cover and was in a firing position. Hardesty turned from the cockpit to the eleven heavily armed soldiers sitting in two rows along the length of the cabin behind him. "Get ready," he yelled. "They're about to fire one of the birds!"

The Blackhawks broke away from the Cobras and the larger HH-53 transports and made a descending turn to the left, preparing to set down in a field of cultivated crops barely a quarter mile from the village. The remaining aircraft hovered in the distance.

⬩ ⬩ ⬩ ▪ ▪ ▪ ▬ ▬ ▬ ▬ ▬ ▬ ▬ ▬ ▪ ▪ ▪ ⬩ ⬩ ⬩

Camilo, sleeping in the abandoned apartment that Salcedo had commandeered at the edge of the village, was awakened by the helicopters and quickly assessed what was happening. He grabbed his FN FAL and rounded up the few guerillas who remained in the village. They rushed to form a screen within the trees, interposing themselves between the Americans and the missiles as the helicopters began to land.

Camilo was surprised to see a missile being prepared to fire and approached Salcedo as the guerillas in the near distance opened fire on the Americans. He called to Salcedo above the mounting din of gunfire. "Have you figured it out?"

Salcedo did not answer immediately. Camilo turned to see one of the guerillas falling in the distance as the battle intensified. He raised his automatic rifle and fired a burst as the Americans drew closer. He knelt to present the Americans a smaller target. "Salcedo!"

"I can fire this one," Salcedo called at last. "Keep the Americans away as long as you can!"

Gunfire slapped at the dirt near Camilo, and he rolled to his left and came up on his knees. Guerillas were throwing grenades and had temporarily stopped the Americans' advance. Camilo saw an American raising his rifle, aiming high at Salcedo. He aimed and fired three times, watching as the American soldier went down before he could get off a shot. At that instant, a bullet hit his upper arm, forcing a scream from him, but he took cover behind a tree and kept firing.

The Americans were reluctant to use explosives because of the missiles. They had fanned out and were gradually using fire-and-maneuver tactics to eliminate the guerillas' first line of defense. As they got to within fifteen yards of the trees, gunfire intensified on both sides. Camilo kept busy, laying down deadly accurate fire to hold the Americans off from Salcedo's exposed position on top of the launcher.

A wood splinter hit him in the face as a near miss struck the tree he sheltered behind.

The Americans had brought a heavy machine gun, and it began to lay waste to the guerillas guarding the second missile as the first two soldiers reached the trees. Salcedo found the critical wires on the small radio transmitter that would start the engine. All he had to do was bypass the transmitter. Reaching into his dungarees, he produced a pair of fine wire cutters. He would need a few moments more.

Camilo slapped a fresh magazine into the FN FAL and fired as two Americans, much too close, neared his position. The first targeted Salcedo, while the second fired at Camilo. Camilo fired a burst and wounded the first soldier while the second took cover. The wounded man tossed something in his direction. He realized with horror that it was a grenade. Camilo caught it and threw it back as the second soldier rose and shot him. The impact slammed him back against a tree and forced him to drop his rifle as the grenade went off at the first soldier's feet. He looked down and saw a bloody hole in his abdomen. He suddenly felt very hot. The soldier who had shot him was now taking aim at Salcedo. He fired, and Salcedo fell from the launcher as he was on the point of completing the firing circuit. Screaming with pain, Camilo snatched up his rifle and fired a three-round burst at the soldier, striking him in the chest and head. Salcedo, bleeding from his back, slowly struggled to his feet and turned toward the launcher. Another American approached, and Camilo laid down withering fire, forcing him to seek cover. Salcedo began to climb onto the launcher again to connect the firing circuit as Camilo held the Americans off. Salcedo had just reached in to grab the key wires when a stun grenade went off nearby and three Americans charged the launcher. Camilo stood up and stopped one of them, firing at him at point-blank range. No sooner had he gone down than the second soldier, Major Hardesty himself, shot Camilo in the chest. Camilo fell back hard, his rifle at his side, and did not move again, as Hardesty stood looking down at him, dumbfounded by how young he was. The third soldier aimed carefully and killed Salcedo with a shot to the back of the head. Salcedo collapsed to the ground, still clutching the disconnected radio transmitter.

All gunfire ceased shortly afterward at 5:53 a.m.

*　　　　　　　　　　　　　　　*

After securing the area, the Americans continued to filter through the trees to confirm there was no possibility of a counterattack. Major Hardesty then posted nine men as a screening force at the edge of the village to keep the civilians back as the Jolly Green Giants hovered into position and lowered cables. The missiles were lifted free of the trees and hauled aboard the helicopters and secured. Once the Jolly Greens had departed, Hardesty and his men raced for the Blackhawks, carrying their wounded and dead. The Blackhawks lifted off and disappeared the way they had come, with the Cobras bringing up the rear.

The entire operation was over and the noise of the American aircraft had completely faded away by 6:15 a.m.

*　　　　　　　　　　　　　　　*

Miguel arrived at Bocuateca around 10:00 a.m. He had seen a thin column of smoke from three miles way, the result of a small fire that had started as a result of the combat at the edge of the village earlier that morning. As he drove in, he saw a number of villagers carrying bodies out of the woods on the east side of the village. He leapt from the jeep like a man on fire when he saw Camilo lying in the dirt. He raced to the boy's body and knelt, unable to comprehend what he was seeing. He touched Camilo's face. It was like touching a block of ice.

"What happened here?" he demanded of one of the villagers who was carrying three of the guerillas' rifles.

"The Americans," the woman said. "They came early this morning to get the missiles. Just before dawn."

"How can you know it was the Americans? It could have been our own Army," Miguel protested.

"No," the woman said. "I heard them talking English … it was the Americans."

Miguel looked among the bodies, seeing several that he recognized. He felt weak. He continued to question the villagers and learned that it had all been over very quickly. The Americans had known exactly where the missiles were. They had taken them away in two big helicopters after the fight with the guerillas.

"Did no one survive?" he asked a man passing by.

"No," the man replied. "The guerillas started shooting first. I saw it. They wanted to stop the Americans getting to the trees, where the missiles were hidden. But the Americans, once they started shooting, they would not stop until no one moved in the trees. They even threatened a few of us who got too close."

Miguel felt light-headed, and went back to sit in the jeep. He wanted to sleep. He was sorry that he had come. Mateo had been right. There was nothing to do.

He was still sitting there thirty minutes later, semiconscious, when Mateo drove up. "My God, what happened here?"

Miguel did not reply right away. Mateo saw the dead guerillas, then let out an obscenity when he saw Camilo's bloody body. He walked back to Miguel. "What the fuck happened?"

"The Americans," Miguel said. "Early this morning."

"But after all this time, how did they know where the missiles were?"

"Didn't you tell me," Miguel said hoarsely, "that Zorrita brought Palmer here?"

Mateo ignored him and walked into the trees, where the scent of gunpowder lingered amidst an unseen halo of death. Among the shell casings and bodies and abandoned weapons, he began to feel sick, for all he could see was Camilo, lying dead. At last he came to the missile launchers, which the Americans had abandoned. He tried to remain calm, to tamp down his emotions. He examined the launchers for clues. There was nothing out of the ordinary about either of them, although one of them was pockmarked with bullet strikes, a few of which had demolished its control console. Salcedo lay dead nearby.

Mateo walked all the way around the launchers, a sudden rage quickly building within him. He kicked the launcher nearest him, with no effect. It was simply too heavy. He kicked it again and again, until he screamed and knelt and put his arms underneath it, seeking to overturn it for no reason other than to satisfy his rage. He was able to lift it momentarily, but it was too heavy for a single man turn to overturn it. As he let it go, his foot kicked something shiny in the dirt. It was a dented liquor flask. Puzzled, Mateo picked it up. He opened it and took a whiff. Definitely whiskey. He poured it out, but even in his highly emotional state he realized that the liquid stopped flowing all too quickly. He put his index finger inside and touched the bottom before the second joint disappeared inside the flask. He removed his finger and shook the flask. Nothing. He took his .38 revolver out of the shoulder holster, dropped the flask to the ground, and shot out one of its bottom corners. Picking it up, he recognized electronic components inside.

He remembered that he not seen the flask on the ground below the launcher initially. He reached underneath the launcher, trying to feel a clamp of some kind, but its undersurface was entirely smooth. Mateo held the flask close to a metal side panel of the launcher and released it. It seemed to leap out of his hand and stuck fast to the launcher. Mateo took the flask and walked back to his jeep. He found Miguel semiconscious, huddled over the wheel of his own jeep. Mateo lifted him bodily and placed him in the back of the jeep. He walked back to where Camilo lay. The boy looked dead, pale with bloody bullet holes in his shirt. He had been hit twice, in the chest and abdomen. Mateo expected the worst as he knelt and touched Camilo's face. Cold. He felt Camilo's neck for a pulse. To his shock, it was faint, but definitely there, his breathing shallow. Mateo picked Camilo up and quickly carried him to the jeep. He hopped in and started it up.

He drove quickly back to Limado, where he left Camilo in Alma's care. Miguel awoke and refused to get out of the jeep once he learned Mateo was headed for Sharks Grotto. He insisted on going. Mateo reluctantly agreed.

That morning, Leighton and Gabriela made love immediately upon waking up. They lay entwined in one another's arms afterward, as if reluctant to start the day. Suddenly Gabriela arose and said brightly, "Let's have a swim and breakfast by the swimming pool. We've never done that."

Dressing was a brief affair, since they were headed to the pool near the cliff face, just outside the lobby. They brought only towels, suntan lotion, and sunglasses. Leighton went shirtless for the first time, openly showing the scars on his shoulder and side from the gunshot wounds he had suffered in Valmonte. They had healed sufficiently for him to swim in chlorine water, and when the resort staff noticed them, he sensed that it only increased his stature with them, for he and Gabriela both had come to realize that they knew exactly who she was and that she was nonetheless safe here. Gabriela could not wait to hit the water and dived in quickly, starting for the opposite side of the pool in a fast breaststroke. Leighton left their things on two of the chaise lounges, jumping in after her a few seconds later. They raced one another for three laps and emerged from the pool laughing like children.

It was beautiful day. Leighton felt sure that whatever happened, whatever Gabriela decided to do, the darkness was behind them.

A waiter came by as they were drying themselves and asked whether they wanted breakfast. They nodded, and he pulled from his vest pocket two wallet-sized menus. They had a light breakfast of scrambled eggs, a few ounces of cold sliced chicken, grapefruit, yogurt, and coffee. Gabriela seemed happy and relaxed.

"Let me see something," Leighton asked.

Gabriela looked puzzled as he gently took her left arm and raised it, then positioned her hand so that it was palm down in a horizontal position.

"Steady as a rock," Leighton said with a smile. She leaned over the small breakfast table between them and gave him a long kiss.

"I must go back to Limado," Gabriela told Leighton. "I can't leave now, when we are so close to victory. If it is as close as it seems, I may be able to leave soon … but not now. I have to be true to what I believe."

"I know," Leighton said, smiling at her. "When do we leave?"

"I don't want you to come with me … unless you truly want to. I don't want you to be unhappy, and it would hurt me if you grew to resent me. Also I don't want you to miss home. I know what that's like. It could come between us."

Leighton got up, sat on her chaise lounge, and cupped her face in his hands. "You are my home."

She embraced him, and they held each other for several moments. "Let's go for a walk," she said at last.

They took their longest walk yet, unarmed, up the coast almost to Catellan, passing fishermens' huts and small boathouses and climbing over a breakwater of piled rocks.

They came to a little café on the beach and stopped there briefly to have pastries and hot chocolate. A radio in the café was playing American music, and Leighton recognized a popular song from home, *It's a Mistake*, by Men at Work:

> *Jump down the shelters to get away*
> *The boys are cockin' up their guns*
> *Tell us General, is it party time?*
> *If it is, can we all come? …*

It was a protest song, about accidental nuclear war, which Reagan had everyone thinking about. But as they left the café, Leighton thought bleakly that it was equally topical given the events in Madrinega, and now Grenada. He wanted to discuss it with Gabriela but was afraid to, she was so recently out of her black funk of depression, and he did not want her slipping back into it. He pushed it out of his mind as they walked slowly back along the water's edge, hand-in-hand, breathing in the salt air, listening to the surf.

When they returned to the bungalow, it was midafternoon and they were both feeling the effects of the sun and sea air. They lay on the bed and napped, waking about an hour before sundown. Leighton ordered a gin martini and a virgin daiquiri from room service. While Gabriela showered, he called the concierge again and dictated a cable to be sent by messenger into Catellan, and from there to William Miller of the World Finance Corporation of San Francisco, California:

> I hereby tender my resignation as a member of the editorial staff of your publication, Development Abroad, to take immediate effect.

The drinks arrived, and Leighton tipped the waiter and paid for the cable as Gabriela emerged from the bathroom, a towel across her torso and another in which she had wrapped her hair.

"Did I hear you sending a cable?"

"Yes. Just cutting my last ties with the States."

"I'll be out in a minute," she said, disappearing into the bedroom. She soon emerged in a black one-piece swimsuit with a single shoulder and had tied her now unruly hair back in a fluffy ponytail.

"Mmm … when did you buy that?"

"It was during one of my bad days, when I wandered around the resort alone."

"It's beautiful."

"I thought we'd go for another swim. In the ocean, not the pool. That chlorine didn't do my hair any good."

"You love the water, don't you?" Leighton asked.

"Since I was a little girl."

Leighton took the tray containing their drinks out to the deck, and Gabriela joined him after grabbing her sunglasses. As they sat down, the telephone rang.

"I'm closer," Gabriela said, and went to answer it. In a moment, she stuck her head outside. "There's a message for me at the concierge desk."

"Is it from Limado?"

"I don't know," she said, grabbing her robe. "I'll be right back."

* * *

Gabriela ascended the steps up the cliff face with a sense of foreboding as the sun slipped down toward the horizon. As she entered the lobby from the side door, she was surprised to see both Mateo, a satchel slung over his shoulder, and Miguel.

Mateo's expression was somber. Miguel looked gaunt, ill.

She rushed to embrace Miguel. "We thought you were dead, Miguel. Thank God. Come, sit down, you don't look well."

"He's not," Mateo said. "He shouldn't be here, but he insisted."

"But what's wrong?"

"Can we talk in private?"

"Yes, Machete is waiting in the bungalow. We can go back—"

"No," Miguel said abruptly. "Another place."

She looked at him and frowned. "The bar," she said hesitantly.

In the bar, they sat down at a table. It was nearly deserted, but they spoke in low tones.

"Miguel, you look terrible. What is it?"

"The Americans found the last two missiles. They attacked Bocuateca this morning at dawn and flew them out of the country."

"But Mateo, why didn't you launch them?"

"I gave the order but we couldn't. Something was wrong with the firing sequence, either the software or an equipment malfunction—I don't know. Salcedo was still trying to trace it when the Americans hit them this morning. He's dead."

"What about Camilo? Is he alright?"

"No, Z. He's not."

She seized Mateo's arm. "Is he wounded?" Her voice went up a few octaves.

"Yes, badly," Mateo said quietly. "He may not live, Z."

She sat back, tears in her eyes. "Will this ever end?"

"I'm sorry. I know you love him. If he lives, he'll be the only survivor."

"So the armory … and the air base. They're still intact," she said, her face reddening with anger.

"Yes," Mateo said. "There's more." He pulled the damaged flask out of the satchel he carried. "I found this near one of the missile launchers. It's some kind of electronic device that I think helped the Americans find the missiles."

"I don't understand."

"It's magnetized. I was one of those who helped haul the launchers aboard the truck the night we stole the missiles. I saw nothing like this."

"Machete?"

"You did take him to see the missiles," Miguel interjected.

"But I can't believe it. He's done so much—more than either of you know. Since we've been here, we've seen Narváez."

"What?" Mateo gasped. "*Here?*"

"Yes. He tried to make a deal with us."

"What happened?"

"I was sure Narváez would try to sell me to the CIA. So we killed him," she whispered. "Raoul covered it up. Disposed of the body."

"We didn't know."

"So you see why it's hard to believe Machete is responsible for Bocuateca. For Camilo."

"Zorrita, no one else could have done it," Mateo said. "We know it wasn't one of our people. He's the only other person who's been allowed to get anywhere near those missiles. And we know he went to see the CIA in Valmonte."

"That was just to give them those missile parts."

"And to pick up a device like this one, perhaps?" Mateo said, nodding at the flask.

"But didn't you go with him when he met with the CIA?"

"No, I couldn't. We had little time. I had to make preparations to get Alma clear of the Secret Police."

She sighed. "Dear God … I meant for you to stay with him."

"I knew that at the time, but it was not possible. It is done now."

"Listen to me carefully, both of you. In light of all that Machete has done, I will not condemn him without proof simply because you, Mateo, did not follow my instructions and allowed him to meet with the CIA alone."

"Z, I know you care for him. But it is possible he has done all the good things we know about, *and* that he has betrayed us, killing Salcedo and three dozen others."

"But Mateo, where is your proof? You bring me suspicions and you have nothing to base them on. If he is an American agent, sent to do such things, why hasn't he tried to kill *me?* I'm the most important target, and he's had plenty of opportunity. No. I will not believe it. There must be some other explanation."

"Suppose we ask him?" Miguel suggested.

"I don't think you should be in that conversation," Mateo said to Miguel slowly. "And this may not be the time."

Zorrita looked confused. "Why do you say such things, Mateo?"

"Z, forgive me," Mateo replied. "But you are blind. Miguel is not objective on this subject. He is jealous of Machete, and it clouds his judgment. We should discuss this only once you have returned to Limado."

"Is this true, Miguel?"

Miguel sat sullen and silent.

"I see," Zorrita said slowly, after a long pause. "Well, Mateo, I am inclined to agree with you … but I do not want this matter to fester. Come with me."

Upon their return to the bungalow, they gathered in the sitting room. Leighton had changed into the Army uniform against the chill night air and came in and congratulated Miguel on his escape from Redención, but the other man barely acknowledged him. Leighton sensed danger and was glad that he had pocketed the Vesta automatic upon seeing Miguel.

"They have come with bad news, I'm afraid," Gabriela began.

"The Americans found the missiles," Mateo said. "They attacked Bocuateca at dawn this morning and took them. The entire guerilla force guarding the missiles are dead, except for Camilo, who may have died since we left him."

"My God," Leighton exclaimed. "Camilo was there?"

"I sent him," Gabriela replied.

"I found this at the site afterward," Mateo said, reaching into his satchel and placing the flask on the table. They all watched Leighton for a reaction. He looked the flask over but remained impassive.

"It's clearly an electronic device of some kind. It may have helped the Americans find the missiles," Mateo continued.

"Possibly," Leighton conceded.

"Machete," Gabriela asked him, "do you know anything about this at all?"

Leighton looked her in the eye. In that instant, Mateo and Miguel did not exist. "No," he said.

Gabriela turned to the others. She was clearly satisfied but waited to see whether they had any more information to bring out.

"You've never seen this before?" Mateo asked, nodding at the flask.

Leighton looked Mateo in the eye. "No. Why do you ask?"

"It was under a missile launcher. We don't know who could have placed it there. You had access to the missiles."

"For two minutes," Leighton replied. "Your own security detail had access to them for weeks, and yet you come to me."

Gabriela looked at them and sighed. "He has a point," she said. "Is there anything else?"

Mateo looked over at Miguel, who still sat sullen and silent.

"No, Zorrita, there's nothing else. I suppose we should be going."

"If there is truly nothing else," Zorrita said to them in a solemn voice, "then I want this matter laid to rest here and now. If you have evidence that Machete, or anyone else, has done wrong at any time, you can bring it to me always. But if all you have are unfounded suspicions, then all that you bring to me is poison. It is bad enough that we have to bury thirty-six more of our comrades, and maybe Camilo, without also turning on each other," she said, almost in tears.

As they all began to rise, Miguel suddenly went berserk, snatching Mateo's satchel and pulling out his .38 revolver. "You lie!" he screamed, pointing the gun at Leighton.

"Miguel, stop it!" Mateo exclaimed. "You are not in your right mind."

"Put the gun down, Miguel," Zorrita said firmly.

"You lie," Miguel said, looking at Leighton with hatred. "I can't prove it, but I know. You fucking American."

"Put it down," Zorrita repeated, louder, taking a step toward Miguel.

"Gabriela, get back!" Leighton shouted. Several things happened at once. Leighton lunged forward to shove Gabriela out of the way as Miguel raised the gun to shoot Leighton, and Gabriela pushed hard in the opposite direction, intent on blocking Miguel's shot with her body, absolutely certain in her belief that Miguel would not shoot her. Mateo seized Miguel's arm, and a struggle ensued.

"Die!" Miguel screamed, as the gun went off. Gabriela went limp in Leighton's arms, a bloody hole in her chest.

Everyone froze for an instant, unable to believe it. Leighton feared that she was already dead. He eased her to the floor, pulled the Vesta and shot Miguel in the forehead twice at point-blank range, spattering himself and Mateo with small droplets of blood. Mateo dropped Miguel and jumped back as Leighton shot him four more times in the chest once he was down, until the gun was empty. Leighton dropped the gun and pounced, punching the lifeless face and drawing still more blood as Mateo tried in vain to pull him off.

"Stop it! Stop it, he's dead!" Mateo shouted. Leighton continued to pummel Miguel until Mateo stabbed him in the leg. He paused but then resumed hitting Miguel, until Mateo jabbed the knife hard into Leighton's side. The pain made him stop and retreat.

Oblivious to his wounds, Leighton came partially to his senses and went to Gabriela, cradling her in his arms. "No," he cried, tears already forming in his eyes. "He wanted me ... he wanted to shoot *me* ..." he sobbed. "You can't ... you have to ... you have to go back to Limado."

He could see she was fading, fighting to stay alive and losing. She looked up at him, her eyes barely able to focus, as her mouth formed a weak smile. She tried to lift her arm, but her strength was failing her rapidly. Her hand fell limp at her side. Each breath she took seemed like a miracle. He could see in her eyes that she was slipping away. Leighton could see her visibly gathering all her strength for one final act, but he could not imagine ...

"Th-ank ... you ... for the ... mist ..." And the light behind her eyes suddenly vanished, her spirit suddenly absent from her body, leaving an almost imperceptibly deflated shell behind, vacant and lifeless.

Leighton held her tight and let out an unholy scream. When he finally fell silent, for him the room was spinning.

Several resort employees crashed through the door, nearly taking it off its hinges. Two of them were armed. Mateo put up his hands. "Get back, get back! There's nothing you can do. It's too late."

"We heard—"

"I know. Please get back," Mateo said, unaware that his face was spattered with blood.

At that moment, Raoul came running in, pushing his way past the others. He looked down at Zorrita and Miguel. "Mother of God," he gasped. "Mateo, are you alright?"

Mateo, slack-jawed, shook his head. "I'm not hit … but I'm far from alright." He took a deep, shuddering breath, fighting to pull himself together.

"That scream," Raoul said, incredulous. "Like something out of a nightmare."

"That is exactly what just happened here," Mateo said, beginning to regain control of himself. "Nightmare. Raoul. Get these people out of here—all but two of them."

Raoul turned. "Okay. You and you. Stay. They rest of you go." The sitting room emptied out.

"Now," Mateo said, his voice quaking, pointing at Miguel, "get him, get him out of here. He was never here, do you understand? Never here."

"Pedro," Raoul barked. "Get a laundry bin, quickly." One of the employees left at a run. Raoul turned to his remaining employee. "Joaquin, go to the bedroom. Wrap the man's body in a comforter. Be ready to get him out of here when Pedro gets back."

"Help me get this one to his feet," Mateo told Raoul. "Try not to get any blood on you."

It took some doing to separate Leighton from Gabriela's body. By the time they did, Pedro had returned with the wheeled laundry bin, and Miguel's body, wrapped in the comforter off the bed, was dropped inside it and wheeled away. Mateo and Raoul pulled Leighton, shattered and almost completely limp, onto his feet—barely. They half-dragged, half-carried him into the bathroom, where Mateo realized for the first time how much blood Leighton had lost. He went into the bedroom and stripped the bed of its pillowcases and one of the bedsheets, while Raoul telephoned up to the concierge to make more formal, dignified arrangements for the removal of Gabriela's body.

Back in the bathroom, Mateo stripped Leighton to his underwear, then grabbed a pillowcase and folded it quickly to make a compress. He tore a length of the bedsheet off and tied it around Leighton's midsection, the source of the worst of the bleeding. He tore a second length and repeated the procedure. He tore a third, shorter, length and used it to make a tourniquet above the stab wound on Leighton's leg, which he had been surprised to discover. He remembered stabbing Leighton only once, but in the horror and confusion of the past half hour he could not be sure. He used the second pillowcase to make a compress on the leg wound and tied it in place with a thin strip torn from the remains of the bedsheet. He had not stopped the bleeding, but he had it under control.

Leighton's hands were covered in blood, both Gabriela's and Miguel's. Mateo turned the water on in the sink, handed Leighton a bar of soap, and told him to wash. Leighton stood there staring at his hands, almost catatonic. Working with him as he would a child, Mateo helped Leighton wash his hands, and saw that Leighton had stripped the skin from most of his knuckles in beating Miguel to almost a pulp.

Raoul appeared in the bathroom doorway. "The man's body will be dealt with. There will be no trace of his having been here."

"Good," Mateo said. He went and looked at Leighton's clothing. There was too much blood on it for it to be useful. "That uniform will have to be burned. I have a uniform in my jeep, I'm going to get it. Take him into the bedroom and for God's sake, *don't let him go back into that front room.*"

Mateo walked past Gabriela's body, uttering a prayer, and he left the bungalow and bounded the stairs two at a time to get to his jeep, which was still parked in the roundabout. He still had the uniform of an Army lieutenant from the air base raid tucked under a tarp in the back, and recovered it. He stopped at the concierge desk on his way back.

"Colonel Borrero's car. Have it brought up to the roundabout," he told the clerk. "And send three triple whiskeys down to Bungalow Nine, quickly."

"Yes, sir."

Moments later, Mateo had recovered his gun from the floor of the sitting room, covered Gabriela with a bedsheet, and seen to it that Leighton was dressed in the lieutenant's uniform and looking presentable. Once Mateo slapped his face, he seemed to come to himself, at least partially. Raoul was busy telephoning, making further arrangements for Gabriela, when two resort employees came in with a stretcher, laid it down, placed her body upon it, methodically ensured that she was fully covered, and quickly carried her out. Two more employees came in with cleaning supplies and towels and efficiently began to remove the considerable amount of blood on the floor.

Only once they finished did Mateo bring Leighton into the kitchenette, within view of the sitting room, sit him down, and place a triple whiskey in front of him. "Raoul."

Raoul joined them.

"To Zorrita." Leighton, the only one sitting, got to his feet.

"No," he said. "To Gabriela."

"To Gabriela," they said in unison, and drank.

"Now," Mateo said. "We will have to engage in a little play acting. The American spy has killed our Zorrita."

Leighton balked. "Hold on—"

"Shut up. I said it was play acting. You will play along. Raoul, if you will go up to the concierge desk. We will talk more later."

Raoul nodded and left.

Minutes later, the side door of the lobby burst open, and Leighton entered with his hands up, being pushed forward by Mateo, who was holding his gun on him. "This American spy has killed our Zorrita," he yelled. "I will see to it that he meets justice. No one is to interfere! You!" Mateo yelled at Raoul. "Where is the car?"

"It is just out there, in the roundabout," Raoul said nervously. "As you ordered."

Mateo quickly hustled Leighton out to the Impala, parked and waiting, and told him to get in the front seat. Mateo kept the gun on him and slipped into the back seat. Leighton started the engine. "Drive," Mateo said in a normal voice.

When they got to the arch at the bottom of the drive, Mateo rolled down the window and fired two shots into the air. He sat back. "Now drive us into Catellan."

As Leighton pulled onto the road to Catellan, he asked, his voice hoarse, "Why did you do that? You know I didn't kill her."

"I'm thinking ahead, to her legacy. It is better that you killed her, rather than one of our own."

"But Mateo, you called me the American spy."

"You see, Palmer, if that's your real name, I'm not all that convinced that you aren't an American spy. It's just a gut feeling. Miguel's mind may have snapped, but he had good instincts. If you are a spy, you're a damn good one, you know how to cover your tracks. If I could prove it, you'd already be dead."

"Why are we going to Catellan?"

"Just drive. You'll see."

"You mean you're going to put out the story that I killed her so the *Frente* can save face? I'm going to be remembered as her *assassin?*"

"It's not just for the good of the *Frente,*" Mateo explained. "The new government, too. And you'll mainly be remembered that way in Madrinega. Maybe in your country. The rest of the world won't care."

"Goddamn it, Mateo. You know … you know I loved her."

"If you truly loved her, you will see that it must be this way," Mateo explained, his voice calm and surprisingly gentle. "We are going to win here. When we do, if you killed her, she will forever be remembered as a Hero of the Revolution. A martyr for the cause. Children will learn about her in school for generations. She will be an inspiration for who knows how many millions. On the other hand, if Miguel killed her, it taints the reputation of both the *Frente* and the Revolution. She will have been just another victim of a sordid romantic triangle, a Chilean beauty found dead in a love nest."

"How can you talk that way about her? You're a cold son of a bitch."

"I'm a realist. But this isn't about me. You must think not of your emotions, but of her. *Her,*" Mateo emphasized, staring at Leighton in the rear view mirror. "Think of Gabriela, and how you want her to be remembered. You'll realize this way is best. Not now. Not tonight. But in time."

"Shit. That's what you meant when you said Miguel had never been there."

"Exactly. She must be a martyr … not a victim of Miguel's jealousy."

They drove in silence for several more miles, until they neared Catellan. It was quite different from Valmonte, the only other city in Madrinega Leighton had seen. The outskirts of the city bore witness to grinding poverty. They passed multiple abandoned businesses that had been boarded up, the wooden panels covered in graffiti, and interspersed among them were the few active merchants who, by the looks of things, were holding on by their fingernails. Debris and garbage littered the sidewalks. A dog, too sick to move, lay dying in the street, and Leighton had to swerve to avoid it. It was nearly 11:00 p.m., yet as Leighton turned onto a four-lane boulevard, an old man in a wheelchair sat motionless next to the concrete median separating the northbound from the southbound lanes. His clothing, a torn T-shirt that had once been white and a pair of jeans whose tattered legs ended halfway up his calves, was little more than rags. He had nothing on his bare feet, and appeared to be intoxicated as he stared at nothing in particular. A few blocks farther on, three young men sat drinking outside a well-lit cantina, their motorcycles parked nearby.

"Some of the few who are gainfully employed, outside the hotels and resorts and the farms," Mateo said bitterly. "They are couriers for the drug cartel that operates in this area. Take a good look, Palmer. As you can see, it is far worse to be poor in the city than out in the countryside. This is what Zorrita was fighting to bring to an end. Along with the rest of us. She was right, Pando will do nothing to change all this, for all his conciliatory gestures. You have seen only Valmonte and a handful of rural villages. This is what most of our cities look like. This is why the guerillas will win."

They drove for mile after mile as Leighton saw more of the same. At last the boulevard rose to an elevated highway.

"Where to now?"

"Stay on this highway. It goes to the airport."

"Why there?"

"I have never known you to ask so many questions, Palmer. One would think you were worried for your safety. Do not worry. The answer to your question is that you are going home."

"What do you mean?"

"I think you're an American agent, and I'm going to put it to the test. I'm going to leave you at the airport, without money, identification, or passport. I'm betting that because you will slowly bleed to death by morning if you don't get proper medical attention, you'll contact whoever you need to contact to get you out of here within the next few hours, maybe sooner."

"What if you're wrong?"

"You can take your chances with the local hospital, maybe avoid arrest by the Secret Police."

"Or bleed to death, because you know the nearest hospital is miles from here."

"Or bleed to death. But you see, I think you're an agent. So I don't believe you will bleed to death, not at all. I say that by morning, you will be long gone."

"What's the point?" Leighton asked, looking at Mateo in the rear view mirror.

"The point," Mateo replied, looking back and fixing his eyes upon Leighton's, "is that I'd like to know whether Miguel was right about you. If he was, then Zorrita's death is as much your doing as it was his. You pulled the trigger and killed her, just as he did. And I'll know it. And you'll know that I know it. More importantly, you'll have to live with that for the rest of your life—the fact that you murdered the woman you loved. And if you ever return to Madrinega for any reason, I'll know that you're ready to die."

Leighton fell silent. He drove into the airport and followed the signs guiding him to the Departures section. In a few moments, he pulled the car up to the curb.

"Just put the brake on and leave it in neutral with the motor running," Mateo instructed. Leighton did.

"Vaya con dios, Señor Palmer."

"Mateo—"

"Get out."

"I loved her, Goddammit."

Leighton got out of the car and limped into the airport, holding the compress to his side as the roar of a departing jetliner filled the air. Inside, he assumed he was being watched as he walked to the nearest telephone booth.

"Hello?"

"Lang?"

"Yes. You're lucky I'm in a charitable mood, Palmer. I don't normally accept collect calls."

Leighton hesitated. The pain in his side was becoming unbearable. He forced himself to say the words, but only because he remembered what she had said to him that day by the river, after their first swim together: *"But a death with meaning is perhaps the best kind."*

"I've killed Zorrita." He felt ill at the utterance of the words; he suddenly tasted copper. But the guerillas intended to blame him for it; he may as well own it. And Mateo, damn him, was right about one thing: This version of events gave her death meaning. "But I've been stabbed. I'm in the airport at Catellan and I need a flight out of here *now* or I'm dead. I have guerillas hot on my tail. They may be watching me now."

"You at a pay phone?"

"Yes."

"Give me the number. I'll call back in five."

Leighton recited the number. Lang repeated it and hung up. An airport security policeman with a drug-sniffing dog passed by at that moment. He looked Leighton over, but the lieutenant's uniform gave him a certain respectability. Leighton glanced down. No blood showed through yet. He stood in the phone booth, trying not to look as though he was in excruciating pain. *Stay awake.*

After an eternity, the phone rang. "It's Lang. There's a flight for Mexico City in twenty minutes leaving from Gate 39. Flight 264. You're booked on it, as Palmer. Don't miss it, it's the last one tonight. Just show up. I've taken care of Customs, give your name and they'll wave you through. Good luck."

Leighton was ushered to his seat by an attractive flight attendant. Beneath the army tunic, the compress felt saturated. A bloodstain about the size of a quarter had seeped through, and he covered it easily with his hand. He sank back into his seat and asked for a blanket. He covered up quickly when the airline attendant handed it to him. Mexicana Airlines Flight 264 took off on schedule with Leighton aboard but losing consciousness.

Don't bleed.

In Mexico City, Leighton never left the airport. Lang had alerted Miller, who had an emergency medical team standing by. They gave Leighton four pints of blood, stabilized him, and hustled him by stretcher aboard a private flight to Miami. After emergency surgery at SONAI's secure medical facility there, Miller had to wait for him to regain consciousness, then spent two hours with Leighton, in violation of the doctor's orders not to overtire him. Tape recorder in hand, Miller debriefed him.

Although he was doped up on painkillers, and would be hospitalized for some time, Leighton had been eager to talk, to get it out, even if he had to do it from a hospital bed. He was devastated by Zorrita's death; needed someone to tell the story to. Someone to listen and believe that he wanted more than anything to have died in her place; it had not yet registered for him that she had died protecting him. That would come in time. Miller made no mention of it, correctly assessing that Leighton was still far too psychologically delicate to hear such an awful truth, for it would only rattle him further. Miller served the functions of friend and confessor. He asked few questions, merely let Leighton talk until he had wound himself down. With part of his brain, Miller was already working on the severely edited version of the audio tape that would become the official record of Leighton's debrief.

When Leighton had nearly finished, he looked at Miller, speaking with greater emphasis now despite mounting pain. "I told Lang the lie the guerillas wanted me to tell, to give her death meaning. Because it gave her life meaning, too. It was the only thing I had left, that I could do for her."

Miller shut the tape recorder off.

"You did a hell of a job, Leighton."

"Bullshit," Leighton spat. "I disobeyed your orders … I resigned … and I got her killed. Camilo, too."

Miller leaned forward, his beside manner gone. "I am the *last* person you will say any of that to," he said, his voice suddenly cold. "You can do yourself a lot of good, if you'll just keep your fucking mouth shut. Right now, you're her assassin, officially, and as repugnant as that may be, it can work to your advantage. So wise up. You loved her and you feel guilty, but you can't go around letting people know you broke the rules and got emotionally involved. I know you need to sleep, but I need to tell you something else before I go."

At that moment a nurse came in, carrying a paper Dixie cup.

"Sir, you really must leave now," she said to Miller. "He should have had his pain meds nearly an hour ago."

Leighton beckoned the nurse. She was a plain woman whose caring nature made her beautiful. She came close. "Thank you," he said in a rasping voice, "but please give us two more minutes. Then kick him out if you have to."

"Sir, you have a major abdominal wound. You have been out of surgery less than twelve hours, and from your other injuries, it looks like someone used you for target practice. You think you can handle the pain now, but when the last of your meds wear off, it'll hit you like a truck. And it'll get much worse, fast."

Leighton grunted suddenly. The nurse could see he was in pain right now. "I know," he said. "Two minutes. Please."

"No," she said firmly. "If all you need is two minutes, you can take the pills now. They'll take at least that long to hit your bloodstream. I won't have you screaming and disturbing all the patients on this floor. You're not alone here, you know." She reached for the pitcher of cold water on the nightstand and poured some into a plastic cup, then handed it to Leighton along with the Dixie cup. "Now. Down the hatch."

Leighton sat up in bed with her help. He looked at the two pills in the Dixie cup, dumped them into his mouth, and drank the water.

The nurse, a veteran, looked at him and said, "Now open your mouth and raise your tongue." Leaning over to carefully inspect his mouth, she confirmed that he had indeed swallowed the pills. After fluffing Leighton's pillow, she straightened and looked at Miller.

"Your two minutes just started." Disgusted, she went out.

"I know you're ready to quit, to walk away from all this," Miller began. "You'd have done it if she had lived, there's no doubt in my mind about that. I can't blame you. But I want you to reconsider. You can do a lot of good in this job, Leighton. Zorrita made a difference in Madrinega, and you helped her. The truth is, we're on the wrong side down there. Vilar's departure proves it, in my opinion. The new crowd may be no better. Speculation in Washington is that Pando's government falls by Christmas."

Miller paused, trying to find the right words.

"I'm sorry for what happened to her, Leighton. I gave you that order, and I'll deny this if you ever repeat it, but sometimes I have to issue orders I disagree with. I can't honestly say you were wrong to disregard it. It won't be easy, but you can go on making a difference. Sometimes you'll have to walk a tightrope, as you did in Madrinega, and sometimes you'll do harm in the midst of doing good, as you did there. As long as the good outweighs the harm, it may be worth it. But only you can make that decision. Think it over ... because I'm recommending you for Neptune Section." Miller stood and walked out, to let Leighton sleep.

Neptune, Leighton thought, as the medication lulled him to sleep. *He's crazy. The elite branch of Operations Division. Grand prize ... for a murder I didn't commit. For Gabriela. Shit.*

CHAPTER 18
A MATTER OF IMPORTANCE

Nine months had passed since Leighton's return from Madrinega, eight since his release from the hospital. His wounds had fully healed, although there had been some nerve damage to his leg that Dr. Bokhari, his agency physician, said might take years for a full recovery. But it did not affect Leighton's physical prowess, his hand-to-hand combat skills, or his ability to pass the rigorous physical examination that had finally cleared him to return to operational status.

Physically. His mental fitness was another matter. Miller had submitted the paperwork for Leighton's promotion to Neptune Section, but Barnaby, the Neptune chief, was holding it up. Barnaby liked to select his own agents, and he had ordered a battery of psychological tests in the hope of screening Leighton out. Barnaby heard the rumor that Leighton had fallen in love with the guerilla leader he'd killed in Madrinega, and he raised questions about Leighton's emotional stability. He had Leighton evaluated by three different psychologists, and their reports were pending.

The process tested Leighton's patience in the extreme. For one thing, it was a promotion he didn't want. Not for killing Gabriela. For another, he'd met some of the Neptune agents, and believed most of them were confirmed malcontents or mental cases of one kind or another. It was the height of hypocrisy to expect him to pass some arbitrary litmus test of "emotional stability." For the time being, despite his disenchantment, Leighton decided to remain with SONAI at Miller's urging. He filled his days rebuilding his physical strength after the toll that Madrinega had taken on him, swimming, cycling, lifting weights, maintaining a careful diet, and visiting the gunnery range once a week. But the activity that benefitted him the most was the resumption of his advanced karate training, for it emphasized not merely fitness and hand-to-hand combat, but also the harmony of body, mind, and spirit, a particular focus that preserved his mental health and what little emotional balance he was able to maintain after Madrinega.

Leighton had undergone plastic surgery to eliminate the crease in the right side of his head, and the scar on his left hand from the Secret Police sniper's attempt on his life outside Panactatlan. The scars from the other two bullet wounds to his shoulder and side, as well as the stab wounds inflicted by Mateo, were left undisturbed. The invisible scars also remained.

Outwardly, he was returning to his old self and maintained a convincing facade at the office. But the crushing grief and depression he felt in the wake of Gabriela's death he kept to himself. He refused to discuss her when questioned by the agency psychiatrist. Dr. Vanessa Byrne, Ph.D, Dartmouth University, was an extremely qualified professional who happened to be beautiful, owing to her African-American and Filipino parentage. Her reputation as being possessed of a demeanor of such softness and caring that melted the most hard-hearted subjects, combined with a disarming yet probing intellect that got them to open up, was dented after six meetings with Leighton.

"Whatever his feelings about the woman," Dr. Byrne reported to Miller, "he's done more than bottle them up. More like locked them away in a vault, under a mile of concrete. I can't get to square one with him, when it comes to her. You ask me if he's emotionally stable. The truth is, he hasn't given me enough information on which to base an opinion. The most I can tell you is that he's learned to put on a very convincing *mask* of emotional stability. I can't say what's beneath it, but whatever it is, he's devoting a lot of energy to hiding it. That takes a strong will, and a lot of discipline. But I can't say it's healthy."

"He's up for promotion to Neptune Section," Miller said, his voice laden with concern.

"I'd rather he took a long leave. But don't worry. All my records will be handed over to your office, as you requested. If I get inquiries from Neptune, I'll send them to you."

For two months, Dr. Byrne prohibited Leighton from using the gunnery range and compelled him to surrender his agency-issued firearms, as a precaution. Avoiding the temptation to resort to alcohol or recreational drugs, Leighton discretely acquired and took melatonin pills to combat what had become chronic insomnia. Only through martial arts and melatonin was he able to get sufficient sleep to remain healthy and functional. But he dreamed of Gabriela often, sometimes awaking deeply disturbed, unable to get back to sleep. On weekends he made solitary trips to the coast to take long walks near the ocean, at Mendocino, Santa Cruz, Monterey, and Santa Monica.

Another month passed. Miller, not yet willing to send Leighton on a full-blown operation because he, too, had lingering doubts about his emotional fitness in the wake of Dr. Bryne's report, assigned him to a passive surveillance detail that involved listening to recordings from a wiretap on a banker suspected of laundering money for a drug cartel. It maintained appearances and bought time, while Barnaby's psychologists argued about the contents of their final report on Leighton, which was several weeks overdue. Barnaby decided that even if the psychologists cleared him, he wanted Miller to assign Leighton one last job, as a final test before he would accept him into Neptune Section. Miller agreed. When it was finally released, the psychological evaluation, while not terribly enthusiastic, deemed Leighton fit, and Miller began to seek an appropriate assignment abroad. Leighton meanwhile maintained his daily training routine once the surveillance job came to an end.

One Saturday afternoon, as Leighton emerged from the house he rented on Euclid Avenue in the Berkeley hills to attend a karate class, he turned from locking up to see a man of medium height in a dark tan suit standing on the brick walkway connecting his front porch to the driveway. He had a dark olive complexion and a moustache, and he regarded Leighton with watchful eyes.

"Señor Leighton?" the man inquired.

Leighton tensed. "No." The standard answer for unexpected strangers. His eyes swept his front yard and the street in both directions. He detected no immediate threats.

"Please do not be alarmed," the man said, opening his hands to reveal his empty palms. "I have reason to believe you are he. I represent … a friend, who would like to speak with you." The man spoke English fluently, but with a definite accent from south of the border. He had not said quite enough for Leighton to pinpoint it. It was irrational, but to Leighton he felt like Madrinega.

"About what?" Leighton asked.

"I was told to say it is a matter of some importance to you."

"To me," Leighton repeated. "Is that all?"

"That is all that I know, yes."

"Have you come alone?" Eyes sweeping the area again.

"Yes, señor."

"Where is this friend?"

"Not far. The Claremont Hotel, within the city limits. If you will be kind enough to follow me in your car."

"Suppose I don't?"

"Then I will leave you in peace and return … I believe the expression is 'empty-handed.'"

"Just like that."

"Yes, señor. This is entirely voluntarily on your part. No harm will come to you, whatever you decide. But I hope you say yes." He smiled, without guile or menace.

"Who is the friend?"

"That, señor, I regret to say I have been explicitly directed not to reveal. But I was told to give you this." He reached into his hip pocket and handed Leighton a folded newspaper. Leighton first noticed that it was entirely in Spanish. Then he saw the front-page banner. He handed the newspaper back.

"Alright," Leighton said. "Lead the way."

Leighton's mysterious visitor had parked across the street in a blue Buick, and he now turned and walked back to it. Leighton got into his metallic grey Volkswagen Scirocco, started the engine, backed it out of the driveway, and followed the Buick as it drove off. True to the man's word, their drive took less than 15 minutes, ending in the parking lot of the Claremont Hotel.

Leighton followed the man into the hotel, nodding at the parking valets, and was led into Limewood, the restaurant and bar whose entrance was on the left of the broad hallway just a few feet from the hotel foyer. The two men passed through the restaurant to the outdoor terrace, which offered a sweeping view of the San Francisco Bay.

Sitting at a table near the railing, looking almost regal as she sipped Perrier, was Rosa Avellar. She looked alluring in a sleeveless burgundy blouse with a cowl-neck collar, matching pumps, and a bone-white skirt that showed off her excellent legs rather well. Her hair was done up in a French roll, with her trademark flash of silver. As always, she projected the aura of a woman of considerable means.

Leighton stopped cold as his escort melted away.

"You look surprised, Señor Palmer ... or perhaps I should call you by your actual name, Señor Leighton. Come, sit down, I am here as a friend."

Leighton sat down opposite her, recovering his composure. "The edition of *El Celador* was a perfect calling card ... but I assumed I'd be meeting some messenger of Roberto's ... not the Grande Dame herself," he said with affection. "How did you find me?"

"It was rather difficult, and expensive ... but Roberto and I know how to locate and hire people who are the very best at what they do. Private investigators, in your case. Roberto unfortunately cannot join us, although he wanted to. He was eager to see you again and sends you his very best regards."

"Please thank him and tell him I'm sorry we could not see each other."

"I will. He is here for an international journalism conference convening in San Francisco. We might have chosen a hotel on that side of the bay, but for you."

"Me? Why?"

Rosa visibly hesitated, thinking about how best to frame her words. Leighton interpreted the delay as reluctance on her part, and said, "I believe you when you say you are here as a friend, but I don't think you went to all the trouble to find me just to say hello."

"You are correct." She nodded, looking somewhat amused. "Your real name is Jeigh. It suits you better than Brian."

Leighton waited.

"Jeigh, she is alive."

Leighton frowned. "What?"

"Come closer."

Leighton sat up, moved his chair to the very edge of the table, and then leaned over it.

"Zorrita is alive," Rosa said in a hushed tone. "We have many friends in the new government since Pando resigned," Rosa began. "There will be a number of reforms now that the *Frente* is the ruling party. They have asked Roberto and I for help, but they are determined for their own reasons to stick to the legend that Zorrita was killed by an American spy."

"I knew that much already," Leighton replied, not yet believing her first words.

"You don't understand. She did not die at all. Or rather, her heart stopped, but she was revived before brain damage could occur, and she remained in a coma for two months."

Leighton sat completely immobile, but he was suddenly breathing heavily. "Are you telling me the truth?"

"Yes. She came out of it just before Christmas last year. It was agreed to maintain the fiction that she was dead, to keep her safe and to help the *Frente* politically. We know that your CIA made inquiries once you left the country, and they were fed the appropriate information, enabling them to confirm her death to their satisfaction. But it was a long recovery, and she has lost a portion of her memory."

"It can't be true, Rosa. I know what I saw. *She died in my arms*. It was the worst day of my life," Leighton said bitterly, anger welling up within him. "You must be wrong."

Rosa Avellar reached across the table and seized Leighton's arm. Her grip was terribly firm.

"*Listen to me.* I wasn't there. Perhaps she did die, or something so near death it was impossible to know the difference. But she was *revived* shortly after she was taken out of that bungalow. Unresponsive, but *breathing,* later diagnosed as comatose. The bullet had lodged near her heart, but didn't pierce it. Sharks Grotto caters to powerful clientele. They'd had medical emergencies there before, and they were equipped to handle even Zorrita's. They used a defibrillator, gave her a blood transfusion, and got her to Valmonte for emergency surgery by helicopter, partly by claiming she was the niece of the Argentinian ambassador. Foreign dignitaries always seem to claim their mistresses are nieces, so the hospital didn't ask questions. More importantly, they didn't alert the government or keep terribly good records."

"I know what I saw," Leighton repeated, staring at a point in space. "I've been living with it for months."

"Don't you think I know that? Why do you think we're sitting here? Or that Roberto and I spent a small fortune to find you? Would we have bothered if we weren't sure of our facts? The last time I saw you, I could see that you cared for her. Deeply. I told Roberto so." She paused. "I know what happened at Sharks Grotto was a horror. I imagine you have suffered a great deal," she said, her tone a soothing reminder that the Avellars considered Leighton a friend. "But I have seen and talked to her myself."

That got Leighton's attention. His eyes locked onto hers for a moment. Then he sat back and looked out at the bay, his eyes darting from one end of the vista to the other and back. "It's been almost *a year.* Why didn't someone tell me?"

"Someone just did," Rosa replied serenely. "It took time to locate you … As I said, it wasn't easy. Your government has taken pains to obscure your identity, your location. And for her, there is an ongoing need for secrecy as well. When she 'died,' that bounty on her hadn't been lifted, remember. And the new government in Valmonte is determined to conceal the truth."

Leighton sighed, feeling bewildered as he struggled simultaneously with various emotions: Relief. Anger. Joy. Fear. Fear, even now, for her. Rosa watched him processing the information.

"She was smuggled out of the country with a new identity," she continued. "We didn't know where, or under what name. But she apparently investigated how to contact you, and decided the only channel she could trust was Roberto and I, your former employers. Not the guerillas, not our government, and definitely not yours. Because we received this, two months ago."

Rosa reached into her purse and withdrew a buff envelope, about five by seven inches in size. "There was a note inside, asking us to get this to you, any way we could."

Leighton took the envelope and laid it on the table between them. He stared at it, noting that it was addressed to the Avellars and bore a Sao Paulo postmark. No return address. He knew that Sao Paulo was the ideal place to lose oneself, the largest city in the Western Hemisphere by population, eight million people, outstripping even New York's seven million. *Smart girl,* Leighton thought with tenderness.

Rosa waited for a moment, watching him. "You aren't going to open it?" she asked.

"I lied to her," Leighton said. "I denied I was an American agent. I got Camilo killed."

"You don't know, then. Camilo survived. He will be attending the University of Madrinega in the fall." Rosa paused. "She has reached out to you. She has begun a new life. Only you can decide what to do now."

"But, Rosa—"

Rosa Avellar held up a hand. "Roberto and I have done what we could. All that we were asked to do. The rest, Jeigh, is up to the two of you … if you have the courage."

The waiter, long delayed, finally arrived. Leighton continued staring at the envelope.

"Please bring this young man whatever he would like, and charge it to my room," Rosa said.

"Yes ma'am. What will you have, sir?"

Leighton glanced up at the waiter and said quietly, "Bring me a double bourbon, please." The waiter nodded and disappeared.

Rosa finished the last of her mineral water and gathered up her purse. "Tell me something. Where did you first meet her?"

Leighton looked at Rosa and frowned. It seemed an odd question. "Where? It was in Valmonte ... in Colinas."

"Yes ... but where in Colinas, exactly? Do you remember?"

"That bridge by the river ... the one with the statue, next to the park."

"The Bridge of the Venus."

"Yes, that was it. Why?"

Rosa smiled. "Because I had a hunch. Call it woman's intuition. There are those who dismiss it as pagan superstition, but there's a legend about that bridge. It says that the spirit of the goddess Venus watches over it, even though people no longer believe in her ... that when a man and a woman meet there for the first time, if they are destined to be together, then they will both know it then and there."

Leighton's laugh was cynical.

"Yes, I thought you would laugh ... but how did you feel when you met her?"

Leighton's laughter faded, as he thought of the sudden intensity of that kiss in the tunnel.

"You don't have to answer me, it isn't important that I know," Rosa went on. "But you might consider it, as you decide whether to open that envelope. It has been a pleasure to see you again. You look quite well ... physically. I will tell Roberto."

Leighton looked up at her as she rose to leave. To a woman of her station, etiquette demanded that men rose when she rose, but she overlooked the breach as Leighton remained seated. She knew she had given him a lot to digest; to her eye, he looked like a man who had lost his way.

"Thank you, Rosa." But she sensed confusion from him, rather than gratitude.

Rosa Avellar stood before him, purse in hand, studying Leighton intensely. At last she said, "I know this news has been a shock ... but I would think a pleasant one. Take your time with it. Think it over carefully," she said, and smiled at him with concern.

She walked around the table until she was behind Leighton, then bent over and put her arms around his neck in an embrace. She could sense his pain. Leighton reached up and touched her forearm, focusing on the envelope once more. "I have a name," she whispered into his ear, continuing to hold him and attracting attention because it seemed so intimate. "Delphine ... Martel ... Voland," she whispered, breathing each word into his ear slowly, meticulously giving each word the correct French pronunciation. "Again. Delphine."

"Delphine," Leighton repeated, whispering it back to her.

"Martel."

"Martel."

"Voland."

"Voland."

"There," she whispered, "now ... you know everything." Her whispering and her embrace were like a balm on his invisible wounds. "Good luck to you, my friend," Rosa said softly, giving him a final squeeze and then releasing him. "Vaya con dios." She straightened up, turned, and walked away.

Leighton suddenly felt better than he had at any time since that last morning with Gabriela by the pool at Sharks Grotto—the last time he had felt any hope at all. His bourbon arrived. He took a sip, and then another, larger, one, then gulped the rest of it down all at once. He set the tumbler down and opened the buff envelope.

Inside there was nothing more than a postcard, a color photograph of an archway that appeared to be the main entrance of a large, imposing building with a tan stone facade. There were colonnades and stone carvings of what appeared to be coats of arms above the archway, and the French tri-color hung from a flagpole on the stone window sill above it. Directly over the archway and directly below the window were large, dark capital letters that stood out against the pale tan stone of the building. They formed the word "SORBONNE." Below that were three more words: "UNIVERSITE DE PARIS."

Leighton turned the postcard over. It bore no name, no return address, no addressee information of any kind. There was only a message in French, printed by hand in blue ink.

> *Si vous voyagez à Paris, vous pouvez de rencontrer de la brume*
> *à cette période de l'année.*

Leighton could not believe it. He read it and reread it, over and over. He recognized her printing from the night she had let him read the report she had transcribed into her notebook from a Morse code message, detailing the fighting at Redención. The same night he made love to her for the first time on that hilltop at Limado under the trees.

> *If you travel to Paris, you may encounter mist this time of year.*

Leighton suddenly felt alive in a way he never expected to experience again. He thought of those final days with her, after she emerged from the grim darkness that had swallowed her upon learning of the death of Maurice Bishop. He stood, left a tip, and went directly to the men's room. In a private toilet stall, walled in white marble behind a shuttered white wooden door, he took out his Zippo. He had not had a cigarette since Madrinega, for the nicotine cravings had died with Gabriela, or when he believed she had died, but he still carried the lighter. He set fire to the postcard, watching it burn until he dropped the last flaming corner of it into the toilet, then flushed the ashes.

Leighton went to the nearest telephone booth, deposited two dimes, and dialed the number for the World Finance Corporation in San Francisco. He'd forgotten it was a toll call, and the operator came on asking him to deposit fifty cents for three minutes. Leighton cursed under his breath, but dropped in two quarters. In a moment he was speaking to Kelly Gradenko. "I'm sorry, Agent, Mr. Miller isn't back from lunch yet."

"Tell him he owes me for Hawaii, yanking me back thirty-six hours into a three-week vacation. He said he'd make it up to me and today's the day. As of now, I'm on leave for a month."

Kelly Gradenko, professional as ever, replied simply, "Enjoy it, Agent 571." Leighton hung up. Digging more change from his pocket, he dialed another number.

"Varig Airlines? I need a reservation on your next nonstop flight, Los Angeles to Sao Paulo. None? Well, what have you got? A stopover in Panama City … I'll take that. First Class. No. No, the fare doesn't matter. Just so it's the next flight."

A quick hop to Los Angeles on PSA would be no problem. She wasn't in Sao Paulo anymore, but it was the ideal place to lose himself, as she had, to vanish into the throng of millions in case anyone tried to track him, as he prepared for the next leg of the journey.

Leighton could not run to her in a straight line. Not if he wanted her to live.

CHAPTER 19
THE FLOWER IN THE GUN

Six days later. Paris, France.

It was late afternoon on the first Friday in August, in a little third floor apartment on the Rue de Monsieur de Prince, just across the Boulevard Saint Michele from the Sorbonne, quite near the Theatre National de l'Odéon. The young woman surveyed her new lodgings. The apartment was bright, freshly painted with walls of yellow ochre and white baseboards, the main room sparsely furnished with a settee covered in red velvet and an antique coffee table, a somewhat higher breakfast table with two wooden chairs next to a window, and a bookcase. The kitchen was almost claustrophobic with a small stove and a tiny refrigerator, but the bedroom was spacious because it was designed for a king-size bed but contained only a double, leaving room not only for a nightstand but a writing desk, a chair and a bureau. The most luxurious feature was the bedroom's walk-in closet. The bathroom, like the kitchen, was a bit tight, the combination bathtub and shower quite near the wash basin with a toilet wedged in between, and a towel rack on the opposite wall too close to the exposed metal heater below for comfort. If she placed her towel carelessly on the rack and it touched the heater, before long she would have a fire. And it was all too easy to burn her legs if they touched the exposed heating coils.

Delphine Voland gazed about her apartment with satisfaction, imperfections and all. Its diminutive size was cozy to her. God knew she had lived in much worse. The walls of the main room were bare save for two items. The first hung above the settee. It was a print, about 55 x 98 cm, of a painting of a violin, bow and sheet of music hanging from a wooden door. The writing in English at the bottom said it was by William N. Harnett, commemorating a display of his work at the National Gallery of Art in Washington, D.C. But the thing Delphine appreciated most about the print was the least prominent thing in it. A letter, tacked to the door toward the very bottom, the name of the addressee virtually illegible, but the Paris postmark above it clearly distinguishable. The only other item on the walls was an unframed oil painting hanging above the breakfast table, *Girl in the Rain,* which Delphine purchased herself from the artist one Sunday on the concrete strip just outside the Montparnasse Metro station for 280 francs. The girl was making her way beneath a white umbrella across a city street that looked awash. She wore a red pullover hat with a white stripe, a white jacket beneath a mid-length taupe dress that buttoned up the front with black shoes, and carried a rust colored purse. Her face was not clearly visible but her attire and shapely legs indicated youth, a female in her 20's. 280 francs was more than Delphine could afford, but she wanted it and was very pleased with the purchase, carrying it back to her apartment on the Metro in its brown paper wrapping with great care.

She went into the bathroom to stand before her only mirror, to check her appearance and brush her long, dark brown hair, which held just a hint of chestnut and had finally grown down past her shoulders. She wore a sleeveless light green cotton blouse with faded black denim jeans, and chestnut colored suede flats. She had put on a few pounds recently, but men still looked at her with desire on the street, in the cafes, and on the Metro. She went into the kitchen, debating whether to serve her guest coffee or wine. It was Friday afternoon, so wine was appropriate. But it was wrong for this occasion.

He would be here soon. She ground coffee beans using a hand crank on an old fashioned wooden grinder, then transferred the aromatic powder into a French press and brewed it, setting out a small ceramic carafe of cream, with sugar, croissants and Gruyere cheese with small plates and a paring knife, technically not the correct knife for cheese but it was sharper and would cut more cleanly. She could plan in such detail even though she was nervous. She had two coffee mugs, one glass and one porcelain, an ancient blue Air France mug that bore a hand-painted image of a Dewoitine 332, a tri-motor airliner that turned heads in September 1933 when it carried ten passengers an astounding 1000 kilometers – so the legend on the mug read. She took the glass mug and set the Air France out for him.

The intercom near the door of her apartment buzzed. She looked up in alarm; she had not expected him so soon, but her wristwatch told her he was right on time. She hurried to press the button and talk, although she told herself not to rush. She couldn't help herself, after all this time.

"Yes?" she said.

"Delphine?"

"Yes."

"It's Brian."

She hesitated. A moment went by.

"Are you there?" he asked. She pressed the talk button.

"No," she said. "No more lies. If you want to come up, you must tell me your name. The truth."

She waited, the side of her face against the wall.

"Delphine," he replied, "My name is Jeigh. Jeigh Leighton. I got your postcard. Please let me come up."

Again she hesitated. She took a step back from the intercom. Then she stepped toward it and pressed the button to buzz him in. She turned to the door of her apartment. She unlocked it and then backed away, standing in the middle of the room near the coffee table. She expected to hear the elevator clank its way to the third floor, to finally hear the outer elevator door rattle open noisily as always. But there was nothing, at first. Then, footsteps. He was taking the stairwell. She felt her heart pounding as the noise grew louder. In a moment, there was a knock on her door.

"Entrez," she said, raising her voice slightly.

The door opened. Leighton stood there. He wore a black leather jacket, dark denim slacks, and black boots. He looked the same. But somehow different.

Leighton gazed at Gabriela dumbfounded. Her hair was darker, longer, her complexion a bit paler, perhaps the months away from the unrelenting sun of Central America. There were lines in her face that had not been there before, but that was to be expected. "My God, it's really you," he said, his voice almost a whisper.

For a moment she couldn't speak. She stared as if he were a stranger. "I made coffee," she said at last, hunching her shoulders a bit awkwardly. "Would you—"

"Yes. Yes, please." He closed the apartment door behind him. He turned back to her.

She had the urge to run to him but controlled herself. "You...you look well," she said.

"You do, too. But different. I may look well...but I haven't been," he replied. "Not without you. Not thinking you were dead."

She looked at the floor. "Let's...let's have coffee," she said nervously, patting her hips.

"Alright."

"Let me take your coat." Leighton removed the leather jacket and she stepped toward him to take it. He tried to embrace her and she allowed it for a moment, still holding his jacket, but then stopped him, placing a hand on his chest as she looked down. She could not make eye contact.

"Let's...let's talk," she said, and as he yielded, releasing her, she shuddered. His jacket slipped from her hands and he embraced her in a fierce hug. She tried to fight him off, then yielded as emotion overtook her. She sobbed quietly into his chest as he held her, the passage of time and distance between them forgotten for just a moment. They stood that way for several moments, her muffled sobs the only sound in the apartment. At last she looked up at him, and Leighton kissed her on the mouth. She responded, but then pushed against him, bent down to retrieve his jacket, and placed it on the settee.

She wiped her eyes and turned to go into the kitchen, and brought out the French press. She poured coffee for him, and he sat down at the table as she poured for herself. As she expected, he admired the artistry of the blue mug, but only for a moment. She went into the kitchen again and returned with spoons. They each doctored their coffees in silence, trying to read one another's energy. Leighton tore off a piece of croissant and began to chew it. Gabriela cut herself a small piece of Gruyere and nibbled at it. They sipped their coffee.

Leighton noticed that all of Gabriela's movements seemed to be smaller. Quieter. In fact, there was a quiet about her that had never existed before. She had changed, that much was certain. He kept silent and waited.

"You look different," she said. "The scar on the right side of your head is gone."

"Plastic surgery."

"That's too bad. It was appealing."

"I never knew you liked it."

"Scars on men are sexy. Yours…gave you distinction. It reminded me of your courage. I meant what I said earlier. No more lies."

"No," Leighton agreed. "No more lies."

She took a sip of coffee. "So … is Jeigh truly your real name?"

"Yes. My mother chose it, British spelling and all."

"I was in a coma."

"Rosa Avellar told me."

"When I came out of it, Mateo came to visit me. He tried to turn me against you. He told me he was convinced you were an American agent. He said you could not have gotten out of Madrinega alive otherwise, because you were badly wounded, no money, no identification. He said he saw to that. He said you were very good…that you had him believing you were one of us. *Are you* an American agent?"

"Yes."

Gabriela looked at him and took a deep breath. She blinked twice, slowly. She stared at him, studying him. Another deep breath. She sipped her coffee and sat back in her chair. Her eyes never left his.

"Why did you go to Madrinega?"

"To recover the cruise missiles."

"Did you know about me before you went there? Did you know I was there?"

"No."

"But your government did."

"No, they didn't. They were looking for you, but they didn't know where you were. It was me. I was the one who found you, by accident."

"Once they found out, did your government order you to kill me?"

"Yes."

"Why didn't you do it?"

"Two reasons," Leighton said slowly. "First, I believed in what you were doing, your reason for being there. When I wrote those articles, I wasn't just playing a role, I believed what I wrote. I saw that you personally could change things. I didn't want anything to stop you."

"You said there were two reasons."

"By the time I got the order…I was just too close to you. It came the morning after the first night we were together. By then it was too late. That night changed everything. I knew that I loved you. That I was on the wrong side, and I was going to have to make a choice."

"The day you just walked away from camp and jumped into the river."

"Yes. I was horrified at what they wanted me to do. I knew I wouldn't do it…but I didn't how to respond, what to tell them."

"What did you tell them?"

"At first I just ignored the order. But eventually I lied to them, told them I couldn't get close enough to you."

She glanced down at his coffee mug, then looked up to bore into his eyes again. "By then, weren't you were sleeping with me every night? Or as often as we could?"

"I didn't tell them that. There was no way in hell I was going to tell them that."

Gabriela broke her stare, looking down at the table as she considered this. "I don't understand you," she said. "You're an American agent. But you refused to kill me. You risked your life to help us. More than once."

"I'm a man first. I loved you. I still do. I believed in what you were doing, from the beginning. That last day, I sent a cable resigning from the agency. I was ready to go back to Limado with you."

"You were?"

"Yes. Don't you remember? That last morning, we talked about it."

"No, I don't remember. There's a time before the coma that I've lost…it's just…gone. It's blank. I'm not sure how long it is. A week, maybe more. The doctor told me it's common to have memory loss after a coma."

"Will it come back?"

"He said often it doesn't, that it's often permanent, but it's impossible to predict."

"Do you remember that we went to Shark's Grotto?"

"Yes, I remember arriving, buying swimsuits that first day, and having dinner…but not much after that."

So Mateo had only told her part of it.

"When you told me you loved me," she asked, "was that just to get me to lead you to the missiles?"

"Gabriela…by the time I realized I loved you, I didn't give a damn about the missiles. I told you what was in my heart."

"But you still worked to find them, to get them out."

"I wasn't going to kill you. I had to give them something."

"But you're still an agent, aren't you?"

"Yes."

"Why, if you resigned?"

"When I thought you were dead, there didn't seem to be any point in quitting. Any point to anything."

"I suppose you couldn't have gone back to Limado anyway, if Mateo didn't trust you. Does your government know where you are now?"

"No. I went to a great deal of trouble to make sure they wouldn't know. They know I'm on holiday, that's all."

"Then you won't turn me in?" She was staring at him, reading him, but something in her manner seemed as trusting as a child. Leighton thought it had to be an act. She couldn't possibly be so trusting, not after all that she had been through. Leighton wondered, without malice, whether she had suffered any brain damage or fundamental personality change as a result of the coma. She was quieter, more reserved than he remembered, but otherwise seemed the same as before. But he reminded himself that he had been with her barely half an hour. There was another

252

possibility. It could be that perhaps, she simply needed desperately to believe in him.

"Gabriela Diaz," he said slowly, "I have killed, trying to keep you safe," he replied, staring into her eyes. "Do you remember the day we drove to Bocuateca?"

"Yes," she said, with a slight hesitation.

"I wouldn't hurt you then. I won't hurt you now."

He slowly reached across the table, and covered her hand with his. She put her other hand on top of his, and he followed suit.

"Everything stopped, when I thought you were gone," he said quietly. "I felt like I died, too. For months, I wished I had."

They rose from the table together, and embraced freely this time, a long, fierce hug, ending in a kiss. She took a step back from him and removed her blouse, then her brassiere. Without a word, she turned and led him to her bedroom.

As they disrobed together they suddenly became frantic, almost frenzied until the instant he entered her, and then they made love slowly, savoring every sensuous pleasure, as if the act so long denied would have to last them a lifetime. Her orgasm, when it came, was long, silent and powerful, her body shuddering against his as her climax seemed to grow more intense with the passing seconds, until at last she let out a tiny whimper, the sound he had learned to listen for in Madrinega. Then she lay still.

Afterward, they slept, awakening long after sundown. She got up first.

"How long can you stay?" she called to him from the kitchen.

"A little over three weeks. I have a month's leave, but I used five days of it getting here."

"That's why they don't know where you are," she said with a little smile, returning to bed to hand him a jelly glass of chilled water.

"Yes." He drank greedily. Sex had made him thirsty.

He set the jelly glass on the night stand and noticed that she looked suddenly somber. The only light in the bedroom came from the kitchen, and the faint glow of streetlights from the window, but he could see her expression clearly.

253

"What's wrong?"

"Maybe we shouldn't have done that," she said, waving a hand over the bed. "I'm not the same, you know. I'm different since the coma."

"I know," Leighton said gently. "I've noticed a few things already. I can't say they make a difference, at least not to me."

"What have you noticed?"

"Your hair is longer, darker."

"It only looks reddish when I'm getting a lot of sun."

"There's a quiet about you now. It wasn't there before. You're more reserved. Your gestures, they're not as dramatic."

"I've gotten fat."

"Even if that were true, it wouldn't matter. But it's ridiculous. You are *not* fat. Your figure has filled out some, that's all. You look sexy. Black men like that look."

As she looked at him, her eyebrows went up. "They do, do they?"

"Tell the truth," Leighton challenged. "Men still look at you, don't they? I mean, the way we look when we want a woman."

"Yes," she admitted, with an embarrassed smile.

"Then it's official. You're not fat. You're curvy. You're more alluring."

"Was I skinny before?"

"Not at all. But it seemed to me we all got less to eat in Madrinega. I remember being hungry a lot of the time."

"Do you think the Americans will ever invade?"

"Madrinega? No. The time when that might have happened has passed. They invaded Grenada instead."

Her expression darkened. "I read about that, and the killing of Maurice Bishop. That was devastating. I knew him."

"I know."

She looked confused. "How do you know?"

"You may not remember," Leighton said gently, "but you told me. At Shark's Grotto. I was with you when you got the news. You had some very bad days afterward."

"I was hard on you, I can tell," she said, her voice apologetic.

Leighton shrugged. "It passed. We were closer, afterward."

Tears welled up in her eyes. "I don't remember any of it."

Leighton put a hand on her shoulder. He kissed her temple. "You don't have to. It's alright."

She wiped her eyes. "I am pleased with the work I did there, and I'm grateful that the movement was successful in forcing a change of government. But I do not miss Madrinega."

She rose, and went into the kitchen, wearing his shirt. She reheated what was left of the coffee on a small burner on the stove. "Come to the settee," she called. Leighton got out of bed and pulled on his underwear. He went into the main room as she poured more coffee for them both. They added more cream, more sugar.

"Tell me about your life here," Leighton asked, once they had settled onto the settee.

"It's quiet. I have a favorite café where I buy pastries and baguettes. I have a job teaching two courses in the College of Music. Fundamentals of Violin Performance, and the other is an introduction to Vivaldi. Nothing especially prestigious, the pay is enough to eat on and save a little. It's a start. I take walks along the Seine. I occasionally see a play or a musical performance. I read in cafes. I'm applying for a position as an Assistant Professor of Music next month. A friend of mine says I have good chance of getting it."

"Just what you wanted."

"Close. I remember talking about whether you would be here with me. I remember that much."

Leighton took her hand. "I'm here," he said quietly.

She embraced him. "I am not the same woman. I can't tell you how I've changed, but I know I'm not the same as I was before the coma. I feel it. Compared to being a guerilla leader, I lead a rather dull life now…but I'm content with it."

"Suppose we get reacquainted over dinner."

"Yes. We know the sex is still good, but there's a lot more to it than that, my friend. Much more. We can begin by talking a walk. Then we can find a place to eat dinner."

"I'd like that."

She leaned forward to pick up her panties from where she had dropped them earlier, then gave him a curious sideways look and smiled.

"What is it?" Leighton asked.

"Nothing," she said. "I'm just glad to see you."

Leighton embraced her. "Jeigh," she sighed, "we have to get to know each other all over again," she said. She separated from him and looked him in the eye. "You have to understand…Zorrita and Gabriela are both dead and gone. I'm truly Delphine Voland now. I have no choice. I'll tell you a secret. Right now I'm terrified you're not going to like Delphine."

Leighton kissed her tenderly on the forehead. "I'll tell *you* a secret. I already do."

They sat quietly for a moment. Then she spoke, hesitantly. "I have nightmares," she said quietly.

Leighton's eyes met hers. "So do I."

"Madrinega's left its mark on both of us, then."

"It looks that way. But I don't think I'll have mine anymore, now that I'm here."

She laughed. "I don't have any special magic."

"You're wrong," Leighton said with feeling. "You are so wrong about that."

"When we go out," she said, holding him close, "you must remember. I'm Delphine. If you forget, it could cost me my life."

"Are you under surveillance?"

"I have to assume that I am."

"I won't forget, Delphine. You'll be safe with me."

They dressed slowly, stopping to kiss one another twice. They left her apartment and walked hand in hand along the Seine in the dark, looking at the illuminated boats on the river, admiring the lights of the Eiffel Tower, and kept walking along the Left Bank for some time, as far as the Musée d'Orsay, then walked back along the Boulevard Saint Germain to have dinner at a Spanish restaurant in the Latin Quarter near the university. They talked about Paris, about how this night was a dream come true for them both, and Leighton discovered he had a passion for this new woman with longer, darker hair, this Delphine, this quieter, openly pensive, slightly plump version of Gabriela, who was just as desirable.

"I have to tell you something," Leighton said, as they lingered over an after-dinner coffee. Most of the other patrons had cleared out of the restaurant.

"We've been having such a good time, but you look so serious all of a sudden."

"We said no more lies. So there can't be any secrets between us."

The woman who was now Delphine Voland did not move. She studied Leighton's face and waited.

"I'm not sure what you know, because of the coma—"

"I know enough."

"Delphine, please listen." Leighton began by telling her how seriously he took her safety, the painstaking precautions he'd taken to lose anyone who might have tried to follow him, starting with flying to Sao Paulo, just as she had. The four other countries he had flown to in as many days, using a different passport each time, until finally he had arrived in Paris, by train.

"I'm confident no one knows I'm here. Which means I'm confident that you are safe."

She reached across the table and grasped his hand. "I knew you would be careful."

"I want to tell you what happened. Everything," Leighton continued, "because I don't think Mateo did. Not all of it."

"Before you do, I want to tell you something first," she said, pushing her empty coffee cup and saucer aside.

"No, please wait—"

"No, I will speak," she said forcefully, and Leighton at last saw a flickering of the old Gabriela, the firebrand guerilla leader determined to have her way. "Mateo went to great lengths to poison my mind against you, it's true. You were an American agent, you were evil, you had manipulated all of us. He even suspected you had almost gotten Camilo killed with the others at Bocuateca. It almost worked. But Camilo tried to see me once he recovered from his wounds, and Mateo blocked it. When I found that out, it made me suspicious. While I was in hiding, before I left the country, I contacted Rosa Avellar for help. She arranged for me to see Camilo.

"Camilo had heard only the official story of what happened at Sharks Grotto, that you shot me, that Miguel was never there and had been killed in the fighting at Redencion. Camilo could not believe the part about you. He was sure you loved me, that you would never hurt me, and he was sure the story the guerillas were putting out was a lie. He'd confronted Mateo, demanding an explanation. Mateo was determined from then on to keep Camilo and I apart. He knew he could not rely on my memory loss being permanent, that Camilo might help me remember, and that the cover story might begin to unravel. Camilo wasn't there and didn't know exactly what had happened, but he had a fierce belief in you. He was convinced Mateo was lying about your actions. He has a wisdom about him, for one so young. He said to me, 'You and Machete were happy together. I saw it. But some people in the world see happiness and their only thought is to destroy it.'

"But Rosa also told me things I remember to this day. It was what led me to contact her again once I escaped to Brazil, asking for her help to contact you. She said it was true, you were an American agent, that you lied to her and her husband, just as you lied to me. But she was absolutely convinced you were a good man, that you actually supported the guerillas, and that you were in love with me. She said she believed I was the one reason you would regret leaving Madrinega.

"So, it's true I don't remember everything about my time there, and maybe that's a blessing. I'm sure some of it was ugly. I'm sure I killed people. We were fighting Vilar, his Army and his Secret Police. I have no doubt there was no choice but to use violence at times. I can't stand the thought of that now, but I sense that before, I just accepted it and moved on. I warned you that I've changed. But the thing I remembered most, once I came out of the coma, was you. And over time – I admit I didn't understand it, but I eventually stopped questioning it – the memory of you became a yearning."

Delphine moved closer to Leighton, until she was physically pressing against him. "We have each other now. It was unlikely, but it's happened...we're together again. I don't think anything else matters. Whatever you want to share with me...maybe it's better left in the past."

Leighton stared at her. *Does she know? Is she determined to pretend otherwise? If she truly lost a part of her memory, she's making it clear she doesn't want it back.*

He mentally reviewed what he'd planned to tell her, none of it pleasant: That they'd murdered Narváez together, and the staff at Sharks Grotto covered it up; that he, Leighton, had signaled the Americans, telling them where to find the missiles; that he hadn't known Camilo would be there with them, in harm's way; that on their last day together Mateo and Miguel showed up at Sharks Grotto, to tell her that the Americans had seized the missiles and wiped out the thirty-odd guerillas guarding them, except for Camilo, who at the time was badly wounded and not expected to live; and to share with her their suspicions that Leighton was an American agent, but that they'd had no proof, and she didn't believe them, probably because of Narváez; that Miguel tried to kill Leighton, and shot Gabriela by mistake once she got between them; and finally that Leighton had killed Miguel in retaliation.

It all amounts to more blood and death, Leighton thought. *Most of the blood on my hands, maybe a little on hers. No good can come of bringing all that into the open.*

Delphine was stroking his cheek. "Have you thought it over?" she asked gently. The sound of her voice was sweet. As she gazed at him, Leighton could feel her trust, her vulnerability, as if they were radiating from her body.

Leighton drew her to him and gave her a long, passionate kiss. "Yeah," he said, when their lips finally parted. "I have."

She rested her head on his shoulder and said, "I came to realize something while I was in hiding, healing and waiting to be smuggled out of the country: that with Vilar gone and the government on the verge of toppling, the *Frente* no longer needed me. And Mateo and most of the guerillas, secretly, would be glad to see me go. I was a woman, after all, and I was a foreigner. By then I was of more use to them as a legend than as a leader. I still am."

They spent a blissful night together in her little apartment, making love by the light of a street lamp that penetrated her bedroom window easily when she left the drapes open. At one point she lay on her back, staring at the ceiling. "Doesn't the violence bother you?" she asked.

"The violence?" Leighton stirred and turned toward her.

"In this life you've chosen."

"I don't like it, or enjoy it. But sometimes it has to be done."

"There is a famous photograph, of a Vietnam War protest on a college campus in your country. It might have been Kent State, but wherever it was, your National Guard had been called in. Soldiers were lined up with rifles facing the students. A girl went up to one of them. She was carrying a flower, a daisy, I think, and she put it stem first into the barrel of his rifle. I know before my coma, I felt as you did. If violence had to be done, then I'd do it and try to give it no more thought. I was a revolutionary, and I truly believed that power comes from the barrel of a gun. I was determined to hold that gun. But not now. Now I want to be the flower in the gun."

Leighton stroked her hair, and she nestled against him and closed her eyes.

◊◊◊◊● ▥ ▤ ▤ ▤ ▥ ▤ ▥ ▥ ▥ ● ◊◊◊◊

In the morning, they rose and showered one at a time in the tiny bathroom, then went out for coffee and eggs in a café nearby before Delphine left to teach her first class of the day. She said goodbye in the café, kissing him lovingly after giving him the key to her apartment and asking him to buy a baguette and a fish for dinner.

"It will be a wonderful day," she said, breezily, gathering up her leather brief.

"Why is that?"

"I have made a discovery…I sleep much better after you have made love to me."

"Are you sure about that?"

She looked back at him in surprise. Then she gave a little smile, and sat down next to him. "Oui," she admitted. "I have made another discovery…I hunger for *you*. You, my love. So you have no need for doubts," she said, touching the key in his palm, then closing his hand around it, "for I have just handed you the key to my heart." And she was off.

Leighton basked in a glow of intoxicating euphoria for several moments. Then it began to subside as he ordered more coffee. He sipped it happily, glad to linger for a time. As he continued to sit there with his coffee, he gradually began to feel pain in his stomach. The food had been excellent. He was absolutely certain that he wanted never to leave her again. But he knew his leave would end, and he had a sense of foreboding that once it did, it would be difficult to return to her. Only when he put the thought out of his mind did his stomach pain ease.

Later than morning, Leighton returned to his hotel to collect his toiletries and a change of clothing. He walked to the Odéon Metro station and caught a train to the Ecole Militaire, emerging from the underground to walk back to his room at the Hotel Derby Eiffel, a small establishment near the Eiffel Tower on the Avenue Duquesne. In Paris, he generally preferred to stay at the Hotel Kleber on the Rue de Belloy, or the Hotel Raphael on the Avenue Kleber, both of them a short walk from the Arc de Triomphe and the Champs-Elysees, the center of things, but they were both larger and more luxurious – the Raphael in particular was a popular five-star hotel – and therefore much more high profile. But everything about this trip had to be discreet, so Leighton had chosen a smaller hotel more likely to be frequented by young foreigners visiting Paris for the first time or those traveling on a budget. At the Hotel Derby Eiffel there would be no VIPs, and Leighton himself was less likely to appear on the radar of the CIA or any of his French intelligence colleagues in Paris.

Delphine had agreed to meet him for lunch, in front of Notre Dame. She said she knew a restaurant near the cathedral, on the Rue Chanoinesse. He entered the hotel lobby, and was walking past the front desk to the elevator when the concierge called out to him.

"A lady called with a message for you, Monsieur."

Leighton accepted the envelope. It was from Delphine. She could not make lunch, but wanted to meet for dinner at the same place at six. Leighton thanked the concierge, pocketed the small envelope and the note scribbled on the hotel's stationery and went up to his room. He quickly shaved and changed clothing and went out again.

He strolled the neighborhood and went into La Commanderie, a restaurant near his hotel. He sat outside on the side walk with a glass of Bordeaux, behind a large glass partition partially covered by faded pale green awning. An hour went by. He felt good. He thought of sitting by the river with Gabriela at Limado, how peaceful it had been. Lunchtime rolled around and he ordered a delicious dish, *Boeuf aux oignons caramélisés,* beef with caramelized onions, along with more wine.

As Leighton sat digesting his meal and sipping wine contentedly, a man walked by, looking immaculate in a tailored grey suit. He was handsome, in his early thirties, with dark hair going prematurely grey, and looked strangely familiar. He was accompanied by a tall, attractive Eurasian woman in a deep burgundy dress with black hair. Her legs were particularly striking. They both wore sunglasses and paused outside the entrance of La Commanderie, where he turned to her and handed her a leather brief. They parted company and the man entered the restaurant, glancing at Leighton but passing him by as he went inside.

Inside, Leighton could hear a waiter greeting the man with familiarity. "Ahh, Monsuier Daranet, how are you today? We have not seen you in some time."

"Very well, Andre. I rarely get time to break free for lunch these days. What looks good on the menu today?"

Daranet. Of course! Leighton rose and went inside, approaching the man, who had by now removed his sunglasses. He recognized him, as he expected to do. "Phillipe? Phillipe Daranet?"

The man turned, his expression curious, and took a good look at Leighton head-on. His face lit up. "Leighton, old friend! My God... what are you doing in Paris? Why did you not let me know you were coming?" They shook hands vigorously.

"It's a long story," Leighton replied.

"Well, fortunately I have plenty of time, for once. Andre, two glasses of your best wine, please. This is a great friend of mine from America. He used to fly the jets from their over-sized aircraft carriers. As daring a man as Saint-Exupery himself!"

"Right away, Monsieur Daranet." Andre said with a nod and a tiny bow.

Daranet joined Leighton outside, and immediately lit a cigarette. He offered one to Leighton.

"No, thanks. I quit last year."

"Unbelievable. You used to go through half a pack a day. You were often begging them from me, as I recall. You have changed. Well, I suppose you are a bit healthier. Now, you must tell me what adventure brings you back to Paris."

"Later," Leighton said. "I want to know about you. You look different, I hardly recognized you. Still fit, but going a little grey. What are you up to these days? The last time we saw each other, you were with the Ministry of Defense." In reality, Daranet had been employed by SDECE, the French equivalent of the CIA, but Leighton wanted to be discreet.

"Well, the work is not terribly different these days," Daranet replied. "But there was a shake-up, a reorganization year before last," he continued, lowering his voice. "SDECE is no more. Now it is DGSE, the Direction Générale de la Sécurité Extérieure. To many it may be a cosmetic change, but some of the old guard were pensioned off, many others fired. There were a few too many cut-throats in the ranks, settling old scores with assassinations and lining their pockets, all of it off the books, you know the sort of thing. When the new minister took over, he said he could not tell the difference between us and the Corsican Mafia," Daranet said with a chuckle. "I tell the tale with humor, because we are old friends and you are a man who appreciates the need for discretion, but it is all true."

Leighton nodded, and raised his glass. "To the loyalty of old friends."

"Indeed." Daranet lifted his glass, and they drank. "And you," he went on, "the last time I saw you – what is it, eight years – you were

263

with the Office of Naval Intelligence, after they took flying away from you. Did that inner ear problem ever clear up?"

"Yes, but by that time I'd been with ONI for over a year. I wasn't inclined to jump through all the hoops needed to get my flight status back. ONI were reluctant to let me go, anyway."

"That was quite intelligent of them. And now?"

"Still in intelligence, but no longer in the Navy. I worked for the DEA for a while."

"And then?" Daranet asked, sipping his wine as he scanned the pedestrians walking by.

"Now it's SONAI," Leighton said quietly. Officially, SONAI did not exist, but he knew Daranet would know of it.

"I heard," Daranet said, not wishing for Leighton to feel compelled to elaborate. He pulled his chair a bit closer to Leighton's, and spoke even more quietly. "It seems we have again found our way into the same line of work. Counter-terrorism, nuclear proliferation, and the related nefarious activities."

Daranet's manner was friendly, but deliberate. He had something more to say.

"Phillipe, it's honestly good to see you. But you didn't just happen by this café, did you?"

Daranet took a drag from his cigarette, and tapped ash into one of La Commanderie's metal ash trays on the table between them. Looking Leighton in the eye, he said, "To tell you the truth, no. Not really. But you haven't told me what you are doing in Paris."

"I could just say that I'm visiting a friend."

"From what I understand, if you said that, it would not be a lie," Daranet said amiably.

"Then that's what I'll say."

"A woman," Daranet said with a knowing smile. "But this one is rather special, and not just to you. Listen, my friend, I can tell you that she is safe here. I am now the number three man in DGSE's Intelligence Directorate, and I know."

Leighton sat back and took a deep breath. He listened and waited.

"We know precisely who she is," Daranet continued quietly, "and we have tracked her from the moment she entered the country, although we did not know her identity right away. We keep watch on her, simply because we know her past and we do not want her riling up the Arabs or the Muslims here in France. There is no indication of that so far, so place your mind at rest…and so long as nothing along those lines occurs, she will be perfectly safe."

"Nothing will," Leighton said. "I have reason to know, those days are behind her."

"That is encouraging," Daranet replied. "We also know about the American contract that was placed on her life before she came here… but frankly, we have no sympathy with the Americans, on this and a number of other issues, we don't give a damn what they want. I give you my word. You saved my life on that operation in Martinique, and one does not forget such things. So long as I remain in the Directorate, and I expect to remain in place for a very long time, neither your people nor any of their right-wing allies will ever learn that she alive and living in France."

"I appreciate that, Phillipe. More than I can say. But why are you telling me this?"

"To answer that, I need to know how much you care for her."

"Imagine the worst. I've already done it, to protect her."

Daranet studied Leighton for a long moment, the smoke from the cigarette in his hand beginning to curl about his head. "That much, eh? I suspected…I received a report that you went to great lengths to conceal your identity as you entered the country. A crime for which, were we not great friends, I would have you arrested. I take it you were covering your tracks in case your own people were tailing you."

Leighton nodded. "I did a great deal more before I arrived. My people think I'm in Brazil."

"Leighton, if you love this woman, truly love her, I have a hard thing to tell you. You are placing her in danger. It would be better if you gave her up."

"Why the hell would I do that?"

"I know how careful and meticulous you are when you set your mind to it. I'm confident you have evaded anyone who might have tried to track you here. This time. In the future…that might not be the case."

"I'm damned careful, Phillipe. I know her life is at stake."

"Yes, it is. And if anyone with bad intentions ever tracks you to her, she's as good as dead."

"You've as much as admitted that you have her under surveillance. You'd let that happen?"

"It is not a bodyguard detail. For that, we'd have to get close enough to her to tip our hand. She'd know we were there."

"She already suspects."

"Yes, but if she knew for certain, what do you think she would do?"

"Run."

"Precisely. And she might run to a less safe situation. I emphasize to you that here in Paris, she has friends. She is safe. As safe as someone like her can be."

"What do you advise?"

"I have told you, my friend. It is why I have come to talk with you. I have seen her, so believe me I understand your feelings. What man has not lost his head over a beautiful woman?"

"Suppose you keep her under surveillance and forget you saw me?" Leighton asked.

"Well, I am in no position to sit in judgment, Mon Ami, far from it," Daranet replied. "But that I cannot do. I think it possible that your emotions are inflamed, yes? And that it has temporarily clouded your judgment, eh? Your pursuit of her places her life in danger…the fact that you have direct connections to more than one American intelligence agency…"

"You're telling me to walk away."

"If you truly love her, it might be best."

"I don't know that I can."

"Then you will both have to take your chances. But don't you think she should make an informed choice? The risk is mainly hers, after all."

"Phillipe," Leighton said slowly, staring at his wine goblet, "let me handle it my own way,"

"Certainement," Daranet replied, nodding and tapping ash from his cigarette. "I have said what I needed to say. I am sorry to come with such tidings, but remember I come as a friend. If you broach the subject, whatever else you tell her, do not let her know that she is being watched. Neither of us can predict her reaction to that news."

Leighton nodded.

"Believe me, old friend, I understand. Enjoy her to the fullest. There are so few things in life that make us feel truly alive. But think carefully about the future. And now, let us have another drink, and talk of pleasanter things. Whiskey this time, what do you say?"

"You are too good a friend for me to say anything but yes, Phillipe."

"Vive l'amour, old friend."

<hr />

Leighton took a long walk through the city after parting company with Daranet. He would have preferred to see his old friend under different circumstances. Their reunion had been amiable, but it left a bad taste in his mouth. He resented being given advice on a matter as private and dear to him as Delphine, but he knew Daranet had been genuine when he said he came as a friend.

He returned to his hotel as dusk was approaching, showered and changed into a tailored blue-grey Armani suit, a pale grey cotton dress shirt, and a navy blue necktie with flecks of powder blue in it. He wore brown English wingtips which he had buffed to a high shine before leaving the hotel to walk to the Metro.

Delphine was waiting for him at a table near the window as he entered the restaurant. She looked stunning in an ochre cowl-neck pullover, a short black leather skirt over black stockings, and black knee-length boots. Leighton was unable to hide his distraction during dinner. She asked him what was wrong, and he struggled to answer her. He had to share the basic thrust of Daranet's concern without alarming her.

Finally, he said, "Each time I visit you there's going to be a risk. A serious risk."

Delphine took a sip of wine and replied, "I know." She knew he had more to say, and waited.

"I've really got to leave SONAI. I can't maintain my connections to them and keep you safe."

"Are you ready to do that?"

"Not yet. It's strange. On one hand I'm a hero because they think I killed you. On another, they think I'm unstable because they suspect I got emotionally involved."

"With me?"

"Yes."

She reached across the table and took his hand. "If they only knew."

"I don't owe them anything. But I'd rather not leave with them thinking I'm 'mental.'"

"I'm not objective on this, my love. I feel the sooner you break away from them, the better."

"I can't disagree."

"You're right about the risk. But don't you think I thought of that before I sent that postcard to the Avellars, asking them to track you down? I knew there was a danger you might lead someone to me. I also knew that you'd know that, that you'd take every precaution. And you have."

"Yes."

"Then let's stop dancing around it. Having you in my life means that I might be killed. I know that. I want you anyway. It's my life and my decision. But you're the other part of the equation. Do you want me, yes or no?"

"You know I do."

"Then what are you going to do?"

"I can't see you again until I'm free of them. That would be safest thing to do."

"I don't know that I like that. Even if you quit, honestly, I'm skeptical that you'll ever be free of them. I know about that world. You never really get out of the life, they say."

Leighton smiled. "You know too much."

"How long would it take you to resign?"

"That's just it. I'm not sure. If I get another assignment under my belt, I can walk away then."

"Jeigh, you can't just put us on hold. Not after all we've both been through." She fixed him with a steady gaze. "For now, I say we go on. Come to me when you can. I'll take my chances if you will."

Leighton's brow furrowed into a frown. He said nothing.

"Unless of course," she added, "you simply want to end it now."

"No," he said at once. "I'm not saying that."

Delphine shrugged and gazed at him with a matter-of-fact expression. "We have three weeks. They'll go quickly so let's enjoy them. But when they end, you'll be faced with the same two choices."

· · · · ▨ ▩ ▩ ▦ ▨ ▨ ▨ ▩ ▨ · · · ·

The three weeks passed swiftly, as Delphine predicted. Leighton spent very little time at the Hotel Derby, practically moving in with her. They were happy in her tiny apartment, cooking together in the claustrophobic kitchen, making love, listening to music, mostly violin recordings, discussing films they had seen at the cinema. They visited the Sacre Couer and said a prayer, and had dinner at a small restaurant down the hill from the basilica. They strolled along the Seine, haunted their share of cafes, and one Sunday they dressed formally and she took him to Mass at Notre Dame.

On his last Saturday in Paris they took the Metro out to Montparnasse, a cold day that threatened to rain but never did, and Leighton bought her an oil painting of two falcons in flight. They enjoyed a heavy lunch of American hamburgers and beer in a pub called Falstaff. Since it was unseasonably cold, the chill had begun to affect them both, and they ducked into Café Odessa nearby for a double shot of Lavagulin before getting back on the Metro to return to her apartment. As they sat together sipping the 16-year-old scotch whiskey, he told her of the legend of the Bridge of the Venus that Rosa Avellar had shared with him. As he talked, Delphine smiled but kept silent, staring into her whiskey. When he finished, she leaned close and whispered into his ear, "Take me home."

They made love on her small bed, having developed through practice the ability to do it with no one falling out onto the floor, a delicate art form. Afterward, they lay clinging to one another fiercely, aware that their time together was growing short. Leighton was due to leave the following day. They slept.

Delphine rose at 10 p.m., hungry, and put on a yellow tank top and boxers with her slippers to go into the kitchen to make empanadas from scratch. After a fashion Leighton rose and went in to help her. She put on a kettle for tea as he diced tomatoes and green bell peppers.

"I love you," she said, looking at him as she reached for a sack of flour in one of the upper cabinets.

"I love you, too," Leighton said.

"You're a fool if you leave me," she said matter-of-factly. "Anything could happen. I could meet someone."

"Yes, I thought of that," Leighton said calmly, using the knife to scrape the diced vegetables from the plate into a bowl. He opened the refrigerator, reached in and pulled out the chicken she had grilled that morning, handing it to her just as she was about to ask for it.

"Then don't go," she said.

Leighton turned and looked at her. He watched her, in her dull yellow tank top and red shorts, as she mixed the water and flour together in a mixing bowl to make dough, seasoning it with ground bay leaves and lemon juice.

"You know I have to start back tomorrow," he replied.

"That's not what I meant and you know it," she retorted softly, picking up the knife to dice the chicken. "Don't just walk away out of fear for my safety. I haven't heard a really good reason why you can't just leave your world of spies."

"There's really only one reason I can't quit right away," Leighton said slowly. "We'll need money to live."

"That's not important. We can live off of my salary."

"Women say that, until the reality hits. You wouldn't be happy with that arrangement, and neither would I. I have assets, but I'll need time to liquidate them."

Delphine looked into his eyes. She was listening intently, breaking her gaze just long enough to put the chicken into a sautee pan with olive oil. The meat began to sizzle as Leighton continued.

"My father started a business, a chemical company, and placed it along with a couple of lucrative patents he owned into a trust," Leighton explained. "When he died, ownership passed through his trust to me. I still hold a controlling interest in the company, but I'm not involved in day-to-day management. I never wanted to be. I used the profits to invest in real estate. I've haven't been concerned about any of this until now, but I'll need to sell most of it off. I need time to wrap things up. Then I can quit."

"How long will it take?"

"No more than a few months. Then I'll come back. For good."

Delphine rushed to him, her hands still white with flour, threw her arms around him and kissed him intensely. Leighton held her tight, as if his life depended on it, and returned her kiss with yet more heated desire. At last he released her.

"As soon as you can, my love," she whispered quietly. "We'll be happy. You'll see."

EPILOGUE

Mateo Avellar, the cousin of Raoul Benitez and estranged younger brother of Roberto Avellar, became the first president of the newly formed Democratic Socialist Republic of Madrinega, once General Humberto Pando resigned and fled the country in December 1983, two months after Zorrita's "death," along with key members of the General Staff known to have been involved in the Panactatlan scandal. The Avellar Administration reconstituted the Parliament, legalized unions, curbed foreign imports, launched a nationwide literacy program, established universal health care, made inroads on land reform, and disbanded the Secret Police. Avellar called on his brother Roberto for the difficult task of navigating the establishment of diplomatic relations with Cuba, Nicaragua, and the United States. He also ensured that Zorrita's revolutionary activities were fully chronicled and became part of required school curriculum, dedicated ten public monuments to her around the country, and with the help of his sister-in-law Rosa Avellar, established the Gabriela Diaz School of Revolutionary Doctrine and Warfare at the University of Madrinega, sealing Zorrita's reputation as a Hero of the Revolution.

Alma Perez, onetime waitress, sniper, and medic to the guerillas, performed emergency surgery on Camilo Aguato under primitive conditions, and saved his life. She would forever attribute his survival to divine intervention, given the far-from-antiseptic conditions at Limado and the fact that she had not yet completed her medical degree at that time. She later returned to complete her medical studies at the University of Madrinega and became a pediatric surgeon. She opened and operated clinics in multiple cities and villages once the new government announced its plan to provide universal free health care. Once the Pando government fell, she never picked up a rifle again. While she became involved in a long-term relationship with Mateo Avellar, she vowed never to wed him while he was president. When he stepped down after eight years in 1992, they were married the same day.

Camilo Aguato, who accompanied Leighton and Mateo on the reconnaissance mission to Taramantes air base and was later seriously wounded in the American assault on Bocuateca, fully recovered from his injuries. After the Revolution, he enrolled at the University of Madrinega, graduated with honors, and became a Professor of Political Science. He then married Henrietta Jimenez, the young guerilla who instructed the other girls in the Limado cell how to field strip an AK-47 assault rifle. He was commissioned by President Avellar with chronicling the history of the Frente Popular de Madrinega, which became an award-winning book entitled *La Frente,* and formed the basis of the school curriculum educating students about Zorrita's contribution to the Revolution. His second book, *My Friend Gabriela: A Personal Account of the Madrinegan Revolution,* won the Nobel Prize for Literature. After serving as the Minister of Culture under Mateo Avellar, Camilo was drafted by the Partido Socialdemócrata and became the second president of the new republic in 1993. At twenty-eight, he was the youngest head of state in Latin America, and he expanded on the policies of his predecessor.

Roberto Avellar, publisher of *El Celador,* won the Pulitzer Prize for his news coverage of the revolutionary struggle in Madrinega, based on several of his stories being published in major American newspapers such as the *New York Clarion* and others. He remained active in journalism for the remainder of his life, and ironically, became a leading figure in the administration of his estranged brother Mateo, helping champion the cause of land reform by selling off half of his significant land holdings to small farmers and ranchers. For this, he sealed his reputation among his wealthy peers as a traitor to his class. He also served as his brother's unofficial envoy, carrying out a series of sensitive diplomatic assignments. Avellar continued to collect rare automobiles, and eventually purchased another 1949 Ford Coupe to replace the one totaled when the Secret Police made an attempt on his life.

Rosa Avellar, known before her marriage as Rosa Marquez, one of Madrinega's leading journalists, served in the Avellar government as the Minister of Public Education. She spearheaded the national literacy program and dramatically expanded Madrinega's public school system, ensuring that poor students in rural and urban areas alike received a high school education that included instruction in history, mathematics, and science. Behind the scenes, she was a driving force in perpetuating Zorrita's legacy by helping shape the curriculum about her. She supported by various means the work of Alma Perez in promoting women's health care and prenatal care, particularly in the country's poorer rural areas. Despite pressure from the Avellar Administration to do so, neither she nor her husband would ever recant their association as onetime employers of Brian Palmer; privately, even before receiving word that she was still alive, they never accepted the official story of his reputed role as Zorrita's assassin.

Brian Palmer, the American spy credited with the killing of Zorrita, alias Gabriela Diaz, was, according to multiple Madrinegan sources, never seen alive again once he was taken at gunpoint by an unnamed guerilla from the Sharks Grotto resort near Catellan. While some accounts allege he was spirited out of the country by the CIA, according to documents in the Madrinega state archives, he was taken to an unknown location, executed, and buried in an unmarked grave. Neither the CIA nor any other American agency ever admitted to any connection with him.

Miguel de Cordoba was quietly buried near Catellan following his death at Shark's Grotto. By presidential order, his body was secretly exhumed and on the third anniversary of the Madrinegan Revolution in 1986, it was interred once again in the City of Redención beneath a monument to him and all the guerillas who gave their lives in the uprising. In his speech at the dedication ceremony cementing the mythology of the *Frente* that Miguel was killed at Redención, President Avellar heralded him as the guerilla's greatest general, second only to Zorrita herself. His name is inscribed first on the monument's large bronze tablet, listing the names of the revolutionaries who died there.

Raoul Estefan continued to work as the General Manager and "fixer" at the Sharks Grotto resort until he had accumulated enough capital, by some accounts through means of questionable legality, to buy it outright. While he resisted unionization, his first act upon taking over as the new owner was to implement a unilateral wage increase for all employees of 28 percent. As tourism to Madrinega increased under the Avellar government, he became a giant in the nation's hospitality industry, eventually acquiring control of Costa Pacifica, the Grotto's major competitor, and purchasing two more hotels on Paradise Island in the Bahamas.

CPSIA information can be obtained
at www.ICGtesting.com
Printed in the USA
JSHW060728211222
35249JS00001B/24